Full Circle

Full Circle

Ayana Ellis

www.urbanbooks.net

Urban Books, LLC
78 East Industry Court
Deer Park, NY 11729

ISBN 13: 978-1-60162-515-1
ISBN 10: 1-60162-515-4

First Mass Paperback Printing July 2012
First Trade Paperback Printing January 2010
Printed in the United States of America

10 9 8 7 6 5 4 3 2 1

*This is a work of fiction. Any references or similari-
ties to actual events, real people, living, or dead, or
to real locales are intended to give the novel a sense
of reality. Any similarity in other names, characters,
places, and incidents is entirely coincidental.*

Distributed by Kensington Publishing Corp.
Submit Wholesale Orders to:
Kensington Publishing Corp.
C/O Penguin Group (USA) Inc.
Attention: Order Processing
405 Murray Hill Parkway
East Rutherford, NJ 07073-2316
Phone: 1-800-526-0275
Fax: 1-800-227-9604

Here's a sneak peek at
Colleen Collins's RIGHT CHEST, WRONG NAME
Available August 1997...

"DARLING, YOU SOUND like a broken cappuccino machine," murmured Charlotte, her voice oozing disapproval.

Russell juggled the receiver while attempting to sit up in bed, but couldn't. If he *sounded* like a wreck over the phone, he could only imagine what he looked like.

"What mischief did you and your friends get into at your bachelor's party last night?" she continued.

She always had a way of saying "your friends" as though they were a pack of degenerate water buffalo. Professors deserved to be several notches higher up on the food chain, he thought. Which he would have said if his tongue wasn't swollen to twice its size.

"You didn't do anything...bad...did you, Russell?"

"Bad." His laugh came out like a bark.

"Bad as in *naughty*."

He heard her piqued tone but knew she'd never admit to such a base emotion as jealousy. Charlotte Maday, the woman he was to wed in a week, came from a family who bled blue. Exhibiting raw emotion was akin to burping in public.

After agreeing to be at her parents' pool party by noon, he untangled himself from the bed sheets and stumbled to the bathroom.

"Pool party," he reminded himself. He'd put on his best front and accommodate Char's request. Make the family rounds, exchange a few pleasantries, play the role she liked best: the erudite, cultured English literature professor. After fulfilling his duties, he'd slink into some lawn chair, preferably one in the shade, and nurse his hangover.

He tossed back a few aspirin and splashed cold water on his face. Grappling for a towel, he squinted into the mirror.

Then he jerked upright and stared at his reflection, blinking back drops of water. "Good Lord. They stuck me in a wind tunnel."

His hair, usually neatly parted and combed, sprang from his head as though he'd been struck by lightning. "Can too many Wild Turkeys do that?" he asked himself as he stared with horror at his reflection.

Something caught his eye in the mirror. Russell's gaze dropped.

"What in the—"

Over his pectoral muscle was a small patch of white. A bandage. Gingerly, he pulled it off.

Underneath, on his skin, was not a wound but a small, neat drawing.

"A red heart?" His voice cracked on the word *heart*. Something—a word?—was scrawled across it.

"Good Lord," he croaked. "I got a tattoo. A heart tattoo with the name Liz on it."

Not Charlotte. Liz!

HARLEQUIN WOMEN KNOW ROMANCE WHEN THEY SEE IT.

And they'll see it on **ROMANCE CLASSICS**, the new 24-hour TV channel devoted to romantic movies and original programs like the special **Harlequin® Showcase of Authors & Stories.**

The **Harlequin® Showcase of Authors & Stories** introduces you to many of your favorite romance authors in a program developed exclusively for Harlequin® readers.

Watch for the **Harlequin® Showcase of Authors & Stories** series beginning in the summer of 1997.

If you're not receiving ROMANCE CLASSICS, call your local cable operator or satellite provider and ask for it today!

Escape to the network of your dreams.

Take 4 bestselling love stories FREE

Plus get a FREE surprise gift!

HE SAID

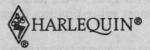

SHE SAID

Explore the mystery of male/female communication in this extraordinary new book from two of your favorite Harlequin authors.

Jasmine Cresswell and Margaret St. George bring you the exciting story of two romantic adversaries—each from their own point of view!

DEV'S STORY. CATHY'S STORY.
As he sees it. As she sees it.
Both sides of the story!

The heat is definitely on, and these two can't stay out of the kitchen!

Don't miss **HE SAID, SHE SAID.**
Available in July wherever Harlequin books are sold.

Let's Celebrate!

LOVE & LAUGHTER™

invites you to
the party of the season!

Grab your popcorn and be prepared to laugh
as we celebrate with **LOVE & LAUGHTER**.

Harlequin's newest series is going Hollywood!

Let us make you laugh with three months of terrific
books, authors and romance, plus a chance to win a
FREE 15-copy video collection of the best romantic
comedies ever made.

For more details look in the back pages of any
Love & Laughter title, from July to September,
at your favorite retail outlet.

Don't forget the popcorn!

Available wherever
Harlequin books are sold.

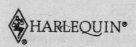

Free Gift Offer

With a Free Gift proof-of-purchase
from any Harlequin® book, you can receive
a beautiful cubic zirconia pendant.

This stunning marquise-shaped stone is a genuine cubic
zirconia—accented by an 18" gold tone necklace.
(Approximate retail value $19.95)

Send for yours today...
compliments of ⬦ HARLEQUIN®

To receive your free gift, a cubic zirconia pendant, send us one original proof-of-purchase, photocopies not accepted, from the back of any Harlequin Romance®, Harlequin Presents®, Harlequin Temptation®, Harlequin Superromance®, Harlequin Intrigue®, Harlequin American Romance®, or Harlequin Historicals® title available at your favorite retail outlet, together with the Free Gift Certificate, plus a check or money order for $1.65 U.S./$2.15 CAN. (do not send cash) to cover postage and handling, payable to Harlequin Free Gift Offer. We will send you the specified gift. Allow 6 to 8 weeks for delivery. Offer good until December 31, 1997, or while quantities last. Offer valid in the U.S. and Canada only.

Free Gift Certificate

Name: _____

Address: _____

City: _____ State/Province: _____ Zip/Postal Code: _____

Mail this certificate, one proof-of-purchase and a check or money order for postage and handling to: HARLEQUIN FREE GIFT OFFER 1997. In the U.S.: 3010 Walden Avenue, P.O. Box 9071, Buffalo NY 14269-9057. In Canada: P.O. Box 604, Fort Erie, Ontario L2Z 5X3.

FREE GIFT OFFER   084-KEZ

ONE PROOF-OF-PURCHASE
To collect your fabulous FREE GIFT, a cubic zirconia pendant, you must include this original proof-of-purchase for each gift with the properly completed Free Gift Certificate.

084-KEZR

This book is dedicated to:
The memory of Michael Anthony Jasper
a.k.a. Mikey April 26, 1978–July 4, 2004
R.I.P.

Reginald "Black Reg" Caraway
and Gwendolyn
"Don't Even Try It!" Wheeler.

You are truly missed by many.
And to Mr. Lawrence "Shake" Francis for
becoming a part of my life for a reason,
season, or a lifetime. By the time this
book comes out I don't know if you'll still
be around so I'm thanking you for that
special moment in time when you were
here. You're a good man. Thank you for
everything, my likkle rude-bwoy.

Acknowledgments

To my past I pay homage. I would be nothing without you.

To the victims of domestic violence, please know that there is a way out. Don't ever think that staying is your only option or that there is no better life awaiting you after being in an abusive relationship. Time heals all wounds, and sometimes even though you are being ridiculed and you don't have support a lot of the time it's because people don't take you wanting "out" seriously. Get serious with yourself and get out of that situation. Fight your way out of that situation and survive by any means necessary. Seek help and shelter and reclaim your life. You are loved, you are special, you are necessary and important to someone and life is beautiful. Live to tell your story and to lend a helping hand to another individual who feels hopeless in this situation. Run and don't look back. No matter how good some days are, know that those dark days of abuse are lurking right around the corner. It doesn't stop, it just takes breaks.

Thank you to those of you who supported me in my time of need but a special thank you to those who did not. Your ignorance of the situation, ridicule, and lack of compassion has only made me strive harder to become a better woman, a stronger woman, and a God-fearing woman.

Last but not least to my daughter, Nia S. Kerr. Mommy goes through the struggle so you won't have to, my ladybug. Live your life full of knowledge and free of ignorance.

FULL CIRCLE

Based on a true story
"Full Circle"

Some grow and see Daddy, jeans baggy
Not giving damn near enough
But Momma seems happy
So baby girl grows up, imitating what she sees
Can't wait to grab her a loser
Soon as she hits her teens
No male role models, Mommy is too strong
To have a man in her house, black woman sometimes we are too strong
So she raises baby girl on her own
But li'l mama knows that she's missing
The male figure in her house, so she goes out sniffing
Trying to find him, in the streets, in dark ghettos and slums
Nobody in the family has a man, she wants to be the first one
She runs into his fist, hit after hit

Her lip is split, she shakes it off and spits
Blood
She's hardened, but beg her pardon, see she's still looking for daddy
So she could distance herself from her mother's life and the burdens she's seen her carry
By any means necessary, she spreads her legs, as he begs to go deeper
Surrounded by a cloud of reefer, begging to please keep her
Painting a canvas on her pretty body, purples and blues
She calls him daddy happily, as she's being abused
She has that father figure in her life, her body numbed and bruised
Momma can't stand it but she knows li'l mama's a product of what she didn't do
Blame Momma, not Daddy, why is that the case?
Li'l mama, has a permanent smile on her face
From wired jaws, once held no flaws, now her scars inside
Are far more deeper than the one he put over her eye
Damaged gem, so many men, got a peek of her internal décor
She's about two men short of being called a whore

Ass is fat from all the pumps and slaps, they begging for more
She goes back and picks a loser that stands in front of the store
'Cause she grew up seeing daddy, jeans baggy
Not giving enough
But momma seemed happy
Hiding times that were rough
When li'l mama asked Mommy tell me what's wrong
Mommy's overprotectiveness couldn't tell her daddy is gone
Instead she paints a pretty picture pretending to be strong
Not knowing li'l girls need knowledge and truth
So they won't try to belong
In circles that will hurt you
Mommy seemed happy
So baby girl will follow Mommy's footsteps quite naturally.

By Ayana Ellis

The Beginning . . .

I got my first taste of heartache from my father. It may sound crazy but I remember being shot from my father's testicles into my mother's womb. I remember the warm feeling of love when they created me. I remember closing my eyes with joy; happy to be born to two parents who loved me and who would raise me right; happy for my mother because she wouldn't have to be a single mother like the rest of her friends. I remember resting in her womb, a tiny embryo of a thing, nestled happily when she called my father and told him the news. Unfortunately, he was not happy. I didn't understand it. After all, weren't they in love? They made love. They laughed, they made memories. My mother and father created me on Valentines Day. I was their love child.

My mother carried me full term, to work, home, to friends' houses. Every day she'd sing to me and I'd kick from inside. I couldn't wait to come out and meet this woman who loved me so. Nine months later when my mother gave birth to me, my daddy was not there. He broke my heart many times before I entered the world. I knew from then that I would probably get into the pattern of messing with the wrong men. When I was born, my daddy was someplace in Miami "with friends" while my mother cried, not because of labor pains but because the man she had loved for four years was nowhere to be found to celebrate the coming of his first daughter. He wasn't there as her feet swelled and she bled from stress, scared that she might lose me. He wasn't there to take her to work or bring her home. He wasn't there to help her with her cravings, he wasn't there to see her face glow with excitement when the baby moved. No, she worked until the ninth month and rode the train every day faithfully.

I remember looking at my father. I was a day old. My auntie called him and told him that I was born. He came "as soon as he heard the news." I knew it was him by the way he held me. Only a dad could hold his child this way. He held me gently and his eyes were watery. He kissed me softly on the lips and said, "Li'l mama" in soft little whispers. He kissed me over and over, then he put me over his shoulder and patted my back. I remember thinking, *I love this man. I forgive you, Daddy, even for future mistakes, I forgive you in advance.* When it was time for me to leave the hospital, I looked up at him from my car seat wondering if he was going to get us out of this ghetto as a good daddy should. My mother had endured a lonely pregnancy. My dad was nowhere to be found during the nine months she carried me. She had such a hard time bringing me into this world, but she did it. She never had a doubt as she carried me for nine months back and forth to work with her. She laughed and talked about me all the time and couldn't wait to see me. Yeah, I heard her talking, I felt the love from day one. I felt the love they had for one another when my father shot me into my mother's womb and settled me there. He aimed for that egg and he held my mother tight and said, 'I love you,' on Valentines Day.

Which is why I would never understand why he left when he learned about me coming. She tried, she tried to be happy, she tried to move on, but she wasn't strong enough. Her pretty face, bodacious behind, pouty mouth, and gracious sex weren't enough to keep my father around the way he should have been. But at the age of twenty-six, my mother was more naïve then most when it came to love. She thought that being a good woman would keep her man close to her. She never dreamed that my father would leave her, especially when she got pregnant. Her loyal heart, her tears, her pain were not enough to make him stay. Giving him the best gift a woman could give a man, a daughter, was not enough to hold my hustler father down. He'd come around when he was damn good and ready. But in the meantime, her bitter heart got the best of her. She thought he loved her. I thought he loved me.

Yeah, my first taste of heartbreak was from my daddy and it's been downhill ever since.

Darren

When Jackie told me that she was pregnant it rocked my world. We had been together for three years and nothing ever happened and I assumed that nothing ever would. I was thirty years old and already had a child from a previous relationship. Me and my son's mother were just beginning to get along; finally, I was free of baby mama drama. My son was four years old by the time I met Jackie. I didn't want to have any more children anytime soon, and if Lorraine found out that I was having another baby she'd give me hell for sure. Besides, I was in the streets and the money was getting good. I didn't need the pressure of having to be home with a new baby and her newly sensitive mother. But Jackie insisted on keeping this child no matter what I said to try to convince her to do otherwise. Initially, out of frustration, I skipped town to clear my head and different situations pulled me further away from her. I didn't mean to let so much time pass before I checked back in. I loved Jackie so much. But money, other women, a minor coke habit, and small bids here and there had me so far removed from our relationship. My life had spiraled out of control and before I knew it, years had gone by and my guilt wouldn't allow me to look into my daughter's eyes, knowing that I had failed her. I could only pray that one day things would change, but for now I was gone and there was no turning back. Not for Jackie, not for Carin, not for love. It was all about getting money and nothing came before that.

PART ONE

Life As a Shorty . . .

1

Carin

The year was 1994 and my *Ready to Die* and *Ill-matic* tapes were on heavy rotation. That was all I seemed to do, blast my music when my mother wasn't home. It was my escape. I loved all kinds of music. Since I spent most of my time alone, music was my company. I didn't think anyone I knew loved music more than I did. Even though I was only fifteen, someway, somehow I found my way inside the Palladium night club most Fridays to see new acts perform. I was more than open when I realized that tonight's guest would be none other than Biggie Smalls singing "Juicy." The first time I went to the Palladium alone the bouncer laughed in my face and told me to take my young ass home. Not to be outdone, the next day I went to Forty-second Street to obtain my fake ID. I came back the next week to see Biggie and he let me in. I wanted to laugh in his face but decided to just enjoy the show.

All night I sipped on a drink called Kamikaze that had me feeling woozy. When the show was over, I caught a cab on Eighth Avenue and headed home, happy to have partied the night away, not having to think about my boring life at home. Music was my freedom. I would come home and tell Sinny of the fun I had at the clubs that I would sneak into and she'd just shake her head, wondering why I would go out alone. That's what I did. I rolled alone. I didn't need a group of girls or a clique. I did what I had to do with or without the help of anyone. Yesenia, or Sinny as I called her, was my best friend. If anyone was a product of her environment, it was Sinny. All she knew was "the block." She never wanted to party or go anywhere if it didn't involve lying up with some dude. Sinny had been sexually active since she was twelve years old, and her life revolved around opening her legs. We had been friends since the sixth grade, but we really became tight during the first year of high school when she began seriously dating a guy who was like a brother to me, named Tron.

I grew up in a project in Brooklyn, and about six blocks down Bushwick Avenue was another project called Williamsburg Houses, where Yesenia and my boyfriend, Chauncey, lived. Through Chauncey was how I met Tron, who started dating Sinny once he and I became friends. I guess you could say I had everything to do with that connection. Every day Sinny and I would meet up at a park outside of her projects, smoking our weed on a bench, waiting for Tron and his cousin, Panama, to come through. I would always play innocent when Chauncey would ask me why I chose to hang around Sinny, Tron, and his cousin so much. At that time I hadn't recognized my infatuation for Panama, but slowly I realized that I had a thing for him.

It was already six in the evening and Tron hadn't come through yet. I was getting antsy. The fall weather was cool and the streets were rather quiet. It seemed as if Sinny and I were always the only two people out in the streets no matter what time of the day it was; me running from my morbid home life, her running behind Tron. I pulled out my small radio and began listening to "Gimme the Loot." As we sat side by side quietly, inhaling the yellow smoke, I bopped my head in agreement to everything this man was saying. Biggie was the truth. "You don't know shit about this." I laughed and started reciting the words.

"I know about that," she said.

"Must be through Tron, 'cause your ass don't have no culture. You don't listen to music, you don't party. I don't get you, Sinny. Why don't you ever come party with me?"

"Don't nobody wanna be up in no sweaty-ass club with all those people!" she snapped.

"Tron got that ass on lockdown, that's the fucking problem."

"No, he doesn't."

"Yes, he does. You're too young to be having some boy tell you what to do and where to go. Please, I wish I would have some guy telling me I can't go somewhere. Where is he anyway?" I asked. I really didn't care where he was, but I was sure that he'd have his cousin with him. Panama was so damn fine! He had a tanned, pecan complexion, hazel eyes, and pretty, dark, wavy hair. He had dark features all over. His eyebrows were thick, his eyelashes were long, and he had the most perfect set of teeth I had ever seen on a boy. And although he was nineteen years old, in my young, fifteen-year-old mind I was going to make him mine. Not that Chauncey would approve, but I was allowed to daydream. I daydreamed about him every night and pictured myself in his arms all the time. He was my first crush. The first time I saw him he was oblivious to my presence as he stood off to the side, irritated with Tron and Sinny's constant bickering. He rushed Tron and threatened to leave him if he didn't come on. He was so sexy in green army fatigues, a black T-shirt, fatigue hat, and black chuckers. I knew that Panama wasn't thinking about me. He wanted someone who would give it up on a regular basis like Sinny did with Tron, and I wasn't ready for that. But when I was ready, it would be given to Chauncey, my boyfriend of a year-and-a-half. There was no doubt in my mind about that, because I loved him. Panama was just an infatuation, but Chauncey was the real deal. Everybody in our neighborhood knew that little fly-ass Chauncey was my man. Girls constantly gave me dirty looks. I'm sure since I was a virgin, Chauncey had to have banged a few of these girls, but his loyalty and respect lay with me and that was all that mattered. Besides, Sinny lived right across the walk from him and she'd tell me if she saw anything funny going on. I loved him dearly. We were more like homie lover friends and our relationship was solid. It was based on friendship. I met Chauncey, a cute, skinny, brown-skinned dude with big lips and a big heart, while hanging out with Sinny one day. I had always noticed him but he seemed withdrawn and shy. Then one day he approached me and asked me where I was from, and the rest was history. We spent most of our time up in his bedroom where he had everything you could ask for. He had plenty of movies and video games, a stereo system, and a queen-sized bed. We would listen to Clue tapes all day and get high. Chauncey wanted nothing more than to keep his head between my legs.

Chauncey always told me that he loved me so much because of my ability to love with my heart and not my eyes. His mother was an alcoholic and was never home. When she was, she was stumbling drunk. When I first met his mother she was babbling drunk, eyes red and glossy, drooling, stuttering and slurring telling me how pretty I was. It was embarrassing to him. I sat his mother down and handed her a glass of water as Chauncey hid his embarrassment behind shades. As she sipped her water I made her bed and asked Chauncey to help me lay her in it.

"She's your mother, we all make mistakes, don't be embarrassed," I said to him as he watched me tuck his mother in. "I won't be here but I'm sure she will have a hangover, so in the morning just get her some black coffee, no sugar. She just needs some love, that's all." I sat on his bed.

Chauncey had always kept me close, but after that incident he held me tight. Because my mom was never home and I had to fend for myself, I'd go to Chauncey's house and cook. He was missing that from his mother so he clung on to me. He'd do anything for me because he knew that I was love, I wasn't going to judge him. I was all for making a bad situation better by any means.

Though he hustled, my mother liked Chauncey and why shouldn't she, he was a good guy, *my* guy. He was just doing what he had to do, considering the hand he was dealt.

"You want to see Panama, huh?" Sinny said, bringing my mind back.

"No!" I laughed.

"Yes, you do. He knows you like him too!"

"You didn't tell him that, did you?" I said, slapping her thigh.

"No, but Tron did. Besides, he ain't stupid, Carin. You act all quiet and shit when he comes around."

I sat there daydreaming about my first crush, wondering what it would be like to just talk to him. The most he ever said to me was "what's up."

About an hour later, I could see Tron and Panama walking through the park on the other end, which gave me time to slim out my jeans and slick the sides of my hair. Courtesy of Chauncey, I was fly with my big earrings, leather jacket, Guess jeans, and fresh sneakers. Tron reached us first, giving me a hug and a kiss on the cheek. Panama brought up the rear and sat next to me in a pair of camouflage fatigue pants, fresh Tims, and a brand new black hoodie. Immediately he started rolling up. Panama and I sat side by side, quietly smoking marijuana but saying nothing until he got fed up and got up off of the bench.

"Where are you going?" I said. *Please don't leave.*

"Oho! You talk?" he said sarcastically and sat back down next to me.

"So you were just going to up and leave and not say anything?"

He smiled at me, wide and handsome. "You're a dime. But you're too young for me." He said it out of nowhere, as if he was contemplating whether he should pursue me. It was embarrassing that he knew I liked him. He couldn't imagine how I sat in my room and thought about him over the slow jams they played on the Hot Five at Nine.

"We can be cool," was all my young heart could muster up saying.

"I'd like that." He winked at me.

"Did you hear that new Biggie Smalls tape?" I asked.

"Nah, you got it?"

"Yup."

"Let me hold it."

I did not want to lend anybody my tape, but this was Panama and I couldn't tell him no. Reluctantly, I took it out of my radio and handed it to him.

"Yo, Tron, look what I got!" he said, showing the tape.

"Carin, that's yours? Oh, you foul, you suppose to be my sister!" he teased.

I shrugged sheepishly and smiled. "You know I can just dub you a copy," I offered.

Panama smiled at me. "You want your tape back?"

"No, I was just saying."

He stuffed the tape in his pocket and winked at me. I kissed my tape good-bye.

"So, you two getting along over there?" Sinny asked me from Tron's lap. She was perched up there like his little bird. Tron, a dark-skinned cutie with good hair and brown eyes, could do better than my girl Sin, I couldn't lie. Sin was boring and she took the tomboy thing too far. She walked with a hunchback, talked like a dude, always dressed like a dude; she acted just like Tron. I couldn't see how that turned him on or any of the guys she was banging behind his back. Sinny was hot in the ass. She had slept with a few of Chauncey's friends who Tron spoke to, and some other guys from her school. Tron was none the wiser. Though I was a tomboy, I didn't take it that far. I carried myself like a girl at all times. But Sin was giving it up more than any girl I knew, and at the end of the day I guess that's what guys wanted.

"We're fine," I said snidely, wishing I had some conversation for Panama. But my young, fifteen-year-old heart didn't have anything to say. Liking boys other than Chauncey sucked.

Sinny and her bright idea decided to announce that since my mother was not home, we should get out of the fall, chill, and sit up in my house. It seemed as if Sinny knew my mother's schedule better than I did. I knew that once my mother left to go to her boyfriend's house, whoever he was at the time, it was rare that she would come back home, especially if she had to go to work the next day. Still and all, I didn't need any surprises with her coming home and seeing these people in her house. I didn't want to seem immature and tell them no because my mother would kill me, so I got off the bench and led the way to my building. I was nervous because he kept staring at me once we got inside my house. His eyes looked through me and undressed me. I was even more nervous when, at the last minute, Sinny and Tron decided to go somewhere else so that they could be alone, which left me with Panama. I knew that it was a setup the minute we got to my front door and Sinny and Tron decided they "had somewhere to go," leaving Panama and me alone.

As soon as we entered my apartment, I headed straight to the bathroom. I touched myself to make sure I smelled kosher. *I do.* I checked my panties to make sure no uninvited guests had arrived. *They haven't.* I brushed my teeth and put on extra deodorant. I rubbed Razac lotion between my thighs and poked my flat chest out.

What am I doing? I can't have sex with him! This is going too far. Chauncey would kill me if I gave it up to someone else first, especially Panama, he hates Panama. I'm going to tell him to leave. No, can't do that, he'd hate me forever and never talk to me again. I'm going to kill Sinny for this. I headed to my bedroom, where Panama was sitting on my bed in a Grambling University T-shirt and boxers. His clothes were draped over my headboard.

"Come here," he said, and instructed me to sit on his lap. Nervously, I did. He put the blunt in my mouth, and as I smoked he began touching me in places I had never been touched. Chauncey had never touched me the way Panama was touching me now. He was aggressive, rough, determined. He slid his large hands up my shirt and revealed my small, adolescent breasts. I was embarrassed as he began sucking on them. I continued to concentrate on the weed I was smoking.

"Take your pants off," he said, and took off his boxers. He put the pillow over his penis. When I was down to my panties and bra, he revealed himself to me. *There is no way he is putting that big thing in me.* I was scared to death when he put my hand on it. "Touch him," he said. I put my hand on it. He laughed.

"Stroke him," he said, taking the blunt from me.

"Stroke?" I asked.

"Yeah, like this," he said, showing me. He was big, long, and thick. I had no problem speaking up.

"I can't do this." I pulled my hand away.

"Why not?"

"I just can't," I said, shying away. He looked at me for a while, then broke out into a huge grin.

"You a V?" He smiled.

"Yes."

"*You are?*" he asked in shock.

"Yes!"

"Oh, shit, I didn't know that. I figured that since you been hanging out with Sinny and shit plus you got a man I thought he was hittin' that. So Chauncey ain't hittin' that?" he said, and put his pants on. I didn't bother to respond and I don't think he cared either way. He said nothing more about it and continued smoking with me in silence.

"When you're ready to give that away, make sure it's with me, you hear?" he stated more than asked. I didn't know what else to say, so I agreed.

We grew closer as the days went on, and he never tried to pursue me sexually again, but there was an understanding that when I was ready it would have to be him. I only agreed verbally so that he wouldn't be mad, but there was no way that was happening. I had a boyfriend. But Panama had a strong presence that demanded attention. And it was only a matter of time before he demanded mine. But at what cost?

2

Carin

I convinced Chauncey to buy me a few pairs of Girbaud jeans after much pouting. He could never tell me no. So as we walked around downtown Brooklyn together, I ran into each store and began picking out all kinds of items beyond what I had asked him for. Chauncey was a doll. Bigger than anything I could wear, I convinced him to take me into Beat Street so that I could get some music.

"What more do you want, Carin, I just bought you a bunch of music about two weeks ago? Nothing new is out yet."

"I know, baby, but my Biggie tape popped so I need a new one. Come on, baby, please? And I need a new pager, they have Sky Pagers now. I don't want this one anymore."

"You spoiled, you know that?" he said, digging in his pocket. "I don't have much money on me, you bought enough shit. Get the tape and we can come back tomorrow to get whatever else you want."

"The new Guess jeans with the pen pocket and a sweater to match. Something pretty that has the color of the jeans in it," I gushed. He rolled his eyes as we headed into the store.

Happily, I ran in the store to get my *Ready to Die* tape. I had been lost the past few weeks without it. Once we left downtown Brooklyn, Chauncey and I stopped at the diner on Grand Street and sat down for a bite to eat. A friend of his entered the diner, and they began conversing off to the side when Panama and Tron entered the deli. My heart sank. They both gave Chauncey dap then made themselves at home at our table. Chauncey looked back briefly but kept handling his business.

"What's up, sexy?" Panama whispered. I tried my best not to smile too hard. I knew that Chauncey was watching through his peripheral. Panama was looking real good today in a money green T-shirt and blue jeans, with some fresh Beef N Broccolis on. He had a mouth full of gold teeth. The gold set off the green in his eyes. He was gorgeous. His dark features took away any thoughts of calling him a pretty boy. He was straight rough and rugged, just how I liked my boys.

"Ain't nothing, boy." I tried my hardest not to smile. But this was a guy that I used to daydream about in my room, never in a million years thinking that he would find interest in me. Now, I no longer had to daydream. He was on to me and feeling me.

"You look cute today. I see you got some bags. Ya man took you shopping and shit?" He smiled big and wide. He knew exactly what to do.

"Yeah."

"That's good, that's good. What you got from Beat Street, you stay with some music," he said, taking my bag out of my hand. He laughed when he saw that I had another Biggie tape.

"Why you ain't just tell me you didn't want to give me the tape?" He smiled.

I shrugged.

Tron laughed. "You so corny, Carin, for real."

"Shut up, where's Sinny?"

"In the house. I told her to stay inside. She comes outside too much. No chick should be out in the streets as much as she is."

"Get the fuck out of here, are you kidding me? And she listened?"

"She knows what's good for her if that ass acts up," he said, raising his pimp hand up.

I shook my head in disbelief. "I can't see it happening. "

"So Chauncey doesn't check you?" Panama inquired.

"Check me? Nobody *checks* me. Shit, my mother doesn't even check me so I'll be damned if some boy is gonna be checking me."

"I like that. But any girl of mine is gonna have to follow rules," Panama said.

"Well, I'm glad I'm not your girl."

"Says who?"

"Excuse you?" I said, feeling some heat. I was glad when Chauncey came to save the day. He sat next to me and put his arm around my shoulders. "What y'all niggas doing on this side?" he asked.

"I came to check Sin and my grandmother, you know? We about to head back to the grimy side of Brooklyn though. I thought I saw Carin in here so I just came to show love, ya heard?" Tron said.

"Right, right, where Sin at anyway?"

"In the crib. Let me know if you see her outside today, too. She on house duty today." Tron said smugly.

Chauncey laughed. "You'sa wild boy."

Tron and Panama both got up to make their exit. Once again they extended their hands for dap to Chauncey, then said their good-byes. "Stay beautiful," Panama said, and winked at me. I looked at Chauncey, who was chewing real hard on his straw, staring Panama down. He didn't say anything to me about it but I knew that it had caused a silent disliking for Panama.

Panama

Tarsha was in my face all day today and I couldn't get to call Carin. I wanted to send a hello to my little shorty. I thought she was kind of fly and wanted to get to know her a little better. Normally I wouldn't ever consider dating a girl that young. But there was something about Carin that had me intrigued. All I could do was think about her now, though, because Tarsha rode shotgun all day and came with me everywhere I went. If I went to a pay phone she was posted up right under me to see who I was calling. I did all that I could to not show her how much she was annoying me. She had been my girl for three years, but for the past four months I had just been hitting it every once in a while for reasons unknown. I even had her name tatted on my chest. I had to get that removed real soon. It was over between me and Tarsha in my mind, but she wasn't giving up easily. I was the best thing that ever happened to her ass. I stayed quiet all day hoping she'd see my lack of interest and fly away. Tarsha was a hot mess, and the only reason I didn't smack her and tell her to get from around me was because Tarsha would fight back. She was nice with hers and if I hit her, she'd fight me tooth and nail all day all night. I was a rugged nigga but I didn't go for that blemished skin shit. Besides, I didn't want Carin to ask me any questions about some other girl. She was my little honey and I had her right where I wanted her. Tarsha was a high school dropout gangster bitch with no ambitions or goals. The more I hung around Carin, the more I realized that all girls from the hood weren't destined to fail. Carin had a bright future, or so it seemed. She was intelligent to say the least. Tarsha cursed every other word, chain-smoked cigarettes and blunts all day, and hung out with the dirtiest crew of bitches you could ever lay eyes on. I pulled hard on my cigarette thinking of a way to get rid of her.

"I got some shit to do," I said simply, and pulled over in front of her building on Mother Gaston.

"Shit to do like what?"

"Never you mind. I'll be back through here later."

"You think I don't know about that bitch in Bushwick? Yeah, your boys talk way too fucking much, Panama, trying to get me jealous they done got you bagged!"

"What girl from Bushwick? Man, ain't nobody seeing no bitch in Bushwick, man, go 'head with that shit," I said, wondering how she heard anything like that. Tarsha exited my car, but not without threatening me and "that bitch" if she ever found out who she was. I wasn't even going to see Carin, I was going to see this next bitch, Emily from Blake Avenue. I pulled off thinking about Emily, a Spanish chick Tron introduced me to. He loved his Boricua mommies. I didn't have a preference, but black girls were my thing. However, Emily was really cute, with long, stringy hair that hung down to her ass, and that ass! She was definitely arm candy. I had been to her house twice and each time she had her parents cook me up a feast. I was loving that shit and they were loving me, only because I looked more like them than I looked like my own people, bastards. Her parents were old and didn't speak much English, so I told her to tell them to take their old asses to bed because when I came over, after dinner I wanted some head in her bedroom. She giggled, then said okay, and with that I was on my way to her house.

I pulled up to the side of her building and walked around the front, ignoring the stares of her neighborhood dudes who were wondering who I was, walking through their territory alone, so brazen and sure of myself. I had 357 reasons to be so sure of myself. I made it to the front of the building when a dude shouted out, "Yo, my man, who you here to see?" Not one to back down I turned to see about five cats on a bench. The "shouter" didn't make himself known so I didn't press the issue. I turned on my heels when a bottle hit my ankle. I took a deep breath and turned around again.

"Sup, sup, who got a problem?" I asked with a big grin on my face. But I was heated and my trigger finger was always itchy.

"Who you coming to see, duke?" a short, stocky, light-skinned dude asked me.

"I'm coming to see you, meng."

"Oh word, me, word." He flicked his cigarette. Immediately I backed my thing out. "This is what it is?" I asked. No one said anything. I eyed them all.

"It's not that serious, Panama."

I nodded in agreement and sarcastically asked for permission to go in the building, but I knew it wasn't going to end just this easily. These niggas knew my name only because of my hood fame. I didn't know any of these clowns. But my name rang bells and my description was unique. Nobody in Brooklyn even fit my description. My eyes that almost glowed in the dark gave me away more than anything, and my height. I was a long, lanky nigga at six foot five with big hands and dark features, with an even darker soul. Ever since both my parents died when I was a child and I was forced to eat on the streets, I had no love for nobody and didn't really care about dying, or killing for that matter. I had killed a few times before and didn't hesitate to squeeze on anybody who I felt was trying to come for me.

"You know how them project elevators is, boy," someone threatened. We all knew that if you had beef, the last thing you wanted was to get caught in a small project elevator. A threat to me was as good as a promise. I wasn't about to let these niggas throw words at me so easily, so I started shooting. The benches cleared, kids were screaming, and everybody was running. The short stocky guy ran backward smiling, no doubt reaching for his piece. While he was reaching I was aiming. He hit the floor with his wig split. I ran and jumped over him, ready to finish him off if he wasn't already. He was a goner, so I headed to my car, screeching off into the night.

Carin

I tried my best to love school, but every time I entered the doors of Martin Luther King Jr. High School my head began to hurt. It wasn't that I wasn't popular or anything. I knew a lot of people and they knew me. Ironically enough,

I was well known because I was the girl who
never came to school. In my freshman year, I
took a liking to one girl named Missy. Missy
kept to herself and wasn't in the riff-raff. She
was the kind of friend I needed. We shared the
same homeroom and soon found that we shared
even more things. She and I both loathed being
at home, her because of her hypocritical parents
who practiced the "word" of God every day,
yet her father committed adultery constantly
and had recently been rumored to be messing
around with much younger girls in the church,
girls our age; and me because of my sourpuss
of a mother who shared no interest in my life
or feelings, just disdained at the sight of me, it
seemed. Today, I dragged myself into this building that was supposed to be the gateway to my
future, running right into a guy named Shane.
Shane was popular for reasons unknown at first.
He was a skinny, silly-acting guy with bad skin.
But as I got to know Shane, I realized just what
it was that had the girls going crazy over him. He
had what you call swagger, and he was getting
money outside of school and had a lot of broth-
ers that the girls in my school wanted to get with.
The girls in King were boy-crazy! I had never
seen anything like it. They dressed up every day
like grown women, and fought over the boys in

the school. It was ridiculous. I had no time for this nonsense.

"Carin, whaddup?" Shane said, throwing his arms around my shoulders and walking with me down the hall.

"Hey, Shane, what's going on, boy?"

"Shit, I haven't seen you in a while, where you been?"

I shrugged. "Home, doing what I do, ain't shit going on in here." I said as people passed by saying, "hello" and "where you been" to me.

"You wanna lose some money?" he asked.

"You ain't saying shit," I said, following him to the G floor where everybody who gambled, gambled.

I spent the next two hours losing money, then winning twice what I lost playing spades. Happily, I counted my $150 when I heard the whistle of the dean, Mr. Pole, blowing. "Douglas, James, Christen, Kirkland!" He yelled the last names of me, Shane, and some other people who immediately took flight. I ran past all of the girls on the G floor who were busy putting on makeup, and finally made it to the front door, where I caught my composure and coolly walked out as if it was the right thing to do. The females in King were all lost to me. Each of them getting old before their time, dressed in heels and red lips, running after boys. Maybe I was the weirdo who would much rather keep myself to myself, and didn't chase boys but wanted to get money with them, have fun with them and do what they did. For that reason alone I was known in school, but I hated coming.

First of all, the lessons seemed remedial. I knew the answers to my tests without ever having to come to school. The teachers also didn't seem to care. They were all there to collect a check and they made it obvious when they never stopped a student from walking out of class such as I did many times. I'd roam the halls until I found myself at the Fifty-ninth Street train station on my way back home to Brooklyn. The only time I'd stay was when Missy would catch me and force me to stay all day. In turn, I'd make her go with me uptown during lunch to cop some weed. She deemed me an addict. I told her to get a grip. It's how I get through life.

I didn't have any neighborhood friends. I spoke to everyone and they spoke to me but I didn't hang out with anybody. I was a loner, a young girl afraid to get attached to anything or anybody it seemed. I was too smart for school and bored with what girls my age did. The few times that I traveled to East New York to go to Missy's house (to my mother's delight), I'd get spooked by her father who seemed to always be lurking. I told Missy that one day I'd eventually drop out and

just get my GED, that four years was a waste
and that I could be doing other things with my
time. It's a mystery to me how the school hadn't
called yet to inform my mother of my excessive
absences. The only person who did call was Missy
who, like me, was in the tenth grade, but she was
on the honor roll.

Friday came and I was happy to not have to
deal with the guilt I felt for not attending classes.
I was free to hang out with my friends and do
what I pleased with no curfew, no eyes watching,
and no pressure.

I was asleep on a Sunday morning when Panama called me and said that he was coming to my
side of Brooklyn, but I paid him no mind because
he said that he was coming to visit me for the
past few days and hadn't shown up yet. I didn't
mind though, because it gave me time to spend
with Chauncey, and in the interim I earned a pair
of Beef N Broccolis and another leather jacket.
Besides, my mother was home this weekend and
she wasn't going for this boy she didn't know
coming over, especially at his age.

But if my mother knew that I spent most my
days at Chauncey's house getting high and laying up she'd hate him. For now, she thought
Chauncey was the best thing since sliced bread

because I had been dating him for a year and I was still a virgin. My mother made sure of that when she took me to the gynecologist for him to examine me externally, pronouncing that I was a virgin. No one had ever looked at me down there so closely and I was embarrassed. I could have gotten her killed for that. I didn't speak to her for weeks.

Chauncey was sitting on the edge of his bed with an album cover on his lap, breaking up some weed. I said nothing as I put my book bag down and kicked off my ACGs. I immediately snatched up the remote and started watching the *Richard Bey Show*. Chauncey didn't greet me or anything. He stayed focused on what he was doing. I could tell he had something on his mind because normally he'd smother me with hugs and kisses as soon as I entered his home. He skilled his blunt and began smoking, still with his back to me he puffed and puffed. A few more minutes went by, then he finally said something.

"I'm not feeling you around the nigga Panama," he said between pulls.

"Here we go." I shifted in the bed to get comfortable. I knew he was about to talk me to death.

"I know Sin is your girl and Tron is your boy and all that, but that nigga Panama ain't nothing to you. I don't want to see you talking to him. If the nigga got a problem with it, tell him I said to come see me. You heard?"

"Chauncey, you can't stop me from talking to people. Why, because he called me beautiful? I mean, shit, ain't I beautiful?"

"Don't play fucking dumb with me, Carin, all right? You heard what I said. I don't want to see you near that nigga. He a grimey nigga first of all, and you not in his league. Stay in your lane."

"Hold on. Now, I don't know what you and Panama got going on, but leave me out of this. I talk to whoever I want to talk to, Chauncey. Why are you acting so insecure anyway?"

Chauncey turned around to face me. He stared at me for a long time then stood up. I waited for him to give me an explanation, but he said nothing. He passed the blunt to me then went to his night stand to pull money out. Swiftly, he counted the twenties and put them in his pocket, tucking the remaining amount back into the drawer. He took the blunt from me and headed out the door, but not before saying, "You heard what I said."

"Yeah, I hear you talking but I'm not Sinny. You can't tell me who to talk to and who not to talk to."

"You want to be that nigga friend bad, huh?"

"What are you talking about? Look, he never did anything to you or me. I've been knowing him for a while now, Chauncey, and he's never stepped out of line. Besides, you never had an issue with him until he called me beautiful, like that's a lie." I laughed.

"It's only a matter of time before he push up, if he didn't already, and I don't need that shit. Look, man, do what the fuck you want since you wanna argue me down over this nigga. Do you, ma." He headed out the door. I put my sneakers back on and decided to leave right behind him. I wasn't about to sit up in his house like an idiot while he walked around with an attitude. But first I went into his drawer and helped myself to sixty dollars. As I left, I passed him in front of his building as he talked to his friend. He didn't call out for me and I didn't say shit to him. I began my trek home, figuring I could have an attitude in my own damn house. We were officially not speaking.

Jackie

I watched Carin every day and could not quite put my finger on what kind of girl she was. I didn't know if she was a fast ass or not. I tried to stay quiet, mainly, and observe her, but to no avail. She was damn good at whatever it was she was doing. I could only pray that she didn't wind up with a loser like her father. She was nothing like me when I was her age, though. I was a girly girl, I wanted love, I wanted a boyfriend, and I wanted a fairytale. Carin was more rugged and she was very mature for her age. She was boy-crazy for sure but she seemed more into their lifestyle than she was into their hearts. She was no girly girl. My daughter loved the streets and the shit that was in it. I was disappointed upon finding out that she had been cutting school, smoking weed, and possibly drinking. I knew that she ran the streets a lot but I figured that she did that on the weekends. Carin was a smart girl, very articulate and well mannered for the most part. She was no product of her environment; though we lived in the projects we didn't act like project people. My work schedule at the hospital as a nurses' aide didn't allow me to see what Carin was doing as much as I needed to. If I didn't go to work, I didn't get paid and there would be no roof over our heads. Though she had her ways, I trusted her to make good decisions.

I worked hard to take care of Carin, more than she would ever know. I didn't make much money, and the extra that I had I needed to maintain myself as a grown woman. I had a man to keep, and I would not allow Tony to leave me like the others before him. I was tired of letting Carin's father, Darren, haunt my dreams and stunt my growth. I knew where to find him, but chose not to. He'd only play games with me and Carin and we were making it without him. It was hard enough raising her on my own. No man wanted to date a woman with a child. Each one thought that I wanted him to play Daddy to Carin when that wasn't the case. So that was why I'd rather visit them than have them come over. Seeing Carin scared most of them away. I had made peace with myself for now, and had accepted the fact that I was a grown, unmarried mother of a young girl, who seemed to be on a path of destruction because of the company she chose to keep. Sinny had "slut" written all over her. The poor girl looked older than her sixteen years. She had been run through already. I worked too hard to chase behind Carin all day. But I decided to take some time off and lay around the house to see what I could find, and I found plenty.

Carin

My mother was always quiet, but today she seemed to have something on her mind. She made being an adult look so miserable. She was always pouting and thinking. It couldn't be that bad. She never smiled. I never saw her go out with any female friends. She was always dragging her ass around the house. My mother wasn't an ugly woman at all, either; she was very attractive with her naturally auburn hair and curvy shape. She had the most perfect set of teeth I had ever seen on anybody, and when she was in a good mood she seemed to be an all right person to hang out with. But she just chose to be so miserable.

"Ma, are you going out today?" I asked as I walked to the bathroom.

"Why?" she asked somberly as she sat on her sofa, twirling a rum and Coke in her hand with her chocolate brown legs crossed. It was about two in the afternoon and the bar was already open. She and her "man" must have been arguing because she was home and she was grumpy. My mother never smiled unless she and her man were getting along, as if the sight of my face wasn't enough reason to smile. The guy she was with now, Tony, was all right. He didn't come around much, but when he called she went running. I wanted to call him myself and tell him to come get this miserable bitch out the house. When she was home she didn't cook, she didn't talk to me, she didn't do anything except watch television, probably praying that this man called. There were never any snacks in the house. And since it was only us two, when she did cook it was always just enough for us to eat that night, no leftovers. The next meal would come a week or two later so I mainly ate out, ordering Chinese food or eating at Chauncey's house.

"No reason," I said, sitting down in the love seat across from her.

"Why? So you can run the streets?" she accused.

I wouldn't have so much time to run the streets if you were home. "No, I was just asking, Ma."

I actually wanted to just sit down and kick it with my mother about boys, school, whatever because my mom was cool when she wasn't pissed about something. We had no beef as mother and daughter, she was just miserable. So as I sat to talk to her, she looked at me and rolled her eyes. I had to laugh, she just couldn't help being feisty. "What you been up to? You look thin," she asked in disgust.

You don't leave food in the house! "I do?"

"Yeah, *you do.* And what is with all of the EZ widers I'm finding in your room? You smoking that shit?" she asked me of the thin paper that you roll marijuana in.

"No!"

"So whose shit is that?"

"I hold it for my friends."

"You must think I'm stupid," she spat.

Must be to not notice I been drinking and smoking weed since I was twelve. I quickly changed the subject. "Ma, I need some clothes."

"Clothes for what? You don't go to school!"

"Yes, I do." *What the fuck is her problem today, dammit? She is on a roll!*

"Oh yeah?" she said, and tossed a Bible-thick stack of cutting cards at me. "So you need clothes for what? To run around with these little hooligans?"

So this is what her attitude is about. "What hooligans?" I said, fumbling with the cards. I fanned through them as if I were playing spades, which is all I did all day in school anyway.

"Carin, you think I'm stupid? You love you some street niggas, but listen, honey, your father was a street nigga so you go 'head and chase them if you want to. I thought I was smart when I waited until I was twenty-six years old to have you. I saw all of my girlfriends getting dumped left and right at sixteen, seventeen, eighteen years old because I thought they were having babies too young and that was why these men were leaving. But no, honey, understand something: age has nothing to do with it. These men chase money and other bitches. You will never be number one, do you understand me? And if you are number one, you will never be the only one.

They all cheat, they all lie, they all leave eventually. None of this shit lasts forever, honey, let me tell you that! You will get left with a fucking baby and bills!" she barked.

So there you have it. This is what it's about. She blames me for my father leaving her. Everything was all good until she decided to have me. Well, fuck you too, lady, you should have aborted me.

"Ma, I'm not even having sex and you know I'm only with Chauncey, the rest of the guys are just my friends!" I said, getting ready to get up. I didn't sign up for this, not today.

"That was how long ago that I took you to the doctor? A lot could have changed since then. For all I know you could have spread your legs right after the exam! You are going to sit there and tell me that you're not having sex with that damn Chauncey as much as you're up in his face? Then you're cutting school, smoking and drinking?"

I wanted to tell her to try staying home more so that she didn't have to judge, but I didn't want her home, not after insinuating that I was out there fucking everybody when I was a virgin. Yes, I had plenty of guy friends. I had no female friends but Sinny and, yeah, she was a big slut, but *I* was no slut. I got up and began walking back to my room to listen to my music.

"Yeah, go back in your room, you think I'm stupid? You wish I would spend my money on you so you can go lay up. Ask them little hooligans you out there with to buy you some clothes. And if your ass goes to jail do not call me! And, Lord, do not call me if you get pregnant because that will only get you a first-class ticket to the streets that you love so much! I'm not raising another baby!" she barked. I slammed my door.

I fucking hate her. Hot tears rolled from my eyes. I sat on my bed and paged Sinny almost immediately, hoping she wasn't with her man or with those girls I didn't like from around her way. Sinny never did call me back, but to my delight, my mother got a phone call and began getting dressed. When she got in the shower I looked in her room and saw an overnight bag. I looked in her pocketbook and took fifty dollars. She never left food in the house. I was always eating somewhere else. When she left, she didn't even offer to leave me twenty dollars, so I didn't feel bad about stealing, as usual. "I'll be back after work tomorrow, be good," she said, and kissed me as she sashayed out the door. Under my breath I said, "Bye bitch."

Once my mother left, I sat in the living room and began ordering videos off of *The Box* on channel thirty-one. I was dozing off on the couch when my house phone rang.

"Yeah, hello."

"If I find you, bitch, I'ma pump two in your ass," a girl's voice said.

"What?" I looked at the phone, then put it back to my ear.

"You heard me."

Then the phone went dead. I looked at the phone again then hung it up.

I had no idea who it could have been. After a few moments I concluded it was probably a wrong number, because I knew Chauncey wasn't fucking around and if so, he wouldn't have some girl calling my mother's phone. As I began to doze off, a slew of thunderous knocks on the door made me jump. I walked slowly to my front door and stood there for a few seconds.

Boom, boom, boom! I looked through the peephole and could only see the top of a man's head.

"Who . . . ?"

"Yo, open the door!" Panama yelled.

Panama? What the hell is he doing popping up here? I swung the door open as he barged in, then slammed my door behind him.

"What if my mother was here?" I asked with my hand on his chest, trying to stop him from coming in.

"She here?" he asked quickly.

"No, but—"

"So shut up. Yo, come here." He grabbed my hand, pulled me down the hall to my bedroom, and lifted my mattress. He pulled a smoking .357 Magnum out of his army fatigue jacket.

"You don't see this here, you hear, *you hear?*" he asked.

I stood there in shock. "Where are you coming from?"

"Don't ask me no questions. Did you hear me, Carin? You don't see this and I been here with you all night, all day. Do . . . you . . . hear me?" He stood so close to me his lips touched my nose.

"Yeah, yeah I got you," I said as he tossed the burner under the mattress.

"Nobody knows this gun is here, Carin, so if somebody find out I know you done ran your mouth. It's food in here?" he asked me calmly as he took off his jacket and kicked off his Timberlands.

"No, and get your jacket off of my bed." I snatched it up and tossed it back at him.

"Go get some Chinese food or something, meng. I need to just relax, you got weed? Never mind, I do. You got liquor?"

I didn't answer him. I just watched him as he called himself trying to order me around my house.

"You couldn't bring all of that over here on your way from doing crime, nigga?" I said.

He laughed at me, then calmed down.

"Boo, do me a favor. My man is in a grey hooptie downstairs, tell him I'm safe, just tell him you're Carin," he said.

He had me at "Boo." I threw on my fresh black 54-11s and his army jacket, and jumped on the elevator. As soon as I came out of the building I saw the grey hooptie packed with dudes. A real black dude by the name of G.O. came out of the car and started walking toward me as I stood at the bottom of the ramp.

"Carin?" he said, and flicked his cigarette. He looked me up and down and smiled.

"Yeah, hi."

"What's up, shorty? My man is good here, right?" He looked up at the nineteen floors then back at me.

"Yeah, he's good here, so what happened?"

"He stashed something in ya crib?" he asked me.

"What happened?" I asked again.

"He's good, right?" he asked me once more.

"Yes, he's fine," I said, annoyed.

"Good. Tell him to hit me on the hip when he leaves you in the morning." He got back in his car.

In the morning . . . He thinks he's spending the night?

***

I tossed and turned all night with Panama in my small twin bed. If my mother doubled back and saw this, *oh my God*. At around two in the morning I got up and sat in the living room. If she came in I'd say he was my friend and he was drunk and sick and I let him have my bed. She'd still spazz out, but not as bad as if she caught us together in bed. At seven I called to make sure she was at work. She was, so I snuggled under Panama and wrapped my adolescent frame around his grown one. Since there wasn't any breakfast in the house, I got up a little while later and walked to the Associated across the street. On the way there I ran into the neighborhood mayor, a guy named Freddie, who lived down the hall from me. He was outside fixing somebody's car.

"Where you going?" he yelled out from under the hood. I didn't even know he had seen me.

"To the store, you need something?"

He dug in his pocket and handed me five dollars. "Bring me back a Heinekin."

"It's nine in the morning, Freddie, you can't be serious."

"Do what I say, little girl!"

"I'm underage, I can't buy beer!" I joked.

"You can buy weed and vodka, though, right? Think I don't know? I know everything!"

"You think you do. Whose car you fixing?"

"Ms. Posner, from the fourteenth floor, and I do know everything just like I know your mother is gonna whoop your ass if she find out you got that nigga up in her house. You know better and you know tenant patrol is nosey as hell!"

"Yeah, and your mama is the president so if anybody snitching it's her. And there is no nigga in my house."

"That tall, light-skinned cat you be creeping with is not in your house?" he said, coming from under the hood and smiling at me.

"Whatever, you need to mind your business. But first, let me get twenty dollars."

He fanned me off. "All these hustling-ass niggas you're running around here with, let me get fifty dollars."

"Come on, Freddie, this nigga is gonna want breakfast." I laughed. He started laughing too. "Shit, I started to get some cereal but if you give me twenty dollars I can feed a muh-fucka."

"Where's my boy, Chauncey? I like the little dude, he seems nice."

I put my hand out for the twenty dollars. Freddie was being too damn nosy. He slammed it in my hand. "Don't forget my beer and I want to see some change, little girl."

"You ain't but five years older than me."

"Yeah, but I'm legal!" he shouted as I walked off. I waved to a few more people on my way to

the supermarket, where I picked up eggs, pancake mix, syrup, bacon, and orange juice. I got
Freddie's beer to him and hurried upstairs.

Panama was already up, smoking on a blunt,
of course, looking through my drawers. He
didn't even jump when I came in. "Um, what are
you doing.?"

"What it look like I'm doing," he said calmly
and closed the drawers. He took the bags from
me and brought them into the kitchen, then took
the items out. "You cooking?" His face lit up.

"Yeah, you hungry, right?"

He smiled and kissed my forehead. "Thanks,
ma, I was real hungry too and was hoping a nigga
ain't have to eat no bullshit. Do you know how to
cook?"

"Yes. I have no choice, I fend for myself around
here."

"That's what I'm talking about." He kissed my
nose. I nearly melted.

"So are you going to tell me what went down?"
I asked. I whipped up the pancake batter and put
the bacon in the frying pan.

"Nope. In life, Carin, the less you know about
certain things the better off you are."

I contemplated asking him again. I didn't want
to push it, but I had every right to know why he
brought a hot piece to *my house* of all places. Why
couldn't he have brought it to some other girl's

house? *He must really like me and trust me,* I figured.

"You can tell me why you brought that gun here or you can take it out of my house. That's the deal," I said seriously and I meant it.

He stared at me for a long time.

"What happened, that's all I want to know."

"I can trust you, right?"

"Of course!" I was getting annoyed.

"I got into some beef earlier. I was going to see my man in his projects and some cats starting talking reckless. One thing led to another and I wound up bodying some clown out there trying to defend his projects or some lame shit. I never understood that 'defend your hood' shit. Niggas better defend themselves." He shrugged.

Murder? I wish I never asked. I had to remain cool. I had heard the stories from one end of BK to the next about him being a wild cowboy, and now he had confirmed it.

For what? I wanted to ask, but you never needed a reason to body someone in Brooklyn. It just didn't matter, you could get clapped for a dollar. He offered no explanation as he continued to eat his food.

"Let me show you something." He pulled that big-ass gun from out of nowhere. "You want to know how to shoot this?" He smiled.

"Do I need to know how?" I asked, staring at it. Something told me that I did not have a choice, that he was going to take me to the roof and teach me how to use this thing.

"Every woman should know how to use a powerful weapon. Come on, let me show you how."

"Can a bitch eat breakfast first?"

After about twenty minutes of shooting off the roof, we came back into the house. "I'm going to keep teaching you how to shoot, too," he said, amped up like a fiend.

"Why would I need to learn how to use a gun, Panama? I just want to graduate high school, get a good job, and live my life." I laughed.

"Yeah, but you still need to know how to use this thing. If you can use this big shit you can shoot anything." He pulled me on to his lap. He was staring me down with those intoxicating eyes when there was a knock on the door.

I knew the damn nosy tenant patrol was going to say something.

"Open the door." He gripped his piece.

What the fuck are you going to do, start shooting? This boy is nuts. I swung the door open without asking who it was, and there stood Chauncey with a bag full of things most likely for me.

"What are you doing here?" I asked. I had thought Chauncey was mad at me. He was the last person I expected to see. We hadn't talked since I left his house yesterday morning, so I figured we'd just cool off for a few days until someone gave in. I wasn't expecting it to be this soon.

"I can't come visit my princess? I bought you some things." He walked in, smiling. He kissed me on the cheek, but his smile faded when he realized my face was grim. "What happened? What's wrong, P?" he asked.

He laid eyes on a very comfortable Panama, who decided to make his presence known by coughing loudly. He was sprawled out on my sofa, smoking a blunt in his boxers. Chauncey stepped out of my mother's apartment and looked me up and down.

"It's not like that, Chauncey." I felt like shit. He wasn't supposed to see this.

"What the fuck did we just talk about yesterday? You sat up in my fucking face telling me that this nigga ain't never try to violate me or you and he's up in your crib in his fucking boxers? Ayo, you act like you don't know this is my fucking girl, son!" Chauncey said to Panama.

Panama stood and put his pants on. "The shit ain't about nothing. I came through last night and fell asleep, that's all."

"He spent the night?" Chauncey's eyes widened.

All I could do was shake my head. "Chauncey, it's not like that."

"This is the kind of company you like to keep? Niggas like this? He fucks *mad bitches*, he is just a grimey-ass nigga, yo, grimey and you ain't ready for that type of dirt, Carin, you hear me? This nigga right here will break your heart, do you dirty, use you. You ain't in his league, princess. This dude will get you caught up in a bunch of nonsense, man! The fuck is you doing, Carin?"

"We are just cool, Chauncey."

"But he laying up in ya crib in the morning in his boxers. You fucked him, Carin?" he asked me with wild eyes. Chauncey was so cute, his little brown-skinned fly self, standing before me in a Columbia jacket and blue jeans with his skull cap covering half his eyes.

"No!"

He laughed a wicked laugh, then walked off. He turned around and tossed the bag at me.

"I'm not going to be a bitch-ass nigga and take the shit back. That's the Guess sweater and the new Guess jeans you wanted," he said, and disappeared into the staircase.

"Let the lame go 'head. Lock the door, it's a draft," Panama snarled as he sat up. I looked at him for a while and couldn't see what Chauncey saw. I was different from other girls. I was a virgin. I was precious and Panama treated me that way. I wasn't trying to hurt Chauncey and I felt bad. I started to put on my sneakers to run after him.

"Fuck that nigga, Carin, close the door. He doesn't know what to do with a dime like you anyway," Panama said, stopping me in my tracks.

I felt bad for what had just happened. Panama obviously didn't as he pulled me to him. I nudged him off of me.

"Come on now, this shit ain't right. That boy never did anything but love me. I need to go talk to him."

"When . . . I . . . leave. Like I would have you running behind some next nigga while I'm here."

"So maybe you need to leave then, P. I need to go handle my business."

"You really love that li'l nigga, huh?" He smirked.

"It's not even about that. Look, I think you should get dressed so I can go squash this thing with me and Chauncey."

Panama began getting dressed. He gave me a long glare. "You're a real loyal person, Carin. Just don't be loyal to a fault," he said, then walked out.

3

Panama

I had been seeing Carin now for a few months and I was feeling her a lot. She took my mind off the hard knock life. She made me laugh, and the sun always seemed to be shining on her side of Brooklyn. We didn't have to do much when we were around one another to have a good time. All she wanted to do was listen to some good music, laugh, smoke, and eat. What I liked most about Carin was that she wasn't a hood rat. She was a nice girl, street but sweet, and she came from a nice home. I knew this the minute I entered her house, expecting it to smell like stale weed and have roaches everywhere. You could tell that she was loved. Her mother was never home, though. Carin said she worked weird hours. Her black leather sofas looked barely sat in and her bedroom was made up of white furniture and a twin bed. She had a few pictures of her and Sinny on the wall, her and Tron, and her and that nigga,

Chauncey. She offered me something to drink whenever I came over, and we almost always ordered in because she would never cook. She probably couldn't but was too embarrassed to admit it, trying to impress me. She wasn't nothing like those girls I grew up around in Brownsville. Through the winter I spent a lot time visiting Shorty when her mother wasn't home, to gain her trust more than anything. I liked her intimately, yes, but I loved money more, and under my influence I knew that I could use her to be on my team and we could get money together, if she wasn't scared. Carin knew how to handle a very powerful weapon. She had it in her to be a real "Bonnie" if she applied herself. She had the innocent look that no one would suspect, but she also had that die-hard street swagger deep inside of her. I could have her riding with me while doing my sticks. We could get a lot of money together if she was wit' it. I watched her intensely as she let shots off the roof. She was excited, yet she kept her cool. I could picture us doing big things. I had to start buttering her up and reeling her in, putting her under my wing. I knew she was sweet on me so it would be easy to influence her into my life of crime. Besides, by the looks of things she could use a few dollars of her own. That chump Chauncey wasn't uppin' no real bread, from what my cousin told me. A girl like her needed a real nigga like me in her life. She had potential and needed to be given all the things girls wanted. I was going to give it to her or, if nothing else, show her how to get it herself. She needed a life of excitement, not a life of lying up under some lame who wasn't even hittin' it.

I knocked on the door with my wide grin, ready with a hug. It's all she ever wanted from me. She made my heart glow. She was precious. I never had anyone smile at me like she did, except for my mother. She let me in and then excused herself to the back. I popped up on her so I was sure she was going to the bathroom to put on some perfume or do whatever girls do. I wasted no time putting my plan in motion when she came out. I pulled her onto my lap as she tried her hardest not to smile or blush.

"Miss me?" I asked her, wrapping my arms around her shoulders.

"Mmm-hmm," she mumbled shyly.

"So gimme a kiss." I puckered my lips. I could feel her crotch get warm on my lap. She was putty in my hands as she leaned over and kissed my lips softly.

"You are so sweet," I said honestly. But I was about to turn her on to the game. A pretty face was just what I needed. The girls from around my way in Brownsville were too damn rough and old looking. They looked like they were up to no damn good.

"Carin, you know what I do, right?"

She stared at me blankly. "You know how I get money, right?" I reiterated.

"I think I do, I'm not really sure," she answered honestly. "I know whatever it is, it ain't legal." She laughed.

"Look, I'm a stick-up kid. That's what I do for a living. I rob niggas," I said simply. "But this is the deal: I need someone like you on my team." I waited for her to respond. She just kept looking to me to finish. "No one would suspect you of a thing. You look innocent as hell. I'm thinking me and you can do business together. I promise you I will keep you out of harm's way."

"What would be my position, Panama? Rob who? You actually think I'm going to be running around here snatching chains and pocketbooks?" She laughed and stood up. "I'm broke but I'm no bum-ass bitch, that's for damn sure." She looked herself up and down for emphasis.

"Do I look like I snatch fucking chains, little girl? Watch your mouth," I said, offended.

"So who do you rob? What's the most money you got out of a jooks, Panama?"

She was questioning my robbing potential like she knew what she was talking about. I had to admire her guts. "Never you mind, just know that I wouldn't be doing it if there wasn't good money involved."

"If the money is so good then why you ain't stop yet?"

"'Cause I didn't get enough and why you questioning me, Carin? You down or what?" I asked her, getting upset. I thought about having a girl on my team and realized a lot of questions and politics would come along with it. I wasn't sure if I wanted that bullshit to interrupt my flow. I often did things alone or with my man, G.O., but Carin's presence would mean more money. I bit my tongue and continued trying to entice her. She was at a real influential age right now and, besides, I knew she cared about me a lot.

"What is my position . . . that's *if* I was down to do this, and what kind of spots are you trying to hit up, Panama?"

She was inquisitive. This shit right here was turning me on. She wasn't a dummy. "Your position would be simply to put the drop on niggas, Carin. Let's say, for instance, I ran up in somebody's crib. Your job would be to straight put the drop on whoever the person is while I get the cash, the jewelry, whatever. That's it, that simple. My man G.O. would be in the car waiting. He got a lead foot and he is focused. Me and you run up in cribs, spots, whatever. I don't wear masks, I don't give a fuck. Now you? You got to keep that pretty face hidden. You're my best kept secret. I promise you I will guard you with my life. Just listen to what I say."

"What's the most amount of money you received from doing this?"

"Sometimes I've gotten disappointed. I bodied a nigga once just for two hundred dollars thinking it was some money in the spot, once I came off with ten thousand dollars. It depends, it's the chance you gotta take, Carin. You can go on one or two with me. I got one set up right now. This nigga named Cat. I hear he keeps a stash at his girl crib—an inside source tells me this. His girl and her moms live together in the East on Hegeman and New Lots in a house. I hear he keeps his guns and most of his cash there so that's the spot I got in mind."

She sighed deeply and lit a joint. She stared out her window for a minute. I sat back, wondering what she was thinking.

Carin

I was listening to Panama and thinking about the dough I could get out of this thing here. I'd be masked up, he'd protect me, and I could get a couple of grand out of it and be straight. He said that he would teach me how to drive, which was something I had always wanted to learn.

"What's my percentage?" I got off his lap and walked to my living room window.

"We split everything three ways among me, you, and G.O." I could tell he thought this was a good idea. His green eyes were even greener with greed. I took a deep toke and looked at him long and hard.

"If I get killed, shot, hurt, or anything bad happens to me, especially if I get nabbed, you better hold me down, avenge my death, do whatever it is you got to do, you hear me, Panama? Don't just leave me fucked up like I was nothing to you."

"Yeah, Carin, I got you, don't worry about it!" he said and stood up, trying to suppress his excitement. But I knew he was ready to break out the confetti.

"I don't know how to drive."

"I got you. By the time I'm done with you, baby, you'll be ready to work for NASCAR or some shit." He laughed.

"I like the gun you left here. I want that one."

"That one got bodies. You get caught with that, we all going down for life. Let me get you a clean one and I'll keep you posted on when the shit is going to go down. In the meantime, just ride with me," he said, and grabbed my hand. "Be my Bonnie."

I smiled. "Only if you'll be my Clyde."

"I got you, Carin." He kissed my forehead.

I took a long toke. *Nah . . . I got me.*

4

Carin

After I agreed to run with Panama, we thought it best that I just go along for the ride for a while to see how things would pan out. I was forced back to school by both my mother and Panama, who insisted that I go or he'd quit me. My life at home was spent eluding my mother's accusing eyes whenever I'd come running into the house sweaty and nervous. After much begging and pleading Chauncey finally forgave me. I spent every day at his house throughout the winter, and when I was not with him I made sure that I called him every hour on the hour. After a while he calmed down and began smiling at me again. It felt good. I couldn't lose Chauncey.

But once the winter was almost over and spring began to tease us, I started to become more involved in my newfound lifestyle. Panama was always buying me things and taking me to the nicest restaurants, and Sinny would disappear so that I could lie and say that I was with her. Our first real date was at Armando's, downtown in Brooklyn Heights. We both dressed up—me in a pretty denim dress, him in khakis and a button-down—and had a nice quiet night sipping wine and holding hands by the promenade. Chauncey had never taken me out on a date before. Panama even began making sure I got my hair profession-ally done every week. I was feeling this big boy who obviously was feeling me too.

"You having a good time tonight?" he asked from across the table.

"Yes." I blushed.

"You look nice." He looked me up and down.

"Thank you."

"I like you, Carin. I just want you to know that. You special to a nigga, you know?"

Being with Panama was like a dream come true. "I like you too."

He poured my wine and handed me my glass. The wine was red and sweet. I liked it a lot. "So, when you gonna leave your man, Carin?"

I nearly spit out my wine. "I have no plans on doing that."

"You got a real nigga like me now, what do you need with Chauncey? He can't do shit for you."

I took a deep breath and set down my glass. "Look, I think that we should just take things slow and let it play out. I like you a lot, Panama, but you know the deal with me and Chauncey, don't put me on the fence."

He chuckled. "That's why I like you. You ain't easily persuaded. You strong."

I smiled.

"So what do you want to do after this?" he asked.

"Go for a walk on the promenade, if that's okay with you."

"Anything you want to do is all right with me. But look, man, you got a time limit on how long you gon' be able to fuck with Chauncey. I'm not gonna share you much longer."

His jealousy was making me feel all mushy inside.

"Okay," was all I could manage to say as Chauncey blew up my pager. I excused myself and called him from a pay phone.

"Yeah, hello."

"Why I gotta page you a million times before you call me back!"

"You actually didn't have to, you act like I have a damn phone on me to call you right back. Where's the fire, boy?"

"Where you at?"

"Out with Missy, why?"

"When you coming home?"

I looked at my fossil watch that read 9:13. "I'll be home around eleven-thirty or so."

"Why so late, what the fuck are yawl doing?"

"We are hanging out, damn!"

"Don't you see her in school?"

"Bye, Chauncey. I will see you in a few hours, all right?"

He just hung up. "Checking in?" Panama said as soon as I sat down. He had already paid the check and was ready to go for our walk. "Come on." He grabbed my hand, and we headed to the promenade.

Panama dropped me off in front of my building around midnight. We sat in his car and kissed for what seemed like hours. His lips were so soft, his hands big and masculine. Each touch sent chills through my body. "Go upstairs, all right? I don't want to hear you was with that lame," he said.

I nodded my head.

"I love you, see you soon."

Did he just say he loves me? "I love you too." I smiled and got out of the car. I watched him pull off, then ran through to the back of the building and headed toward Chauncey's house.

Chauncey was aggravated, but I quickly changed his mood by sitting on his lap and smothering him with kisses. "What's the matter, brown sugar?" I giggled. I was feeling good.

"You seem real happy, what did you do?"

"What, I can't be happy to see my man?"

"Oh, I'm your man now, you must want something."

"Uh-uh, I just love you, that's all. You're so good to me."

He eyed me suspiciously. "You look nice."

"Thanks, I got it from T.J. Maxx."

"It's nice, you look real pretty. I like when you dress up in dresses and shit. You never dress up when you come see me."

"You never take me out, Chauncey. Maybe if we start going out then I'll start wearing dresses."

"Is that right?"

"Yes." I stood up and took off my shoes. As soon as I lay down, Chauncey began rubbing my feet. "Wake me up around four so I can get home before my mother, okay?"

"All right, princess, I love you." He smiled.

"I love you too, baby," I said, drifting off into a sweet daydream of Panama making love to me.

After the first few jobs, Panama had the idea to hook me up with this guy he believed we could get a grip from. Plenty of times I had gotten phone numbers from guys and just sent Panama and G.O. to do what they do, but this particular guy I had to get close to and actually tolerate.

His name was Monk. I staked him out for three weeks before making contact. Monk was from Canarsie, Brooklyn. He wasn't cute at all. He looked like what his name sounded like.

I stood outside the barbershop in Starrett City where he was getting his hair cut. I was dressed uncomfortably in a tight pair of Gap jeans and a tight T-shirt. My hair was slicked in the tightest ponytail you could imagine, giving me the ghetto chinky-eyed look. I was posted up by his Maxima. All I could think about was getting home and putting on some comfortable jeans. Every day I posted up by the barbershop with a tight getup on just so he could get familiar with my face. I would see him looking at me periodically from the barber chair, but today he was smiling at me, *finally*. When he came out, he immediately asked who I was waiting for.

"Excuse me?" I asked, because I totally forgot what I was supposed to say.

"Why are you posted up in front of my car, shorty?" He smiled his ugly, raggedy-tooth smile. But I could tell Monk had money. His Sergio Tacchini suit was fresh and unique, he wore a heavy gold bracelet and ring, always kept a fresh haircut, and had a souped-up Maxima, a two-door Acura coupe, and a moped.

I touched the hood of his car. "Oh, this yours? I didn't mean to lean all on your shit."

I am going to kill Panama for having me play this dumb car hopping role.

"Yeah, this is mine, sweetheart, you wanna ride?" He smiled, knowing all too well how girls threw themselves at his mercy to ride shotgun.

"Yeah, okay." I smiled and batted my eyes. I walked to the passenger side, his eyes glued to my ass. Monk had to be at least twenty-seven, so I didn't know what he was doing looking at my young ass . . . *pervert.*

"So, what's your name shorty, who was you waiting for?"

"My name is Keesh. A friend of mine told me to meet her at that shop and I been waiting for almost an hour and she didn't show up. I'm not from Brooklyn so I don't know what buses to take home or anything like that."

"Oh, word, where you from?"

"Staten Island."

"So who house you going to now? I know you're not going all the way out to Staten Island."

"My family is out in Queens."

"You know what part of Queens?"

"Yeah, Corona."

"Okay, where about?"

"Um, something like One Hundred First Street and Fifty-seventh Avenue."

"I know where that is. So, Keesh, you mad cute, how old are you?"

"Seventeen."

"*Seventeen, nice.* You mixed or something? You look like you got a little bit of Espanola in you or something." He laughed.

"No, I'm all black."

"Oh, I'm Monk," he finally introduced himself.

When we parked in front of the fictitious house, Monk turned toward me. "You know, I been seeing you in front of that shop for the past week or so. I've been checking you out, shorty."

I smiled awkwardly. I hoped he wouldn't try to kiss me or something.

"Oh, yeah," was all I could say.

"Yeah." He smiled that raggedy-tooth smile again. Monk's skin was oily and bumpy, his hair was of a bad grade, and his lips were big and dry. Jesus, he was fucking ugly.

"Can I get your beeper number?" He touched my pager, trying to be sexy. "How long you gonna be out in Queens?"

"For a while, back and forth. Here you go," I said, jotting my number down quickly and passing it to him. He eyed it.

"My code is one." He smiled.

"One? What makes you think that code is available?" I said, sliding out of the car.

He laughed. "All right then, zero-one is my code. When can I take you out?"

"Hit me on the hip." I slammed his car door and strutted past the front of his car. He rolled the window down as he was about to pull off. "I like what I see, shorty." He winked. I winked back and almost vomited. When he pulled off, I walked to the pay phone and hit Panama to come get me.

After a few dinner-and-a-movie dates with Monk, I knew that he felt that he had earned the right to hit it. Monk kept throwing hints about wanting to show me his crib in Harlem and watching movies there on his leather sectional and fifty-inch screen TV that "niggas knew nothing about," he'd always brag. He started picking me up in different cars, no doubt playing me like a chicken, thinking I was pressed to get it. One night, I slid on a black stretch miniskirt, riding boots, and a fitted, long-sleeved shirt, and wore my hair in my signature bun style but with bangs. I sprayed myself with my mother's Chanel N° 5 perfume and greased my body up nice with baby oil. I packed my bags with FDS and feminine wipes, just in case Panama didn't get there in time and Monk got closer to the pussy than I anticipated. I told Monk that I was running around and that I'd meet him in Canarsie. He agreed.

I hopped in a cab and had the driver drop me off a block away. Panama and G.O. were following behind me. As I walked down the block I could see Monk leaning on his car, talking to two guys. One of them spotted me and alerted him. He got off the car and gave both of the guys pounds, and they jumped in a car that was double-parked. They waited until I got up close, no doubt wanting to see what I looked like. When they got a good enough look they honked the horn twice and pulled off, smiling. Monk smiled too and threw up the peace sign, then grabbed me around my twenty-four-inch waist.

"You look real good, yo." His breath smelled of cigarettes and beer. "Come on, I'm ready to get my night started." He snickered and opened the door of his coupe for me to get in.

We pulled up in front of a brownstone on 145th and St. Nicholas, and by the time I got there I was buzzing. While en route, Monk and I sipped E&J and I had my joint. I could see Panama and G.O. parking on the opposite side of the street with their headlights off. Happily, Monk jogged up the steps to his apartment on the quiet and dark Harlem block. We entered through the second floor and the first room was the living room. It was nice how he had it decorated in money green and beige. Everything was nice and neat. You could tell that Monk was getting money but what I needed to know was where it was at. "Where is your bathroom?" I asked.

"Right upstairs, the last door on the left," he said, occupied with his stereo system. "Take your shoes off." I complied and jogged up the stairs lightly, immediately opening doors and looking around as much as I could. There was a spare room with a few boxes in it, a small bed, and a small television. In the closet I saw about six or seven sneaker boxes. I opened one and saw papers. I opened the other, saw a few bills, and got nervous so I ran to the bathroom before Monk got suspicious. I assumed that in the rest of the boxes there was cash.

When I came back down the steps, Monk was laid out on the sofa in his jeans and a wife beater, flicking through the channels with the radio on the Quiet Storm. All I kept thinking about was him putting those big, nasty, dry lips on me. I sat next to him and smiled. "This is a nice place you have here."

"Nobody comes to this spot, so you know you gotta be special." He smiled.

Ugh.

"So I'm special?" I asked as he passed me a plastic cup of brown liquor. This nigga thought he was getting somebody drunk and vulnerable. I sipped it slow and chased it with Sprite.

"You want some more weed?" he asked.

"No, I'm good." I was never big on smoking with strangers. I didn't trust people like that.

"You sure? I got you, you know. You don't have to worry, get right, get comfortable," he assured me.

Yeah right.

"Okay." I played easily influenced and guzzled down the E&J. I had been drinking longer than I care to admit, so Monk had the wrong one if he thought he could get me tipsy. I knew how to handle my liquor, especially around strangers. "So what movies do you have for us to watch?" I asked as he handed me another drink.

He fanned his hand at the television and turned it off. "I'm thinking we can make our own movies, get to know one another." He smiled rottenly.

You gotta be fucking kidding me.

"Is that right?" I said.

"Mmm-hmm. I think you're pretty. I like you, Keesh. You like me?"

I almost asked him who he was calling Keesh, then I remembered this dumb name that Panama had given me.

No! Hell fucking no!

"Yeah, I do, if I didn't I wouldn't be here," I said, sipping my drink. I wanted him out of my face. He turned the radio up as Hi-Five sang "Quality Time." I sucked my teeth, knowing he was going to try to get romantic on me.

"What's wrong?"

"Nothing," I lied as his hand went up my thigh. He loosened my shirt from my waistband and ran his hand across my breasts, pushing me back against the sofa slowly. "Relax," he said, biting his bottom lip, trying to be sexy. The next thing I know, he was sucking my breasts and fondling my pussy. *Where the fuck is Panama and G.O.?*

Panama

"Come on," G.O. said and took his gat off safety. I skipped across the street first, dressed in dark blue with a skully on. G.O. came up behind me and tucked himself on the side of the door. I rang the bell and knocked loudly.

Carin

I know that's Panama and them. I wish this fool would get off of me, this is disgusting! I was thinking as he sucked on my breasts so nastily and rubbed my clit so hard. He grabbed my hand

and put it on his dick. This was awful. I lay there with my shirt wide open and my pants unzipped. I was disgusted. I didn't like this feeling at all, and once I told Panama about this he'd have Monk's neck for sure.

"Rub this, you ever had a dick as fat as this?" he asked, still biting his bottom lip. He was in animal mode as he dry humped me on the couch.

"No." I put my hand on his chest to stop him. "See who is at the door so they could stop knocking and ringing the bell. It's fucking up my mood."

"You wait right there, I'ma tear that young pussy up."

He smiled and headed to the door. I got up and ran into the kitchen.

Panama

"Here he comes," I mumbled to G.O. I gripped my pistol tight. I could see Monk peeking, trying to identify my face. "Yo," he said from behind the bullet proof glass doors.

"Hi, does Shelly live here?" I said innocently and inaudibly.

"Who?"

"Shelly."

"The fuck he say?" I heard Monk mumble. He cracked the door a bit to hear me better.

"Shelly, does Shells live here?" I asked.

"Nah, don't no Shell live here," he said, about to close the door in my face.

I put my foot in the door quick and could see Carin creeping up on Monk with a pot and a kitchen knife. She whacked him upside his head with the pot as hard as she could. His knees buckled and I put him in the fiend while Carin put the knife to his neck. G.O. ran in.

Carin

"Let's go!" Panama said for me to lead the way. I ran ahead of Panama, leaving G.O. to handle Monk. We ran through the house, with me leading Panama to that suspicious room.

"I think the shit is in here," I said, opening the closet. We came across seven sneaker boxes with money in them.

"Where else?" Panama said greedily as he scooped the money into a plastic bag.

"I don't know, let me check the mattress." I ran to the bedroom. I lifted the mattress and found three knots of money wrapped tightly in rubber bands, all hundreds. "Come on, Panama!" I said.

"Check the other rooms."

I sucked my teeth at his greed. We found nothing else.

"A'ight, come on," he instructed.

We ran down the steps, me heading to the car. G.O. had tied Monk up and taped his mouth. As I was walking out, I could hear G.O. pistol whipping him and Panama telling him to chill with laughter in his voice. As soon as I got to the car, I saw them running down the steps. With ease they got in the car and we pulled off. Panama gave me the three knots, and he and G.O. evenly split what was in the box.

I was thoroughly disgusted with how far things had almost gone with Monk. The more I thought about it, the creepier I felt.

"What the hell took yawl niggas so long? This dude almost got some cootie-cat!" I said from the backseat.

"What do you mean *almost?*"

"I mean like he was fondling me and sucking on me and shit. Oh my God, he is disgusting!" I shivered for emphasis.

"He did all that to you?" Panama said, slowing down.

"What are you doing?" G.O. asked.

"I'm ready to go back to kill that nigga. He was touching you like that? What else he did to you?"

G.O. and I both knew that once Panama got started, he wouldn't stop. And I was his precious little doll. For someone else to have touched me in a way that only he did pissed him off.

"Let's just go. Next time don't take so long, that's all."

Panama glared at me through the rearview mirror. His eyes were tiny green slits. He lit a cigarette and began to drive slow as if he was contemplating.

"G.O., get behind the wheel and take us back to that nigga crib, fuck that." G.O. took a deep breath, but did as he was told.

"Panama, just leave that shit alone, all right?" But my pleas fell on deaf ears. We wound up back in front of Monk's brownstone, where Panama ran upstairs without saying a word. Five minutes later he came back downstairs with his right hand covered in blood. Since we had heard no shots, I could only assume that he stabbed Monk.

"He's done off, let's go."

G.O., with his lead foot, hit the gas, getting us to Brooklyn in what seemed like ten minutes.

"Um, what did you go upstairs and do to that boy?"

"Let's just say his ass won't be sucking on nothing ever again. Leave it alone, ma."

Chauncey had been bugging me to come to his house. I hadn't seen him in a while and because I had to go get money, I was addicted. I was always

on the run, *literally*. Panama had me running up
in bodegas and all kinds of spots. He would just
go off on a whim. We could be on our way out to
just have dinner and a movie, and he'd say, "Carin, come with me." After a few months I knew
what "come with me" meant.

Sin was always paging me off the hook with
411. I couldn't tell her that I was out there "sticking" because Sin had a big mouth. She glorified
shit like that. She'd run her mouth and get me
nabbed. She didn't have to do this, her parents
spoiled her. She was in the street because she
wanted to be, and she was a wannabe. She was
trying to be something she wasn't. The little bit
of street cred that she did have was because of
Tron. Other than that, Sin was nobody trying to
be somebody.

My mother wasn't giving me shit, so I had to
go find a way and I'll be damned if I got money
lying on my back. I was too young to get a decent
job and wasn't trying to be packing nobody's
groceries for chump change. Every ten minutes,
she or Chauncey was paging me. The paging
made me more nervous than anything, so I always left my pager at home when doing my thing
with Panama. We had gone on several small
jobs, splitting things three ways, me only getting
$500 here and $200 there after the $3,000 I got
from the Monk thing. I was spending my money

on partying, treating Sinny to clubs because she said that was the only way she'd go, that spending money to be packed like sardines in some club was stupid. I had a good time just throwing money away. There was nobody flyer than me on this side of town. I got eyes rolled at me, things said to me, and I even began to see new faces around my way of girls grilling me. I guess that was supposed to intimidate me and have me tuck my jewels in. No such thing would happen, especially when I roamed the streets with Panama. People were scared to speak to me when he was there. And when I wasn't with him, I kept a piece on me almost always (unless I was going to see Chauncey), and I wasn't afraid to use it. I had officially become a gun-happy chick. I loved the power I felt having one in my possession.

We had to wait for the opportune moment to get the Big Fish, as Panama called it, and I was fine with that because after this so-called Big Fish I was done with it. I wouldn't lie; I got a rush out of what I was doing. I didn't have to hurt anybody and we got paid. What better way to make a living? But I was done. It was time to get focused on my life. I needed to finish up school and force myself to go to college so I could make something of myself, and not wind up a loser like the rest of the broads in my neighborhood who were pushing strollers and running behind niggas stuck on welfare. What we didn't know was that the day we caught our Big Fish, the drama would pop off.

Panama called me early one Sunday morning after having been on a hiatus for about two months from robbing.

"Carin, get up. It's on," he said with greed in his voice, but not like the other times. This morning Panama sounded like he was on to something.

"What's on?" I said, sitting up.

"You, baby, you! It's show time. I'll see you in about an hour. Meet me up the block by Katz drug store, not in front of your building, and bring that thing downstairs, too," he said of the .357 he left in my house, then the phone went dead.

I lay in my bed for a while wondering why Panama was so excited. He really loved robbing folks. Panama was an all-around nutcase. But people respected him in the streets because he was thorough. His name rang bells all over. He was known as a murderer, a stick-up kid, a basket case. He didn't give a shit about anybody and if he did care about you consider yourself lucky. He only had love for a handful of people and I was one of them. We had gone on plenty of jobs together, and each time, Panama wickedly put his burner to anybody who got in the way. He didn't even wear masks, he didn't care. It was amazing to see him in action, so cold and heartless one minute, then adoring and gentle the next, when he would be up under me, kissing me and holding me, whispering sweet nothings in my ear.

My mom had been giving me the evil eye a lot lately so I knew I had to slow down before she began questioning me. She began to grow suspicious of the clothes and the jewelry. It was making her dislike Chauncey, oddly enough. She figured he was out doing wrong to be able to afford these things for me. She said nothing with her mouth though, just her eyes. She was watching, always watching. It was odd for me to be leaving my house on a Sunday morning when I didn't go to church, but I had to go. I wrote a quick note, then called Missy so she could act as my alibi. Nobody knew. I got up and peeked in my mother's room; she was sound asleep. Quickly, I showered, threw on some Gap sweats and a long john–style shirt, made my ponytail pretty, and slid my feet into a pair of black low top Reebok classics. I waited for about twenty minutes before G.O. pulled up with Panama and a strange female in the car.

"This is Ashanti. Ashanti, this here is Cee-Cee." I looked at him and at G.O. G.O gave me the "go with the flow" look in the rearview. "Hey," I said to Ashanti.

"Hi."

Ashanti looked really young and lost. She was my age, maybe a year or two older, but she just had a naïve look in her eyes. One thing I did notice was that she looked comfortable, like she had been here before. My problem was this third party getting thrown into the mix. I didn't know who she was and didn't give a fuck. I was glad they didn't tell her my real name, and that he was smart enough to have me meet him a few blocks from my house. All I could think was, *let me find out Panama getting sloppy.*

"Look, Ashanti is going to go to Simone's crib, that's Cat girl. Ashanti's brother and Cat fuck wit' one another on the money tip, and Ashanti said that the nigga just dropped off like thirty thousand dollars to Simone's house. We comin' to get that thirty. We'll give Ashanti five of that thirty for her input, a'ight?"

I shrugged, it didn't matter. The money I was getting was more than I could imagine at that age.

"So, boom, Ashanti is going to go visit Simone and your job is this, boo: when Ashanti goes inside, you're going to knock on the door and Simone is going to answer. When she does, it's show time don't waste no time," he said, which was his motto. I laughed every time he said it. When we got closer to the house Panama offered me some chocolate. I told him no. I didn't like to be high when doing this, especially knowing now that he *wasn't* going inside with me and that I would be in the hands of a stranger. I wanted to be on point 100 percent.

Ashanti had already gone inside and was being two-faced. *Bitches. Who could you trust these days?* After about twenty minutes I made my way to Simone's door.

I knocked four times before she appeared at the door, laughing. Simone and Ashanti were having jokes about something. The thick ghetto chick stood in front of me, hair still in doobie pins, dressed in pajama pants and a camisole with her hands on her hips. I stood with my hands behind my back, holding my weapon. I held her stare. "Yes," she asked me in all her stink girl attitude.

I didn't like her demeanor. I had never had to run up on a female until today and I could tell that she was sleeping on me because of how I looked. I said the motto to myself, *It's show time don't waste no time*, then I pulled out my piece and grabbed her wickedly by the throat like I'd seen Panama and G.O. do many times. I put the gun in her mouth and backed her into the apartment. I pushed her down on the sofa and backed up, aiming the gun at her and Ashanti. Ashanti was playing her part. *Grimey bitch*. She sat there holding up both her hands.

"Put your hands down, stupid. Who's here?" I asked, gritting my teeth.

"Nobody, just me and her," she said, motioning toward Ashanti. I gave Ashanti the look to let me know which bedroom the stash was in. She was hesitating and playing the scared role.

"I'm just here visiting her. I don't have shit to do with whatever she's into," she said.

"I want the both of yawl to get the fuck up and go in the room," I said. Ashanti got up first, leading the way to the bedroom. Simone followed her with her hands still up. She sat on the bed. I heard a noise behind me. I turned real quick then looked at Simone.

"Who the fuck is here, I said?"

"My man, he's asleep, that's it."

"Oh, bitch, you trying to be funny? Didn't I ask you who was here?" I whispered. My eyes narrowed at Ashanti. I didn't trust this bitch because I did not know her. I looked around and saw jewelry on the dresser.

"Them earrings are nice, what else you got in here?" I said, walking up to her dresser. I scooped up her Figueroa link and her bamboos. I didn't need any of it, I was just playing a grimey role.

"Nothing," she said.

"Nothing? You, what you got?" I asked Ashanti.

"Nothing," she said. I was contemplating my next move when I heard her man's footsteps. I put my gun down before he could see. He was rubbing his eyes as he walked into the room so he didn't see what I had in my hand.

"Who you?" the guy I presumed to be Cat said to me.

"I'm Cee-Cee." Quickly, I went from pretty thug to an L7. I stood there smiling at him, knowing he'd relax a little bit.

"This is my friend from the GED program I go to," Ashanti said.

"Oh. Yo, Simone, get up and cook a nigga some breakfast, I'm hungry. I'm about to be out. Ashanti, where ya brother at? I been paging him since yesterday."

"He's probably with his girl. You know how he gets when he's around her."

"Yeah, all whipped and shit. Tell him to get at me. Simone, come on, put some pep in ya step." He clapped and walked away.

"Okay," Simone said. I could tell she wanted Cat to read her eyes. I'd have to pop him *and* her if she said one wrong fucking thing. The air was thick. I stood against her dresser with my hand behind my back until I heard the bathroom door close.

I had to think fast. Ashanti obviously didn't want to incriminate herself, which was making it harder for me to get the cash and get the fuck out of there. Cat was up now so it was hard for me to do anything, but at this point it was do or die.

"Where's the stash at?" I said, putting the steel to Simone's ribs.

"What stash?" she asked nervously.

"Bitch, come up off it before I gotta do something stupid."

Simone looked at Ashanti. Ashanti looked at me. I slapped Simone with the gun. "Let's go before ya man comes back out for his breakfast," I whispered.

"I'm back, shorty," I heard him say. I turned around and found Cat standing there, pointing his piece at me. This was not part of the plan. I told Simone to stand up. She did. I kept my piece on her and stood behind her.

"Shorty, I don't want to do nothing foul to you, just tell me who sent you because I know you didn't do this on your own. I don't wanna pop you, I don't," he said calmly. I had to think quickly. I'd never had anybody point a gun at me before. I didn't like how it felt now that the shoe was on the other foot. I needed Panama here with me, not this young, scared chick. Ashanti stood up and continued to play scared.

"Shanni, just chill, I got this. Go in the other room and page your brother zero zero seven, he'll call right back now. Shorty ain't leaving until she tells me who sent her and where they at. Whoever sent her is gonna have to come inside to get her," he said, keeping his cool. Ashanti eased out of the room damn near shaking. This bitch was really an actress. Cat started to walk toward me. I cocked my pistol back.

"Don't make me," I snarled.

"What you got sent here for? Ain't nothing up in this house." He smiled cockily. I smiled cockily too, as Ashanti pulled out her piece and put it to the back of his head.

"Shanni, what are you doing?" Simone said. Cat's smile dropped.

"Put your gun down now," Ashanti ordered.

"What the fuck are you doing, Shanni?" Cat said, attempting to turn around.

Ashanti shot one up in the air. "You think I'm playing with you? Pass that thing back this way *now* Cat, you know how I get down." Cat did as he was told and Ashanti pushed the piece down in the waist of her jeans.

"Lift up the mattress, both of yawl," she instructed.

Reluctantly, they followed orders, revealing guns and money, lots of it. I snatched up the big Conway bag in the corner.

"Fill it up, hurry up now, gimme them guns right there, too," I said.

Panama was paging me off the hook. I hoped he was going to sit tight. Me and Ashanti had this.

Simone put the money in the bag. I told Simone to walk outside to the car and hand it over, while Ashanti and I kept the drop on Cat. As she headed out we guided Cat to the front door so we could keep an eye on them both. When Simone came back, Ashanti and I backed out of the house slowly, guns drawn.

"You just killed your brother," Cat said to Ashanti.

"He ain't got shit to do with this."

"He does now." He continued standing in the doorway with a sinister smirk on his face.

I walked out of the house swiftly. I wanted to get out of there. My heart was beating fast and my nerves were shot. Something told me that shit was about to hit the fan. As soon as I was a few feet away from our car, shots rang out from what seemed like down the block, and I hit the pavement. This shit was crazy. I didn't want to die. I promised myself that this was the last run I'd go on if God spared our lives. Cat came out of the house shooting too, and he was stopping at nothing. I peeked up and saw Cat motioning to his goons with his guns. Panama ran up to me and dragged me by my collar. "Get the fuck in the car and get under the seat!" he yelled as he fired shots up the block while shielding me. He then hopped in and yelled for G.O. to drive. When G.O. tried to pull off, Cat shot through the window, hitting G.O. in his shoulder, then he sent a few more shots to the back. Glass was shattering everywhere as G.O. sent as many shots as he could with his hurt arm. Ashanti popped her head up once and sent a few slugs, so I did what I had to do. Through my window I let off two shots. One hit Cat in the stomach. He instantly stumbled back and fell against a parked car. The other hit his man in the neck. He dropped to his knees and I prayed to God that none of them died.

"G.O., drive this fucking car out of here now!" I yelled. I noticed that Ashanti was quietly ducking down in the back seat. Panama was still shooting. We pulled off, and that's when I realized that Ashanti had been hit dead in the forehead. I looked behind to see Simone running out of the house, screaming, the phone in her hand, calling 911 I was sure . . . I could only hope.

5

Carin

I was crying my head off as G.O. drove the car like a maniac. Ashanti was with me in the backseat, *dead*. Panama and G.O. were on the fritz. My throat was tight and dry.

"We have to take her to the hospital," I whispered. No one heard me, or they pretended not to hear me. I tapped Panama from the backseat. "You heard me."

"Shut the fuck up, I know she dead, meng! I know this shit! Just shut the fuck up," he yelled. I began to cry harder. Ashanti's eyes were popped wide open as if the bullet had caught her by surprise. I shut her eyes. I began to pray and repent. This was too much. I was done with Panama and his "sticks." We finally came across a wooded area out by the Belt Parkway somewhere. Panama and G.O. opened the trunk and pulled out two big dirty rugs. I moved all the way to the other end of the car as they dragged Ashanti's lifeless body out and dropped her on to the carpet. Quickly, they rolled her up and tied up the carpet. "We'll be back," Panama said as they struggled to bring her into the wooded area. I sat in the car, scared, for well over a half-hour until the boys returned.

"What did yawl do with her?" I asked.

"What do you think, Carin? Use your fucking head, meng," was all Panama said.

G.O. pulled over about ten blocks later and he and Panama switched positions. G.O. lay on my lap in the backseat, moaning in agony. I pulled off his shirt and wrapped it around his shoulder tightly to stop the bleeding. "What are we going to do with him?" I asked calmly.

"Nothing, we gon' lay low for a minute. Just take care of him back there," Panama mumbled. He was chain-smoking, and driving like someone was in labor. I sat still, wondering if I had left two niggas for dead.

We wound up in Jamaica Queens at a small, run-down house. A dirty dog was in the yard barking like crazy. Panama got out first and knocked on the basement door. I saw him talking to someone, then he jogged lightly to the car.

"Son, come on." He pulled out G.O. G.O. held his arm and walked to the door. There was blood everywhere. Panama jumped back to the car and told me to get up front. We drove for about five minutes, then he asked me for the piece. "Where the burner at, Carin?"

I took it from under the seat and gave it to him. He cleaned it off, then got out of the car. He disappeared around the corner and came back without it.

"Get out."

I obeyed, and walked with him. We got into another car four blocks away, drove back to the dilapidated house, and went inside.

A little Mexican dude was over G.O., sewing up his shoulder. I saw a hot pair of tweezers and a bullet with blood on it on a small table next to some Jack Daniels. These niggas were crazy.

"So what happened?" the Mexican guy asked.

Panama started telling the story. The guy laughed the entire time, as if it was nothing new.

"Yo, you owe shorty your life, B!" he said, and tightened the stitch on G.O. Panama looked at me and winked. I was still on edge just wanting to go home and lay down for a while. How could they be so calm when there could possibly be dead bodies back in Brooklyn, and what was going to come of this Ashanti situation? I expressed this to Panama, who agreed that I'd had a long day.

"Ya think?" I said sarcastically.

"Son, I'ma come back and get you, let me take her home," he said, ushering me out of the basement, his hand on my back.

"A'ight. Yo, Cee-Cee, I owe you one. I will never forget this." G.O. winked. I gave a fake salute and walked out.

By the time Panama and I got home it was about three in the afternoon and I had blood all over my clothes. "I can't go in the house like this," I said, looking at my shirt. I was shaking terribly. Panama leaned in and wrapped his arms around me.

"You did good, girl. Don't worry. I'm not going to let anything happen to you so don't worry, okay?"

All I could do was nod. At this point it was out of Panama's hands. His handsome face, good hair, and pretty eyes could not, as they'd done many other times before, make me forget about what was important. We sat in the car in front of my building discussing the details of the robbery for a little while longer, then pulled off so I could get a shirt from Jimmy Jazz. Since I couldn't get out of the car, Panama ran inside the store and got me a change of clothes. In the backseat of his hooptie, I cleaned up as much as I could with baby wipes and changed my clothes. Panama disposed of my soiled threads down a sewer on Broadway and Flushing by Woodhull Hospital.

"You all right, baby girl?" he said, squeezing my hand.

All I could do was shake my head. I had seen too much and had done too much. "I want out."

"You can stop whenever you want, baby. As a matter of fact, yeah, I want you out too. If something ever happened to you, Carin, that's my word I'd lose it. I love you, li'l mama." He winked his signature wink and smiled at me. I began to cry.

"Shhh, don't cry, baby. I'm not going to let nothing happen to you, believe that. If them boys come for me I'll take the heat for everything. You a soldier, Carin, you went in harder than I ever expected. You deserve everything, baby. Damn, Ashanti is dead. They're coming to get me for sure." He leaned back in his seat, rubbing his head.

"I didn't mean for shorty to get popped, damn that shit is fucked up."

"What about the two guys?"

"Fuck them niggas, Carin. You did what you had to do, a'ight? So think of it like that. Don't go home all stressed out thinking about karma and all that bullshit, let me worry about that."

I shook my head in pity. I was sick.

"Go get some rest, lay low, and I'll call you. If anything happens to me someone will let you know. Either that or you'll hear about it on the news, but I can't be around you at all, baby, not for a while."

I hugged him tight and kissed his lips. "You be safe, baby, and beep me zero zero seven daily so I know you're okay, all right?"

"You got it, ma. I love you, baby.

When I got upstairs, I heard men's voices in the hallway. I peeked around the corner and saw three plain clothes talking to my mother. She was in the hallway with her arms folded, staring at them as they spoke. "I don't have any sons, and my daughter damn sure isn't running around here shooting at people off of the roof. If she knows something I'll have her call you, but other than that I can't tell you much."

I saw the detective hand her a card. "Have your daughter call us. It's nothing serious just that we have gotten some complaints. You have a nice day."

"Sure, you too." My mother scowled and closed her door softly. As the men neared the elevator I crept back into the other staircase and waited for them to get on before I walked to my door. When I walked in, my mother was on the phone telling my aunt (I'm sure) about what had just happened. She paused when I walked in. "Here she goes now, let me call you back."

I kept walking to my room as she hung up.

"Where are you coming from?" she asked accusingly as she stood in my doorway and watched me undress. I had my back to her, thankfully, because there was blood on my stomach.

"You ain't get my note?"

"I got your fucking note, but where are you coming from?"

"Church, Ma, I went to church with Missy and now I'm home. What happened?" I said, throwing on a pajama shirt.

"You just up and went to church all of a sudden and dressed like that?" She eyed me suspiciously.

"Yeah. You know in Missy's church you can wear what you want, stop tripping," I said, trying to make her laugh.

I knew she didn't believe me as she squinted her eyes at me and pointed, but she didn't say anything. She had no proof.

"The cops just left here talking about some shootout. They said that tenant patrol called the cops because someone keeps shooting off the roof and that you are the one who has strange people come to the building."

"Ma, with all due respect, if you were home more often you'd see that I don't have anything to do with no guns and shooting. Do I even look like I'm into that, Mommy?"

"No, you don't, but those boys you run with sure as hell look grimey. Carin, I pray you're not dumb enough to be doing no bullshit and having no criminals in my house."

I sucked my teeth. "Come on now, Ma."

She stood there, staring at me.

"So what was service about?" she said, and folded her arms in interest. *Dammit*. I tried to suppress a laugh, then her phone rang.

"I want to hear all about it, hold on, baby." She ran to the phone. I'd be taking a nap by the time she came back to hear my story.

Two weeks had gone by since the Cat episode and I hadn't heard anything. There was nothing on the news or elsewhere. I had a few stacks stashed in my mattress. I did a little bit of shopping here and there but nothing that would alarm Chauncey. I was missing Panama like crazy. Though we were stick-up partners, he was also my emotional lover. He made me feel the way a boy my age could not. The way he held me, talked to me, the things he promised me, the way he protected me, made me feel like no other. I loved Panama and I knew that he loved me too. I loved him in a way that I didn't love Chauncey. It was hard to explain.

One summer day, about two months after the Cat incident, I was sitting outside with Chauncey in his projects when Tron, Panama, G.O., and Sinny walked up. Tron sent Sinny to the store and the three thugs walked up to me.

G.O. had that smile on his face that let me know he was still on a high from how I blasted on Cat and his man. Panama held a stone expression showing his hate for my man, and, as always, Tron was smiling that grimey gold-toothed smile. Since Chauncey and Tron were cool, they gave each other a pound, and Tron kissed me on the cheek.

"Sup, Bonnie." Tron smiled. I rolled my eyes as Chauncey looked at me in bewilderment.

"Bonnie, huh? That's what they call you nowadays, princess?" Chauncey asked uneasily. I ignored him and asked the fellas where they were coming from.

"How you been, Carin?" G.O. asked. I hadn't seen him since the incident. I looked at the bullet mark on his shoulder.

"Panama." I greeted him with a head nod.

"Shorty, long time no see." He smiled wickedly.

He extended his pound to Chauncey, who declined. Chauncey moved closer to me and asked Tron what was good for the weekend. I gave Panama a look to let him know to chill out. Chauncey caught this and got upset.

"Carin, go upstairs, I'll be up there in a minute."

I looked at him like he was crazy. "Go upstairs for what?"

"It's a beautiful spring day. Why would you send this beautiful flower upstairs on such a lovely day? You can't hide the sunshine, meng." Panama chewed on his straw.

Chauncey looked at me, then back at Panama. He spat at the ground. "You got a problem with me?"

Panama looked around then back at Chauncey. "You talking to me, li'l nigga?"

"You two cut the bullshit, come on now," I said, but it was useless with two men standing toe-to-toe ready to get it on. It had been a long time coming.

"You and my girl got some secrets or some shit?" Chauncey asked.

"Chauncey, just chill!" I said. Chauncey glared at me.

"This the nigga who's buying you all this shit?" he said, flicking my heavy, long bizmark chain with the Jesus piece. He looked back at Panama.

Panama stepped in Chauncey's face. Tron stepped between them. There was silence. "You's a li'l nigga, Chauncey. A li'l nigga. Big paws on a puppy, that's all," Panama said.

"Fuck you." Chauncey spat again from the corner of his mouth and threw his hands up. Panama looked at G.O., then back to me.

He swung on Chauncey. Chauncey ducked from Panama's swing and caught him in the jaw. I was kind of happy that Chauncey was getting his off. The two of them were scuffling like crazy, drawing attention. I was pissed, but I couldn't be mad at Chauncey. Panama had overstepped his boundaries one too many times. I jumped in between them once Tron and G.O. had pulled them apart.

"What the hell is wrong with you, boy, you crazy?" I slapped Panama. He held his face and looked at me.

"Carin, you serious?" Panama asked me.

"You are way out of line and you know it," I barked. I wasn't about to have Panama come to my side of town and fuck up what me and Chauncey had. What me and Panama did was our thing, but Chauncey was my home and nobody was getting in the way of that. While Tron was calming Chauncey down, Panama leaned over and whispered something in my ear that would change my life.

Panama informed me that Cat had succumbed to his wounds a week after he had been shot, and that detectives had been flashing pictures of him, trying to link him to some other murders and robberies. I felt like shit, I felt like dying my damn self. I wasn't a killer. I was simply defending myself in a situation that I should not have been in in the first place. The wake had come and gone, and word on the street was that they were looking for Panama and "the bitch" he was with. Panama thought it was best that he stay away from me for a while in case he was being followed. Ashanti's brother was on the run from Cat's crew as well. But while he was running, he was surely trying to run into Panama.

Thoughts of Ashanti lying in the backseat with her eyes wide shut haunted me at night. The fact that I took a life haunted me even more. I wasn't the same anymore. I felt it. I became sheltered and paranoid. I chain-smoked marijuana to try to forget about everything, but the more I smoked the more I remembered. I dozed off on the couch this particular day with tears in my eyes, and was awakened by my mother's presence.

"Did you go to school today?" she whispered, taking off her coat and holding her pocketbook. She was looking down at me with her burgundy lipstick and bloodshot eyes. My mother was tired, but of what I did not know because she damn sure wasn't taking care of me.

"Yeah." I looked up at her with red eyes.

She knew I was lying, but had no proof, so she gave up.

"Some guy keeps calling here for you."

"What's his name?" I said, sitting up.

"I don't know, I didn't ask," she said, walking away.

"Well, what did he say?"

"He just asked to talk to you. I said you were asleep. He called three times and said for you to call him."

"Ma, that really says nothing if you didn't get a name."

"You lucky I didn't curse his ass out! You have a beeper, don't you? I want you to stay away from my phone, dammit. You don't pay any bills in here."

Here we go.

"Running around with these street niggas. You are a young lady, try acting like one!" she shouted at the top of her lungs.

"Ma, do you see any girls in this area for me to hang with? There is nothing but boys in the neighborhood. We are in the ghetto, ma, the ghetto!"

"Don't hand me that shit, you got girls in your school, girls in this building!"

"I hang with them! What about Missy? That's my girl! But I can have different kinds of friends, can't I?"

"You and that damn Sinny. She got the right name, Sin . . . No good, the both of you. I know one thing though; you better finish school and get the fuck out of my house."

As she began talking that ol' bullshit, I began to dress. It was the usual routine of roaming the streets, nowhere to go, but anywhere was better than being home.

6

Carin

Since I wasn't running the streets I had nothing to do. My time had been action packed with adventure because of Panama and now that was over. I couldn't even see him the way I wanted to. I spent days with Chauncey and nights daydreaming about Panama, wondering if he was missing me the way I missed him. Sinny was never around when I called, and Missy was Missy, a homebody with her head in the books, where mine needed to be. I had a closet full of fly shit and nowhere to go, so that pushed me to go to school even more. But tonight I wanted to go party, so I called information to find out who was going to be at my favorite hot spot. To my delight, Jay-Z and Biggie Smalls were scheduled to perform. I had my hair done in a pretty French roll, and rested my gold in jewelry cleaner. A mint green cashmere sweater that showed a little bit of my belly, and fitted jeans were the attire for the night. I'd throw on my hard leather Pelle and leather Durangos and rock out tonight.

I took a cab to the Palladium where the bouncer recognized my face. "Where you been, honey?" He smiled and hugged me as he checked someone's ID.

"I been around." I smiled.

"You looking pretty, li'l mama, you ready for the party?"

"You know it." I dug for my money and ID. He fanned me off and lifted the rope for me to enter. I got a drink at the bar and got a nice quaint spot in the corner of the stage so that I could see the performance clearly. The music was good tonight and the fellas were checking me out. I got a few phone numbers as I killed time before the show.

Jay-Z came out in a denim suit and Timberlands, and Biggie had on a black sweatshirt with a B on it, and blue jeans. They attacked one another verbally on the Brooklyn's Finest track, Jay stumbling over his words as he held a bottle of Cristal in his hand. Big, looking larger than life, also held a bottle. The crowd was going crazy! I was wishing that Sinny or Chauncey was here to witness this moment. It would be talked about for years to come. Once the show was over, I made my way through the crowd as everyone continued to party. I hated to be the last to leave a club, so on the way out I bought a spray-painted photo of Jay and Big, and hailed a taxi to take me over the Williamsburg Bridge. Tonight was a good night.

The next morning I woke up ready to go to Chauncey's house to brag about my star-studded night, and noticed how grey the skies were. I was beginning to think that only in my part of town was there rarely any sunshine. The skies always seemed gloomy and there was always some kind of chill in the air. I got dressed and headed into the streets to see what was going on. The wind was cutting through my thin leather jacket and blowing my oversized earrings all over the place. I flipped up my collar and tucked my earrings in, and stuffed my chain under my shirt and my hands deep into my jeans pockets.

When I got to Chauncey's building, I could see figures in the hall. I tugged at the doorknob and knocked for them to let me in. I knew they had to be some neighborhood dudes. Chauncey opened the door and was standing there with Sinny and an unfamiliar female. I immediately sensed something wasn't right. The girl continued sizing me up as I did her. She was dirty, wearing a dirty pair of aqua blue Guess jeans, a dirty leather jacket, just dirty, trying to be clean but she wasn't. She didn't sit right with me. *Where did Sinny find this chick?*

"Sup, yawl," I said. No smile, no phoniness.

"Sup," Chauncey said, and put his arms around me, immediately trying to lead me upstairs.

"What are you doing in the hallway? I thought I told you that I didn't like for you to hang out in the halls."

"I ran into them on my way back from Harlem. I just got here not even five minutes ago, Princess," he assured me.

"Sin, what's up. I was paging you today." I looked back over my shoulder to Sinny.

"Ain't nothing." Sinny averted her eyes. I was going to just head upstairs to lie down but I felt the need to say something. Something was tugging at my instincts. Sinny wasn't acting like herself. I knew that maybe through the course of me running with Panama she may have found a new friend, but Sinny and me were girls to the end and I still made time to speak with her daily, even if I didn't see her.

We all stood quietly for an extra twenty seconds, then the girl spoke up.

"You fuck with Panama?" she asked me out of nowhere.

"Who, me?" I said for lack of anything better to say. She had caught me off guard.

"You know who I am?" she asked.

"Nah. I don't believe I do." I put my hand in my jacket pocket tight on my orange box cutter. "I'm Panama's wife!"

Ain't no way in hell Panama could be fucking with the likes of this bitch.

I didn't want Chauncey to think anything so I played it cool. "Oh, okay, that's cool."

"Didn't I tell you if I ever ran into you I was going to pump two in your ass?" she said, reaching. Then I remembered the phone call I had gotten some time ago.

"Yo, what the fuck are you doing, girl, chill with that!" Chauncey said, stepping to her. I backed up. Chauncey pushed me behind him. I had nothing to prove to a dusty bitch with a gun.

"I'ma tell you like this, you better stay the fuck from around my man or next time you gon' feel this."

I was at a loss for words.

"Let's go," she said to Sinny, who didn't look my way, she just tagged behind. But not before I was going to get in her ass.

"Let's go!" the girl yelled like a mad woman.

"Sinny, that's what's up?" I asked her, my voice cracking. I was hurt. Sin was my girl.

"Let her go, Carin, just let her go." Chauncey pulled me back inside.

I felt humiliated for dissing Chauncey for this dude who was claiming some dirty bitch. We walked up to his apartment so that I could calm down. I sat on the edge of his bed and began to cry out of nervousness more than anything. He sat next to me but didn't touch me. He just let his hands dangle between his legs while he looked at me with disappointment.

"What is that girl's name?" I asked.

"Tarsha, why? What are you going to do, run behind this broad and fight for that nigga Panama?" he asked.

"Not now, Chauncey."

"Don't 'not now, Chauncey' me, Carin! What are you doing?" He grabbed me by the chin to look at him. He had worry and disappointment in his eyes. I felt bad for letting him down over and over.

"Now what, Carin? Do you see where all this shit is going? Sinny done flipped on you for this bitch!" It cut like a knife to know that Sinny had betrayed me in this fashion. He stood in front of me ranting on and on about me running around with Panama and not going to school. "Panama don't give a fuck about you. He got a girl, or whatever you want to call that shit, and you're the only one doing some dumb shit that doesn't concern you. You got a man, Carin, you forgot?"

"No, Chauncey, how could I ever forget about you?"

He lay back on the bed with his hood still on and his hands behind his head. I couldn't even look at him.

"Carin, come here." He pulled me to him. I lay under his armpit. "What are you looking for, huh? What is it that you need?"

"Nothing, I'm not looking for anything," I said, not sure. I knew there was a void in me that needed to be filled, but I just didn't know how that hole had gotten there.

"Stay away from Panama or it's over. I don't want to hear shit about shit now. You know what it is. I catch you around him and it's over, you hear me?"

"Yes."

"Say, 'yes, Chauncey.'"

"Yes, Chauncey."

He got up, took his sweater off, and turned on the television. We sat there in silence for a while when I realized that I needed to get home and page Panama. I was going to curse his ass out.

"I'm out, Chauncey, I have to go," I said, jumping up and putting my coat back on.

"Where are you going? You go out there and that bitch catch you she will clap you, Carin. Does she look like she won't?"

"Call me a cab," I said on second thought, and waited since he had the phone. Chauncey didn't wait with me like he normally did, and I didn't care right now. When I got home, I jumped on the pay phone in front of my building and paged Panama first.

"Who is this?" he said when he called me back. I was freezing, rocking from side to side as I spoke to him with one hand in my pocket.

"Panama, who the hell is Tarsha?"

"What are you talking about?"

"Where's Tron? Where's my brother?" I yelled. I was hysterical.

"He's right here, but calm down. What are you talking about?"

"I go to see Chauncey and next thing you know I got this chick pulling out guns on me, talking about stay away from you. I don't get down like that, Panama, I'm not into all of this fighting over guys and all of this. I mean, is this the kinds of bitches you fuck with? Motherfucka, I went out in a blaze for you and this is how you fucking do me, you son of a bitch?"

Panama was quiet for a while as I breathed heavily.

"I didn't have nothing to do with her pulling out on you, Carin, you don't even believe that shit yourself. I didn't have anything to do with that."

"You know what, Panama, I should have never fucked with you from the gate. Chauncey was right. You are a grimey, lowdown, dirty-ass nigga."

"Carin, where you at?" I heard him yelling out on the other end but I just hung up. *Fuck him!* I grunted then headed to my house.

I sat in the house, thinking about the mess I had gotten myself into. All I wanted now was for everyone to leave me alone. I kept having dreams of trying to finish school and the cops looking for me there or rolling up on me in the street. I was in way over my head, and although Panama had said he'd take care of it, I didn't want to hear it. What he talked in the streets might be different from what he'd say in one of those small, hot rooms in downtown Brooklyn. Two days after that situation with his girl, I calmed down enough to hear his version of events. Panama came to my house with a bag of groceries and toiletries for the house. I got the food part but didn't understand the toilet paper and dishwashing liquid.

"You never seem to have enough of this shit when I come over." He laughed and began stuffing things under the sink and in the kitchen. He brought paper towels and air freshener, too. He doubled up the plastic bags and put them under the sink, then made himself comfy on the couch. He grabbed my hand softly, sat me down on the couch, and apologized.

"Carin, you know why I care for you so much?"

I shrugged.

"You remind me a lot of my mother. My mother and father died in a fire at a basement party when I was four years old. My family members bounced me around until finally my aunt Sheila, Tron's mother, took me in for a while but only out of obligation. My entire life I never had no family and I had to eat the best way I knew how. I robbed, I begged, I stole, you name it I did it to eat. It wasn't until I turned fourteen that I started fucking with girls and I would eat at their houses. Where I grew up, bitches is only about status and reps. Bitches loved me 'cause of my looks and my reps. I always been the underdog. I never came across a woman who looked at me with pure adoration except for my moms, until I came across you, Carin. I want you all to myself. I miss my mother, I miss that feeling, and you look so much like her it's crazy, and you're maternal, too. I don't know if you know that, but you just give off this motherly thing. I'ma call you mama bear."

"Mama bear?"

"Yeah. Look, I'm not trying to scare you, shorty, I'm just saying what's on my mind. You're pure, your love. You're special. No matter what you do in this life, B, don't let no nigga take that from you, you hear me?"

"Yes."

"You strong-minded. All these raggedy broads falling for peer pressure and shit, nah, you ain't like them. You are you! Stay true to you. I love you, Carin, that's my word. I will protect you with all that I have. Trust me when I tell you that I didn't know anything about that girl coming over."

"Who the hell is she?"

"I use to deal with her. But listen, meng, she ain't important. I checked her ass for stepping to you so you don't have to worry about that ever happening again."

"Can you believe Sinny though?"

He shook his head. "Tron got in her ass about that, believe that. He fucked her up good behind that."

"I don't understand why she would bring that girl to Chauncey's, and, Panama, what are you doing even fucking with somebody like her? She is dirty!"

"I was young and dumb but that's over. All I want is you, Carin." He smiled that big smile. He told me that he loved me and would never let anything happen to me. I believed him. As much as he had put me in harm's way, I felt safe with him.

Later on that night, after Panama left my house, I had calmed down enough to get my thoughts together. I began thinking about Sinny, wondering why she would do this to me. I went to all of our little spots in the hood and could not find her. She wasn't at the deli on Grand Street, or on the wall in front of Eastern District High School. She was probably hiding from me as she should because if she knew me, she'd know that when I caught her I was going to beat her ass senseless. Walking home from the "chocolate spot," a game room that clearly sold the best chocolate marijuana in town, I spotted Sinny and a girl from her projects coming out of a bodega. I put my blunt out, jogged up to her, and tapped her on her shoulder. She was stunned to see me after allowing so many weeks to pass. She smiled faintly.

"What's up with you, Sinny?" I grilled her down. Sinny was a punk and had always been. She was a Puerto Rican girl who thought she was black because she had a black boyfriend. Everyone in the hood knew that about her.

"Carin, let me tell you how that shit went down, yo, I wasn't being foul. She asked me did I know you because she heard that P was seeing some girl from Bushwick. Then I told her I knew you and she wanted to come through to see you."

"So you bring this bitch to my man house none-theless?"

"I didn't mean to. She kind of followed me."

I had to laugh. Sinny was such a pussy. "So you let this broad put the pressure on you to come to my hood to see me? You're supposed to be my best friend!" I hauled off and slapped her. She held her face. Her friend laughed. "You and I will never be friends again, you backstab-bing bitch. This bitch had a gun. She could have killed me, you stupid fucking bitch!" I began to hurl punches at Sinny the more I thought about the danger she put me in. Sinny finally hit the ground where I began to stomp her out. The girl she was with just stood off on the side, covering her mouth. I would never do that to her or any-one I considered a friend. I hated disloyalty. She didn't even fight me back. I was mad that I even wasted my good punches on this spineless cow-ard. Breathless, I left Sinny cowering behind a car as I walked home to take a nap. That chapter of my life was over.

Panama

I knew that I was looking fly in a beige jeans suit with my hair freshly cut and a fresh pair of cheese Timberlands. I had just copped a brand new nugget watch and my chain was thick and long. It was a partly cloudy day but there would be no rain, no drama, no robbing, and hopefully no murders today. I didn't want to beef with Tarsha or explain to Emily why I couldn't come to her house anymore. She had no idea that I was involved in that murder around her way. She hated that I had to take her to the Galaxy Hotel all the time, but either she'd like it or leave me the fuck alone, period. But today wasn't about that bitch or anyone else for that matter. Today was about my sweet shorty, Carin. I loved that girl. Some time had gone by since we had been dating exclusively without the stick-ups and crime. We had laid low off of that for a while since the Ds were on me. I spent most of my time in the house or in Williamsburg at my grandmother's with Tron, hoping I'd run into bitch-ass Chauncey. I never would, though. I spent a lot of time wooing Carin, taking her out when she could get away from that lame-ass man of hers, meeting her at school and driving her home, even taking her to school in the mornings just to make sure that she went. I knew she struggled with school but I wanted her to achieve and feel good about herself, and as long as I took her or promised I'd pick her up, she'd be in that building, getting her education. I didn't want her to let a rotten nigga like me ruin her life. Even if we were to be together one day exclusively, I wanted her to have her shit together, to give me something to show off. For once in my life, I needed something to be proud of, and a girl like Carin was it.

I knew Carin wanted me to hit it like yesterday. I was trying to stall her out and see if it was what she really wanted. She was seventeen now and developing quickly. She was no longer a tomboy but a fly little honey with a cute shape and a nice smile with bowlegs that had been hiding in those baggy jeans. She stuck her ass out and arched her back whenever she sat down next to me or on my lap, and when I spoke to her she had lust all in her young eyes. How could she not, with that nigga Chauncey not slinging no dick to her ass after all this time? I was glad she put it out there because I was definitely taking that.

"I'm serious. How about this weekend when my mother goes to her boyfriend's house, you come over, bring some chocolate, we get high, and you, um . . . you know, take this from me," she said the last time I was at her house.

"Yeah, you sure you want this?"

"Yeah." She shrugged.

"What about your man?" I mocked.

"You want this or not?" I could tell that she wasn't really sure, but it was too late; she'd said it and I was snatching that.

"Yeah, I want it. I'll be by Friday night for that." I smiled and pulled her up on my lap.

Carin grabbed my face and tapped her lips with mine, then slid her warm, soft tongue in my mouth and kissed me slow.

"I'ma give it you slow just like that, baby," I told her.

Carin

From one extreme to the next I sat back and waited for Panama to call me. Tonight was the night he'd make me a woman. We had a bond that was undeniable. I felt it in my bones that I was doing the right thing. My mind was made up and there was no turning back. Missy had asked me a million times was I ready, did I have condoms, did I know how big he was, how bad it was going to hurt. We had even gone out to Strawberries yesterday picking out a little outfit for me to wear. I sat up on the phone with Missy until ten at night, then told her I needed to prepare myself mentally for this and that I'd call her tomorrow with the details. As if the mood couldn't get any more set, a light rain began to fall. I was amped up. I'd be making love for the first time, in the rain. I'd have a story of romance to share. According to Missy, boys couldn't tell if you had sex before so I planned on lying to Chauncey if I needed to. The time was right and Panama was the one. Chauncey was taking too long and I wasn't pressing him. Nervously, I sat on my bed and watched television. I checked my outfit out a million times, sprayed my bed with FDS, and sprinkled baby powder on my mattress. I waited until eleven o'clock, but Panama did not show up. I paged him back to back, nine one one, four one one and got no answer. I even paged G.O. to see if they were together. Neither of them called me back. I sat on the edge of my bed dressed in my cheap panty and bra set from Strawberries, my hair slicked back into a tight, neat bun with "Let's Jam" holding up my sides, my big earrings on, and my body drenched in my mother's Chanel N° 5 perfume. I was ready to get it on, but after waiting for Panama until one in the morning I wound up falling asleep.

I'm a firm believer that everything happens for a reason, but I was still pissed off that Panama stood me up. I couldn't even function I was so damn angry, so I decided to call Chauncey and go chill with him but he said he had other plans. I continued getting dressed anyway as I spoke to him. "Other plans like what?"

"Like going out," he said coldly.

"With who?" I paused upon realizing he was serious.

"Why do you care? You're busy running behind that grimey-ass nigga, never you mind what I'm doing. Go run behind him. I hope his girl don't air you out. I told you I wasn't trying to hear you fucking with him. I'm out."

"Who told you I was fucking with him, Chauncey? I don't fuck with him!"

"Whatever, B," Chauncey said to me with a chuckle. I guess I deserved this but my pride wouldn't allow me to humble myself.

"Fuck you then, Chauncey."

"No, go fuck Panama."

"I sure will!" But he didn't hear me. He had already hung up on me. I wanted to cry. I had nobody. Panama had stood me up. Sinny and I were no longer friends. Chauncey was on the verge of quitting me, rightfully so. I needed to just go back to school and get my life together and move on. Missy had been calling me off the hook trying to convince me to get my ass back in class but I had more important things to do. But I had every intention of going back to school.

I didn't even want to smoke. I kept seeing Cat fall to his knees. My mother would be mortified if she got wind of any of this. I didn't even want the money anymore that I hid in my closet. It was blood money. I didn't want anything to do with anything. I paged Panama nine one one, I wanted to tell him that it was over. I wanted him out of my life once and for all. An hour later, the house phone rang.

I knew it was him with some sorry excuse why he stood me up the night before. He could forget about it, he should have gotten it while it was hot. I didn't want to have sex with him anymore.

"Hello," I said with attitude.

"You know that I didn't even go out last night. I was just trying to hurt you," Chauncey said as soon as I picked up. I knew he couldn't stay mad at me for long. I promised myself that I was done with Panama, though I couldn't deny that I was pissed he hadn't even called me with a an explanation. I was going to hold on to Chauncey, because although he hustled he was so good to me. For a guy who was only seventeen, he was dedicated to me when he could have been running wild like the rest of the hood. I was almost positive that he got his nut off elsewhere, but out of respect for me I never heard anything, and he patiently waited for me. Here I was ready to give it to some nigga who in truth didn't even love me.

I ignored his comment. "Your mother cooked?"

"You are something else, Carin. Yeah, she cooked." He laughed.

"What did she cook?"

"Chicken and macaroni."

"I'll be there in a few. Pay for my cab, and be outside."

"You are mad lazy and bossy! You can't walk down Bushwick Avenue? Man, it's only six blocks! I'll meet you halfway."

"It's late and it's six *long-ass* blocks. Pay for my cab, see you in about ten minutes."

"A'ight, man." He hung up and I called my cab.

Chauncey killed me when he tried to make his room all grown up to get me in the mood. It was cute how he lit incense, had that awful blue light-bulb in his room, and Keith Sweat was always on the radio. Tonight I guess he planned on giving me oral. That was the basis of our relationship. I'd come to his house and he'd go down on me almost every night, but he would never take it to that next step, and I surely wasn't going down on him. I wondered when he planned on trying to go all the way. I was glad at this very second that my hot ass didn't let Panama hit it. I dozed off with a full belly in Chauncey's queen-sized bed, and for the first time in a long time I felt safe and at peace. There weren't any outside distractions. I just wanted to be here with him and forget about any crushes and excitement. It was at this very moment that it became clear to me that this is where I needed to be. I didn't need to run around being reckless, not for another day. I got rid of the bad seeds in my life and was afforded another opportunity at happiness.

Momentarily, I'd open my eyes to find Chauncey lying next to me just staring at me with adoration in his eyes. I caused him pain and uneasiness for no reason at all when all he ever did was be good to me. He answered my every beck and call, he bought me things, tolerated my immaturity, and bigger than that, he never ever pressured me for sex. He was satisfied with giving me oral all the time because he felt I wasn't ready. When he told me that he'd wait for me, he meant it. He said I should wait until I graduated high school.

"Go back to sleep, princess, I was just looking at you, checking you out. I love your stank ass," he said in his smooth, cute voice.

"I love you too," I heard myself say. His eyes widened and he reached over and turned on the light. "Since when?" he said excitedly.

"You are so silly, Chauncey. I love you, now don't go making a big mess out of it."

"You love me? Me? You sure?"

"Right now? Yes." I giggled. He turned the lights back off and hugged me close to his chest.

"We are going to be all right, Carin, you just gotta learn how to leave some bullshit alone. You know what I mean?"

"It's already done, Chauncey."

He said nothing more, he just lay there with me in his arms for the first time in a while, breathing easy. He couldn't stop kissing my forehead.

At around one in the morning, my pager was vibrating like crazy as Chauncey stood over me, growling.

"Who would be calling you like that this time of the morning?" he asked me, fully dressed.

"Where are you going?"

"Back downstairs for a minute to talk to my man, collect some money. Your pager been going off for a second now, P, who's paging you?"

"I'm sorry."

I meant that sincerely and tried to ignore my pager, but it kept going off. I picked it up and saw the word duplicate. "Can I use your phone?"

"To call back some nigga? You buggin'." He pulled his fitted hat down lower on his head.

"I don't know who this is, Chauncey!" I said.

He tossed the phone at me and walked out as I called the number.

"Hello, somebody beep Carin?"

"Yeah, this is Hamp, you don't know me but I know you. I called to tell you that G.O. and Panama got locked up."

"Hey, what's going on?" I said, trying to sound natural. I knew Chauncey had stopped at the front door to listen.

"Yeah, sorry, I meant to call you Friday but I got caught up. But, yo, the boy is locked up."

"Locked up?" My heart fell. "What do you mean *locked up*? When are you going to talk to Panama again?"

"Tomorrow sometime, do you need me to tell him something?" he asked me.

Chauncey stood in the door way chewing his tongue. "Um, no, nope, just to call me when things get situated," I said.

"All right then, keep ya head up. I'll be in touch." He hung up.

I jumped out of bed and slid my small feet into my black low top Air Force Ones.

"I guess you just now getting the news about your boy, huh?"

I just stared at him wishing I could tell him the hell I was going through. I wish I could hide in his arms forever. But I had to leave and go lay down with my thoughts.

"Go 'head, just be safe. When am I going to see you again?"

"Tomorrow, I promise you. Just remember what we spoke about earlier. I meant it. I'm done. I do love you, Chauncey, and I want this to work. I have so much that I need to confide in you about, baby, just give me a day or two, please." I ran out into the night as I heard the cab honking the horn. All the way home I was nervous thinking about why Panama was locked up. It could be anything, as much dirt as he did. I prayed that I wasn't next.

Panama

I wish I could bring Carin over to my house but these girls would kill her if they caught her coming through here. Brownsville girls were ruthless when it came to the boys they grew up with, they felt as if they owned us. My little one-bedroom apartment wasn't bad, especially for only $200 a month through my homegirl's section 8 hookup. It was my down low spot that nobody really knew I had. Everybody thought I still lived with Tron and his mother on the other side of the projects. I was fresh in my beige jeans suit and my hair cut, my waves were spinning, and I was dancing in the mirror. G.O. shook his head at me and I didn't even entertain him. I had some pussy to go conquer.

"Young girl got your nose open," he said, looking at his pager. "She paging me now for you, why you not hitting her back?" he asked me, shoving his pager back onto his hip.

"She's thirsty right now. I'll call her back when I'm in front of her building, she ain't going anywhere. I'll just take that from her real quick and you know once I do I get to hit that any time I want for life." I laughed smugly. G.O. laughed too.

"So what's her man been doing with her all this time? She must be sucking his dick or something!"

"I don't know, man. *I don't even care* what that nigga doing to her. I know what *I'ma do* to that ass. Her little ass been getting fat, too, I noticed that shit the other day when I was in her crib and she had on these little sweat shorts."

"Carin is cool people, though, she thorough," G.O. said.

"Mmm-hmm, that she is, and untapped!" I said, thinking about what I was going to have Carin doing once I got inside of her.

"A'ight then, I'm hittin' up this house party over in Tilden with Rah and 'em tonight. Pick up a few chickens and what not."

"You go do that. I got a well-cooked Cornish hen that's fresh out the oven waiting for me. I wonder what she's going to put on. You know she probably ran out and got some shit for the kid to impress me, her little young hot ass can't wait to get popped!"

G.O. laughed some more and stood up to check his pager. "That's Rah and 'em now. I'm out, son. Be easy on the young'un, we need her to be mobile," he said, giving me a pound.

"Hold up. I'm going downstairs with you, let me call a cab."

When I got downstairs, it was drizzling and G.O. and a few dudes from around the way were all in front of the building talking shit and getting ready for the house party. "You not rolling?" a guy named Stacks asked.

"I got shit to do, meng, shit that you need to be doing instead of hanging with a bunch of niggas, meng."

"You going to check shorty from Bushwick?" Rah asked.

"And you know this!" I said proudly.

"Look here come Tarsh," G.O. said, rolling his eyes. He put out his cigarette and dug his hands into his pockets as Tarsha walked up with a crew of hood rats. I loathed that bitch Tarsha. She was so beneath me, and I don't even know what ever made me fuck with her on the level I did. I'm glad she never kept any of those babies when she got pregnant.

"Sup, yawl?" she said, sipping on a Tropical Fantasy soda. I didn't speak to her or her peoples. I barely acknowledged the dirty hood rats.

"You can't speak, Panama? You too good to speak now?" she started.

"Oh, boy, don't start your shit," G.O. said.

"I ain't startin'. The little light-skinned bitch got this nigga forgetting what's *really* hood. Nigga done went upside my head over that bitch!" Tarsha went on.

"Get out my face, meng," I snarled, then turned my head because Tarsha was right up on me, touching my chain and playing me close. I wanted to punch the bitch in her face and just knock her out.

"She fuck you like how I fuck you, Panama?" she asked me, reminding me of how many times I played myself fucking Tarsha, sometimes raw. But that was long ago. I was getting disgusted. Tarsha was a dirty piece of hood trash, just worthless; no goals, no life. She just rolled with a bunch of baby-mama, Section 8 welfare bitches whose idea for a better life was having more kids so that they could get cheap housing. Back in the day, she fought every single girl who came through the projects to see me. She was pissed that I defended

Carin the way I did and almost tried to take her head off when I found out she stepped to her. I beat her ass real good behind that one.

"You taking her somewhere tonight, nigga, you got on cologne?" she teased.

"Cologne? What the fuck are you doing with cologne on?" one of Tarsha's cronies, Melody, asked.

"Yawl some dumb bitches, Mel. Where ya kids at, meng? Go make a bottle or something," I said.

"Fuck you, Panama. My kids is with they grandmother where they belong."

G.O. gave me a pound. "Yo, I'm out. You waiting for a cab or something? I can't be around these bitches another second."

"Oh, like them bitches you fuck with in Seth-low is any better," Tarsha said.

"Anything is better then yawl pecka-heads," Rah said.

"Shut up, Rah, wit' your burning ass!" Mel said.

"Burnin? Bitch, you don't even know who your baby father is so shut the fuck up."

"I know who he is, he's up north."

"Word," Rah said, making the guys laugh.

"Where the fuck is the cab?" I asked, peeking my head out from under the awning.

"Oh shit, one time!" someone said. I didn't even know who said it. All I knew was that I had to get in the building. Police were jumping over ropes, slamming niggas up against the walls, tackling them across benches, even hemming the bitches up. From where I was standing I had nowhere to run but back into the building and up to my stash house. I put my foot against the wall and pulled the heavy project door hard, breaking the lock, and high tailed it up the steps. I got to the ninth floor and was out of breath. As soon as I got upstairs, I walked a little slower to catch my breath. I reached my door and went inside.

"Think think think, meng, think!" I said. "Fuck!" I looked around with my hands on my hips. Before I could blink, the door was kicked in. "Don't you fuckin move!" was all I heard. Flash lights were on me and four guns were aimed at my head.

"Put your hands in the air and don't move!"

How the fuck I'm putting my hands in the air and not moving. I slowly dropped to my knees with the guns following me down to the ground. As soon as it was deemed safe, an officer rushed over and cuffed me.

7

Carin

I woke up this morning in tears. I was scared especially when I watched the news and saw that they found Ashanti Melkhi's body. Her face popped up on the screen and I began to break out into hives. *How did I manage to get caught up in this life?* I started thinking about my father and his other children and I wondered if he sheltered them, provided for them and cared for them and kept them out of situations like this. I wondered if they too sat in a project window feeling uninspired, wondering what tomorrow would bring. I wondered how he could just walk out of my life and not even look back to see if I ate, had clothes on my back, was breathing, or if I needed a nickel. The more I thought about it, the more pissed off I started to get.

I walked over to my bed and sat down, trying not to cry. I kept thinking back to when I was younger. I remembered my father and that's why it hurt. Although I was small the last time I saw him, I remembered his hugs and kisses and I needed them now. I yearned for and craved my father's love. But he'd abandoned me without reason.

I pulled hard on the chocolate and stared out the window. I got so high I thought that I saw a dead pigeon flying with one wing. I was home alone; my mother was at work as usual. She had been in some kind of mood ever since she and her man broke up. From what I could overhear her telling my aunt, she done fucked up on yet another dude. How many had it been? If we barely spoke when they were together, we weren't going to say shit to each other now. Her mood would only worsen. She was a torn, bitter woman. My mother and I didn't have any *personal* beefs. I just sensed that something had gone wrong in her life and it left her drained, broken, and silent. I'm sure my father had everything to do with it. But life went on, or at least I pretended that it did. The music in my head and heart, playing sad songs of yearning, happy songs of promise, was all I had to get me through.

My mother didn't even concern herself with how I ate. I don't think she *didn't care* how I ate, I just think she knew I'd eat. I was a hustler, a survivor, so I'd be damned if I did without. I smoked my weed and blew out the window while looking outside. I watched little girls play in the parking lot of an abandoned building, crackheads copping, thugs slap boxing, Puerto Ricans in loud cars driving down the narrow street, old ladies scowling, old perverts hollering at the little girls playing tag in the parking lot, girls like me sitting on the bench in a daze, smiling, laughing, trying to be young but having so much on their minds. The radiator was hot; the heat was nothing to fuck with, especially in the projects. It seemed as if NYCHA was trying to cook niggas out of their leases. I got tired of the scenery so I began to read the Bible, no verse in particular, just surfing through it, trying to convince God that I was into Him, but, truth be told, I didn't know Him. I looked at the pages in His good book and wanted the words to find me, but they didn't. As I held the book, I took a toke and sipped on Hennessey straight. Sipping Hennessey, reading the Bible, smoking a joint, early in the afternoon. What a sight.

My pity party was interrupted by a hard but slow knock at the door. I figured that it was Chauncey. I needed him now. I just wanted him to hug the pain away. I put the joint out on the wall right by my front door, dusted off the ashes, opened the door, and blew smoke in two detective's faces. They threw cuffs on me and pinned me against the wall, wearing nothing but Chauncey's long, grey T-shirt, my high was immediately gone.

"What did I do?" I asked with my face pressed against the wall. The detective started off being rough, but for whatever reason changed his mind and sat me on the couch, while two other officers ran to the back and began to search.

"You have the right to remain silent." One of them flung a piece of paper at me that I assumed was a warrant. They ransacked my house. They made off $4,000 in cash that I had left from the Cat robbery.

I silently cried all the way downtown and was lead into the interrogation room at the Eighty-third precinct. Quietly, a Spanish detective by the name of Ramos came in the room and sat across from me with his arms folded.

"Hello," he said, and stared me down. I didn't say anything, I just wanted to know what was going to happen to me.

"Do you know why you're here?" he asked.

"No."

"You sure? 'Cause *I* know why you're here."

"I need to make a phone call," I said. He rolled his eyes, threw down a mug shot of Panama, and tapped it with his large index finger. "You know this guy?" he asked matter-of-factly.

"Yes, I do." I knew there was no sense in lying. If they knew where to find me then they knew who I knew.

"Is this your boyfriend?" he asked.

"No, he's a friend."

"A friend, huh? Friends do this?" he said, throwing out a picture of Panama and me in the backseat of his Honda making out. I remembered it being the same day Ashanti and Cat were killed. He had been comforting me.

"Look, young lady, from what I hear about you you're a well-liked girl. Don't go throwing your life away over this loser. We have been watching him for a long time, and I'll tell you another thing. He has a girlfriend and she's not too happy with the closeness you and he have. She is pissed and willing to tell all. Tell us what you know and we'll cut you loose. You want to play the ride-or-die chick? You go to jail, bottom line." He leaned back in his chair, folding his hands.

"I don't know anything and neither does this so-called girlfriend of Panama's," I said.

"So where did you get the money?"

"I have a boyfriend. I'd like to call my mother."

"You want your mommy. Were you thinking about your mommy when you were out there robbing and killing people?"

"I never killed anybody. I don't know what you're talking about!"

The detective eyed me seriously. He then threw down a picture of Ashanti, Byron Murrows, a.k.a. Cat, and Ricky Moore. "Any of these people look familiar to you?" he asked me.

I was getting sick. I didn't know if he was playing mind games with me, if Panama snitched on me, or what. I was going to deny everything until they came up with proof, fuck it. I'd send Panama to hell if he tried to pin anything on me. I didn't think he'd be that stupid and never took him to be the snitch type, but when you're facing life you'd do some desperate shit.

"No, I don't know these people."

"Not even her?"

Thoughts of Ashanti in the backseat came at me like a raging bull. Thinking of how they wrapped her body up and buried her in the woods made my skin crawl. It was inhumane. I tried hard not to cry. That poor girl didn't deserve a gun shot to the head. She wasn't supposed to die and get thrown in a ditch like that. I kept talking to myself: *Carin, don't cry, don't cry, don't fold, take this shit to your grave, make them show you proof it's your word against everybody's right now.* I didn't have time to be spending in prison. I was only seventeen, I had my entire life ahead of me. I hadn't yet gotten to enjoy the things a girl my age should enjoy.

"You know something? Everybody is saving their own ass, so don't be a hero, Carin. Tell us what you know and you can walk out of here free."

"I don't know shit, so do what yawl got to do," I said finally.

I prayed that Panama hadn't snitched. I sucked my teeth and demanded my phone call. "I know my rights." He escorted me to a phone where I called my mother, but she wasn't home yet. I left her a detailed message, hoping that this one time in her life she'd be there for me.

The judge set my bail to $120,000 dollars. My mother had to come up with $12,000 of that. I knew she didn't have that kind of money, and if she did she had no intention of spending it on my bail. Maybe Aunt Maxine and her husband could come up with some of it.

G.O., Panama, and I had different court dates. I couldn't even communicate with them to find out what was what. I tried calling Tron to find out if Panama had told him anything, but he wasn't taking my calls for whatever reason, and calling Sinny would be like calling the cops. I regretted whooping her ass. Maybe if I would have just let it slide I would have been able to call her now. But it was too late for regrets. Besides, she probably had everything to do with the cops coming to my door. After that beat down she probably told Tarsha everything she knew and Tarsha, in turn, a scorned woman, sent them to my house with Sinny's help. I believed in my heart that's how it happened. Panama wasn't no bitch, not to my knowledge, so I couldn't see him putting anything on me. They set my bail so high because they wanted Panama's ass bad. They didn't even give him or G.O. bail. I was sick on the hard bench eating nasty cheese sandwiches. I was stinky, dirty, tired, constipated, embarrassed, and fed up, and I wanted to go the fuck home. I couldn't even call Chauncey because I was too embarrassed, and once he found out who had gotten me into this trouble he would surely turn his back on me. I couldn't dare call Missy's house from the pen, her sanctified parents would have a holy shit fit. Where the fuck was my mother?

Jackie

When I walked inside I put my keys down on the table and opened the refrigerator. There was nothing in there. Pissed now, I headed to Carin's room to see if she was there sleeping off her high. She really thought I was stupid, like I didn't know she was out there smoking reefers. On the way down the hall I noticed the condition of my room, knowing damn well I hadn't left it like this. My mattress was flipped over, clothes were everywhere. I ran out of my room and into Carin's; her room looked even worse.

For a minute I stood there in bewilderment, wondering what had happened. My heart began to beat fast. Had we been robbed? Was Carin okay? I ran to my room to page her and saw my message light blinking. I hit the button and listened to my daughter as she spoke calmly and evenly into the phone so that I could hear every word.

"Ma, it's me. They got me down at the Eighty-third precinct and if you don't get me bailed out, they are going to send me to Rikers. Ma, you have to come get me. I can't be in jail! They have me down here on some gun charges, accomplice to murder, armed robbery. Mommy, please come get me, I swear I didn't do anything. Call Detective Ramos at the Eighty-third. My bail is twelve thousand."

I sat on my bed and shook my head. Where was I suppose to get $12,000 from? What did I tell Carin about messing with those damn thugs who won't even bail her out? The first thing I did was page Chauncey. With all of the money he been spending on her, I was sure he could at least come up with $3,000. I'd put up $3,000 and get the rest from my sister and Carin's father. And when I bailed Carin out I was going to put my foot in her ass, then put her out. I was done with her and her nonsense. She had been nothing but a damn obstacle from the day she came into this world, blocking the life her father and I had, then any life I had after him, and she wasn't even a good child. She constantly had me worried, running that streets with that crowd of hers. I was bailing her out and then I was done with her. I had a man in my life I needed to tend to and I wasn't going to let Carin and her juvenile issues get in the way. She was my child so I'd hand her the rope, but after that she was on her own.

Chauncey

I hadn't heard from Carin in some days and truthfully, it was all right. I was tired of her playing me for Panama. I didn't care if she wasn't giving either of us pussy. She was disrespecting me in my face by hanging out with him, especially after the fight we had. I was sick of her. I loved her but I was done with her. She was starting to go down a path no girl of mine should go down. She was losing her quality. So when I saw her paging me nine one one, nine one one, I ignored her. I rolled over and went to sleep. I was moving on, once and for all.

Darren

I was staring at the pictures of my daughter that her mother had been so gracious to send. I couldn't believe how much Carin looked like me. She was so pretty, but lately her mother had been telling me that Carin was keeping the wrong company, and she was afraid for her safety. I knew it was time to step up and step in. I hadn't been a father to her all of these years, but I figured it wasn't too late. The fact that my sister ran into Jackie in Macy's four years ago was nothing short of a blessing, because I had been thinking about my daughter so much over the years. Even though I knew how to get in contact with them I knew that Jackie was not going to allow me to see her, not after how I did them both.

So when Jackie ran into my sister at Macy's and gave up her phone number for me to call, I was delighted. I called her and she told me that she would not allow me to come back into Carin's life unless I was willing to be there full time. She still took the time to send me pictures of all the years I'd missed. I felt like shit, having my daughter grow up without me. All the years of me just being selfish and getting too caught up. I still loved Jackie very much, and Carin was my love child. But I got scared and I got carried away and I hurt Jackie and Carin to the point where I was too afraid to come around, and one day turned to weeks, then months, then years. But I was ready now to help my daughter walk into womanhood with her head held high, not with a baby in her hand or as a high school dropout. I knew her rebellious ways were due to my absence and it killed me every day. I stared at the picture of Carin. She looked just like me, except she had her mother's smile and big legs. I had to save my daughter from being a statistic and, most importantly, from getting caught up in the streets with a nigga like me. Though I made an honest living now, I had put a lot of women through hell and didn't want that for my daughter. But after I got the phone call from Jackie I realized I was too late. My karma had begun to come back, but on my daughter.

My heart sank as she told me the current state of our daughter. I had the money to bail her out and I was going to do just that, but I couldn't believe that it had come to this.

"Jackie, are you sleeping on the job? How the hell did this happen?"

"Excuse me?" she said. I could see her standing there with her eyes opened wide, blinking a million times per second in astonishment at what I had just said. "At least I showed up to the fucking job, Darren, where the fuck you been all this time?" she yelled.

"Jackie, how did my daughter wind up in jail? What is she in jail for?"

"Look, I don't know the full details, all right? Are you going to help us out or not?"

"Sit tight, I'm on my way to you now. I'll call you when I get in my car."

I did eighty toward the Holland Tunnel to go get my baby girl.

Carin

At eleven in the morning, I was released on bail. When I came out of the precinct I saw my mother standing there, her eyes red from anger, lack of sleep, and worry. I didn't put my head down; I had to hold my head up. I looked back at her, confused. I wasn't sure if I wanted her to comfort me or if I should get angry. "Ma, I'm so sorry," I said. She hugged me for a long time but didn't say anything, then held my hand as we walked out into the cool morning air. I was hungry and I wanted to take a long, hot shower.

"We are going to that car across the street," she said. I eyed the smoke grey BMW and the man in the driver's seat who, I was sure, my mother was seeing. I wondered why she was so calm. When I got to the car I stopped, unsure of whether I should get in. The driver got out. I noticed how handsome he was. Finally she had gotten a man with some kind of street swagger. He looked really young. I smiled inside. But then my smile started to quiver as I stared at this man who had tears in his eyes. He came from around the driver side and faced me.

Until that day, I thought I looked exactly like my mother, just a lighter version. This man in front of me had my complexion, my nose, my eyes, my mouth. When he hugged me I pushed him away. He said nothing, but gritted his teeth. The same fucking thing I do when I'm at a loss of words or contemplating something to do or say. "I bet you're hungry, you hungry?" he said, smiling sadly.

I stared at him for a long time. My mother held on to the back door and watched us as she dabbed her eyes with a tissue.

"How you doin' there, li'l mama?" he said to me.

I felt embarrassed that after all of these years my father showed up, and here I was coming out of jail in a raggedy T-shirt, with uncombed hair, smelling like hot nickels. He reached out to me, grabbed my hands, and gently pulled me toward him. I kept my head down. I was too vulnerable, I couldn't look at him. I wanted to cry and hug him tight, but I didn't want to show him how much he meant to me just to have him leave me again. He put my arms around his waist and rubbed my back. This time, I accepted his hug. I didn't have time to throw a princess fit and be mad. I needed someone to hug me and hold me down because my ass was going to jail.

My father hired a lawyer and was with me for every court date, sometimes with his girlfriend. He and I were getting to know one another despite the situation, and I even confided in him my role in each of the situations. I didn't even tell my mother because she would flip, but my father was from the street and the more he knew, the more he could help me out. I had a lot of questions to ask him but that could wait. I had plenty of time when I got to jail, to write and ask him everything.

After a six month trial, the prosecutors pinned the illegal possession of a fire arm, manslaughter, and armed robberies on Panama and G.O. They both were hit with eight and a half to fifteen years. I was tried as an adult, charged with being an accomplice, and sentenced to one year. The day I turned myself in for sentencing had to be the saddest day of my life. My mother cried, my father hugged her, and his girlfriend rubbed his shoulder as I walked into the courtroom.

"Baby, with good behavior you'll be home in eight months, so maintain. I'll be there to see you every single weekend and I'll keep money on your books, I promise you," my father said as he hugged me tight.

My mother couldn't stop crying. I wondered why she was putting on such a show for my father. Or maybe it was for his girlfriend, who, by the way, seemed so precious by the way she carried herself. She was a girly girl; she was into her looks and her hair and she gave off a nice vibe. She seemed to be younger than my mother, and the vision of her and my dad together did something to my emotions. My mom was no doubt being a damn actress for her audience.

"My baby is going to jail?" my mother kept saying over and over. I started to get pissed at her. I blamed it on my parents. If they had been there for me more, I would not have gone out in the streets looking for attention and getting into trouble. The court officers cuffed me and took me to my temporary destiny, and all I could hear was my mother wailing in the background. I knew I was going to have a rough ride. None of them had been there for me before, so I doubted they'd be there for me now.

My first week in Rose M. Singer, the women's prison on Rikers Island was downright fucking scary. Since they had tried me as an adult, I was among murderers, rapists, all kinds of nasty, dirty dykes and butches. I was scared for my life. I was nothing like these women. My mother worked hard, I was smart and I wasn't dirty or abandoned . . . well, to a certain degree. My cellmate was an older lady who had to be in her forties. She looked young and had a young spirit. She was chocolate brown with a short haircut that was growing out. She had been there for eight months already and was due to go upstate in a few months. "Hey, I'm Mizz BK," she said. I laughed inside. This old lady was wild if she thought I was going to call her that.

"Hi, I'm Carin." I threw my shit on the hard-ass bed. I wanted to just scream, *"Get me outta here!"* but I knew I just had to do my time and keep it moving.

To my surprise this "Mizz BK," which I refused to call her, knew everybody and she was well respected. Word was her son was a big-time hustler and she went to jail for him to avoid him going to jail for life. She was doing five years straight, no parole, and no probation. But her son always put money on her books and a lot of the other female inmates', so they loved her and they loved her son. He was a handsome dude. She showed me pictures and one time we both got a visit at the same time, me by my dad and her from her son, and it was wild how her son looked so much like my father. We joked about it often and she would always tell me that back in the day, she'd had sex with my father and that her son was my brother. I called her by her government name, Li'l. She hated it but accepted it. When I told her what I was in for she looked shocked. "You don't look like you'd hurt a fly!" she said, hopping up on the top bunk and opening her mail.

She read a little bit, then ripped up the letter. "Anyway, listen here, this jail shit ain't cute. Do your time and get the hell out of here and leave them niggas alone. I'm telling you, stay away from these street niggas. Well, just learn to choose the ones that ain't in no shit. What happened to your co-d's, they snitched?"

"No, everybody rode it out. I just want to get out of here," I said, laying on my bunk and thinking about Chauncey. I wondered what he was up to. I had written a letter to him some time ago explaining what had gone down, but he never wrote me back. I couldn't blame him. I had played myself.

"Douglas!" the guard came and called my name. I sat up slowly, hoping that miraculously the charges had been dropped against me and I would be going home. *Yeah, right.* "You got a visit."

I always got visits so I wasn't surprised to be getting one now. I knew it would be my father or possibly my mother since she hadn't made it up here yet, but this time I was totally surprised at the person who sat at the table waiting for me.

Chauncey

I could not believe what Carin had let Panama do to her. When I didn't hear from her I knew something had to be wrong. At first I figured she had her head buried in the books, especially when I got word that Panama was locked up. I let her ride for a little while. But then when I finally broke down and called her house and her mother told me she was in jail, I was disappointed like crazy. Soon after that I got a letter from her telling me a halfassed story about what had happened.

I stared at the envelope for a while, at her name on it with the address to Rose M. Singer Center on Rikers Island. I thought the worst when I opened the letter. Carin had always been a smart girl. I used to see her come through my projects with Sinny all the time and was hesitant at first because anybody who rolled with Sinny was trash. But the more I watched her the more I realized she wasn't a hood rat, so one day I had to push up. I could never forget how she smiled when I spoke to her.

She spoke slowly and clearly as if she wanted people to understand everything she had to say. Our talks when she came through the projects turned into late-night phone calls, then to her waiting for Sinny at my house, to her always wanting to be at my house. We had been tight ever since, and the fact that she hadn't been tampered with was a plus in my eyes. I was no doubt making her my girl. So to see her in this predicament was heartbreaking. As mad as I was, I had to go see her, even if it was for the last time. I sat at a small table among a bunch of inmates, waiting to see my princess come through one of the small doors by the C.O. desk. There my baby girl stood, looking around to see who was visiting her. I stood up and put my hands in my pockets. I was mad that she had let herself go down like this. She was still fly in Reebok classics and a navy blue Nautica sweat suit. When she saw me, she got nervous but walked toward me anyway. I greeted her with a long, warm hug and a kiss. The first couple of moments we said nothing to one another, but the silence said so much. Then I broke the ice with a simple, "So how are you doing?"

"I'm good. How are you?" she asked me distantly. I noticed that she couldn't look me in the eye, so I reached across the table and held her hand.

"Carin, it's all right. If I was that mad at you I wouldn't be here. What the fuck happened though? How you wind up here?"

Carin

I told Chauncey *everything* that went down. He sat back in his chair with his head down, listening. When I was done I waited for him to tell me "I told you so," but he didn't. Instead, he asked me who was taking care of me in here.

"My father. Can you believe it?" I laughed and sat back.

"Get the fuck outta here, where he come from?" he said, laughing too. He knew all too well the pain I carried with not having my father around.

I shrugged. "My mother found him and he bailed me out. He sends me food packages, clothes, the whole shit every week. I can't complain. He's holding me down. My mother hasn't been up here at all yet, but I'm not surprised."

"You know it has to be hard for her to see you like this, Carin."

"Chauncey, please, she doesn't write me and she doesn't take my calls, either."

"Damn, princess. This is fucked up, you know, you being in here and all that," he whispered.

"Who did you think you were? I mean, why did you even fuck with them cats like that when you know how grimey they are?" he said, getting mad at me like I knew he would.

"Chauncey, despite what you want to think, Panama has never disrespected me in any way."

"If he cared about you so much why did he have you out there like that? You could have gotten yourself killed! I would never have put you out there like that. I do my shit but you would never know because I love you enough to not want you worrying about me. *I* love you, Carin, *not him*."

"Chauncey, I know this. I know you love me. Everything you're telling me right now, I know. I'm over it. Look, it's all water under the bridge now. It's over. I'm going to come home and do the right thing."

Chauncey rolled his eyes. He was pissed. I reached over and touched his hand. "Look at this shit, man, you don't belong in here," he said, looking around. "I hope you do come home and go straight."

"I promise."

"Anybody try to fuck you?" he joked, trying to lighten the mood.

"Hell no! Not yet at least."

We shared a good laugh at that one, and I told him about Mizz BK keeping me under her wing.

"I love you. Call me if you need anything. I'm here. I'll be up to see you again soon."

"I know you got me, Chauncey, and thank you for always being there for me. I never did deserve you." I winked.

He smiled at me and kissed my hand, then the visit was over and so was Chauncey. I knew he wouldn't visit me again. I saw the disappointment and coldness in his eyes when he stood up to say good-bye. A part of him was probably happy that I was on lockdown. I had broken his heart and knew that he was never coming back to me. I had lost him for good.

8

Carin

I served eight out of twelve months in prison. I had a few scuffles because a few women wanted to "rep their hood" and all that ignorant shit. Most of my scuffles came from jealousy because I got visits often, and as many packages and as much commissary as the books would allow. I never starved in prison so I had a lot of women trying to take from me because I was a young girl and I looked sweet. How surprised they were to find out that looks could be deceiving. The day that I was released was so invigorating. I wanted Chauncey to come get me so that I could get a nice take down before I went anywhere, but I hadn't heard from him except for once right after he visited. He wasn't taking my calls and he didn't respond to any of the five letters I sent, so I got the hint. My best friend from school, Missy, couldn't make it because she had to go to Kingdom Hall with her pedophile father and scary mother, so I just told my father to pick me up. He was standing outside of his car smiling at me and holding his arms open for a hug with a huge bouquet of flowers. Now that I was coming home, I wasn't sure about him all over again.

"You did it, baby!" he said, and picked me up.

I didn't feel that same feeling I felt before. I was angry all over again, wondering if he was going to abandon me now that he had done his good deed. "Can I please get me a home-cooked meal?"

"Your mother got something nice for you," he said, opening my car door.

"My mother? I didn't know I had one!" I was getting angrier by the minute. I had some words for my mother when I saw her.

He gritted his teeth and looked at me. "You are going to be all right, *trust me.*"

The reality of being in prison was hitting me as I drove home with my father. Things hadn't changed. I wasn't "corrected," because I didn't think I had an issue before I got knocked. I just planned on coming home and moving on with my life as a normal girl. I was nineteen years old. It was time to act like an adult. My father was just talking a mile a minute as we drove. I looked at him as he spoke. My heart had forgiven him.

I was always soft on the inside but hard on the outside. My mind couldn't get around the whole situation, though. Granted, he was there for me, but did that make up for nineteen entire years?

Every so often he'd pat my hand at the light.

"You know, Carin, don't ever think my absence was due to me not loving you. I mean, the streets can make a man lose sight of everything that is important. I'm no longer out there doing the things that I did as a young man. I'm stable, I'm good now. Now, hear me out, I'm not making excuses, but that's just how the shit is, which is why I want you to find you a good guy, a legit dude, you know?"

"I hear you, Daddy, but right now I'm not thinking about any boys." Which was a lie. My teenage hormones had been raging inside of those prison walls. The first thing I planned on doing once I ate a home-cooked meal and kicked it with my folks was to call Chauncey and give him what he had been waiting for all these years. I hoped that he still wanted it. I didn't care that he didn't return my letters or pick up when I called. I needed to get laid and he was the chosen one.

When I came home my mother was in the kitchen on the phone talking to my aunt. She

never sent me anything, not even a hello through
my father. She hung up the phone and stopped
in front of me with her hands on her hips, smiling. She had her hair cut in a short, sassy style,
and it was dyed a pretty brownish red color and
she looked more slender. She looked real nice
standing in the kitchen with black leggings and a
man's button-down shirt. She was happy. I wondered if it was because I hadn't been around. She
had fancy new furniture and everything. She had
paintings on the wall and new dish sets.

"So, you're home, baby, how you feeling? You
look good!" She smiled. She didn't even hug me,
she just kept her hands on her hips. I didn't bother
to try to hug her either. Fuck it.

"I'm good, what you cooked?" I said, opening
the pots.

"Pepper-steak, your favorite."

My favorite was baked chicken but I didn't even
bother to correct her. I instantly grabbed a plate
and made a big dish. This bitch was acting like
she saw me just yesterday. I sat and ate quietly as
my parents sat on the sofa, whispering vigorously.
When I was done I had the craving for a joint and
some Hennessey.

"Ma, you got something to drink in here?" I
said, opening the refrigerator.

"Yeah, baby, in the fridge there's water, juice,
iced tea—"

"I mean like a real drink, some alcohol."

"What? No! You are not of age to drink!" she said, and laughed nervously. My mother seemed to be acting so phony to me, but I couldn't put my finger on why. I belched and put my plate in the sink, then walked to the back and lay down in my bed for a while.

About two hours later, I came out of my room to have the inevitable conversation with my "parents." I sat down across from them and demanded some kind of explanation.

"We were young when we had you, Carin. I was living a life that wouldn't allow me to settle down. I want you to know that my absence had nothing to do with the birth of you. I loved your mother."

"But you left her when she got pregnant with me. I'm confused because from what I was told, you had a son before me and you took good care of him. Then you went back to that same woman and had a little girl after me. I also heard that you take care of them. So, who was I, the outside child?"

My parents looked at one another. "Tell her the truth, Darren." My mother crossed her legs.

"At the time your mother got pregnant with you, I was with my son's mother, but your mother didn't know. I was a coward for denying that you existed all these years. But your brother and little sister know that they have a sister."

I shook my head in disbelief. "So I was the child who wasn't supposed to be here. I bet you wish my mother would have aborted me, huh?"

"No, baby, nothing like that. Baby, look, I missed so much of your life. I owe you so much, Carin. I owe you a lifetime of making you believe that I love you." He hugged me.

"Dad, I know you love me. Shit happens, right?" I smiled.

But inside I hurt like hell. I had missed him throughout the years. The torture of being in Sinny's house with both of her parents, the irony of watching my mother wither away because heartache was too much to bear, me running the streets searching for something, wanting, needing him. I was in pain and I was just happy that he was here trying to right his wrongs. I just wasn't sure if he was here to stay.

He smiled at me. "I'm blessed to have you as a daughter."

"Where are your son and other daughter?"

I saw my mother cringe at my words.

"Their mother took them and moved to Maryland. I talk to them often but I don't see them. Your little sister's name is Justine and your brother's name is Jacob. Justine is fifteen, Jacob is twenty-five. He's my li'l man." He beamed with pride. "Carin, I think you need to come stay with me for a while, see how you like it and decide if you want to be here or with me. Your mother and I have talked about this, and we think it's best that from this point on you live with me. But if you don't like it you can come back. Right, Jackie?"

"Why would I want to go live with you? No, thank you, *Dad.*" I got up. My mother began to talk.

"Carin, baby, it's for the best."

I couldn't believe my ears. My mother had to be on some shit.

"Mommy, how would you know what's best for me, huh? I had to go out there and rob and steal to survive. How do you know what's best for me when all you did was leave me here alone to figure shit out on my own!"

"No! You *chose* to go out there robbing and stealing. If you went to school and did what you were supposed to I would have given you things, but no, you chose the streets, you chose to get you a boyfriend and have him do for you and not me!"

"You were suppose to do it for me regardless, not pass off that responsibility to someone else!

Mommy, you were never home and when you were home you didn't even talk to me. What are you talking about? You never left money on the table, you never asked me what I ate, you never had talks with me, nothing! All you did was threaten me that if I got into any trouble you would not be there and how true is that!"

"Carin, baby, I got a nice place for you to live. Nobody is trying to get rid of you so don't take it like that, honey," my father said, trying to break the beef.

"Carin, I know I haven't been the best mother but I have a lot going on right now and it's best that you go with your father. He is trying to do right. I raised you for eighteen years, now go on and spend time with your father. It's time I live my life."

"Live your life? You haven't done shit *but* live your life since I was born! I raised my damn self. And why can't I go stay with Aunt Max? I don't want to move out of Brooklyn! And where were you through my entire bid, huh? You were *that* busy, Ma?"

"Carin, this room in the back is yours if you feel the need to come back," she said softly. I was confused. I was mad, I was hurt.

"Am I in your way? Have I ever been in your way to do anything? The minute my father comes

back you want to push me to him? You didn't
come see me when I was away, write me . . . nothing."

I was hot when her only come back to that was
to shrug and sip her drink. I stared at her for a
long time.

"Ma, you know what? Fuck you, Ma, fuck you
for real. I see why he left you, you're a selfish
bitch!"

My mother jumped up, snatched me by my
shirt, and balled up her fist to swing at me. My
father jumped between us and grabbed her
arm. I had my fist balled too. I'd straight snuff
my mother if she hit me. It was about to be on!
That's the level of respect I had for her at that
moment. I was mad and hurt, Jackie could get it.

'You ain't nobody! You ain't no real mother!
You haven't done shit for me, never!" I yelled.
Jackie was still gripping my shirt so I punched
her hand for her to let me go.

"Little girl, I swear to God I will fuck you up in
this house this evening!"

"Get the fuck off me, get off my shirt!" I said,
prying her hands off of me.

"Carin, chill out!" my father's voice boomed
angrily. "Watch it, all right? She is still your
mother." He snatched my mother's grasp off my
shirt and pushed her to sit down.

"Who are you to be coming up in here like Daddy of the Year? You sentenced me to a lifetime of pain when you left us. I went to jail because of you! You held me down while I was away. Was it the guilt? Would you have come to see about me if I didn't go to jail? Huh?"

"Carin, I am still your father, little girl," he said stepping up to me.

I stepped up to match him and looked him in the face. "I don't need you and I damn sure don't need her. I'm out of here, both of yawl are fucking nuts if you think you can just pawn me off. First you walk out of my life, then you come back because your baby mother wants to walk out now. You don't want me here? I'm gone, but I'm *not* going to live with this chump." I grabbed my keys off the table and headed to I don't know where. My father came into the hallway behind me as I bawled heavily by the elevator.

"Carin, I promise you I will make it up to you, baby girl. Please give me a chance. I love you, Carin, I love you. You know sometimes a man gets caught up."

"Daddy, please with the excuses, please! You don't know how rough it was for me, Daddy. You don't know the loneliness I felt in my heart missing you. You don't know how dark my days have been. You don't know what that empty space felt like."

My father hugged me tight, then he too began to sob.

"Baby, I didn't mean it. I'm here now. I promise you I'm here now. It's my turn to raise you. I got you for life, please, baby girl. Let me take care of you. I don't want anything to happen to you. God is giving me another chance. Let me be a father. I can show you a better life. You don't have to run to these niggas in the street for shit, you hear me?"

"I was looking for you out there in those streets, Daddy. I swear I was looking for you. Why'd you leave us like that? Huh? Why'd you leave us? You didn't come see me. You said you were on your way the last time I spoke to you and you show up thirteen years later. What kind of man are you?" I cried louder and louder. I could hear my mother coming down the hall toward us.

"Don't let her touch me. I swear, Daddy, don't fuckin' let her touch me."

"Carin, what have I done so wrong to you?" I could hear my mother say.

I was inconsolable. It was something from deep down inside. My father hugged me and we rocked side to side by the elevator.

"Darren, I don't know why she hates me so much." I could hear my mother say, then she sucked her teeth and walked off as my father rubbed my back.

"I got you, Carin, I got you."

I was already tired of hearing men tell me that.

PART TWO

Street to Chic

9

Carin

The night I moved in with my father, his girlfriend, Tyra, and her son, Farrod, they were there to greet me with open arms. My room had already been set up with my own telephone line, a cherry wood queen-sized bedroom set, and a TV, stereo system, and flowers. "I just want you to be comfortable. Just ask for it and it is yours," my father said.

"Welcome home," Tyra said, hugging me. She seemed so sweet and she was so pretty. She favored Holly Robinson Peete. Farrod was equally warm, and a chocolate cutie at that.

"When you get up in the morning, take yourself to the mall and treat yourself to some things," my father said softly once Tyra and Farrod left us alone. He had no idea how I got down with the spending. The next morning I eagerly got up at nine and was ready to go.

"Don't worry about the limit. Just call me when you're done so I can pick you up, all right?"

"Okay," I said, eager to run to the mall and bust up all of his money. I was happy that he sent me to the mall alone so I could walk around, take my time, and pick out the things I liked. I was always a fan of jewelry, so after purchasing tons of clothes, shoes, and underclothes, I eyed a nice set of bangle bracelets with a necklace and earrings. The total cost was $3,000. There was only one way to find out if my father had that kind of cash on his card. I went in and purchased it. The card was approved. I put my jewelry on right there, and at that moment I was feeling really good about myself.

I went to the pay phone and called my dad to let him know he could come get me. As I sat in the food court, I saw a guy eyeing me. He stood there and just looked me up and down for a good twenty seconds. I rolled my eyes and turned my back to him, praying that my father hurried up. I didn't know how "Jersey" guys got down but I did know how Brooklyn operated, so I was hoping I didn't get got with all of this jewelry on and all of these shopping bags.

The guy made his way to me and asked, "Do I know you?"

"No, I don't think so."

"You sure? Because the way you were eyeballing me back there I figured maybe I owed you money or we met before or something." He was trying to keep a straight face, but I was serious. As much dirt as I did, I didn't know if he knew me from somewhere or not.

"No, I'm sorry. I don't know you and you don't know me."

"Oh, okay. Well, what's your name?" he almost whispered. He was smooth and nice looking. I liked how his clothes fit him. He stood about five foot eleven with a fresh haircut, wearing a jeans suit and a new pair of cheese Tims, his complexion golden.

"Carin," I said, trying to fight back my smile.

"Monty."

"Nice to meet you, Monty."

"You live out here?" he asked.

"Yeah, I came out here to shop."

"All by yourself?" he asked, looking around.

"Yes."

"Do you have a man?"

"No."

"Kids?"

"No." I laughed at his bluntness.

"So that's two things we have in common. I don't have a man or kids either."

Is he serious?

"So are you going to buy me something? I see you got a lot of shit."

"No, were you buying *me* something?" I challenged.

He looked me up and down. "I see that brick in your pocket. You hustle or some shit?" he said as I stood up.

"No!" I laughed hysterically; he did too.

"So what do you do?" he asked.

"Why don't we save that for our first date?"

He rubbed his goatee and smiled. "Who said I was taking you on a date?"

"Then why are you standing here?"

He laughed again. "Let's exchange numbers."

"When is a good time to call you?" I asked.

"Any time is good for you, beautiful. Beep me, call me, find me, stalk me, do whatever it is that you do."

I just laughed. He was funny, and handsome, despite a defect in his right eye. It was almost entirely shut. I couldn't tell if he had gotten into a fight or if it was permanent. Either way, he was still handsome.

"Be good." He began walking backward while still eyeing me. I smiled as I looked at his number. I tucked it in my back pocket, or so I thought. The number hit the floor and got trampled by strangers. When I got home the first thing I did was check my back pocket so I could call him. "Where is it?" I turned my jeans inside out, but to no avail. "Damn!" I sulked around for three days until Monty called me.

Monty

I forgot about shorty in the mall as soon as I turned and walked away. I had to get Tionne home. She was in my car waiting for me, but I'd had to run in and see about li'l mama walking through with the tight jeans and the sexy gap. I had been seeing Tionne off and on for years. To me she was just that neighborhood freak. Tionne wanted more, but although at one point we were much closer, it just wasn't like that. I could never make a girl like her my main. She was a whore, bottom line. She felt me slipping away and did anything to spend time with me. Like now, taking her to the mall all the way out in Jersey because her car was broken. One thing I couldn't deny was that Tionne had the bomb sex. She would do anything I asked her to in bed. I kept her around for that reason alone, but I wasn't even hitting it on the regular anymore. Tionne being desperate was a turnoff to me.

I started talking to my main man Rick on the phone, telling him how I was caught up in Jersey with Tionne and how I just bagged a cutie with a gap between her legs. I was really tired of Tionne sweating me. If it weren't for her brother, Barry, who was my man, I would have disrespected her a long time ago. I never made her my girl so that should have told her something. She was sitting in the passenger seat, glossing her lips. *Damn, the head she gives with that mouth . . . What we need to do is put that mouth on a better bitch. Damn.*

"Look what I bought," she said, pulling out some trashy lingerie. I didn't know whether to be turned on or off. I decided to turn it off.

"Nice," I said without emotion, and pulled out of the lot.

Currently I was single, just bouncing around, hitting and running. Since I knew Tionne the longest and she lived the closest, she got the most of me and that made her feel special. But she was not special. She was just a hood rat with expensive tastes, who would do anything to get close to me because I had money. Word travels fast, and Tionne being the gold digger she was had gotten word that I was worth roughly a million dollars because of a childhood injury. She was pretty, dark skinned, thick, had "good hair," a fat ass, nice smile, was fly as hell, and dated nothing but hustlers. She must have thought she hit the jackpot when she met me. The only privilege Tionne got was to be associated with a rich nigga like me. She got nothing else from me. I loved kids, so here and there I'd buy shit for her kids because as a man that's what I do. But that's as far as it would go. If she needed her hair done, I'd go to the salon and pay the beautician myself. The same went for manicures and pedicures. But I didn't take the bitch shopping or on vacation. Only a woman I considered wifey material would get such treatment, and I hadn't met her yet. No bitch could get a dime from me. The most money I ever spent on a bitch was $299 for a suite on special at the Sheraton, and that was because a nigga like me had expensive tastes and would not be caught dead in a shabby-ass hotel. I never bought no broad shit. If we ate at expensive restaurants, it was because that's what I wanted to do for myself. If we drank expensive champagne, it's because it's what I wanted.

I hadn't found the one yet and right now I was kind of looking. I had a lot of money, and sleeping around was getting kind of boring. I got all the pussy a young man could stand, but I wasn't impressed. I wanted a girl so I could spoil her rotten and parade her around. I wanted to have a little me eventually, too, and had to make sure that the woman I tied myself to for life was a good woman, worthy of being the mother of any future children I would have. More importantly,

I wanted a woman who knew nothing about my inheritance.

I noticed that the little honey from the mall hadn't called me as my pager went off. I thought it was her for four days in a row, but each time it was somebody else who I really didn't care to speak to. I decided to do some shit that I never did before. I called her first, but it was more out of boredom. I couldn't stop thinking about that gap between her legs. It probably tasted so sweet. She answered on the third ring.

"You're too young to play games," I said as soon as she picked up.

"Hello? Who's this?"

"Who you want it to be?" I sat back, twirling my keys on my finger.

"Who is this?"

"This is Monty."

"Monty, how are you?"

"I guess you're too pretty to be calling some guy first, huh?"

"No, I'm not on it like that. How you doing, everything cool?"

"Everything is cool with me, Carin, I'm just calling to say hi."

"Well, hi," she said.

I had to laugh. I looked at the phone then spoke again. "So when can I take you out?"

"Whenever, it doesn't matter."

What is up with this tough-ass chick?

"Can I pick you up around eight?" I asked her, not believing that I was chasing.

"That works for me."

"Eight it is, let me get your address. I'll come out to Jersey and scoop you."

Carin

As soon as I hung up the phone with Monty I started screaming and jumping around like a jackass. Monty was so fly and so damn handsome. I was back in the game! I couldn't wait to call Jetta, my friend from across the hall, and Missy, about this new guy who was all that to me.

I searched through my closet and decided on some fitted white short shorts and a baby blue, tight T-shirt. I parted my hair down the middle and pulled it back into a tight ponytail à la Sade. I ran up the block and bought a pair of powder blue Air Max from the neighborhood sneaker store. My father was in his den with Tyra so I was able to leave without question. He just asked me who I would be with and then told me to come home at a decent hour. Monty called me from his cell phone every twenty minutes to let me know how close he was to me. Then he bitched about me living too far and said I should move closer to him. What a jerk. He pulled up in front of my building in his slick black-on-black Lexus. He didn't look my way, he just waited for me to walk to him. I walked in front of his car so he could take it all in. Carin was looking mighty fine these days! I got in the car and asked him why he didn't open the car door for me.

"You seem a little too rough around the edges for all that, but next time I will." He smiled.

Silently we drove until I asked Monty to pull over at a McDonald's.

"Why would you want to eat that shit?" he asked, driving past it.

"What are you doing? Why aren't you going through the drive-thru?"

"Because I'm taking you someplace to eat," he said, annoyed.

"You're acting like you told me where we were going and I decided I wanted McDonald's!"

"You're acting like you was never on a date before. Common sense should tell you if a man is picking you up then he is taking you out to eat, silly."

"Don't call me silly, you don't know me like that," I said, pissed off at Monty's comfort level. "So where are we going to eat and how do you know I'm going to want that to eat?"

"We are going to my man house. His mother is a mean cook. I want you to meet my people."

"Hmph, there goes thinking I'm special."

"What do you mean by that?" he said, staring at me while he drove.

"You just met me and already you're bringing me to your man's mother's house? How many chicks do you bring there and tell them that they're special?"

"First of all, my man mother does not play that shit up in her house so I don't just bring anybody through there."

"So you see something special in me, is that it?" I said sarcastically. I knew Monty liked me and I knew just this quick that he thought I was something special. I seemed to have that affect on any guy I came across.

"As a matter of fact, I do. Believe what you want, but I do. I don't know why, but I get a good vibe from you. If you don't want to go there, tell me before we get on the expressway and I'll take you to a restaurant or something. Or McDonald's, it ain't nothing to me. If you a McDonald's kind of broad then I'll get you a number two, it ain't nothing."

I didn't say anything. I just let him drive. I could have chewed him out but decided not to. He thought he knew me.

We pulled up to a beautiful house out by Green Acres Mall. Two women were standing in front. They immediately looked me up and down as I got out of the car. Monty waited for me, then held my waist as we walked up the steps. Being polite, I said hello.

"They get younger and younger, huh, Monty?" one said.

Here we go, I thought as I stood in the foyer waiting for Monty to accommodate the girl.

"Behave yourself, I'm telling you. *Not her,*" was all Monty said. He caught up with me, but I was already being encountered by Monty's friend, Rick.

"What's your name, sweetheart?" he said, smiling softly.

"Carin," I said sweetly, and smiled only because he was smiling at me so genuinely. He gave off a really good vibe. He grabbed my hand and put his other arm around my shoulder.

"What are you doing?" Monty smiled at Rick.

"This one right here? I see you falling in love with." He gave my shoulders a squeeze.

"Is that right? What makes you think that?" Monty said.

"I don't know. She just seems different from the rest. No disrespect, Carin," Rick said, staring at me. I started to laugh.

"Carin, you could go have a seat right through those doors, I'm coming." Monty pointed the way. I walked slowly, not knowing where I was going, and wound up standing outside of the dining room, watching two women set up.

One was a short, light-skinned woman with a huge forehead. Her daughter stood next to her with an equally large forehead. It was then that I noticed how large Rick's forehead was. The daughter gave me a half-assed smile and continued setting the table. *What is wrong with these bitches? Can't they just say hello? Damn!*

"Hello," Rick's mother said, a little annoyed at me. I didn't mean to be rude and not speak, I was just caught up in hateful bitches.

"My apologies, my name is Carin." I extended my hand.

She extended hers also. "Shirley," she said.

"Nice to meet you, you have a beautiful home."

"Thank you." She finally smiled.

"Monty, so this is your girlfriend?" she asked brazenly as she put her cheek out for him to kiss. Monty put his arm around Shirley.

"Maybe one day. I have to do a background check and all that, you know what I'm saying, ma?" He laughed.

"Mmm-hmm, these young girls be tripping these days, watch 'em," she said smugly.

All I could think was *Damn, old bitches hate, too!*

Dinner was wonderful: pot roast, potatoes, macaroni, salad, chicken kabobs, and enough Hennessey to last through five games of spades. Everyone was tipsy and full, migrating to the living room to get comfortable. I excused myself and went to the bathroom to make sure I looked as cute as I had when I left. When I came back out, Monty was in a solo chair waiting for me. He tapped his knees for me to cop a squat. I really didn't want to be on Broadway like that, but he insisted, so I complied. I was feeling tipsy and just didn't give a shit. I didn't have to see these people again.

"Monty, what's up with the trip to Jamaica, man? You didn't even put your money up for that and we know you got it!" Rick said from across the room.

"For real, you're not going with us?" Rick's sister asked.

"You want to go to Jamaica?" he turned and asked me.

"Me?"

"Yeah, you, silly."

"I'm not going to be too much silly, ya hear? Go to Jamaica when?"

"The end of next month," Rick said, smiling. I liked Rick. He seemed to be real cool.

"Well, who's going?" I asked.

"It don't matter. Do you want to go, yes or no? Ayo, Rick, I'm only going if Carin go," Monty said, putting me on the spot.

"Come on, Carin, go please? You'll be safe, we are all family," he pressed.

I was really concerned about what I would tell my father. But I wanted to go. I would think of something within the next thirty days, so I said yes.

We reached Montego Bay, Jamaica at ten o'clock Friday morning and it was beautiful. I had never seen anything like it. It was my first vacation ever and I was feeling good. I got my hair done up in small bronze and brown, wet and wavy micro braids because I had every intention of swimming.

Monty quickly pulled my luggage through the airport; he was so excited. He pointed out different things to me, promising me that we would have a good time. Rick wound up canceling because his girlfriend didn't want to go. I was happy. I didn't like any of Rick's female affiliates.

"I can hardly wait. This is my first time going away," I gushed as I held his forearm.

"Are you serious? What kind of dudes were you fucking with that nobody ever took you away anywhere? Man, stick with me, shorty, you'll be around the world and back. The envy of all women, stick with me." He smiled and put his arm around my shoulder, kissing me on the top of my head.

Our suite was beautiful! We had a Jacuzzi, terrace, sky light, double-headed showers and a king-sized bed. I took a long, hot shower getting ready to go to Dunns River, thinking about my life and where it was heading. I thought about my mother and how she just let life pass me and her by. We didn't do anything the eighteen years I was living with her. I was hurt by how she just let my father take me as if I was that much trouble. I decided to close that chapter of my life because right now I was starting something new, out in Jamaica with a fly young stunner who seemed to be smitten with me. I didn't really know him like that, but we had become so connected over the past six weeks, it was as if I'd known him for years. I didn't care. I felt miles away from that life I once knew when I barely ate, had to rob to stay fly, had to fight every day because some girl was jealous of me, had to cry for attention. I had a man and I had my dad and right now they were all I needed.

I was so caught up in my thoughts that I barely realized the water was turning cold. I turned the shower off and stepped onto a towel that I placed on the floor. I walked into the beautiful main room of the five-star hotel, with my braids hanging loosely and prettily down my back, to find Monty on his cell phone counting stacks of money on the bed. I made a noise so that he wouldn't think I was being nosy. He looked at me and smiled and kept talking. I sat at the dresser and began to lotion my body, looking at him through the mirror.

Monty

I liked Carin because she appeared to be so normal and laid back. A lot of things didn't excite her. I picked her up in my Lexus GS the first time I met her, in my Range Rover the next, lastly surprising her by taking her for a ride on my bike. Her eyes didn't twinkle, her pussy didn't get wet, and she didn't flinch. She was just too official for me. I couldn't wait for her to get out of the shower so I could kiss her up and hug her. Six weeks we had been dating and at every attempt to get in her drawers she turned me down. I didn't get the sense that she was playing hard to get, and was more pleased when she told me that she had never had sex before. She was exactly what I needed and to my delight, she had never been tampered with before. I had met my wife. I would be her first, her last, her everything. She was going to be my doll baby.

Carin

"Carin, come here." I got up and walked to the bed, body still wrapped in a towel. "You ever seen so much money?"

"Yeah."

"Where?" he asked in disbelief.

"You have no idea. I can look at that and tell you how much money that is."

"If you're no less than two stacks off, I'll give you half of what this is."

I looked at it for a minute. I'd counted money enough times to know what I was looking at just by glancing.

"Come on, how much, doll baby?" he said, fanning two bricks at me.

"They're all twenties?"

"Yup." He kissed them. I laughed.

"All right, I'll say in each hand you got about seven stacks. So, all together, I'll say you're roughly working with about, um . . . twelve or thirteen thousand."

"Lucky guess, I got some tens and fives in there. It's ten stacks. Here," he said, giving me one hand. "You think you know money, huh?" He smiled.

"I do."

"That's nice to know. I can't be with a broad who act like she never had shit before. But I know something you never had before." He winked. I blushed.

"You don't know what I had," I said, walking away to get ready so we could hit the streets.

He fanned me off. "You talk big shit, little girl. Come on, all I want is a kiss. You're not ready for anything else, that's why I'm not even pressing you like that."

I leaned in and kissed him lightly on the lips.

"You truly are precious, huh?"

"I guess."

"Here, let me show you how to kiss a man." He cupped my face delicately and sucked gently on my bottom lip, then parted my lips with his tongue and entered my mouth slowly. I followed his lead and did to him whatever he did to me. He ran his fingers through my hair and moaned as he kissed me. I started feeling hot so I pulled away slowly.

"Nice," he said.

***

We were in Jamaica four days and Monty hadn't tried anything except for a kiss. I was disappointed. At night he'd hold me and just nuzzle his head in my neck, but that was it. I was even more upset that he would not tell me what had happened to his eye. I didn't like secrets. Tomorrow we were going home and I wanted to feel him, or anybody, inside of me. I guess he was being a gentleman and I guess that's what I needed, but at the same time I needed him and I wasn't going to be the one to push up. This morning we woke up to breakfast in bed: champagne and orange juice, cheese omelets, ackee, and salt fish with plantains. It was delicious. The mimosa had me feeling sexy, high, and horny. I was lying in the bed enjoying a good stretch after the delicious meal, when Monty climbed on top of me and began kissing me. My insides starting doing the cabbage patch.

"You didn't think I'd leave this island without making love to the most beautiful female on it, did you?" he said his lips touching my ear.

"No," I whispered, half yawning from my stretch.

"You think you're ready for this?"

"Maybe, I don't know." *It's about damn time.*

"Tell me when you want me to stop." He put his head between my legs. It felt warm as his soft lips kissed mine gently. I thought back to the only guy to give me oral, Chauncey. I thought that he was the one to invent oral sex. But I knew better now that someone else was between my thighs. His lips felt like warm butter. He nuzzled his nose in my pubic hair and took deep sniffs. "Smells like flowers," he whispered. He sucked me delicately as I went crazy but kept my cool from the foreign feeling. I clutched the sheets and closed my eyes. Soon enough I had my first real orgasm.

Monty picked me up and took me to the terrace. He laid me down on the floor and kissed me all over as the sun shone on our bodies and the sheer drapes tickled our sides. The air was still and quiet and you could hear the ocean applaud our lovemaking with swishing sounds. He entered me slowly. The thought of condoms came and went, and I knew better but didn't care at this time. He entered me inch by inch.

"I'm going to be your first, your last, your everything."

"Mmm-hmm," I moaned.

"It hurt?" he asked me.

"A little," I lied. It hurt like hell. Monty had a monster dick. Granted, I wasn't experienced, but I was no dummy. He had girth and length. I closed my eyes tight and covered my mouth.

"It'll feel good soon, just let me get it all in," he promised. He knocked on my entrance a few times with the head, getting me wet.

"Knock-knock," he said and opened me up a little bit more. He got it all in and began to make circles inside of me. "Open up your legs some more, don't be scared."

I couldn't, this was torture.

"Knock-knock, let me in."

I giggled. He smiled, then bit his bottom lip as he plunged deeper.

"Yeah, that's it, follow Daddy's lead, I won't steer you wrong." I wrapped my arms around his neck tightly. It was beginning to burn. He cracked my legs open and held them out like two big fish he had caught; he seemed to be watching his penis go in and out of me. He was getting turned on. He dropped my legs and lifted my head up, cradling it to his chest.

"Damn, Carin, damn you so tight." He moaned.

"Slow down," I said.

He obeyed. "Daddy's sorry, he doesn't want to hurt you."

He really wants me to call him Daddy, huh? I thought. *I'm not calling him no damn Daddy.*

He slowed it down and it became lovemaking again. He whispered four-letter curse words in my ear and held me tight. I didn't know what he wanted me to do, so I just followed his lead like he said. We were going at it for a real long time.

I didn't know that this was what it would be like. He pulled his penis out of me and in one motion propped me up on my knees. He stuck it back in and grabbed a fistful of my hair. I didn't move, didn't know what to do. He plunged in me deep and slowly, kissing my neck and back. He hit the bottom of my pussy. I felt something shift and it made me feel violated, but in a good way. I let out a painful noise as he kissed my shoulder and said, "Baby, I'm sorry." But he kept on doing what he was doing.

"I knew you'd like that, ya pretty ass," he said, slapping it. Soon after, he was bucking fast, then coming all over my back. We lay there still for a while, him on top of me breathing heavily, rubbing my hair. A million thoughts were going through my mind as this guy lay on my back, satisfied, whispering in my ear, "*Let me love you.*" I couldn't stop panting. It took so much out of me to have sex with him. This was a dick that would take some getting use to. Monty breathed heavily into the nook of my neck, but he made sure to tell me how "this was his" before he fell into a deep slumber.

The morning after we made love was even better than our lovemaking. Monty ordered room service as I slowly lathered my body in soap, reminiscing on the night we had. A real man had made love to my body on an exotic island. Life was turning around for me, and my past was floating away in the distance.

When I stepped out of the shower, Monty was setting up our breakfast. He sat me on his lap and kissed my bare shoulder.

"Good morning, baby," he whispered. I smiled. It was all I could do. I was in bliss. He fed me fruit and eggs and wiped my mouth. We sipped mimosas and sat out on the balcony, watching the ocean. "I want to take away your pain. I see it in your eyes," he said, out of nowhere. "Talk to me, tell me about your life." For the first time ever, my feelings were important. A man actually wanted to know what I was feeling inside. I got comfortable on his lap and laid my head back as the sun beat on my neck. The tears began to fall. He listened to me with his heart. He didn't rush me to speak, he just sat back and waited until I was ready to talk.

"I never felt like my mother cared about me. When my dad left her, she became cold and distant to herself, and to me. She didn't do the things with me that mothers do with their daughters. She didn't dress me up and take me out, she didn't talk to me about boys and clothes, she didn't care about anything I did. So I didn't care. My dad was never around. He came into the picture only when my mother had had enough and I turned eighteen."

"So how did this affect you and the men in your life?" he asked.

I shrugged. "I'm not really sure. All I know is that I don't want to be lonely like my mother. I don't want a man who's going to leave me like my father did. I need something steady and sure, someone with a loyal heart like mine." The tears rolled down fast and steady. "I don't want to live my life searching. I want love to find me and stay."

"I think it has."

"I sure do hope so."

"I'm never going to neglect you like your mother did or leave you like your father did. I am here to stay, Carin, always and forever, I promise you. I got you, baby." He gave me a squeeze. I hated how those words always haunted me. But not as much as Ashanti's face.

10

Carin

I was starting to hide things from my dad that I knew he wouldn't approve of, like Monty. My father had more than outdone himself with the lifestyle he provided for me and the genuine love he gave me. He deserved the respect of knowing certain aspects of my life, regardless of how he wasn't around in the past. I just knew that he would not like Monty. I knew he'd think Monty wasn't good enough for me. The summer was ending and, aside from my trip to Jamaica, I hadn't done much of anything. I had lied and told him that I was going with Missy. It was easy to pull off because Missy worked and went to college and she didn't live anywhere near me.

My dad liked that I'd become friends with Jetta, because he saw her often and said she didn't appear to be fast or anything like that. She was a slim, brown-skinned girl with a big smile and moles all over her face. We would sit up for hours in my room and I would tell her all of my war stories, of course leaving out a few things. We clicked immediately.

When I came back from Jamaica we sat up and I told her all about Monty and how he gave me money and made love to me. I had finally found someone who would take care of me. But I couldn't bring Monty over like I wanted to because my father wouldn't like him, I knew he wouldn't. So, for now, Monty would be my secret.

My secret got revealed sooner than I had planned. Monty felt that I was hiding something and decided to come to my house to get dressed the night I was going to meet his family. I was cutting it close; my father would be home in twenty minutes. I didn't want them to meet by surprise. I wanted it to be when I was ready to defend Monty—there were still some things about him that concerned me. Like he still hadn't told me what he did for a living and what was wrong with his right eye. I didn't know if I was dealing with a thug, a drug dealer, or what, and coming from where I came from I wanted nothing to do with any of it. Having some hood or street in you was always fine by me, but I didn't want a cowboy or anyone who could be potentially dangerous.

I was nervous about meeting his family. He told me that he had a family full of women. His grandmother owned a six-family building in Brooklyn and it was occupied by him, his sister, and all of his aunts. *Bitches,* was all I could think, but if this was my "boyfriend" then I guess I had to meet the women he loved. I ran down the steps at top speed and snatched up my small Coach pouch on the way out.

"Let's go, Monty! It doesn't take that long to get ready!" I stood impatiently by the door.

"I gotta piss, hold up."

You're really getting on my damn nerves, Monty.

He came out of the bathroom, wiping his hands with napkins. "Is there a reason why you're rushing me?" he asked, knowing good and goddamn well why I was rushing him.

"You know why. I told you that I don't want my father to catch you in his house without having met you first."

"Too late." Monty smiled as we heard the key in the door.

My father had taken one look at Monty and decided that he didn't like him. I could tell by the way he started gritting his teeth because I do the same thing. He was making his jaw jump yet trying to appear calm. I don't know if it was the tattoos on Monty's forearm or expensive jewelry he wore. Maybe he felt as if he was looking in the mirror. Maybe it was the constant ringing of his cell phone or his cocky attitude. Maybe it was his Lexus that he had parked outside. My father looked at us and smiled. "So this is your boyfriend?" he asked.

"Something like that," I said.

"Where did you two meet? Have a seat." Monty and I sat side by side.

"I met her at the mall," Monty spoke up.

"Oh, okay. So, Monty, what do you do?" My father cut right to the chase. This was the part I didn't want to deal with. I had no idea what Monty did and now the moment of truth was about to happen.

"Well, all I can say is that I do not have to work because I am financially blessed right now." Monty smiled.

"Financially blessed, huh? That's your black-on-black GS outside?"

"Yeah."

"That's a hot ride there, son. I remember when I was young and used to hustle. I had all the hot-test cars, the hottest chicks. Shit, in the midst of all that I even had Carin. Her mother was a dime back then. You ever seen her mother?"

"No." Monty smiled.

"Yeah, Jackie was bad. French vanilla–like complexion, li'l button nose, and, man, she was just so good at what she did, you know what I mean?"

Monty warmed up to my father.

"Yeah, I know what you mean," he said.

I, on the other hand, had no idea why my father was talking about my mother's sex game.

"She was my main girl. My *main*. I had a baby mother that I could go back and forth to and I did that the entire time I was with Carin's mother. But Jackie was my baby, you know what I mean? But I broke her heart, living that fast life, getting caught up. I made a baby and for eighteen years I was out of Carin's life. The life will have you lose focus on what's really important, make you hurt people who don't deserve it, you feel me?"

"I don't hustle," Monty said point-blank, realizing where my father was going.

Tyra came in then, and Monty's eyes widened with pleasure.

"Is that your mother?" he asked, impressed and no doubt taken aback by Tyra's beauty.

"My stepmother," I said.

"Hello!" she said, and leaned in to kiss my father.

"Hey, baby, this here is Monty, Carin's *boyfriend*," he said snidely.

"Nice to meet you." She smiled.

"Likewise." Monty extended his hand for a shake. My father's chest swelled.

"How old are you, son, if you don't mind my asking?"

"Twenty-three."

"Twenty-three years old. You know Carin is nineteen, right?"

"Soon to be twenty, I am not a baby," I said.

I could tell my father was having a hard time swallowing Monty. He couldn't stop staring at him.

"Daddy, look, we have to get going," I said, trying to break the ice between them.

"I love my daughter, Monty. I love her more than any woman in this world, even my mother. This here is my heart, you feel me? Do you have little sisters or children?"

"No, sir, I don't. I just have one grown sister."

"I love my daughter and I will protect her by all means."

"I understand that, I can't blame you. Carin is a beautiful girl inside and out and I'll do my best to protect her also. I have her best interests at heart. I plan to spoil her and love her. I mean, I took her to Jamaica already. Carin isn't some fly-by-night to me. I know as a father you are concerned, but I assure you, she is in good hands."

I could tell my father couldn't get past the Jamaica part.

Monty and his big braggadocios mouth.

"Jamaica? When was this?"

"In June!" he replied as if he thought my father knew.

I didn't have anything to say. My father was burning a hole in my face with his eyes.

"Monty, I need to talk to my daughter before she leaves, can you give us a second?"

Monty fixed his pants then looked at me. "No problem. Carin, Daddy'll be in the car." He leaned over to kiss me, then Monty peeled off a few hundreds and handed them to me. I know he only did that to piss off my father. Why was he trying to piss off my father?

He kissed me on the cheek once more with his eyes on my father.

"Daddy, can we talk about this later?" I knew he wanted to go in on me because I'd lied about Jamaica, but now was not the time.

"I know what she likes," Monty kept on. I wished he'd shut up.

My father looked from me to Monty.

"I'll be home early," was all I could say, then we left. I lived with my father and I would respect his rules, yes, but he had to also understand that I was used to my freedom, used to doing what I wanted, and there was no way he could try to put a hold on me now at nineteen. No way.

When we got in the car, Monty lit a cigarette and turned the radio on. I punched the button and turned it back off.

"What the fuck is your problem?" I barked.

"What?"

"What do you mean *what?* What the hell was all that about?"

"Your father needs to respect that you are grown and you have a man. He is going to treat you like a little girl as long as you continue acting like one."

"Look, let's get one thing straight, okay? You *will not* cause any conflict between me and my dad. I don't appreciate that fly shit you pulled back there, it was uncalled for."

"Your father needs to respect that you have a man."

"Do I have a man? Since when? I wasn't aware that I had a man, or that you *were* a man." I tossed his money back at him. He stared down at it in his lap.

"I was never the kind of chick who could be bought and never will be, so you remember that you have to always step your game up fucking with me. I have no problem getting money,

Monty. I'm a survivor, you hear me? Don't ever try to play my father like that again!"

Monty flicked his cigarette out the window and pulled off. He didn't say anything except, "You got it."

I was so upset that he decided that we shouldn't meet his mother today after all.

I realized that I had spent a lot of time running around with Monty and not enough time getting my life in order. Since I had gotten my GED in prison, it was easy for me to enroll in school. I decided to go to business school to get my office mannerisms together. I wasn't sure what I wanted to do, I just knew I needed to learn basic office skills to get a starter job. I'd gain experience and build my way up from there. Six months after enrolling in Katharine Gibbs I was offered a job as a receptionist at an accounting firm. It paid twelve dollars per hour. I took it because I needed my own income. Monty protested for as long as he could until I convinced him that I just wanted to feel I was doing something positive for myself. He understood my need for independence, but told me that if my job got in the way of "his time" he would make me quit. I continued going to school part-time. I felt good about myself. I was accomplishing things on my own.

Also, I loved going to Monty's house! The feeling of having a boyfriend who actually had his own house was appealing to me. I was the kind of girl who was supposed to have a man who was about his business because I was about mine. Monty's condo in Kew Gardens Queens was fly. The best part about the condo was my hot curlers in the bathroom and my panties hanging from the shower. I left all of my things laying around and loved Monty for not caring. I came first and he never let another woman get one up on me. He'd always quote Jay-Z to me: "You gotta know you're thoroughly respected . . . by me."

One night, I was sitting on his couch painting my toenails when he stood in front of me and folded his arms. I didn't look up at him, but asked, "What?"

"Carin, can you cook?"

"I sure can."

"So when are you going to feed your man?"

"When you tell me what you do for a living and what the hell happened to your eye, maybe I'll cook whatever you want, deal?"

He sat next to me, dangling a Corona between his legs. "I need to know if I can trust you before I tell you what I do, Carin."

"You can trust me and you know this."

"But you never know." He sipped.

"Well, don't tell me what you do or how you get money. But if I find out it's drugs, I'm gone, end of story. I don't want that life."

"I can respect that. I can do so much more for you than what I am doing. I just have to make sure that I can trust you with what I got."

"*I said* you can trust me, Monty, but whenever you're comfortable, let me know what's going on. Just don't wait too long." Then I left it alone. I continued painting my toes as Monty continued staring at me.

Things were good between Monty and me. I couldn't complain. We had an active relationship, we did a lot together, the sex was good and we were experimenting more and more every day. We always took short trips out of town, to Vegas, Mexico, wherever. By now my father knew what it was, so I didn't have to lie about where I was going. Monty's family was real cool and the women turned out fine. But his grandparents were my favorite people, especially his grandfather. We shared the same birthday, and every day I'd sit outside with him on the stoop and feed him bananas. Grandaddy was elderly and because everyone worked mainly at night, I would be there to keep him company. We spent most days laughing on the stoop as he told me old war stories of him in 'Nam and about his love for his wife, Felicia. Since I didn't know my grandfather on either side of my family, I adopted him as my own. He would crack me up with baby stories of Monty, then ask me, "What do you see in that boy, his ol' crazy self." I'd just laugh and admire Monty from afar, watching him talk, politic, or do whatever he was doing at the time. He was my baby and our love was real.

My only problem with Monty was how he showed entirely too much love to these girls who lived on his mother's block in Brooklyn. We spent a lot of time there mainly because that's where Monty's friends were. I was getting tired of coming over to Monty's and having to deal with the jealous females. I was sick of the snickering, the smirks, and the extra special "hellos" he'd get whenever I was around. I was no fool; there was no doubt in my mind that he had to have had some dealings with one of these females or someone they knew, because it just wasn't natural. I was new to this neighborhood but I wasn't new to the hood. I had to say something to him.

One night, I got off the train, tired from working and school. I had been up since seven in the morning and didn't reach Brooklyn until ten at night. I could see Monty holding court on the corner. I squinted to see who was surrounding him. As usual, there were the three females up in his face, laughing. I had yet to tell him that these same females always had something slick to say when they saw me. I walked right up to Monty and broke up the little circle by handing him my book bag. He smiled at me but I did not smile back. The three females didn't budge.

"Excuse me!" I said. One girl looked at Monty as if he was supposed to check me. I looked back at her.

"Excuse me," I said again. Monty told the girl to back up.

"What's the matter with you?" he said, kissing my cheek. I motioned my head for him to start walking toward the house. Once out of earshot, I went in through clenched teeth.

"Now, I haven't been saying anything but that doesn't mean that I'm not annoyed. I am so tired of coming over here and having to deal with these females, Monty. Every time I come home, they are in your face! And did I tell you that for the past two months they always having something smart to say when they see me? I don't have time for this."

"Come on now, I've known these people since I was a kid, you don't have to stress none of these broads! You think I'm fucking with one of them?"

"I really don't care, but I'm not the one for disrespect," I said, thinking about what I did to Sinny when I caught her alone after that whole Panama-Tarsha incident. I beat Sinny down so bad that her mother tried to make her press charges. Of course, they didn't have to once I had gotten locked up. I wasn't the one to play with.

"Carin, you don't have to worry about no other broads, not ever. And another thing, I have been meaning to tell you this too, I'm getting real tired of your mouth," he said, slinging my bag over his shoulder and proceeding down the block to the apartment.

"I'm asking you nicely to please check your fan club, that's all. It's not enough that when I see them they're snickering and whispering and carrying on. You better check them. I don't know why you feel the need to have these broads on your dick all the time. You need that much attention? Don't I give you enough attention?"

"You know what? You seem like you're in the mood to start some shit, Carin. Take the car keys and go home. I don't want to be around you right now, you're getting on my nerves." He began fumbling in his pocket for his keys.

"Because I'm checking you about these bitches you want to send me home? If it were me you would not be having some dudes up in my face all damn day and you know it! You know what? I'm tired, so I will go home."

Not one to be played or dismissed, I headed to the apartment to get my pocketbook and to kick it with his mother real quick, then I would be out. Monty followed me, his steps quick and angry. I stopped short and faced him once we got inside the vestibule. He looked down at me. He was staring at me and his lips were kind of trembling.

"What? Give me the keys!" I said, and folded my arms.

"I'm going to tell you for the last time, Carin. I don't like how you talk to me. Stop talking to me like I'm some kind of lame, you hear me?"

"I'm suppose to be scared, Monty?"

"No, I don't want you to be scared of me, but you need to listen."

"I don't have to listen to you, you are not my—"

Before I could finish, his open hand was across my face. My head hit the mailbox.

"Shut up, shut the fuck up, Carin! You talk too damn much. Now take your ass home," he snarled through his teeth, and stormed out. I stood by the mailbox holding my mouth.

I couldn't believe he hit me. I waited a few seconds before I went upstairs.

"He hit me," I said over and over, convincing myself not to cry. My lips burned. I knew there had to be a mark of some sort on my face because Monty had slapped me really hard. "Fuck this," I said, and manned up. I was going to go outside and check him for that. I made my way up the block and saw him talking to the same three females. My jealousy soared but I kept it in check. I walked up to him and stood there. I said nothing. I waited to see how he would move. The girls looked at me then at Monty.

"What's up?" he asked me. I didn't say anything, I just walked away, hoping that he was smart enough to follow.

Once he caught up to me I turned around.

"Don't hit me again, Monty," I said, looking up at him.

"Stop talking to me the way you do and I won't."

"No, this is not open for discussion; do not put your fucking hands on me again!" I said seriously.

"You got that, I just had to shut you up real quick 'cause this mouth of yours . . . man!"

"I'm over it. It happened once and it doesn't happen again and I mean it."

"You see what I mean? This demanding shit. Stop talking to me like that!" he said.

"This is my face, my body! That's not being demanding! I just want to make this clear to you. I have never had a man hit me, not even my daddy, so please for the safety of us both, do not put your hands on me again, you hear me?"

"Yes, boss," he said.

"Give me the keys. I'm still going home. I'm not standing out here while you kee-kee with these broads." I stuck out my hand.

"I'm going home with you. You think I'd rather be outside talking to some birds than go home with my fine-ass girl? All this ass and fineness and I'm out here in the street?" He picked me up slightly.

"All right now, Daddy." I smiled.

"*Oh,* after all this time you want to call me Daddy?" He was smiling a mile wide now.

"You're my sugar daddy!" I said, kissing his cheek.

"Do you know how much I love you, Carin?"

"Yes."

"I don't think you do. I love you. I don't see myself without you, baby. Do you love me, Carin?"

"Yes, you know I do."

"So how come you haven't gone down on me yet?"

"Monty!"

"I'm serious now, Carin, when are you going to give me some head? It's been eight months since we've been together."

"I still don't know what you do for a living!"

"You know what? You're right, this is what I'll do. Tomorrow, I'm going to take you out and tell you what I do for a living."

"Yeah, okay." I twisted my mouth.

"No, for real. I'm going to tell you everything that you need to know. Tomorrow is the day."

He hugged me as I thought to myself how wrong I felt for allowing him to hit me. But it was only one time, and I told him I didn't like it, so I knew he wouldn't do it again.

11

Monty

Rick came with me to pick out the ring for Carin. I thought she was the most precious thing. I loved her independence and her class. I loved her intelligence and articulateness. She wasn't run-through or worn out. I was open that in this day and age in the hood, I was somebody's first. She was worthy of anything that I could give her. She was exactly what I was looking for in a woman. Though my family adored her, my mother expressed her concern because of my settlement, and my aunts were on the prowl. They wanted me to run background checks on Carin and the whole nine. It was cool when we were dating, but now that I was talking marriage they wanted to really know her. With my reputation and my age, getting married was a big deal. Rick rubbed my shoulders roughly as I opened the tiny box and stared at its contents.

"You're doing a good thing. Aye, listen you are my main man, we get bitches together, it's what we do, and if I'm telling you to do it, then it has to be good reason. I haven't seen you this happy since we were kids. Marry her, man, fuck it, what do you have to lose?"

"I'm too young to be married. I'm only twenty-four."

"So what! Look, Carin is a class act, she's nothing like Tionne or even like half the broads you came across. They all were jump-offs. Listen, I know you not worrying about what the homies will say. The homies are cool as long as it's Carin. Besides, bitches love a man with a ring on his finger." Rick laughed.

I gave him a pound. "Well, since you put it like that, no doubt!"

Carin's ring was a four-karat single solitaire. Classy, just like Carin, on a simple gold band. "She's going to love that!" Rick beamed.

"She's going to be shocked. I know she's not expecting this."

"You got a winner."

"Thanks, man, thanks."

I held it up and looked at it. "She better like this shit for four-five thousand fucking dollars!" I laughed nervously.

"You got coats that cost more than that, be easy, man."

"She's worth it though, she is worth every dime. Fuck it, I'll get her some earrings and a necklace to match." My heart and my gut told me I was doing the right thing as I whipped out my knot and counted it in front of two disgusted white women.

Monty

I sat in the back of the restaurant as my family and friends, and Carin's father, stepmother, stepbrother, and two best friends hid behind a curtain where they sat at their own respective tables. I wanted everyone to experience this night. Carin walked in looking beautiful. I had never seen her hair like that. I couldn't stop smiling as she got closer to me.

"Hey, beautiful," I said, and stood up to kiss her.

"Sup, handsome." She smiled sexily.

"You look like a model or something, Carin, what's up with the 'do?" I touched her hair.

"You like?"

"I love, baby, *I love*." I bit my bottom lip. "Feels nice. It's sewn in?"

"Yeah."

"So I can pull on that shit all night." I gave it a nice tug.

"Monty!" She slapped my hand away and sat down when I pulled out her chair.

"You know you're my little dirty."

The moment before I asked Carin to marry me, so many things passed through my mind. I wasn't sure if she was going to stay with me because of what I was about to tell her. But she deserved to know the truth, and if I didn't tell her something she was going to leave me. I didn't want that. I got my money because of a lawsuit I won as an infant. It cost me 60 percent of my sight in my right eye, but because of that I was well-off and never had to worry about money. Everybody in my neighborhood knew about my settlement. Everybody knew except for Carin. She was a breath of fresh air, and I needed her way more than she could ever imagine.

Carin was sitting across from me talking a mile a minute about how tight her weave was and about a pair of shoes that she saw and how she hadn't been to the movies and how she planned on painting an accent wall in my condo. I dug my hand into my pocket and leaned back in my seat, and watching Carin sip her third glass of Sangria.

Alcoholic ass. I laughed. She looked at me, winked, and raised her glass.

"Here's to the most handsome man I have *ever* laid eyes on, even with that slanted eye of yours. It makes you that much sexier, it gives you character, and I love kissing it every night. This is to us and life and I can't wait to take your fine ass home and treat you like my bitch." She laughed. I wanted to laugh with her but I was so caught up in the moment, I fell into a zone.

"Monty, what's up, baby?"

"Nothing, baby, nothing. I just love you so much, that's all." I wiped my eyes. I couldn't believe I was tearing up. She stared at me intensely, waiting for me to continue.

"I know that if you ever left me, if I ever hurt you, if anything happened to you, that would be the end of me, I lie to you not."

"Baby, I'm not going anywhere, why are you talking like that?" she asked worriedly.

I coaxed myself to take the ring out right then. I opened the box and put it on the table. She pulled her hand away from me and covered her mouth. The tears began to fall. I started talking as she reached for the box.

"Carin, making you happy brings me more joy than the love you give me. Every time I buy you something, make love to you, see you smile, I just love you so much more. I know you love me and you got my back, and I need a woman who will have my back."

As I spoke, she slid the ring on. "See that shit right there, Carin? You wearing my ring? That makes me proud as a man. See how happy you are right now? That's the shit that matters most to me in life, your happiness. Will you please be Mrs. Carin Douglas-Johnson?"

Carin was so busy crying and throwing back flutes of Sangria out of nervousness she couldn't answer. I had to laugh when I peeked back and saw the faces through the curtains. Other patrons in the restaurant were now looking. I got on one knee. I was smiling a mile wide. I could see her heart beating and hear her screaming inside. She was hysterical. I took a napkin off of the table and blotted her eyes, careful not to mess up her perfect makeup job.

"Let me do this the right way, on my knees, begging for you to be with me forever. Carin, will you spend the rest of your life in total bliss, allowing me to shower you and pamper you with everything a woman should have? Will you allow me to care for you, raise our children, and show you the finer things? Will you allow me to protect you, respect you, and shield you from harm's way? Will you allow me the honor of waking up next to you every morning and going to bed with you every night? I promise I'll come home every day, I'll come home at respectable hours, I'll put you first, keep you first, compliment everything you do. Carin, you are my heartbeat, girl."

She began bawling and hugging me around the neck. She got down on her knees so our eyes could meet.

"Monty, you are my joy. Yes, I'll marry you, baby. I'll marry you over and over and over!" she squealed.

I picked my fiancée up off the ground and held her tight as everyone came running out, screaming, "Congratulations!"

12

Carin

I was somebody's fiancée now. I wish my mother could see me now so I could show her that this was how to live life as a young woman. This was the treatment you should get. Marriage first, baby later. That's where she had gone wrong, having some man's baby first before making him give her everything her heart could desire. I knew she always felt I wouldn't amount to much, especially once I did that short bid, but the problem between us was that I knew I would be something. I was no black girl lost.

I spent most of my time in Brooklyn because it was easier to get to school and work from there. We normally would go to Queens on the weekends and lay up, where I'd always cook a nice Sunday dinner. Friday and Saturday we went out. I had so much stuff that I didn't even remember half the bags I had at home in Queens, with garments in them that had never been worn. Monty enjoyed shopping for me. It was the highlight of his day to come home with the latest whatever, dress me up in it, and parade me around like some kind of trophy. I'd have much rathered he put cash in my hand. I was a money kind of girl, but however he wanted to do it was fine with me. I had a job so my finances were straight, and I didn't pay any bills. Monty took care of everything. And every morning it was a joy to go to work knowing that I didn't really need a job. I would strategically put on one of my jewelry sets, slide my feet in the most expensive shoes a girl could wear, and dress myself up in the hottest name brand that was out at the time. I went to work and school immaculate every day. My hair was always done differently and I had enough leathers and fur coats to have PETA come after me. There was nothing in this world that I didn't have. Today I decided that with my suit I would wear my Cartier necklace and bracelet set with the diamonds in them. I was feeling real executive-like. I was extremely hyper today, feeling good about myself when as usual the trains were messed up and I wound up at Broadway Junction at an ungodly hour. I went to a pay phone by the A train platform and paged Monty nine one one a million times just to find that the phone didn't ring back. I didn't want to go outside

in the dark to hail a cab, so I figured I'd be safer if
I went upstairs and took the L or J train. As I rode
up the escalator, I saw three girls coming up the
escalator behind me. I turned my ring around. I
couldn't take my jewelry off without being obvious so I just prayed that they weren't going to do
me any harm. I wished I had my piece on me. I
had to remember to go to my father's house and
get it out of my safe.

I finally reached the top when one of them
ran past me quickly and snatched my black
leather Coach bag. I immediately ran after her but
couldn't run too fast in my loafers. I was pissed.
Another one of the females came up behind me
and put me in a choke hold as the third one began
digging through my pockets. The girl who had my
purse dug in it and came off with only $200 and
my credit card, which I was going to cancel as
soon as I got in the house. The one that was tapping my pockets ordered me to take off my jewelry. I thought about other options. None of them
had a gun but I did realize that the one tapping
me had a razor under her tongue. I shook my head
and took off my bracelet. The one who had me
in the choke hold snatched my thick necklace so
hard that it almost choked me. It was hard trying
to snatch that thick necklace off. "The earrings,
too!" the one who had my bag whispered. She

tossed my expensive bag to the side and snatched my earrings off in one swipe, almost tearing my earlobe. Just like that, $6,000 gone.

"Aye, what's going on?" someone coming off of the escalator said and just like that the three girls ran off into the night with my jewels. Thank God they didn't touch my ring.

They ran off toward the J train so I went back downstairs and hailed a cab like I should have done in the first place. When I pulled up on the block, I saw Monty posted up with his fan club. I was livid. I walked up to him and slapped him on his back. "You didn't get none of my fucking pages?" I yelled. Everybody started looking upon seeing me so frantic and hyper. Normally I was laid-back. I'd just come through, flash my mega-watt smile, and watch everyone watch me until I disappeared inside.

"Who are you talking to, what is wrong with you?" He gave me a cold look. "And where the fuck you coming from, huh?" he said, looking at his watch.

"Did you not get my pages? Just answer that."

"Yes, but I couldn't call you back. Where were you paging me from?"

"The Junction, had you paged me to a number, Monty, you could have known that I needed

you to come get me and had you come to get me,
I would not have gotten robbed!" I yelled.

"Robbed by who, you all right?"

"No, I'm not all fucking right. They took my
damn Cartier set, my credit cards, and they man-
gled my brand new Coach Hobo, and your ass is
out here talking to these dusty-ass bitches as usual.
Why the fuck don't you pick me up from school,
anyway?"

"Come on, let's go upstairs, you're upset."

I caught one of the girls smirking at me, probably happy I got robbed. Jealous bum-ass bitches,
I hated them all!

I threw my bags down and kicked off my shoes
when I got upstairs.

"Did they hurt you? Was it guys or girls?"

"Three girls, and they ain't do shit but snatch
my shit." I told him the story.

"Damn, baby. Well, that shit ain't about shit.
I'll get you a new set this weekend." He winked.

"You just don't get it, do you. Fuck it, Monty.
You'll buy me a new life too the next time someone decides they want to kill me for this shit?"

Monty rubbed his face and looked at me.

"Why don't you cook something, that'll make
you feel better."

I thought he was playing so I ignored him. But
then he said it again while actually looking in the
freezer for something to thaw out.

"Excuse you? You were home all day, if you didn't cook then too bad because I'm not hungry. I just got fucking robbed and you're talking about me cooking." I walked by him to get some water.

"Carin, please go cook," he said, standing in the threshold of the kitchen as I guzzled water straight from the container.

"If you weren't out with your little fan club then maybe you would have remembered to at least take the food out to thaw. It's nine o'clock at night. Nothing is getting thawed out tonight, buddy, so you dead on that home cooked meal shit," I said sarcastically. I walked past him again and headed toward our bedroom. I began to undress as Monty stood there, watching me.

"Your man is hungry," he said. But I was done talking to him about this dinner thing. I rolled my eyes and stretched, and in the middle of a yawn Monty put me in a choke hold and threw me on the floor.

"Let me explain something to you, *bitch*, I run shit. I take care of you. Now, when I say cook, you fucking cook, I don't care if it's four in the damn morning, you hear me?" he said as I stared up at him from the floor.

I sat there, dumbfounded, as he stood over me with his fist balled as if he was about to strike me.

"What is wrong with you?" I asked, looking up at him and holding my throat.

"You are my fiancée, right?"

"Yeah!"

"I take care of you, right?"

"Not really, I work!"

Slap! He went clean across my face as hard as he could.

"I could be with *any bitch* I want, but I chose you. I keep you fly, I feed you, I fuck you constantly, and I keep you up to par. The least you could fucking do is cook a nigga some dinner. Get your ass up and cook for me! I don't want to hear that bullshit about you take care of yourself. You can't afford minks and diamonds on that bullshit salary of yours!"

"I thought I told you not to touch me like that again!" I said, getting up from the floor.

"I thought we had the agreement that if I take care of you, you take care of me!" he said, and hemmed me up against the wall.

"I work hard all day, why can't you cook for me? This shit needs to go both ways!" I yelled.

"Carin, go cook, and I am not going to tell you again." He let me go. But I was adamant about not cooking, so as soon as I had enough distance between us I looked at him and told him I wasn't cooking shit.

***

I had no idea what really happened. All I remember was Monty over me yelling and cursing and then me waking up in his arms as he slept like a baby. He was holding me so tight I couldn't move at all. I had to literally pry his arms and legs from around me. My head was aching and I still had on half of my work clothes. I stripped, then headed to the bathroom for some cold tap water. I looked in the mirror and was frightened by what I saw. I threw my hands up to my face and touched it tenderly.

Oh my God, what happened? My face was purple; my cheeks looked like I had an apple in each one. I touched them softly. *He did not do this to me. He did not do this to me!* I kept telling myself over and over. I ran to Monty and shook him awake.

"Wake your fucking ass up!" I said, and punched him in the head.

He jumped up.

"What did you do to me?" I said, wide-eyed in the mirror. He stood behind me, covering his mouth.

"Look what you did to my face!" I said, and began swinging at him. He held my tiny wrists and pleaded for me to stop.

"Carin, please, calm down. I'm so sorry." He tried to pull me to him.

I continued squirming. I kicked him hard in the knee twice but he didn't let me go.

"Monty, how could you do this to me?"

"Carin, I am so sorry. I was drunk, I'm sorry."

"Sorry? You're a woman beater now? Let me go!"

"I was drunk, baby. I lost a lot gambling and damn, baby, I'm so sorry," he said, and pulled me to him. I had no idea what to think of this. I didn't know what Monty was capable of if he could do something like this to me. I backed away from him and started scrambling around the room for my things.

"Where are you going?"

"Home." I began ransacking my closet for the most valuable items first.

"To Queens, right?"

"No, *home* to my father's house."

"Carin, you can't go back there. I promised him I'd take care of you. You can't go back to Jersey, come here, baby," he said, grabbing me. "This is home!"

"No, *this* is bullshit! I'm not going to be with some man who hits me when he is drunk or otherwise. I'm out of here, Monty. Look at me, look at my face. How the fuck am I going to go anywhere looking like this, you stupid motherfucka! Huh?" I yelled, and swung at him again.

"Carin, if you go home, your father will not let us see one another anymore. Do you want that, baby?"

"Maybe that's for the best, Monty. This is something I will *not* tolerate." I began to cry as I looked in the mirror. Then reality hit me. If I went home like this, there would be bloodshed for sure. My father would come at Monty, guns blazing.

I can't go home like this.

"Just stay 'til it goes down, Carin. I don't want your family to flip out. Just, please, stay 'til it goes down."

"Get up and take me to Queens now before your family sees my face. Let's go! And you're sleeping in the living room when we get back to Kew Gardens. I do not want to come to Brooklyn anymore!" I said.

"Okay, okay, whatever you want. Just please don't leave me, Carin, I'm sorry." He started getting dressed.

Whatever I wanted was right. The gifts were coming in lumps. I ran out of places to keep my clothes. I gave a lot of my things to Jetta because Missy was too big for my clothes, but I gave her plenty of shoes. I was cleaning out my closet on a Saturday afternoon when Monty came in the house singing "Ain't No Nigga" after being gone from nine o'clock in the morning. I didn't even care where he was. A week had gone by and my face was just returning to normal. That image would never leave my mind.

He dropped a shopping bag on the bed and pulled me up off of the floor by my arm. "Here, I bought you some leathers," he said.

I pulled out a hard, black leather jacket and a brown one. "Thanks," I said simply, and turned to go back to my cleaning. Monty grabbed my arm.

"I know what'll float your boat. Come here, let me show you something."

Reluctantly, I put the jackets down and followed him to the front of the house. All the gifts in the world would not make me forget about how my face looked that day. Unenthused, I looked across the street and saw a cranberry-colored, four-door Lexus GS with a bow on it. My eyes widened. "Tell me you didn't buy me a car, boy!"

"No more trains, no more getting robbed, no more waiting on me. With all these minks and diamonds, you shouldn't be on the train."

"I don't even have my license!" I said, grabbing his hand and running outside.

"I'll buy you your license. Let's go upstate tomorrow. I got a hookup."

***

When I was absolutely sure that I had no marks on my face, I drove my brand new Lexus to New Jersey to show my family. This car was the shit and it felt like being in an airplane! I was stunting as I came out of the Holland Tunnel with my shades on and my bangs blowing in the wind. I had my *Reasonable Doubt* CD playing as I cruised around Jersey for a while before heading to my father's house. I just wanted the feeling of being in this car, driving around. I drove like a pro, thanks to Panama. I thought about him often and planned on visiting him one day soon. I parked my car in the underground garage and headed upstairs in the plush elevator of my father's building. Using my key, I entered the apartment to find that nobody was home. I went in the kitchen, made myself a sandwich, and cracked open my father's unopened Hennessy. It felt good to be home. I went upstairs to my bedroom to find it untouched. It was just how I'd left it. If I ever had to come back home it would never be a problem. I loved it here. I loved it everywhere! I was a lucky girl. I heard the key open the door. Someone had come in. I peeked out to see Farrod tossing his keys on the credenza and taking off his fitted cap.

"Psst, hey, you!" I extended my arm for a hug. His face lit up as he walked to me.

"What's up, ma, what you doing here?"

"I just came by to visit, what's going on?" I asked as he held me in his arms.

"You, how you been?" He grabbed my left hand to see my ring. "This bullshit," he said, dropping my hand. I laughed and grabbed his hand again, leading him to the living room.

"You in here drinking up your father shit. What's going on, why are you here?" he said, pouring himself a drink too.

"I can't come by and visit my family?"

"I keep telling you I am not your family." He threw back two shots, one after the other.

"You wanna talk about it, brother? You throwing back them shots like you got some shit on your mind, meng." I laughed.

"It's my girl, Kim. She is so fucking paranoid and insecure. I can't deal with her asking me where I am and what I'm doing all day. I can't shit without her bugging my fucking nerves, B, the shit is frustrating. She's a good girl, she's lovely, I love her, but she gotta ease up with that insecure shit."

"Where is she now?"

"Working. I didn't even tell her that I had the day off. She would have taken the day off too. And then my other boo decided she wanna go marry some ballin'-ass nigga like my job at the Gap wasn't good enough for her." He laughed.

"That is too funny."I chuckled, pouring myself another drink.

"But real talk, Carin, you broke my heart when you got engaged. I was digging you."

"You should have said something. You slow you blow."

"Nah, you seemed real high maintenance and I can't afford you. Look at you, you got a big-ass rock, Chanel shades on your head, Fendi flip-flops, Cartier sets on and shit."

"And a brand new cranberry-colored GS outside!"

"He copped you a GS? Like Jay-Z?"

"Mmm-hmm." I grinned. But then I thought about what Monty had done to my face the other day. I held my smile, though, because Farrod seemed excited. I wasn't sure if it was right to be with Monty after that. He had hit me twice already.

"Wow, you living the life, huh?"

I shrugged and took off my shirt. "It's hot in here."

"So you just gon' sit there in your bra in my face?"

"So," I shrugged. I wasn't checking for Farrod in that way. He was a cutie, yes, but I had Monty now. I was a one man kind of girl. Farrod wiped his finger down my cleavage.

"You sweating." He smiled. His touch was nice. I wanted him to do it again but I didn't say anything. We sat quietly after that and sipped our Hennessy, both probably looking for an excuse to do what our hormones were screaming for us to do.

"You're still sweating," he said after another drink.

"I can't do this, Farrod. I love you like a brother. Let's not cross the line. As much as I want to, it would complicate things down the line, I'm sure."

He shrugged as he leaned over and sucked the sweat off of my cleavage.

"I just had to do that. I respect it, though."

I burst out laughing. "Farrod, come downstairs and let me show you my car!"

It was the perfect way to avoid doing something that I would probably regret.

When I got home that night, Monty was on the steps with his grandparents and his mother. I got out and kissed his cheek first. He rolled his eyes at me and continued smoking his cigarette.

"Where you coming from?" his mother, Pamela, asked me.

"My dad's house. I went to show off my new wheels!" I squealed. "Hey, Granddaddy, you had your bananas today?" I said, kissing his cheeks.

"No, nobody fed me my bananas, nobody feed me 'cept you, Carin. They trying to kill me," he joked.

"You better hush before I take you out, old man," his wife said.

"Why you sitting over there all sour in the face? What's wrong with you?" I asked Monty. He made me sick how he'd get all salty whenever I went somewhere without him.

"He was mad because he couldn't find you," Granddaddy said. Everybody laughed, except Monty.

"Well, I left him a note and he knows my father's number and where he lives, so I don't see the issue."

Pamela fanned her son off and got up. "Shit, you did all that? You a better woman than me. He'll be all right. You're not his child, you can do what you want to 'cause he sure as hell does what he wants."

Monty glared at his mother.

"Where's Sharon at?"

"Working a double," Monty finally said.

"Well, I'm going upstairs, guys, I am tired. I will see you all later," Pamela announced. Everyone said good night, and Monty and I strolled to the corner store.

"How's your family doing?" he asked.

"Everybody is good."

"So, what did yawl do?"

"Nothing, just sat around and shot the shit, why?"

"You couldn't call me?"

"For what, Monty? I was out. If you wanted me you needed to call me." I reached for a water in the freezer.

"Next time you go out, check in. That's the rules."

"Rules, baby, I'm not good with rules." I laughed. He didn't.

"I'll give you whatever you want, Carin, just do what I say."

"The same goes for you. Do what I say." I held my ground.

Driving to the city was senseless because of traffic and parking, so even though I had this sexy new vehicle, I only drove it on weekends or whenever I wasn't going to work. I left work extremely tired today, wishing that I had driven, and had every intention of going home and straight to sleep. It was just my luck that the L train was out of service again, so without a second thought, I hailed a cab. It was hot, and I was tired and very aggravated that the train had been delayed. When I pulled up in front of my house, Monty, Ski, Jomar, and Rick were sitting on the stoop. I got out, smiled at everyone, and said hello. They all smiled back and Jomar grabbed my hand, helping me up the stairs, something Monty should have done. Rick grabbed my hand briefly. They were all giving me the attention that Monty used to give me. Yet I tried to remain positive and good to my man. After all, it was either that or wind up alone like my mother.

"Hey, Monty baby." I leaned in to give him a kiss.

"I'll see you upstairs in a minute," he said, and smiled at me.

"Okay." I headed upstairs and began to undress. I had planned on sitting outside but since he dismissed me I wasn't going to protest. I just headed upstairs. I turned the shower on and let the water run for a while. I just wanted that hot steam to hit my back and shoulders. It had been a stressful day. Once that water hit me, my shoulders slumped down and I began to relax, damn near falling asleep standing up. Too good to be true, I could hear Monty stomping through the apartment with his long ass yelling my name. I ignored him and tried my best to salvage a few more seconds in the shower. *What does he want?*

Monty pulled the shower curtains back so hard they ripped. I stood there covering my breasts. "What did you do that for?"

Monty didn't answer me. He bit his bottom lip and balled up his fist. "Where the fuck are you coming from so late, huh?"

"Monty, I know you're not tripping over the time. I got stuck on the train."

"So where did you get a cab at?"

"The Junction, what is wrong with you?"

"You coming home jumping in the shower, you think I'm stupid?"

"That's what I do every day, what are you tripping about?"

Monty snatched me out of the shower and dragged me to the bedroom. He threw me on the bed wet and naked.

"You lying to me, Carin, huh? You know how it looks for my woman to be coming out of a cab this time of night? You got a fucking car. I paid for that shit in cash, no car payments, no nothing. Why you don't drive your car, huh? You don't wanna be spotted?"

"Lying about what? Spotted? Monty, you better not put your fucking hands on me!" I yelled.

"Or what?" he said, jumping on top of me, slapping me over and over in my face. I began to scream and kick him but he held my hands down and kept on slapping me . . . *hard*. My face was still wet and it was stinging. "If you have to drive that fucking train yourself you better get home on fucking time, you hear me?" he whispered sinisterly to me as he kept on slapping my face until it was numb.

"Not my face," was all I could say as I cried. I wanted to fight back so bad but his slaps took the energy out of me. He literally slapped the shit out of me each time. He ran his fingers through my hair and got a good grip on it. I was so tired of him pulling my fucking hair out. He had his fist balled up to strike me but I was saved by a knock on the door. Monty backed up from me.

"Put on some clothes," he said, and fixed himself up. I could hear Rick's voice as I threw on sweats and a T-shirt.

Monty

I remembered when, as a child, I'd go visit my father every summer in Connecticut. He had this beautiful girlfriend named Harriet. She was tall and dark skinned with short, curly hair and a beautiful shape. Even at the age of five I recognized beauty when I saw it. She seemed really nice and was always hospitable to me when I came for the summer. She cooked for me, cleaned up be-

hind me, and showered me with hugs and kisses.
I looked forward to seeing her every summer and
would tell my mother about her all the time. My
mother could never contain her jealousy and even
tried to ban me from going to see my father every
summer. My father wasn't having it and fought
my mother for partial custody, so I continued to
go there every summer until I was twelve years
old; until that fateful night.

When I'd go to visit my father, I noticed that
Harriet was very subservient. She waited on my
father hand and foot, but when she didn't move
fast enough my father would drag her around
and knock her upside her head. I never told my
mother because my father said that I wouldn't be
able to come over anymore if my mother found
out. Summer after summer, my dad would beat
this tall, beautiful woman down to her knees,
slapping her, cursing at her, kicking her around.
"Son, when they don't listen, you have to treat
them this way. A woman should listen to her
man, and as long as you pay the bills, a woman
is supposed to do whatever you ask of her. You
don't ever let a woman tell you no or make you
wait for nothing! If she comes out her face, talks
to you any old kind of way, or doesn't do what
she is supposed to do, you put foot to her ass, you

hear me? She deserved that shit. She don't fucking listen and I work hard and take care of this
woman!" is what he drilled in my head after each
ass whooping he inflicted upon poor Harriet.

The last summer I went to Connecticut, I noticed that Harriet barely spoke to me. She kept
to herself and barely came out of her room. She
wasn't her usual bubbly sweet self any more and
she looked tired. My father was his normal macho
self, feet up on the table, drinking a beer as Harriet made the world revolve around him. Apparently, on this day, she didn't let the world revolve
around him fast enough. So my father jumped up
without warning and began to beat her. I didn't
even remember what it was about. Harriet went
screaming for me to get out of the house. She ran
past me and looked me in my eyes with a look I
could never explain, but she warned me to get
out of the house and get help now. Not one to
go against my father I stood still, watching the
debacle of my dad chase his woman around the
house, catching her, and beating her. He beat her
to the point where I had to call 911. As my father
shook off his knuckles and grabbed his second
wind, Harriet came running out of the bedroom
like a raging bull and began shooting off a pistol.
Four shots hit my father in his chest and he died
with his eyes open. They say you deserve it when

you die like that. I didn't know if she planned on killing me but I'm glad I called 911 when I did. They were on the scene to take me home and take Harriet away in cuffs. She was sentenced to only a year in prison. Something about battered woman's syndrome. I never heard about her again. All I knew was that women were wicked when they were ready, and they were fucking hard-headed, and I'd kill one of them before they killed me like Harriet did my father.

I hated when niggas questioned me on how I treated my girl. It was none of their business. Rick was up in my face wanting to see Carin, actually trying to walk past me in my house.

"I could hear her screaming all the way outside, what the fuck are you doing to her in here?"

"Rick, it's under control. Me and Carin just had a little fight, I'll be outside in a minute."

"Monty, man, this shit ain't cool. You can't be beating on her like that. This is not the first time you put your hands on her, but make it your last. Don't hit her while I'm around."

I sized Rick up. "You serious? This is my woman, I don't interfere with you and Sade so do not come in my house telling me how to handle mines."

"You don't have to interfere with me and Sade 'cause I don't treat her the way you treat Carin. You dead-ass wrong for this and you know it."

"Rick, go 'head, all right? Nobody was up here hitting Carin. I pressed her for coming home late, she thought I was about to hit her, and she started screaming."

"Monty, don't put your hands on her," Rick said to me again.

"Yo, go 'head with that shit, Rick. I'll be down in a minute," I said, giving him his cue to exit my house.

Carin

It was then that I came out of the room acting like I didn't know Rick was there. I wanted someone to see what Monty did to me behind closed doors. For them to hear it was enough. But he was so good in dressing me in diamonds and furs and designer clothes nobody seemed to notice the bruises under my clothes.

"Oh, hey, Rick I didn't know you were here," I mumbled, fixing my hair. My mouth was busted and my head was aching horribly. Rick didn't speak; he looked at Monty.

"Carin, what's up, mommy, how was your day?" He pulled me to him like a big brother does a little sister.

"Oh, it was fine. The trains were all fucked up so I got home late, but other than that, my day was cool." I smiled. He stared at me for a while. I could see the anger in his eyes, but he kept his cool.

"Are you hungry? We all are about to head up to the Spanish restaurant on Broadway to get some food, you want something?"

"Nah, she's good, she needs to cook," Monty said.

"Cook? Man, it's late, who the hell is cooking this time of day, in this heat? What do you want, C?" Rick asked me, wiping the blood off my mouth with the tip of his T-shirt.

"Man, she's all right," Monty said, pushing Rick's hand from my mouth.

"I'll have steak and onions, yellow rice, and an avocado salad," I said happily.

Rick tapped Monty. "Come on, let's go get this girl something to eat. She has been out working hard all day. We ate good so she gotta eat good. You want something to drink?"

"Can you go to that spot on Myrtle and bring me back a Blue Hawaiian with an extra shot?"

"Yeah," Rick said, and headed out.

Monty told Rick he'd see him downstairs.

"You stay acting like you're a fucking victim. You love the attention, huh?" Monty said as I headed into the living room. I ignored him and turned on the television. "You are going to quit that fucking job. Give your boss his two weeks tomorrow!" he said, and walked out.

I wasn't quitting my job. It was the only time I had away from Monty. He could hang it up if he thought I was giving up school or work. The next day I decided I needed to see Farrod. I hadn't seen him in some months, but we spoke all the time. I wondered if I could confide in him about Monty abusing me. I needed to talk to someone but I was embarrassed, more so because I still loved the man and wanted to be with him. I didn't think anybody would understand that logic. I knew for sure that Missy and Jetta wouldn't understand. I didn't need to be judged; I needed to be heard and understood right now. I waited for Farrod across the street from his job and I could see him coming out of his building. He looked so good and happy. His girlfriend, Kim, was a lucky woman. He seemed to have gotten a shade darker and his facial hair did him justice.

"Damn, Carin, what's up with you? You don't love me anymore!" he said as soon as he got near me.

I chuckled and walked next to him slowly with my hands in my pockets.

"How have you been?"

"I've been good, and by the looks of things so have you. So what brings you here?"

"Can we walk and talk?" I asked.

"Yeah, no doubt. I know a spot over here by Bryant Park, come on," he said, walking slightly ahead of me.

"Okay, so talk to me, and what did you do to your hair?" He lightly stroked the nape of my neck.

I didn't want to talk about my hair and how I had cut it boy short. I just needed some fresh air.

"What's up with that cat, Monty? He treating you good?"

We sat there silently as I pondered if I should speak the truth or front for Farrod. I needed to talk to someone about what was going on with me in case something happened, because each fight was worse and I swore that the next blow was going to kill me. My friends surely wouldn't understand. All they saw were the fancy clothes and jewelry. They thought I was living it up.

"He's fine, just fine!" I said, trying to sound upbeat.

"Yeah, I bet. So what brings you to my job after all this time? I haven't seen you since that night you came over upset over something he did to you."

I was just thinking back to the first time I saw Monty, trying to see if I missed any signs of him being so abusive. It felt so good to be out smelling the fresh air. I sat like that for a long time, trying hard to hold on to this moment of sanity. A long, hot tear rolled out of my right eye. It was bold and strong. I felt my nose begin to burn. I was so unhappy but too ashamed to go home.

"I'm so depressed." The words rolled off my tongue without permission.

"Why?"

"Monty is not being good to me," I said simply.

"What is he not doing? Is he stepping out on you?"

"Probably, but that's not it. He's changed, Farrod."

"He not hitting it anymore?" he asked.

"He's hitting it too much, that's the problem. He hits me for wearing orange, for not cooking enough, for taking a shower at night, for breathing. I don't know what happened! He just changed on me."

"Wait, this nigga beats on you, Carin?" he said, turning toward me. He grabbed my shoulder and turned me to him.

I nodded my head then wiped my eyes. I could feel a storm coming on.

"How long has this been happening?"

"It seems like right after we got engaged he just changed." I began to cry. I couldn't hold it back anymore.

Farrod hugged me. "I knew it, I knew that nigga was up to no good. I knew it and your father knew it. So this is why you don't come around?"

"He won't let me eat, sleep, or shit without him!" I said.

"Carin, you know you have to leave him, right?"

"This is going to sound crazy, but I love him, I do, and I just want him to be the way he used to be. I know he loves me, Farrod, he's just going through something right now."

"You're willing to die waiting for the old Monty to come back? What if this is him and the man you met was just a representative?"

"I love him so much, Farrod, I do. It'll be fine."

"You're making excuses, Carin."

"No, I'm not. If I can only get him to stop drinking."

"Come here." He hugged me tight. "You have to leave that man alone, Carin, you are better than this. If your father found out about this, he'd—"

"I haven't seen my dad in months," I said, cutting him off.

"And it's breaking his heart, but you can't go like this. Go home, get some rest, and come see your pops this weekend. You don't even see your friends or anything. When was the last time you went out with your girls and had a good time?"

"I promise I will come this weekend," I said, getting up. "I need to head back to work. He wants me to quit my job."

"If you quit your job, you are going to die, you hear me?"

I put my head down, but he lifted it up. "You are so much better than this. You have family that loves you, you don't have to deal with this shit."

"I know, Farrod, I'll take care of it in time."

"Well, next weekend get your shit together because we all are going to do something, me, your father, Kim . . ."

"Kim, huh?" I laughed.

"What? You got yours, I can't get mine?"

"Bye, Farrod. Don't tell anyone I'm coming, let it be a surprise."

"Yes, a surprise indeed," he said, watching me as I walked off.

13

Carin

I hadn't seen my father in months. Every time he asked me to come visit I'd put on my happy face and brag about not having the time because Monty was spoiling me so much and keeping me so busy. I told him that I did see Farrod and Missy, so that he wouldn't grow suspicious. He was eager to see me but happy that I was doing okay. But I knew that my time was running out, so I made my way to Jersey to see him. I was driving in my pretty car, with my expensive ring and my classy haircut, donning hundred-dollar jeans, two-hundred dollar loafers, looking damn good in my favorite Li'l Kim vintage Versace shades. They were my favorite because they were black and big and could cover a black eye real good. Though I didn't have a black eye today, my eyes had dark circles around them. I hoped that my makeup was doing a good job. I blasted Faith Evans's debut CD, and put "Is It a Game" on repeat all the way to Jersey. When I pulled up at my dad's, I checked myself out in the mirror. I looked good from what I could see. I still had my key so I let myself in. Tyra was in the living room on her knees, looking for something under the sofa.

"Darren, reach under this sofa and get that brush for me, I have been looking for that brush for so long!" she said, getting up. I stood there, smiling.

She hugged me. "Carin! What are you doing here, girl, and have you been eating? Feels like I can break you, and what have you done to your hair?"

"You like it?"

"I love it! I wanted to do that but your father won't let me. This is beautiful! You look like Halle Berry but prettier!" she said, hugging me again.

"So how is the soon-to-be married life treating you?"

"I'm doing okay, I can't complain," I said, stepping back and putting my hands in my back pockets. I had been engaged to Monty for about fifteen months and it seemed as if right after he put that ring on my finger he started putting rings around my eye.

"Just *okay?* Girl, I thought you were going to roll up in here with a big belly and baby shower invitations as long as you been away. I know you guys must be trying by now." She winked.

"Yup. We are," I said, trying to seem upbeat. I hoped it was working.

She gave me a look that told me Farrod had told her something. "Carin, now, you know I'm not one to get in your business, but . . ."

"Tyra, I'm here to visit my family and my girls and to have a good time. Please, not tonight." I put my hand up.

"Carin, baby, please don't stay there any longer than you have to, it's not okay for a man to hit on you and that's all I'm going to say about that."

"Where's my father?" I asked, changing the subject.

She let out a defeated sigh. "He went to the store. That should be him coming in now."

Monty

I sat on the sofa watching videos for a minute after Carin left. I walked around the house, bored, not really wanting to get up with anybody. I didn't want Carin to go to her family's house so they could put shit all in her head about where she needed to be, but I figured I'd let her go out for a while so I could do me. I looked at my hands and began flexing my fingers. I went into my bedroom and sat down on my bed. Staring at me was a picture of me and Carin coming off of a cruise. I took the picture down and touched her face. I loved Carin, despite how she felt or what she thought, she was my air and I couldn't and wouldn't live without her. I put the picture back up and lit a cigarette. Bored, I did what most niggas do when wifey is away. I went out to play.

"Whaddup, I'll be to you in about a half, did you cook?"

"You know I did," Tionne cooed into the phone.

"Make sure you don't have a bunch of salt in my food, you heard?"

"No, I learned to cook just how you like it, baby. Bring the drinks."

I hung up and jumped in the shower. Tionne was something to do.

Driving ten minutes away to Tionne's, I thought about maybe taking Carin on a surprise vacation. It brought me joy to spend money on my baby doll but lately nothing I brought home lit her face up the way it used to. I didn't even want to be at Tionne's house right now. I had a few options instead of going to Tionne's house but I wasn't in the mood to spend dough on Crystal, this high maintenance bitch I met in the city two months ago while shopping. She was a lawyer and had her own money, but was looking for a bad boy to spend his dough on her. I copped her a pair of

Fendi pumps once, only because we were in the city and she kept hinting at them. I could've told her to get the fuck out of here, but just to style on her I copped her a pair and Carin a pair, but I got Carin a bag and belt to match. Crystal was cool but the sex wasn't all that good. She spent so much time trying to be pretty and not mess up her hair that we couldn't get wild the way we wanted. I didn't feel like that shit tonight. Then there was Lu-lu, the Spanish chick from the lower east side. She was a straight Puerto Rican hood rat who smoked a lot of weed, drank, cursed at her parents, and shit like that. I met her in the sneaker store off of Delancey Street. She had big-ass hips and a fat ass and she was hood fly. Lu-lu was mad cool. She cursed a lot and would always call me with her heavy Puerto Rican accent: "Yo, Monty, when the fuck you gon' come see a bitch, what the fuck?" I'd just laugh. I'd shoot to see her on the low and fuck her on her twin bed with the rosary beads hanging from the headboard, while her son was asleep in the next room. She was a real rat but she took anal well and could cook her ass off. But tonight I didn't feel like ditching her son or even traveling. I wanted to throw on some sweats with no drawers and get in and out like a crack house, keep it moving. Tionne was my only other option.

I got to Tionne's house at around six with a gallon of Hennessey. That's all she needed to get right. She put her kids to bed and was walking around in a black silk robe and some nasty lingerie, as usual. Tionne was always ready to fuck. I headed to her bedroom and took my shoes and shirt off. She took them from me and put them in the closet, then came in the room with a hot plate of fish, greens, and corn on the cob.

"Thanks." I devoured my food.

"Damn, baby, you hungry? Wifey ain't cook again?"

Sometimes Tionne pissed me off because I'd tell her little shit and she always tried to use it against me or Carin.

"She's out visiting family," I said between bites.

"She should have made sure you had food before she left." She got up and put on a porno.

"Turn that shit off. I'm trying to eat."

Carin

If my father found out Monty was abusing me I knew first hand he'd kill him. So I was hoping it didn't get out. But now that Tyra knew it was only a matter of time that he found out, if he didn't know already, so I braced myself for whatever it was he had to say.

"Princess, what did you do to your hair?" he said, squeezing me and rocking from side to side.

"You like?" I said, spinning around and posing for him.

"Well, you know I don't agree with a woman cutting her hair, but, yeah! Yeah, I like it. You look so grown."

"I am though, Daddy."

"Yeah, but like a woman grown. I mean, this is nice, Carin, how long ago did you do this?"

"A month or two ago. How have you been, Daddy?"

"Fine, you know me, how have *you* been is the question. Why haven't you called me or come to visit? That boy treating you okay?"

"Yeah, you know Monty."

"Which is why I asked if he's treating you okay." He chuckled.

"Yes, he is, things are fine," I said following him into the kitchen with his bags.

"Good, well enough of him, my baby girl is here! Did you call your friends?"

"No, not yet."

"Well, call them up, I'm going to cook something nice for you girls to just sit in here and eat and talk and catch up. I miss you so much, baby!" my father said, hugging me tightly. He kissed me on the top of my head and looked at me. I

wanted to come home and start over. I wanted
my dad back, I wanted Tyra back, and I wanted
my friends back. But I was strong and didn't cry.
I wanted to tell them all to help me but I was too
embarrassed. I hugged my father so tightly that
he got concerned. "You okay, princess?"

I couldn't let him go. I needed him to protect
me but I didn't want him to hurt Monty. I wanted
to scream, "Daddy please save me before he kills
me!" But instead I smiled as genuinely as I could
as I held my father's hands. It took everything
in me not to bawl. "I'm fine, Daddy, I just can't
believe I got so caught up. I missed you!"

"It's okay, as long as you're happy and you're
here now, just don't let it happen again, okay?"

"I won't, I promise." I finally let him go.

My father and Tyra disappeared into the
kitchen and I went upstairs to look in my bedroom. It was just how I left it. Neat. I stood in the
doorway and felt a hand around my waist, then
a kiss on my neck. "Welcome home." Farrod sat
me down on my bed. He held my hand.

"Carin, I love you. I don't want to see you hurt
and I definitely don't want to see you getting
your ass beat by some man. I'm not going to
lecture you, but you know what you need to do,
Carin. Don't let this shit get the best of you and
don't let your pride keep you someplace that you

know is no good for you. Now, I ain't condoning this shit, but I'm here for you whenever you need to talk or escape."

"Thank you, Farrod, I appreciate you. It feels so good to be home."

He smiled at me warmly.

"Yeah I'm glad you didn't renege. The girls are downstairs. I picked Missy up at Journal Square. Her car is out of commission and you know Jetta stalking ass was right across the hall."

I was excited. I ran down to see Jetta and Missy sitting on the sofa.

"Hey girls!" I screamed. They both yelled and ran up to me.

"What the fuck did you do to your hair, Carin?" Jetta said, hugging me tight around my neck.

"You like?"

"Hell, yeah! That shit looks hot!" Missy said.

"Yeah, that's fly, Carin," Jetta agreed. "I want to get my hair cut like that! But damn all that, where the hell you been, nobody can call you, come see you, the fuck is that about?" Jetta said, cursing up a storm. Missy rolled her eyes. She couldn't stomach Jetta most of the time. She accused her of wanting to be like me.

"You know how it is when you're in love," I said. Farrod excused himself.

"Well, you can still come up for air and see if we are okay. I mean, damn, Carin, and you don't call or anything!" Jetta continued.

"Well, all of that has changed now. I'm here now and I won't do that again. I'm up for air."

"That's nice to know," Missy said sourly. I know I hurt her by disappearing. Missy was my sister.

"I'm so sowwy, Missy poo, forgive me peeez?" I said in a baby voice, wrapping my arms around her waist. She smirked and hugged me back, but she didn't say anything.

"So, what's new, what's been going on?" I said eagerly, sitting down. I wanted to hear all about what they were doing, who they were dating, and things like that.

"Did you girls see my car?" I said.

"No, you got a car?" Jetta jumped up excitedly.

"Yeah, come on, let me show you guys. Come on, Missy!"

Jetta and I hightailed it out the door as Missy dragged behind.

"Please don't tell me he got you one of those Mazda 929s like everybody is driving," Missy said.

"Nope."

"He got you a Beemer?" Jetta asked.

"Uh-uh, you'll see." I giggled.

We all ran out of the building. "Which car do you think is mine?" I asked.

The girls looked around for a while then Jetta nailed it.

"That is you right there I can see you in it, oh my God!" she said, running to my car. I hit the alarm from behind.

Missy walked up to it. "It's nice."

"Nice? Bitch, this is better than nice, dammit, *that car* is nice," I said, pointing to the silver Acura across the street. "This shit right here is hard! Come on get in!" I said, tossing Missy the keys. But she was being so sour, I snatched my keys back from her. "Fuck it, Jetta, you drive, Missy get your ass in the back," I joked.

"I'll get the fuck out, fuck it." She got out.

"Ew, why you acting so stink?" Jetta said, firing up the ignition.

"I'm gonna go upstairs and lie down. I got cramps."

"Yeah, you sick all right. Sick because of this car. Let's ride, baby!" Jetta screamed and pulled off, leaving Missy on the corner.

Jetta filled me with stories of her and Kenny and all the fights and making up they did over the months. She talked me to death about her beloved Kenny until we got upstairs. Farrod was on his cell phone for the most part asking Kim why she hadn't made it to the house yet and my dad and Tyra sat at the dining room table drinking red wine and playing blackjack. "Where's Missy?" I asked, looking around.

"Oh, she went home, she said she'd call you later."

"She went home? She knew I was just taking Jetta for a joy ride, why did she leave?"

"Jealous." Jetta handed me my keys.

"Naw, not Missy, she's not that type," I said, wondering why she really left.

My father and Tyra were laughing quietly and touching hands across the table the way Monty and I used to. My father made shrimp scampi and egg noodles, and we all had Malibu and pineapple afterward. Around midnight I drifted off to sleep with a smile on my face. It felt so good to be home.

Monty

"Damn, girl."

Tionne was riding me backward and doing some shit with her pussy muscles. I lay back with my hands behind my head watching her move like a pro. Tionne was downright nasty. I was fucking her when she was big and pregnant, too. "I'm coming, Monty," she announced. She grabbed my ankles and started bucking wild. I was coming too.

"Jump off this dick and suck it," I commanded her. She snatched the condom off and sucked me until I came. I looked down at her with disdain. I had no respect for half the bitches I fucked with, only Carin. I glanced at the clock. It was midnight and Carin hadn't called my cell at all. I wondered if she was home yet. "Yo, bring me a rag," I said to Tionne as she tried to cuddle up under me. I started dialing Carin as soon as she walked off.

"Who are you calling?" she asked, tossing the rag at me.

I ignored her and called home. Nobody answered. I got dressed and slid my feet into my Tims.

"Where are you going?" she asked with her hands on her hips.

I let out a gasp and rolled my eyes. I put on my fitted hat and snatched up the keys to my Lexus.

"You running home to wifey now?" she said, putting on a pair of pajama pants. I ignored her and kept walking toward the front door. She followed me like a puppy and watched me as I hopped into my car, the black one to Carin's cranberry-colored one. I didn't even say bye. Tionne knew what it was. I honked the horn as I pulled off. She waved from the door and disappeared inside. I got home in about fifteen minutes and checked the caller ID. Carin hadn't called or anything so I called her. Her *brother* answered the phone.

"Hello, Darren?"

"No, this is Farrod, who's this?"

"Monty, how you doin', man, is Carin there?"

"Carin is asleep, I'll tell her to call you in the morning when she wakes up."

"Can you wake her up? I need to ask her something."

"Nah, she been asleep for a minute."

Who did this bitch-ass nigga think he was, telling me I couldn't talk to my wife?

"My man, it's important. I need to talk to my wife. Can you wake her up, please?"

"She's not your wife yet and anyway no, she's sleeping, so I'm not waking her up. I'll tell her you called, though." He hung up.

I was hot. I slammed the phone down and called a cab to take me to Jersey. I didn't know why this nigga had an attitude with me, but I was going to ring Carin's neck for it because I knew she had everything to do with that shit.

Carin

I was sleeping soundly on my father's big, plush sofa. I had no worries, no pain, nobody touching me in the middle of the night. I wanted this feeling back. But when I woke up for a brief second, Monty was standing over me looking like the devil. He was standing over me wearing all black from head to toe, and a diamond-encrusted necklace. Farrod was behind him, unable to see Monty's face. I smiled and stretched. "Hey, baby, what time is it?"

"Two in the morning," he said curtly.

"Really?" I jumped up. Farrod stood next to Monty.

"I told you she was sleeping. Why are you here?" Farrod snapped.

Monty just stood stiffly and allowed his eyes to follow me around the room as I scrambled for my things.

"Sometime tonight, Carin. I don't know why I had to come all the way out here to get you anyway," he said in a low tone.

"Okay, baby!" I smiled nervously.

Farrod sucked his teeth. "Man, fuck this shit, what's up with you putting your hands on my sister?"

"Farrod, stay out of it!" I said.

"Nah, Carin, you running around the house all nervous and shit. You popping up here like what? Why couldn't she just stay asleep in her family's house?" Farrod said, stepping in his face. Monty was eerily quiet. He put his hands in his pockets and sucked his teeth.

"Ain't nobody hitting your sister, go 'head with all that."

"She told me you beat on her, so what's up? Hit me, motherfucka!" Farrod said, beating his chest.

"You're going to wake my father!" I hushed.

"So what! Wake that nigga up," Monty said.

"Please, do not wake my father, please!"

"Hit a man, motherfucka!" Farrod said again.

"Farrod, please, stay out of this," I pleaded as I slid my feet into my loafers. I tried to hold on to Monty's shoulder for support but he shrugged me off.

"Let's go!" he said, walking away. I hopped behind him trying to put my shoe on when Farrod grabbed my arm. "Look at you running behind him. Carin, you don't have to deal with this shit, you hear me? And the next time you tell me that this dude is hitting you, it's going to be some shit."

"Carin, let's go now!" Monty snarled.

"I'll call you tomorrow, it's okay!" I smiled. He didn't say anything, he just let us out and slammed the door.

Monty was quiet all the way home as he drove at a flowing speed and appeared "easy," but I didn't let my guard down. "Monty, you didn't have to come check on me, baby. I told you where I was going to be."

He continued to ignore me. When we got to the house, he parked, and just when I was about to get out of the car he grabbed my shirt.

"I should fuck you up *one* for not coming home, *two* having your bitch-ass brother step to me, and *three* for telling our business. You think I won't pop one in that bitch-ass nigga *and* your pops? You know who you fucking with, Carin?"

"Monty, you're overexaggerating." I whispered. I tried to be calm. I didn't want him to start swinging.

"Am I?" he said, and back-slapped me, still holding on to the collar of my shirt so that I could not move. I felt the blood trickling down my lip. I stared at the ground. He punched me in the head twice then told me to get the fuck upstairs. I don't know why we couldn't just go to our condo, why we had to be here where the world could see how he treated me. I would be okay if nobody could see what he did to me. I just wanted to hide and deal with this abuse on my own. I could hear his aunt Sharon yelling into the street.

"Monty, get over here!" she yelled after him, but he pulled off in my car.

"Come here, baby, come on," his grandmother said. I began to cry. His sister, Yvonne, hushed me.

"Sleep in my house tonight," she offered.

"No, I got her." Sharon pulled me upstairs.

"No, I want to go in my own house," I said, but Sharon was having none of that. She pulled me into Pam's house, yelling for her to wake up.

"Sharon, don't wake her. She is going to flip out!" I said, still trying to pull away from her.

"She needs to see what her son is doing to you. Now, I love my nephew but this is crazy. What is he mad for now? I saw how he hit you just now, what the fuck did he do that for? Where are you coming from?"

"I was in Jersey at my father's house and I fell asleep. Next thing you know I wake up and Monty is standing over me looking all crazy."

"This shit has got to stop."

Pamela came out of her room in all of her flowing, silk nighttime garb. "What is it?" She yawned.

"Pam, look at her!" Sharon said, turning me toward her. She stared at me for a second and rolled her eyes at me in disgust. I know she was tired of having these woman-to-woman talks with me about leaving her son.

"Monty hit you again? What the hell happened?"

About an hour later, as Sharon, Pamela, and I sat up in the living room talking about men, love, life, and why I should get the hell out of dodge, we heard Monty trying to get in, but the chain was on. He banged on the door lightly at first.

"Ma! Carin in there!" he asked sweetly as if nothing ever happened. We tried to ignore him but knew he'd wake the neighbors if we didn't let him in.

"Let him in, ma," I said.

Sharon sucked her teeth. "My nephew knows not to fuck with me. I'll get the door and let me tell you, if he hits you tonight it's going to be some shit!" she said. I stood up when I heard his voice get closer. I could hear Sharon mumbling something to him then they both entered the living room.

"Why you got the chain on?" He smiled as he walked in.

"Monty, you hit this girl tonight and you're going to jail!" Pamela said immediately.

"Ma, *please*." He looked at me. "Why aren't you sleeping in our apartment?"

"I was up talking to your aunt."

"Well, come on, it's time to go to bed." He stood, waiting for me to budge. "Come on, I'm not going to hit you." He put his hand out for me to grab it, as if I could trust him.

"She doesn't have to go to bed if she doesn't want to. What the fuck you mean it's time for her to go to bed? She ain't no baby," Pamela barked.

"Ma, I am tired, I'm going to bed, okay?" I tried to smile. I could see the pain in her eyes.

"Well, let me talk to you first, go on, Monty, she's coming!" Pamela said. Monty walked off and headed next door.

"Carin, I love you like you're one of my own. We get our nails done together, our hair done, we shop, we cook, and we talk. You are not just Monty's girlfriend. I love you and that is why I am telling you that you need to leave my son alone. He is going to hurt you really bad one day and I can't have that shit on my conscience."

"I don't understand why he is acting this way, Pamela. It's like out of nowhere he just flipped!"

"It doesn't matter why, what matters is that he ain't gon' change. You're not the first woman he hit."

"I'm not?"

"No. Look Monty has a serious, serious problem with his hands, you hear me? If you know like I know you'd leave his ass alone. You are too young to be going through this."

"Why are you telling me this now?" I said, looking at her.

"My son asked me not to say anything to you. He figured he had it all under control and I promised him that if he didn't touch you I wouldn't say anything."

Sharon was fed up. She stared at me for a second. "Look at your face. Look at how pretty you are. What is he hitting you in the face for? Is he mad that you're pretty or something? I just don't understand that shit. Look, I have to get some rest. I have been working doubles back to back. I get off at two tomorrow, okay? Let's go shopping, on Monty. Fuck that."

Pamela got up and fixed her head scarf.

"I don't want to hear no shit tonight. I have to go to work. It doesn't make no damn sense how you two fight. You need to get somebody to whoop his ass real good. You better get away from Monty ass if you know like I know." She walked away. It seemed as if everybody was turning their back on me over Monty.

Pain is what I felt in my heart for this man I thought I could trust. I never had anyone betray me the way that he was doing right now. The pain in my heart was becoming overwhelming and I knew that I couldn't go on like this. I had to find the right time to get away from Monty but he was always angry, always a ticking time bomb and me announcing that I was leaving wasn't going to be a good look for me, so I stayed quiet waiting for the opportune moment to say my good-byes. I headed to my apartment in a daze. I was just so damn torn down and tired. *I hate you, Monty, I fucking wish you'd die!* I thought as I undressed. I could feel his eyes on me as I put on my nightgown.

"I want some pussy."

"I'm not in the mood." I crawled into the bed.

"I don't give a fuck, Carin. Your man wants some pussy."

"Monty, not tonight."

"This is *my pussy*, I gotta take it?"

"I said *no*."

He mushed me in the back of my head. "I don't want no dead pussy from you. You don't want to fuck me? I'll get it from someone else."

At this point I wish he would but I knew Monty was never leaving me. He'd stay with me just to make me miserable if nothing else. I sat up half of the night just thinking, wondering what was becoming of me. Never in a million years would anyone think that I'd allow a man to treat me this way. I knew he'd chase me, pursue me, make my life hell, and go hard if I left him, until I came back. I just couldn't fight that fight right now, so for now I just prayed that he'd stop. I knew that he loved me so I knew eventually that he would stop.

***

I had to be a fool to think that Farrod or Tyra wouldn't tell my father that Monty was beating on me. I was sitting on my sofa, finally out in Queens where I could get some rest from the glares, ridicule, embarrassment, and smirks, when my father surprised us both when he knocked lightly on the door. I hadn't seen him in about a month.

"Hi, Daddy!" I said nervously, because I knew that he was only here for one reason. He had never come to my house before so for him to come unannounced I already knew what it was.

"Where's that punk motherfucka!" he yelled.

"Daddy, what is wrong?" I said, playing dumb, trying to close the door.

"You letting this punk beat on you? Pack your shit and let's go now!" my father yelled.

Monty came out of the bedroom.

"She ain't going nowhere, get out my house."

"Look, you fucking punk, you think because you're putting your dick in my daughter you own her? If you ever so much as yell at her again I'll fucking kill you."

"Daddy, I have this under control."

Monty pushed me to the side and stood toe-to-toe with my father. "I don't like threats, old man."

"What are you going to do about it, bitch?" my father said.

Monty did the unthinkable and snuffed my father. I was floored.

I pushed him, and in a rage he smacked me to the wall. "Nobody comes here disrespecting me, you crazy?" Monty yelled.

"Daddy, get up!" I said, pulling my father up. Daddy and Monty went blow for blow until Daddy finally knocked Monty out cold on his ass. I began to cry. This was going all wrong.

"Daddy, you can't just come to my house with this drama, I can handle myself!" I yelled.

"Carin, what are you doing letting some man beat on you?"

"Daddy, we had a few fights, so what!"

"A fight and abuse are two different things, Carin, and from what I heard from his own mother you have been getting your ass beat for a minute now. Yes, I called his mother and she told me everything! She said that this man beats on you damn near every fucking day. Carin, baby, you are going home now. I'm not leaving you here."

"All of a sudden you care? Where were you when I needed you back then, huh? Don't put on your cape now, coming in my house telling me how to run my relationship. I need you to leave, Daddy, now!"

"I knew I didn't like this motherfucka for a reason. Get your shit. Let's go! You got him brainwashing you and shit. Let's go!"

Monty began to get up.

"You weren't raised like this!"

"She wasn't raised at all, especially not by your fucking ass. Now you wanna come save the fucking day?" Monty said.

"I am fine. You need to leave now before it goes down up in here. Leave!" I said.

"You think I'm leaving you here to deal with this clown? Let's go now and I'm not going to tell you again. I didn't bring you out here for this shit!" he said, grabbing me roughly by the arm. I was trying to squirm away.

"Get the fuck out of my house," Monty said.

"If I need you I will call you. Now go!" I said, pulling away. My father stared Monty down.

"What is it that you need or want, princess? What is it? Why are you letting him beat on you? Is it something I did or didn't do?"

"Daddy, this has nothing to do with you and everyone is exaggerating. It is not that serious. If it was don't you think I would be home? You know me, you know how I get down." I said, trying to lighten the mood. I could tell that it worked just a little bit.

"If you put your hands on my daughter again, so help me God. I'll be around. I will be popping up!" my father said.

"You see where she chose to stay," Monty snarled, and put his arm around my waist. My father started to jump in Monty's ass again. I put my hand on his chest.

"Daddy, I love you, and if I need you I will call you. I know you got my back. I know you do." I opened the door for my father. I looked by the stairwell and saw two goons standing there. Monty came to the door and looked out.

"Oh, yeah, old man?" he said, eyeing the two goons.

"You punk motherfucka. I ever catch you without my daughter around I'ma show you what it is, boy. Out of love for my daughter I'ma let you breathe. Carin, just say the fucking word, you heard me?"

My heartbroken father gave me a kiss and a hug like he'd never see me again. He looked at Monty and pointed. I knew I had to leave Monty before my father really hurt him. I know he spared Monty's life for my sake. I closed the door and leaned against it. Monty glared at me, rubbing his jaw. *You got knocked . . . the fuck out!* I wanted to yell. It took everything in me not to laugh.

"You think that shit is funny?" he snapped.

Can he see me smiling inside? He must know that I'm hysterical inside.

"You two need to learn to get along if not for anything else than for me."

"I should smack the shit outta you just on the strength of your father coming to my crib with this bullshit."

"Smack me for what?"

"Shut the fuck up, Carin, before I smack you."

"Smack me then, bitch," I heard myself say.

Monty laughed at me. "What?" he said, and started laughing hysterically. He was doubled over, holding his stomach, really laughing. He looked up at me with wet eyes. He was on the bed trying to catch his breath.

"Yo, I swear to God, Carin, you made me laugh just now how hard you said it. You ready to throw down with me today, huh? Your daddy came so you're feeling froggy, huh?" he said, and punched me in the stomach, knocking the wind right out of me. I dropped to my knees and fell over on my side.

"I suggest you keep your fucking family out of our business. It's not going to benefit you none," he said stepping over me and heading into the living room.

14

Carin

Embarrassment is what I was feeling at this
phase in my relationship now that everyone
knew what my relationship was about. I could no
longer hide behind designer shades and butter
leathers. It was out there, the entire neighborhood knew, and my family and friends knew that
Monty was beating on me. My father had put
it out there full throttle about what was going
on. They were stressing me to come over but I
wouldn't, not with my eye still dark from the last
fight Monty and I had. It had been a week, the
swelling was down, but now my eye was purple
and on top of that my arms were bruised up
and down. He punched me in my eye because I
didn't do the laundry. But how could I do laundry with a fractured wrist? Since I couldn't hold
the phone, I put Missy on speaker while I folded
clothes as she went on and on about her new
boyfriend, Drew, who was taking her on trips

all over the place, and how much he loved her. She was especially pleased that he wasn't into *wordly things*. I was happy that she found someone who knew what she needed. I was happy for anybody who was in love and happy because I remembered that feeling. It felt good. Everybody should experience that at least once.

"He is not into all this shit that everybody is into, you know, this obsession with fashion and labels."

"That's wonderful, Missy. You're not that kind of female so you don't need that kind of man."

"Girl, we are going to Antigua next month, isn't that great? He loves to travel and do other things with his money as opposed to keeping up with the Joneses. That's some young boy shit anyway," she squealed.

"That's wonderful, Missy. I sure could use a vacation. I'm so busy with work and school. So where did you meet this Drew?"

Ignoring me, she asked, "How come you're working, anyway? I thought your man had all this money."

"I work because I need my own."

"Shit, I would not be working if my man had dough like Monty. Then again, you need your own money, fucking with Monty. He probably doesn't have as much money as he *claims* or he wouldn't condone you working. I'm so happy my man isn't on that old bullshit. Girl, I'm surprised you even going for that shit."

I didn't like how Missy was coming at me. Maybe I was on the defensive because I knew that she was right. Either way, I wasn't in the mood for this shit right now.

"Let me go, Missy. I have things to do around the house."

"You sound down, are you okay? I'm going to come over to see you."

I took note that Missy never came over any other time except for when I sounded down and out. I didn't need her gloating over my distress right now to make herself feel good, so I declined her visit.

"I'm doing okay, I'm just tired. I've been folding clothes for the past hour while talking to you and I still have homework to do."

"Okay, well, I'm going to the mall to do some shopping. Life is good, isn't it? Call me when you have some free time, love."

"Will do, bye." I hung up and felt a pain in my chest. Stress was getting to me. I popped three Ibuprofens and tried to relax, but could not because Monster Monty decided that he wanted to be pissed about something. I was in no mood to talk or guess what was wrong with him, as he liked me to do. He was such a big pussy. I was two seconds from coming out of retirement and pumping two in his ass. But my love for him wouldn't allow me to.

I continued putting away our clothes as he stomped around the house, kicking things over, slamming closet doors, and sucking his teeth. The house was clean and dinner was cooked. There was nothing for him to beef about. I even said "hi" when he came in the house. I covered all bases so that he would not fuck with me, but he found a reason to anyway. I bit my tongue and finally asked him what was wrong, and he had the nerve to tell me to leave him the fuck alone.

"Fine" was all I said, and it was all he needed to go off.

"What the fuck did you say?"

"I said fine, you don't feel like talking, so fuck it." I began watching TV. I was exhausted from house chores. With not enough reason to really go in, he snatched the remote from my hand and threw it. I wanted to laugh so bad but decided to just watch what was on the TV anyway. *An infomercial, how dreadful.* My body hurt and I was tired and I was not about to fight with him. He started making up things to complain about, looking for a reason to go off.

"You are so fucking miserable, why don't you take your angry ass back outside." I rolled my eyes in disgust.

"This is my fucking house!" he yelled.

"So I'll leave, shit you ain't saying nothing but a word."

Monty said, "You think you can get away from me that easily, bitch, please."

I shook my head. He was a psycho.

Monty had become so neurotic that when I'd come home from work or school he had my minutes down to a science. The clock would read 6:42 and like clockwork the house phone rang. I already knew it was him.

"I'm home," I would say as soon as I picked up.

He wouldn't say anything, he would just hang up. He had confirmed that I was home.

Happy that classes were cancelled, I rushed home, early for the first time in a long time. Bigger than that, Monty said he'd be out of town for the entire day handling some business. I knew that I'd be home alone for a while and oh how I looked forward to that. It had gotten dark early today, the streets were desolate, and everyone seemed to be indoors. My aura today was at peace. Giddily, I began to undress quickly. Monty was not home! I wanted to just soak in the tub and relax my mind. I planned on giving myself a facial, perhaps even a pedicure. As soon as my toe hit the water, there was a knock at the door. I wasn't going to answer it, but figured I would see who it was. By the way they were knocking I could tell they didn't plan on going anywhere. I tiptoed and saw Missy standing on the other side of the door. I was happy to see her, but I would have preferred being alone.

"What are you doing here?" I smiled, tightening my long, silk Victoria's Secret robe.

"I can't seem to catch you any other time. I miss you.

Jetta couldn't come, she is really sick with the flu. Girl, I am going to Antigua in five days so I wanted to come see you before I left." *Her and this damn Antigua.*

"Carin, is that a black eye?"

"No, no, I'm just tired," I said, rubbing my eye and exposing my bruised wrists.

"What is this?" she said, grabbing my arms.

"Ow, Missy."

She pulled my sleeves up and saw all my black-and-blues.

"Carin, why are you letting him do this to you?"

"Missy, stay out of this, and please don't ask me those questions. Shit, it's not like me and Monty don't throw down in here. He gets fucked up too. Besides, he has a lot on his mind right now."

"Yeah, like whooping your ass! I knew there was something I didn't like about him. How long has he been beating you, Carin? I mean, damn, I didn't know it was this serious!" Missy said, sitting on a leather recliner in my bedroom.

I leaned on my dresser across from her and folded my arms, waiting for judgment to come.

"Carin, any man that can hit you that hard or at all has got to be nuts."

"No, he isn't. He just has a problem right now, please don't judge him. He's good people inside; remember how we used to be?"

"Yes, but that was then and this is now, look at you! You don't even look the same anymore. Where is that glow? Where is fly-ass Carin?"

"Missy, I'm still dressing and getting my hair done up. What are you talking about?" I tried to joke.

"No, I'm talking about that swagger, that smile, that shit that you do, Carin. Where my girl at?" she said softly and looked me in my eyes. "I know she's in there somewhere. Damn, you letting this nigga take it all from you. You're not even looking the way you used to look. I remembered being slightly jealous of you but, shit, now? For what?" she said, looking around my bedroom. "This is where yawl live? I expected to see some other shit. And he is worth how much?"

"First of all, this is just our little hood spot, our condo is in Queens."

"His condo, unless he put your name on it."

We both paused, me trying to let her statement sink in and her probably gloating in my distress now that she looked at it through a magnifying glass.

"Damn, is the shit he buys you that important for you to deal with this?"

"Excuse me? You think I'm with Monty for money?"

"I'm saying I know he does a lot for you, so maybe you're afraid to leave him because then you won't get those things anymore."

"Missy, look at me. Do I not know how to get money? You think I need to be with some dude beating my ass just to get fly? Come on now, don't insult me. I love Monty and that is why I am with him, nothing more and nothing less. It's bad now, I know, but it will get better. I know it will, just give it time. Have my back, please, and don't judge me," I said, opening my bedroom door. Like the boogie man, Monty was standing there drinking a soda. My heart skipped a beat.

"You know I got your back, Carin, but you're playing yourself, you know this, right? Girl, I don't know what I'd do if my man treated me the way Monty treated you. I guess because he spends all of this money on you he thinks he

owns you, huh? You know how these niggas are,"
Missy said, not seeing Monty yet.

"This is why I don't let yawl bitches come
around, because you're always trying to corrupt
her," Monty said.

"Hey, baby!" I smiled. He hugged me tight and
kissed me passionately. Missy rolled her eyes.

"That's all good, but what is up with the bruises
on my girl?" she boldly asked.

"It's none of your business, Missy. I hear you
in here talking about your man and shit. You
need to go tend to that nigga and stop being so
concerned with me and Carin."

"Why do you think it's right to put your hands
on her like that, Monty?"

"Missy, just chill out and mind your business,
please. As a matter of fact, I think you should go.
Me and Carin got things to do."

"*Gladly*. Carin . . . I'll be around much more,
you hear me, girl? I will call you upon my return
from Antigua," she said for the millionth time.

"What are you going to do, Missy, huh? Tell
me please, what you are going to do by coming
around here. I don't have to let you in my house."

"This is Carin's house too!"

"Says who? Her name ain't on shit in here.
This is *my shit*."

"Oh, so she's your fiancée but half your shit
isn't hers?" Missy argued.

"She's not my wife *yet*," Monty threw back.

"Thank fucking God for that. She'd be a fool to marry your demented fucking ass."

"Missy, it's okay, go on," I said, ushering her out the door. Monty looked at her, smiling.

"Yeah, okay," she said, and walked out. Before the door could even close Monty started talking shit.

"I don't want her back here. I don't need your friends corrupting your mind. Missy's fat fucking ass need to go lose some weight and stop worrying about you. That bitch is jealous of you, Carin. She wishes she had all of the shit you had, trust me. Now, Jetta, I fucks with Jetta, she's cool, but I don't want you fucking with Missy, that bitch is a germ," he said, kicking his sneakers off. He took off his chain and his hat and put them on the dining room table. "You cooked?" he asked.

"You told me not to, you said that you were going to be gone all day," I said, walking behind him into the kitchen. I began seasoning the steak that I had taken out to thaw that morning. He had obviously changed his mind and wanted me to cook.

Not to be outdone, Monty booked a trip for us to go to San Juan a week after Missy was at my house. So when she came back from her trip, we were on ours. I knew that's why he did it, even though he denied. He claimed to have been thinking about taking me away for some time.

"I just want my baby to have the best and have no reason to sweat the next bitch. If an average bitch like Missy can go on vacation with some bum-ass nigga whose bread ain't nowhere near as long as mine, why can't you?" was his logic. For five days Monty and I lay on the sexy beaches of Puerto Rico, and when we came home, love was in the air. We were happy. I was tanned, and looking and feeling prettier than I ever felt. It was Monty's idea that I go out. So I called up Missy and Jetta, who were wondering where I had been the past week. I'd surprise them both with gifts I brought back for them when we linked up to go out. I bought them both scarf dresses. When I got out of the shower, Monty was in my closet pulling out different things he thought I should wear. I agreed with two out of the five he pulled out and decided on a midnight blue sheer Versace pants suit that fit me like a glove. My hair was short, jet black and funky; I swooped my bangs to the side and spiked up the middle, my sides tapered down to perfection. I snatched up the keys to my pretty car. "Monty, I'm out!" I shouted as I stuffed my purse with cash, feminine wipes, and lip stick. Monty came out of the living room sloppily eating a bowl of cereal.

"Have fun, be safe, and don't let the sun catch you." He kissed my lips, getting milk all over me.

"Stop!" I said, and mushed him.

He slapped my ass and opened the door for me. "I'll miss you, don't get too drunk, and if you can't drive call me and I'll come get you. Where are you going again?" he said, standing in the doorway with his wife beater on and boxers, and his Yankee cap sitting on top of his head any old kind of way.

"The Tunnel. What are you doing tonight?" I asked him from the bottom of the stairs.

"I'm staying local. If niggas want to go out I might but I don't have anything planned. I'll hit you up if anything."

"Okay, bye, baby." I exited the building. I knew Monty was going to go to the window. He watched me as I crossed the street to my car.

"You look good, girl, where you going, baby?" he flirted.

"I got a man, go 'head with that shit!" I yelled and hit the alarm to my car. I could feel the girls on the block staring me down, hating on us.

"Hey, Monty!" Peaches sang from the stoop.

"Whaddup. Ayo, miss, excuse me, can I get your math before you pull off?" he said, shutting Peaches down.

"No! I'm good." I laughed at "math." Monty was an idiot.

"You sure? I'm saying I got dough, you need a nigga with some dough?"

"My man is filthy!" I shouted and got in my car. "But maybe one of these bum-ass bitches around here might get wit' you!" I saw him laughing. I rolled down the window and put on my *Reasonable Doubt* CD. "While I'm watching every nigga watching me closely, my shit is butter for the bread they tryin'a toast me," Jay-Z sang. I turned it up real loud and opened my sunroof, although it was late evening. I put the peace sign up through the sunroof and honked my horn. Monty blew a kiss and ducked back in the window. I got to Missy's house in about forty-five minutes because of traffic, and she said that Jetta just called her from the train station saying she was three minutes away. Missy looked nice in a dark purple satin short set with silver sandals and her long thick hair up in a tight ponytail. She had on thick silver hoops and silver accessories.

"Hey, mama, what's up?" I kissed her cheek and walked in.

"Nothing, girl, just doing the finishing touches on my toes. My trip was the bomb, bitch. I was trying to call you to tell you all about it but you were nowhere to be found," she said, waddling to the sofa with tissue between her toes. She hadn't acknowledged my tan yet.

"So where the hell were you?" She looked up at me. I handed her the dress.

"What's this?"

"Girl, while you were calling me I was in Puerto Rico! Monty surprised me with a trip!" I gushed.

Missy frowned. She couldn't even contain her jealousy.

"I brought you back a dress. So tell me about Antigua, boo, how was it?" I said, sitting down, ready to hear her story.

"It was nice." She smiled. She no longer wanted to tell me about her trip because I had gone on one.

"Well, do you like the dress, bitch?" I asked with attitude. I couldn't believe how she was acting. She pulled it out of the bag and put it up to her.

"My black ass in reds and oranges?" She laughed. "I like it, it's nice. So, yeah, girl, I had to go to Macy's and get this outfit. DKNY was having a crazy sale. Isn't this fly? I only paid one hundred fifty dollars for it."

"It's nice, that purple is real pretty on you, Missy."

"You look fly too." She sat down.

"Thank you, darling, it's what I do."

"What is that you're wearing? I saw that same outfit on Thirty-fourth Street in the mall. That's cute!"

"Um, no, this is Versace, the sandals are Chanel, I don't know about no store on Thirty-fourth Street in some mall, boo. I'm strictly Fifth Avenue all day. Monty would have it no other way."

"Go 'head girl, shit, you are living the life," she said almost sarcastically.

"*Hardly*, you got drinks in here? I'm trying to start before I get to the club. You know that shit is going to be packed, right?" I said, changing the subject and wishing Jetta would get here.

"Yes! Some special guests are suppose to be there. I can't wait to see who!"

Jetta walked in right on time wearing the shortest black mini dress known to man. Missy sucked her teeth as soon as Jetta walked in. Jetta ignored her and did a waltz toward me.

"You like?" she sang.

"Yes, but are you going to be comfortable?" I said, looking her up and down. Her hair looked pretty in flat twists in the front and a curly weave in the back.

"I sure am. This is what I do. And what is this you have on?"

"Just a little something. Here, I brought you something."

Jetta opened the bag and her eyes widened at the sight of the pretty green dress. "This is beautiful, Carin, where you get this?"

"I went to Puerto Rico."

"You did, when?"

"I just came back yesterday morning."

"Wow, I love this dress, mama, thanks, boo." Jetta kissed my cheek as I thought *Now that's how a friend acts.*

"What time are we heading out of here? I'm ready to go see my future baby daddy!" Jetta laughed and plopped down on the sofa.

"Carin, pass my flip-flops. I'll let them dry in the car," Missy said of her toes.

"Are you sure? The last thing you need is for them to get smudged in the car," Jetta said.

"I'm straight, I'm putting my feet up on the dashboard."

"Um, boo, I drive a Lexus not a hooptie. I'ma need you to let your feet dry in the house, not on my dashboard."

"Oh, boy, you can't give a bitch shit without her trying to stunt. How the fuck is my polish gonna get on your dashboard. Damn," Missy snapped.

"Somebody is acting stanka dank dank!" Jetta whispered.

I squinted my eyes at Missy, who pretended not to notice as she slid her feet into her flip-flops.

The line at the Tunnel was around the corner. There were half-naked women everywhere, guys flooded the block in the flyest gear from Coogie Sweaters to Avirex leathers (even though it was warm) to the flyest jeans suits and sweat suits. Everybody had on loud jewelry and luxury cars were double parked for blocks and blocks. I parked my Lexus in a lot two blocks away for thirty dollars for the night and got in line. "This is the shit I can't deal with, this line shit," Missy complained. I thought to myself that she was right. We all looked way too fly to have to wait in line. "Wait right here." I made my way down the long block. I could feel everyone staring at me hard. I knew I looked hot in my expensive outfit and I saw a few females who deserved their props too. The Tunnel was no place for slackers. It was a straight baller haven and gold digger heaven. If you weren't fly and rocking whatever they were singing or rapping about on the radio, don't even bother coming. Although it was nighttime, every female had designer shades sitting on the top of their heads, ears draped in diamonds, DKNY shirts, sneakers, jeans, Versace this, Adrienne Vittadini that. I strutted my stuff down the long block and you could hear a pin drop. Four bouncers were at the door being nasty and turning away the poor. I stopped in front of the one who was kind of off to the side and motioned for him to move closer. "What's the cover charge to get in?"

"One hundred dollars." He motioned for someone to come through the ropes.

"Seventy-five you said?"

He ignored me.

"Main man, I got two friends at the very end of the line. I'll give you two-fifty for your pockets if you let us skip the line."

He looked me up and down and smiled. He just motioned his head and lifted the ropes. I waved down the block for Jetta and Missy to come on.

"How much for VIP?" I asked.

"A bottle for every third person. A bottle of Dom is four hundred dollars."

"Here," I said, peeling off the money. I watched the girls roll their eyes and fold their arms as Missy and Jetta waltzed down the block to the front. The bouncer rushed us in. The last thing people in line wanted to see was some other people getting in before them because of money.

I passed my ticket to another bouncer inside and he lifted the ropes to let us into the VIP section. Shortly after, a server brought our bottle of champagne.

Soon, there were more bottles of champagne than one could count. The DJ was playing every song that he could think of to keep the crowd hype and he was doing a good job. I waved my flute in the air as Biggie's "Get Money" came on. People were on their feet waving champagne flutes and plastic cups, two-stepping and smiling. The night was fly and Mase was about to perform. The ladies went crazy when Puffy and Mase came out singing a string of their hits. It was total mayhem in the Tunnel. But when Foxy Brown came out with Jay and performed "Ain't No Nigga" they almost had to shut the club down. Bottles were popping everywhere, people were screaming and jumping up and down as all the ladies including myself screamed the chorus. I wondered if I was the only one truly living this rap song.

"I need to go to the ladies' room, do any of you have to go?" I said, easing my way through the small VIP section.

"No, I'm good," Missy said.

"Me too," Jetta said, smiling up in some guy's face. My girls and I were having a wonderful time, *this* was life. I walked through the tightly packed crowd still with my flute of champagne, sipping as I made my way to the ladies' room, when I ran smack into Peaches. She was with a crew of girls who all looked like they sucked dick to get the bullshit outfits they had on, or had to wait for the first or the third before going on Pitkin Avenue or something. They all had on cheap DKNY T-shirts and jeans with DKNY sneakers. I pretended not to see them, but Peaches shouted me out.

"Hey, Carin." She smiled nastily. I looked her up and down and kept it moving, sipping out of my flute.

"That's why your man is with another bitch right now!" she yelled to my back as I kept it moving. I made it to the bathroom and peed as quickly as I could so I could make it back to my girls. I was drunk and feeling real good, the best I felt in a while, and was not about to let anybody mess up my night. I squeezed in the booth hurriedly and scanned the room for the rats, then spotted them by the bar.

"Jetta, Missy come here. You see those bitches right there at the bar?" I pointed and explained to them who they were.

"So you think that they are jealous of you?" Missy said.

"Why wouldn't they be, I mean, look at all the things Carin has, including Monty!" Jetta backed me up.

"So what, she's not getting anything the average woman can't go and get!"

"Still, Missy, you know those girls are jealous of her and they probably want Monty or a dude like him."

Missy sucked her teeth. "Want Monty for what, he ain't about shit. All this hood rich shit is not blinding anyone to the fact that he's a woman beater."

"What are you going there for, Missy? Nobody's even talking about all of that!" Jetta defended me. I stood off to the side wondering why Missy was spewing so much venom toward me when she was supposed to be my best friend.

"Look, I'm just letting you know that these are females from around the way and for whatever reason they don't like me. One of them just said something to me and so I'm putting you on just in case."

"I'm not fighting anybody, I'm telling you now," Missy said.

I watched Peaches watching me up in VIP with envy in her eyes. I smiled at her and winked then turned my back and started dancing with a honey to Total's "Can't You See." I knew she was going to run back and tell my man, but so what.

Hot, sweaty, but still looking fly, me, Jetta, and Missy walked out of the Tunnel at four in the morning among the throngs of patrons. Everyone had a good time tonight seeing as how the club was about to get shut down permanently. The guys who were in the booth with us gave us all hugs and one of them exchanged numbers with Jetta.

"Shorty, can I get your number?" one of them asked me.

"No. I'm engaged, but if I wasn't then *you know*." I flashed my ring and smiled.

He grabbed my hand. "That's a big rock."

"Ain't it?" I laughed. I was feeling good. Missy rolled her eyes and didn't know that I saw.

"You ladies need a ride home?" he offered.

"My Lex is parked in the lot," I said only because Peaches and her crew were right up on us. "But thank you anyway for the offer." She bumped past me real hard.

The guys waited for me to say something. I looked at Peaches and laughed. "Bum ass," I mumbled, and began walking to my car. Missy and Jetta walked behind me. As I caught up to Peaches and her goons she eyed me.

"What?" I said.

"What?" Peaches's friend said, stepping in front of me. I was toe-to-toe with this beer-smelling welfare bitch and had every intention of laying her ass out if she wanted it. Jetta and Missy stepped up on my side.

"Don't waste my time. Do something if you got the heart," I said, staring her down.

"Whatever, bitch." She walked off, switching extra hard.

Not one to press a fight, I let her walk off knowing that I'd have more drama to deal with at home. But I kept my eye on Peaches because I knew she was sneaky.

As if waiting for the right time to embarrass me, Peaches shouted out, "I would beat your ass but your man does enough of that, you dumb bitch. That's why he's home right now fucking my friend!"

"Let me catch you hailing a cab, I'ma hit you with my Lexus, you bum bitch," I yelled, causing laughter on the sidewalk.

"Yeah, whatever, you think you're all that, that's why you're getting played, you silly bitch."

"You know what?" I ran up to her in my Chanel heels. She stood straight up and immediately threw her hands up. I reached over her fists and grabbed her by her hair and threw her to the ground. I anticipated feeling her friends jump on me but nobody did anything.

"Let it be a fair one, it's a fair one!" I could hear Jetta saying. A lot of commotion was going on around me. I could have easily hospitalized Peaches but I wanted to humiliate her, so I grabbed the back of her collar and ragged her all around the ground then put my foot on her forehead and kicked her to the concrete. She was sitting on her ass trying to get up. I stood over her angry, more angry at Monty then anybody else, but I was going to take it out on any and everybody else.

"Say something else, bitch, I'll stomp your fucking face into this ground, say something else about who my man is fucking."

She got up to fix herself and backed up.

"This shit ain't over, bitch. I'ma see you around the way."

"See me now! I'm here, see me now!"

Jetta and Missy pulled my arm. "Come on, Carin, let them go," Missy said.

The bouncers came and yelled for us to clear the sidewalk. "Yawl gotta go, take this shit down the block or back to Brooklyn, but not in front of here, let's go!" he yelled, clapping his hand and pointing for emphasis.

I fixed my shirt, slicked my sides then I hot stepped it to my car with my girls beside me, slamming the doors thinking if Monty really was out fucking some next bitch. I turned my radio up loud blasting Mobb Deep's "Shook Ones" and stopped at the light as Peaches and her girls crossed the street heading for the train. I honked the horn loud and they looked.

"Yawl need a ride?" Jetta asked from the backseat. They continued to walk slowly.

"Get the fuck out the street before I run yawl bum asses over, move!" I said, making my car jerk at them. Jetta and Missy were hysterical. I was dead serious.

"You think she's telling the truth about Monty fucking around?" Jetta asked as I turned the music down and hit the West Side Highway.

The rest of the ride was quiet as we were all drunk and tired and me being drunk tired. For some reason I felt that Missy was a little too entertained, so I dropped her off first. I didn't need her around me another second. Once I dropped Jetta off I stepped on the gas and did ninety home. When I pulled up on the block it was 4:46 A.M. to be exact. Monty's truck and bike were in the lot but his Lex was gone. He wasn't home. I ran upstairs and took a shower but not before blowing his phone up. He didn't call back but instead showed up a half-hour later feigning fatigue.

Monty

"Monty, this is me here, you know I ain't fucking nobody but you," she said sucking on my neck and licking me up the side of my face. Tionne was so damn nasty. I knew good and well Tionne fucked other dudes and I didn't care, but when I came around they disappeared and that was the end of that. I left my stain on that pussy and had been fucking Tionne for years before I had even met Carin and anybody who was anybody knew that. As she straddled me I could feel her making her butt cheeks jump around.

"Come on, baby, you know you want to feel me raw. You ain't never feel me raw in all of these years," she purred. "I'm safe I promise you." She eased down on my dick, staring me dead in the eyes. *I was playing myself this shit would never happen again.* My thoughts were replaced by Tionne grinding herself so far down on my dick she was swallowing me with her big, seasoned pussy. I grabbed her hips and pulled her down on it as far as I could, then fell back on the bed to let her do her thing. This was the quickest I had ever come. I couldn't control it the shit was feeling good. I could feel Tionne tightening her muscles around me. I pushed her off of me violently to make sure none of my seed was near her and jerked my dick hard as I came. She was on the side panting and grilling me. I didn't care. Bad enough I went raw, I wasn't about to risk this bitch getting pregnant by me with her fertile ass. "Damn, you gotta be so fucking rude?" she said, and got up off the bed.

"Man, go 'head, go get me a rag," I said, mad at myself for going raw with her.

"Get the shit yourself." She walked over to her dresser to get a T-shirt. I lay back down so I could shut my eyes for a hot second. Coming over here was a waste of time tonight.

"Yo, wake me up around three-thirty," I said.

"Yeah, whatever," she said, walking out of the room with an attitude.

"Tionne, don't play. Wake me up, I got shit to do."

"Where are you coming from?" Carin said as soon as I walked through the door. She was standing right at the door with a T-shirt on, looking riled up. I couldn't even say that I was out because of what I had on. "I was at the gambling spot on Sumpter." Which was where Tionne lived, but Carin didn't know that.

"Gambling spot, huh?"

That dumb bitch didn't wake me up on purpose.

"You were out fucking around on me tonight?" Carin was up in my face looking mad as hell. I never saw her look so upset, not even when I'd slap her or something.

"No, I wasn't out fucking around on you. Do I look like I was out fucking around, Carin? I was bored so I went to the spot, lost a couple of dollars, nothing major and that was it, we was drinking and shit," I said, trying to get past her. She tiptoed up to me and sniffed me hard.

"I don't smell any alcohol on you! Come here." She grabbed my T-shirt by the bottom and with her other hand pulled my sweats down. I jumped back. "What are you doing?"

"Monty, don't fucking play with me, come here!" she said, pulling me closer to her.

"Carin, chill!" I said, trying to pry her tiny manicured hands off of me, but she had the vice grip.

"Let me smell your dick, come here."

"What?"

"You heard me, let me smell it." She fought with me to get in my pants. She was determined, because she reached in and grabbed a hold of my dick and squeezed it hard. *"I will snatch this shit out the socket, Monty. Move your hands, move!"* she yelled. Her eyes were red and although she smelled like she had come fresh out the shower she was still drunk. I tried to laugh her off but she wasn't playing as she squatted and sniffed all up in my balls, underneath them, around them, and examined my dick.

"What the fuck is this?"

What did she find? "What?"

She peeled something white and crusty off of my pubic hairs. I was busted. "What the fuck is this shit, Monty?" she said, staring at me with wild eyes.

I took it from her and looked at it. I didn't wash because I figured I'd come home before her and take a shower. She examined it with me. "What the fuck is that shit?" she said and smacked it out of my hand. "Huh? What the fuck is that, Monty?"

I shrugged like a kid who had gotten caught doing something wrong. "I don't know, soap or some shit."

"That wasn't no fucking soap, you think I'm stupid?" she said and hauled off and slapped me so hard in my ear it started ringing. I held it as I tried my best to convince her that I wasn't out doing dirt.

"Carin, are you serious? I was not out fucking around and if I was why would I come home at this hour, without washing my ass at that?"

"I know what the fuck that is and I saw your girl Peaches at the Tunnel tonight. She made it clear to me where the fuck you were tonight."

"Peaches? How the hell would she know where I was? Man, Carin, you don't see that these bitches do shit to piss you off? Are you going to let them win? Huh? These bitches is on my dick hard and you know it and they all want to be you, all of them wants to be in your shoes and you're going to fall for the okey doke? Come on, Carin." I pulled my pants up. *I hope she's buying it.*

She looked at me and pointed.

"All the hell you put me through I swear to God if I find out that you're fucking around on me it's going to be some slow singing and flower bringing. You coming from some bitch house I don't care *what you want to say.*"

"Come here, silly." I grabbed her from behind as she tried to walk away. "Stop." She tried to squirm away but I held her tight and sucked on her neck 'til she calmed down. I reached my hand around the front and fondled her breasts. Immediately she crawled into bed and took off her T-shirt. I stripped down and dove into her. She was drunk as hell and her limbs were weak. She just lay there moaning in ecstasy as I pummeled her to orgasm. Carin fell right to sleep after she came. She climbed on top of me and laid her head on my chest. I wrapped my arms around her and stared at the ceiling for a while thinking about what I did tonight, then realized it was done so there was no reason to stress it. I fell asleep too.

Carin

Angry was how I felt when I got up the next morning. I was so angry that I couldn't seem to think straight. I was still tipsy from my champagne campaign and needed to sober up a little bit so I began to brew coffee. While it brewed, I jumped in the shower real quick, washed my hair, and tried to revitalize myself. As drunk as I was last night I remembered everything that happened and I wasn't done with Mr. Monty. I knew that he was out fucking around and I knew that what I found on his balls was a remnant of his romp. I was hot behind having that altercation with Peaches and coming home to a freshly fucked Monty. He was making a fool out of me. I sat across from him on my chaise and sipped my coffee with my jet black hair slicked back with mousse. He peeked up at me periodically when he felt me grilling him down over my cup, then finally he closed the paper and leaned back in the sofa. "So how was your night? You came home on your secret squirrel shit and didn't even tell me about your night. My man D was there he said Jigga had the spot jumping. How was it, baby?" he asked. I took a long hot slurp then stared him down.

"You're a damn liar, I hate you!"

Monty

I jumped up and started fanning my shirt. I couldn't believe she threw the hot coffee on me. I tore my shirt off and ripped my do-rag off of my head. My chest and the side of my face were burning. Carin stood there, holding the cup in her hand, standing as if she was ready to slap me with the cup.

I was too much in shock to realize that she was up on me trying to break the cup on my jaw.

I swung at her. She ducked and caught me with a left.

"Motherfucka, as loyal and good as I am to you, you out there cheating, you rat bastard! Beating on me isn't enough?"

I tried to grab her but she rushed me and put her head in my stomach so I couldn't hit her. I was trying to pick her up and slam her on the sofa. Carin was strong. I pushed her off of me and threw her on to the couch. She jumped right back up and slapped me across the face. She was on fire.

"You think I'm stupid? Huh? You think I'm dumb! You think you can just play me out like this in front of all these bitches? These dirty rotten hood rat bitches? This is what you disrespect me for, you faggot?" she yelled, and threw the mug at me. I ducked as she ran to our bedroom.

I rubbed my head for a while and could hear Carin in the room tearing shit up. I jogged in there cautiously and saw her pulling clothes out of the closet. I wanted to beat her ass so bad but my guilt allowed me to just let her get her shit off. She was throwing jewelry everywhere. I caught my diamond bone bracelet and put it on the table.

"What are you doing? Carin, that's my word if you destroy anything in this house I'ma hurt you."

"You think I give a fuck about this shit," she said under her breath. "I never needed you for shit. You chose to dress me up in all this shit. I don't need you," she snarled as she tore minks and leathers out of the closet. She sifted through the Dutch Master box on our table that I threw coins in and lit a match quicker than I could notice and tossed it on the clothes. The match didn't cause any damage; it went out as soon as it landed on top of the leather jacket.

"Carin, I wish you *would* burn my fucking clothes. You ain't crazy. I'm not even going to watch you do that shit, I'm turning my back." I walked to the living room.

Carin

I looked around until I found a piece of paper and lit it. I let the fire get nice and big and I dropped it on the pile of clothes that was on our floor. Once it started burning I snatched up my car keys and my bank card, and put on a pair of fitted DKNY jeans and sneakers, a tank top, and a cropped denim jacket. My hair was air drying and short so it was cool. "Fuck you, Monty!" I yelled across the fire. I ran out the back door in our apartment and he caught up with me in the hallway through the front door and grabbed my jacket collar. Ski came out of the apartment oblivious to what was going on as I headed out. "You smell smoke?" he asked as Sharon came running downstairs.

"Get your girl, Sharon, get your girl. I'ma kill her! This bitch right here set my shit on fire," Monty said, struggling with me on the staircase trying to drag me upstairs but I held on to the banister for dear life. "Get off of me." I dug my nails into his hand.

"Let her go, man, go put that fire out!" Ski said as Monty ran into the apartment to try to stop the small fire.

Sharon ran with me downstairs to my car. "Carin, are you crazy, he is going to kill you. What did you burn?" she asked me as I drove around the corner and parked.

"I can't deal with his shit, Sharon, this is too fucking much. It's just ridiculous already. I'm gone for good. He can have all this shit and these bitches. They think I got it easy? They want him that bad? They can have him. I bet you they'll be ready to send his ass right back."

"What the hell happened?"

"I go out to the club last night and wound up getting it on with some hood rats 'cause apparently Monty is fucking their friend. Then I come home and this nigga has dried-up nut on his balls. What kind of nasty shit is that?"

"Wow, Carin, I'm going to talk to him, all right?" was all she said.

"Suit yourself, but I am done. This is just a bit much for me, honey. I can do without this shit." I dropped her off at the corner.

"So where you going now?"

"I don't know. I just need to clear my head."

"Call me later. I'll hop in my ride and get up with you, maybe we can go have some drinks or something. I'll talk to my nephew, though, you know he'll listen to me."

"Do you, I'm gone." I watched Sharon walk down the block before I pulled off. I saw Monty come outside as soon as she got to the stoop. I could tell by the way Sharon's long hair was flying wildly all over the place that Monty had spotted my car and was popping shit, so I drove off. I drove around for a while debating about where I should go. I thought about going to my father's house but I didn't need them in my business. Missy would only underhandedly ridicule me and Jetta was too naïve to understand that all because I had all of the material things a girl could ask for. I drove and drove until I remembered that I had the keys to the condo in Queens. *That's where I'm going.* I drove at an easier pace now that I had a destination. I parked my car two blocks away in the cut and ran upstairs. I turned the lights on and looked around for a while. This place was untouched. I kicked my shoes off and placed them by the front door because the carpet was beige. I had a few things over here but not enough to get me by past a week. I'd figure out what to do when the week was up. I'd probably have Sharon get me some things and bring them to me.

I went into the half room and turned the lights on and looked around. I opened up the boxes Monty had stacked up in the closet. Old sneakers, guns, a few dollars, a box of bullets, some receipts, bank statements, and finally a box of pictures. I tossed them around, coming across miscellaneous pictures of Monty, myself, and family members, then at least ten pictures of this one female with her dark black nasty pussy spread out with her fingers posing, sucking her fingers, making sex faces, ass up in the air. I snarled at the sight of this classless cunt my man was fucking on the regular behind my back. I found pictures of us, some real old ones, more pictures of Monty, and a few other miscellaneous bitches. *So this is what he does when I'm at work all day.* I put the pictures back in the box and started bawling tears of anger.

Monty

It had been over a week and Carin hadn't shown any signs of coming home. I lit a cigarette and headed out to sit on the stoop to clear my head. I couldn't let Carin walk out of my life. After a while my stomach started hurting so I went back upstairs and turned the game on when Tionne started blowing up my phone. Ski came outside right when I was about to call Tionne so I didn't bother. He gave me dap and sat next to me as I chain-smoked cigarettes.

"Damn, look at Mesha, she getting thick," I said about a girl from around the way who happened to be walking down the block. Ski filled me in on who was hitting that.

"Wow, that's crazy," I said upon learning of the grown-ass dude sexing young Mesha.

"When her brother comes home he gon' kill that nigga." Ski laughed and started smoking his cig too. "What's up with wifey, she back yet?"

I shook my head while I blew smoke out of my nose. "I don't think she's coming back."

"Not for nothing but can you blame her? I never seen no broad take from a nigga what Carin takes from you. That's home team. How you treat home team like that?"

I shrugged. "I don't know what comes over me sometimes. I can't explain it but I love Carin, you know I love Carin. I never treated no woman as good as I treat Carin."

"Or as bad."

"Yeah, but she's gone now."

"She'll be back, she just need time to get it together. You can't keep wiling her out like that though, it's embarrassing, that shit looks crazy to see her so bruised up. You can't keep beating on her like that, son, you gon' kill her one of these days."

"I can't have that."

"Right."

Carin

Confusion was what I felt as the days went on and my heart played ping-pong between love and hate. Why was I even contemplating going back to Monty? I had every reason not to go back but my heart was slowly dragging me back to Monty. Two solid weeks had gone by and I felt that it was enough time for him to be shook up and scared and ready to have me back home, but not without an ultimatum. It was time that we came to a conclusion. Either he was going to change his ways or I was leaving for good. So I hopped in my car and decided to head to Bushwick. I couldn't believe that it would start to rain now! The day I chose to go home and talk to Monty it decided to rain when I was halfway to the damn house. I thought about turning back but decided that today would be the perfect day to sit down and talk to him. My windshield wipers did nothing for me, so I had to drive two miles per hour or risk hydroplaning on the Grand Central. I fixed my seat and just got comfortable. My usual twenty-minute drive looked like it was going to take me about an hour with traffic and weather.

Monty

My stomach was hurting me real bad today. I didn't know if it was from stress or what but I knew that I didn't need any outside food. I walked next door to my mother's apartment and she was in bed watching TV. She didn't turn upon hearing me enter, she just asked, "What."

"You not cooking, Ma? I'm hungry."

"Had you not beat that child half to death you'd have a home cooked meal. You're grown and I'm not your woman, I'm not cooking you shit. Close my door on your way out." I sucked my teeth and ran upstairs to Sharon, who, as usual was sipping a drink on her way to work. She was dressed in her corrections uniform looking pretty as ever. My aunt was the shit to me. Just about everything she bought, I ran out and got for Carin. They had a friendly competition going on.

"What's up, Monty?" she asked as she brushed her sides with a toothbrush.

"Nothing now I see you going to work. I'm hungry."

"See if Mommy cooked," she said of her mother, my grandmother.

"I'm not going down there to hear them preaching to me about beating on Carin and shit."

"Have you talked to her?"

"Nope, not in two weeks."

Sharon grabbed her large Fendi purse and the keys to her money green Lexus, the equivalent to mine and Carin's. "She's just hurting right now, nephew, you can't be fucking her up and cheating. I mean, damn pick one!"

"I know, Sharon, but you know how my temper is. You got the same temper. Don't nobody say shit when you get drunk and be in here fucking up your man." I chuckled.

"Right, but he's a man and he's a pussy for letting me beat on him." She laughed as I followed her out of the house. "But Carin is family, Monty. She's one of us and we want her around for a while and so do you. So calm down with that hitting. I know you're young, you gon' fuck around, but stop that hitting. I can't stand that shit. I'm out, boy, I'll call Carin from work and see if she's saying anything that'll benefit you."

"All right, Sharon." I let her go.

I headed back to my house hungry thinking about Lulu. But I wasn't going all the way to the lower east side to eat. I didn't want Tionne to come over but I needed some cooked food. Against my better judgment, I told Tionne to swing by and drop off some dinner that she cooked. She happily obliged and said she'd be there soon. I had no idea she was next door at Peaches'; she got to me in five minutes. Tionne looked nice today for some reason. She had all that hair and weave pulled back into a tight ponytail and it was long and bushy. She had on a DKNY ski suit with a pair of Air Max. She was a little wet from the rain.

"You don't look too well, are you okay?" she asked.

"I got a stomachache. What did you cook?" I said, peeling off the foil. She kicked her shoes off and took her hair out of the ponytail. I wanted to be like, "Why are you getting comfortable, you can't stay here!" Carin or no Carin I wasn't about to have some next bitch, especially Tionne of all people, in our bed. This was still our house. I was happy that nobody in the building saw her come in. They loved Carin so much they would probably call her and tell her. I saw that Tionne cooked up beef cube steak, potatoes, and white rice. I couldn't even eat it as good as it was. My stomach was fucked up. I put the plate up on the dresser and doubled over.

"Monty, what's up?" Tionne knelt in front of me. I curled up in the bed and told Tionne to make me some tea. Happy to be playing wifey for a New York minute, she ran into the kitchen and made my tea. She came out while the water was boiling and sat on the edge of my bed, trying to make the best of her fifteen minutes of fame.

"You need anything, baby?" She put her hands on my stomach and began rubbing my belly.

"No, just the tea, and put that food in the fridge for me, please."

Carin

Finally I reached Bushwick Avenue but even that was a little backed up. Luckily, we stayed not too far off of the Jackie Robinson so I just cut over, hit Broadway, and came up Granite not having to be bothered with Bushwick Avenue traffic. The rain let up out of nowhere and the sun was even coming out. It was shining bright and had pretty much dried up the streets, though remnants of the rain were still visible. I was pretty nervous about seeing Monty. It had been two solid weeks of no communication and the last time I saw him I was trying to burn his ass up in our apartment. I was still pissed but pretty much over it and ready to move on, with or without him. I was just coming over for some kind of clarity or closure.

The hallways of the building were quiet. I saw that all of Monty's vehicles were parked up so I knew he was around here somewhere. I turned the knob and the door was locked. So I used my key and entered. I put my bag on the table and walked to the back of the apartment to our bedroom. I flipped the light switch on and could not believe what I was looking at. I just stared at this female sucking on Monty's dick hungrily even though I made my presence known. Monty looked like he'd seen a ghost. He mushed the girl off of him and pulled his pants up, jumping out of the bed.

"Come on. Get up out of my bed." He deliberately stood in front of me, probably sensing that I was going to pop off.

"Carin, what are you doing here?" he said, walking up to me.

My heart was in my shoes as I stuffed my feet back into my sneakers. It had only been two weeks and he had the nerve to have some strange woman in the house. Monty came out of the room behind me. I couldn't even look at him but I did look past him to see the woman pinning her hair up in a ponytail while sliding her feet into her sneakers.

I knew exactly who she was. She just smiled at me wickedly and finished wrapping up her hair.

"Monty, the food is in the fridge, feel better, baby."

"She just came over to bring me some food. I was laid up sick," he said, immediately trying to explain.

"And she wound up with her mouth on your dick? It's useless to try to work things out with you! You have no respect for me at all." I grabbed my purse and tried to leave. Monty grabbed me and pulled me to his chest.

"Don't leave me, Carin, I need you, please."

"Don't leave you, what the fuck do you mean don't leave you?" Tionne barked. "I'm here sucking on your dick and you're begging this bitch not to leave you?"

My eyes widened at the nerve of this woman acting like she was upset at my husband for begging me to stay. I looked at Monty to handle the situation. He turned to look at her.

She laughed nervously. "All right, Monty, I got your number. You and wifey here have a nice day. I'll be around."

I wanted to say something but couldn't think of anything to say that wouldn't make me look stupid. Monty slammed the door behind Tionne and pulled me to him.

I couldn't breathe buried in his big chest. I dropped my bag, trying to push him off of me.

"You don't need me, Monty, you just need somebody, *anybody*, it just so happens to be me. You don't love me, I don't care what you say, you don't love me!" I tried not to cry because I didn't want to show any weakness. I wiggled away from him.

"How can I ever in my life make love to you again after what I just saw? You let her in our bed after two weeks? What kind of respect do you have for me or for us?"

He grabbed my hand and dropped to his knees hugging me around my legs.

"Carin, I swear I won't let them win. You can't leave me."

"Let them win. What do you mean *let them win?* This is not a competition! This is my heart that you're fucking with and you're wasting my time."

He squeezed my legs tighter.

"I love you, Carin. I won't hit you no more, I won't cheat on you no more. I promise you it's just me and you from this point on. We can go to Vegas and get married and just move somewhere, anywhere, just don't leave me, baby, please, and don't hate me. I can't live without you, Carin. Remember how we used to be?"

I pushed Monty's head away from my crotch and he stood up wiping the tears from his eyes as Ski walked in.

Ski looked at him like he was a maniac for being on his knees begging.

"Carin, this woman has been on me for years, baby, years, ask anybody. Look, there is no excuse for what you just saw, baby, I'm sorry."

"You're always fucking sorry. I'm sorry too. I'm sorry that I put up with your shit so much that you feel as if you can do anything to me and I'll take it. I just came to tell you that it's over between us, Monty. I can't do this anymore."

"Carin, please. Ski, leave us alone, we need a minute."

"There is nothing you can give me, Monty. You won't stop cheating, you won't stop hitting me, it's hopeless and I'm tired. I just caught some bitch in our bed giving you head! You think I'll ever sleep in that bed again? Are you fucking serious?"

"We can go buy an entire bedroom set tomorrow, I promise you. You can pick out whatever bed you want just please give me one more chance, just one." He hugged my knees. I had never seen Monty beg like this before. So I stayed.

15

Carin

I was alone. Everyone began to back away from me because they couldn't stand Monty. I didn't come out of the house often because I was always bruised up or just tired. When help was extended to me I didn't take it and I was too embarrassed to beg for it now. I made my bed and I had to lie in it. I kept my head buried in the books and at work for the most part, and when I came home I just cooked and watched televison. The most action I had was going upstairs to Sharon so we could compare clothes and jewelry. About a month later I was hanging out of the window getting some fresh air when I spotted Peaches on the stoop with some other girls. In a twisted kind of way I envied them. They were free spirits, roaming around, doing what they wanted to do. They dated without fear, came and went as they pleased. They were young and having fun. Meanwhile, I was holed up in the house, half the time dressed to the nines with the entire neighborhood jealous of me. I didn't even know these people and they didn't know me. If they did they would know that being jealous of me was foolish. I had a heavy heart, I had demons, I had pain that nobody could reach. I thought Monty could but as the days went on I realized that he could not.

As the months went by, girls walked past me and rolled their eyes, they grabbed their men tighter when I stepped on the scene. They envied me because of the material things that I had but I would trade it all to just be free. Underneath my vintage Versace shades were black eyes and blood clots, my fancy haircut housed knots and stitches, my crimson lipstick covered up split lips, my fancy jewelry was nothing but guilt gifts, trips out of town were just so that I could heal out of the public eye. But they hated me anyway. They'd trade their lives to walk a mile in my Gucci sneakers. They'd sell their souls and take these beatings just as long as they could look fly. They hated me and I hated them. I hated them for not realizing how good they had it. I hated their ignorance and I hated how much I feared this man I had once loved. Every time I ran away he found me and dragged me back home. And once I got home, he beat me for trying to get away in the first place.

Monty pulled up and Peaches called out to him. He ignored her and came running up the stairs with urgency. I figured he was coming in the house to grab something and run right back out so I stayed in the window so I could ignore him. He busted through the front door calling my name like his pants were on fire. I shut the window and turned to him and met his big hands across my face. He backed me down by the window and I moved because I could just see myself falling out the window and dying.

"You dirty bitch," he snarled at me. I said nothing but held my face.

"I want you out of my fucking house and out of my life!"

He grabbed me by my shirt and tossed me across the room. My back hit the wall and some wind got knocked out of me. He picked up my body like a rag doll and held me by my throat. I dug my nails into his eyes and spit in his face. He dropped me as I ran into the kitchen to breathe but to also grab a knife. He came behind me and stopped at the site of me shaking, holding the knife.

"What are you going to do with that?" he said, biting his bottom lip.

"I fucking hate you, Monty. I swear to everything I love if you come near me I'm stabbing you."

"That's your word, Carin?"

"Yeah, that's my word, bitch."

Monty lunged toward me and I swung the knife, catching him in his arm. "You dirty bitch, you burned me, you fucking burned me!" he was yelling as he slapped me to the ground and kicked me repeatedly. I still held the knife in my hand. He stopped kicking me and picked me up. He snatched the knife from me and tossed it in the sink. I had no idea what he was talking about but at that moment, it didn't matter. I had to defend myself.

"Get your shit and get the fuck out of my house!" he said, pushing me to the bedroom. I walked slowly, scanning the room for something to hit him with and my eyes came across a Corona bottle on the dresser. When I got in the room he stood by the door with his arms folded.

"What do you mean I burned you? What the fuck are you talking about?"

"I don't want to talk about it, just get your shit and leave." It was obvious that someone had burnt Monty and he was trying to put the blame on me.

"Why are you doing this to me?" I began to cry and feel sorry for myself. I could see his arm bleeding through his T-shirt. I wish I had cut his throat. "Some dirty bitch burnt you and you're trying to blame that shit on me? Why are you do-ing this to us, Monty?"

He wiped his face and covered his eyes. "Just go, Carin."

I took that opportunity to crack the bottle on the dresser. He opened his eyes upon the sound of glass breaking but I was on him. I swung and caught him in the neck, opening his skin. I knew he'd need stitches, the cut was deep. He held his neck then looked at his hands. I picked up the VCR that was on the television and hit him over the head with it. He hit the floor but jumped up quickly and chased me back into the kitchen, catching me before I could grab a knife. He wrapped his arms around my throat and choked me until I stopped breathing. That was the last thing I remembered.

When I came to, Monty was sitting at the edge of our bed, staring at the TV. My head was throbbing and I didn't want him to know that I was awake. I wanted to stare at him for a while and muster up some hate but I could not. I just wanted to know why he was turning into this monster. He stood up and stretched and I could see the huge white bandage on his neck where he obviously needed stitches. He was now staring at me. I kept my eyes barely opened so he wouldn't know I was awake. He leaned in and kissed my forehead and whispered, "I love you." He then grabbed his car keys and left the house.

Monty

I didn't even know that I was choking Carin so hard that she would pass out. I thought that she was being a drama queen when her body heavily hit the floor, but first her head banged against the dresser, then she dropped to the floor. I crouched down over her and opened her eyes. I saw nothing but white. I panicked. I ran into the kitchen and got a wet paper towel and began wiping her face. She wasn't budging. I picked her up and put her on the bed. I didn't know what to do. "Shit, think, think."

I watched her for a little while longer then put my finger under her nose. She wasn't breathing. I started sweating. Two minutes had gone by but it seemed like hours.

"Come on, Carin, baby, wake up, wake up, girl, come on," I said, watching the large knot form on her pretty forehead. I went into the kitchen and filled paper towels up with ice to put on her forehead. It was then she began to wake up. I sat her up and tapped her face gently. "You up, baby?" Her head fell back and her eyes began to flutter.

"I'm sorry, baby, I'm sorry," I said, hugging her tight. I could hear her breathing become steady. I thanked God.

Carin

Mornings were the best time of the day for me. It was the only time I could be alone and sneak some me time in before I started my day. I'd lie in bed and daydream about how much fun I used to have with Chauncey. Life was so simple until I let Panama in. We were young and dumb and meant no harm but it cost him eight years of his life and cost me a lifetime of looking over my shoulder expecting karma to show its face. I would also just lie there and take a moment to myself because once I was up Monty would take over and control my every move. So the mornings to me were sacred, pure, mine. I'd play sleep sometimes 'til 11:30 or until my stomach would start grumbling and I was forced to get up and use the bathroom and make breakfast.

Days after that huge fight, Monty admitted that he had unprotected sex and caught an STD but he didn't say with whom. I knew it was Tionne. That bitch looked like she was burning. We got into another physical altercation behind that and I was relieved that I had not been infected, but I had to take antibiotics anyway. But as time went on, Monty was still on a rampage with his ranting and raving. I had enough of him. *Really this time.* I was waiting for him to get at me. I had so much rage and anger inside of me and he was the only one who needed to get the short end of this stick. So when I heard him yelling, "Carin, get your fucking ass in here and cook me some breakfast!" I didn't jump up and ask him what was wrong. I had plans to go to the park and read a book. I needed time to just relax my mind, enjoy the fresh air, and see the outside world for a little while. The area we lived in was beautiful and I wanted to take advantage of the parks, the small shops, and the restaurants out in Queens today. I didn't care if Monty came or not, this is what I had planned for my day, so I walked out of the house and headed to the park. Five minutes after I sat down Monty came behind me. He obviously was following me to see where I was going. I could see his horns poking out of his head from a mile away. He was no longer Money Monty to me. Inside I called him Monty the Monster.

"Bitch, you think you're fucking funny?" he said, walking up on me. Exasperated, I opened my book. I couldn't believe how he called me out of my name every other word.

"Monty, not today," I said with my eyes glued to my book, but through my peripheral vision I was watching his hands. His fists were already balled up and he was ready to strike me.

"Or what? You're going to tell your bitch-ass pops or your brother? Or what, Carin, what? Are you going to try and turn my family against me some more?" he said, punching the book out of my hand.

"It is too early in the morning for this shit! Just leave me alone, okay?" I said, still not looking at him. I wanted to cry. He was just picking on me for no reason like he had no control over himself but I had to stand strong.

"Get your ass up." He grabbed me by the neck of my tank top. He dragged me to the back of the park instead of outside of the park toward our home. He pushed me away from him and I grabbed on to a tree so I wouldn't fall. He stared at me long and hard. "I asked you to make me something to eat," he said calmly.

My eyes began to well up with tears as I stared at him. I wanted him to see how frightened I was of him and maybe he'd change his mind about beating me. But when I saw that look in his eyes, I knew there was no getting out of it. The only way he'd feel better is if he got his shit off first by beating on me. He pounced on me like a cougar and began beating me non-stop as I tried my best to kick him off of me and swing. But every time I swung it angered him and he'd hit me harder and harder until I lay there on the ground unable to move. I just felt so helpless. "Monty, stop!" I yelled over and over until he silenced me with a blow to the mouth. The pain of that blow numbed me as I held my bloody mouth and he continued kicking me and dragging me around in the dirt. I clawed at his face and began digging my nails right under his eyes. He slapped my hand away and I kicked him in the nuts. He doubled over briefly as I got up and tried to run. Monty tackled me into the dirt and the side of my face hit the ground. He grabbed me by a good chunk of hair and bent my head back. "Bitch, you think you tough? You trying to fight me back?" he said, yanking my head back so hard I thought he broke my neck. I snatched up a pipe on my way up and swung it at him, hitting him in the neck. He still held on to me as I hit him repeatedly. "Get off of me!" I yelled, and spit on him.

"You spitting now, bitch?" He snarled and just started dragging me around by my hair, humiliating me. He kept dragging me until I finally dropped down to my knees with his hand still in my hair. He let me go and pushed me down.

"Get the fuck home and make my breakfast, Carin. I pay the fucking bills, I take care of you, I run shit! I don't give a fuck how tough you think you are, bitch, you are not a man. I wear the fucking pants in this bitch. " He left me on the ground.

As I lay on the ground in the park all I could think of was die, die, die. But I didn't know if I was speaking to myself or to Monty. All I knew was that somebody needed to die in order for this pain to end. *I can't die like this, I can't die at the hands of no man. I can't.* All I kept thinking about was the faces at my funeral, shaking their heads in amazement as to how Carin could let a man beat her to death. I had my pride and a reputation of some sort. Even if they didn't have the facts straight, people knew me, they knew my affiliates, they knew my capabilities. And so with that I found the strength to get up and fix myself up. I was beaten badly and bruised. But I had to get home. I had to walk through the throngs of passersby in this bourgeois neighborhood as some stared and some had the balls to ask me was I okay. "I'm fine," was all I could say as I pressed on to my fancy building with the doorman whose eyes popped open upon seeing me. He was used to seeing me dressed to the nines in designer clothes but today I entered my prestigious building with a bra on, blood on my chest, knees dripping, lips swollen, eyes black and blue, bald spots, and torn earlobes.

"Mrs. Johnson, are you okay?" he asked me, using Monty's last name.

"I'm fine."

"Do you need an ambulance?"

"I'll let you know if you need to call one once I get upstairs Vance, thank you." He watched me until I got upstairs.

Murder was on my mind as I walked to our condo. I was no doubt going to kill Monty today. I was going to empty six shots in his face and call the cops and wait for them to come and arrest me. I was going to watch him die slow such as he did me. When I got to the house, I found Monty lying face up on the bed with his hands behind his head, resting He looked at me and I didn't see a hint of sorrow or empathy.

"You finally made it home, now go clean yourself up and cook. All this shit coulda been avoided."

"You are going to rot in hell."

"Bitch, you will be right with me, bet that because your ass ain't going nowhere! When I met your sorry ass nobody wanted you, you steady crying to me. I see why your mother treated you fucked up, because you're a lazy, stupid bitch and your father left your ass 'cause he knew your ass would be nothing. Why the fuck I took your hood rat ass in I will never know but you're here now, so as long as you're walking around here in designer shit you will be cooking for me every fucking night. I don't give a fuck how tired you are, who just got robbed, how bad your cramps are, you make sure your fucking man eats! Shit, I keep telling you, all you are is a fat ass and a cute face. Won't no other nigga want your fucking ass. It don't get no better than this."

I didn't say anything. I walked to his closet where he kept his safe and his guns. My love for guns was something that I kept a secret. If Panama didn't teach me anything else he taught me how to use any gun that was ever made. As I reached up in his closet a number of things crossed my mind. I knew what the inside of a prison looked like and I never wanted to go back there again. I knew what it was like to bust my gun, that wasn't an issue. But to pull the trigger on someone I loved was no easy feat, but Monty had to be stopped. He was out of control.

"Get out of my closet," he said.

I did. I walked up on him and aimed hard.

"Say something and your ass is grass." I held the gun to his head. Monty stared at me for a long time. His face held no expression as if he wasn't sure if he should piss me off or not. He looked right at me as the gun rested between his eyes.

"Carin, put that shit down before you kill me."

I stared at him long and hard. At this moment I could really pull this trigger but I'd be sick later,

I know I would. But I had to shake him up, give him a blast from the past.

"Fuck you, Monty, you need to die, you bastard, look at me! Look at what you've done to me! I thought you loved me."

"Carin, we can talk about this but put the gun down." He sat up slowly with his hands up.

"Don't try to be funny, Monty, you grab this gun and I'm squeezing."

He looked straight down the barrel of the gun then at me. His eyes were unreadable still. He was probably planning on how he was going to tear me a new asshole once this blew over.

"You will go to jail for a long time if you pull that trigger."

"Nah, this is self-defense. I can kill you right fucking now, you asshole! I did time before, it ain't nothing."

He smirked. "You did time."

I gun butted him. "It's funny? Is that funny? Yeah, that's funny!" I said, and hit him again. "Now you got two lumps!

There's a lot about me you don't fucking know, boy, and I'm trying my hardest to spare your fucking life but you keep pulling me in. You keep trying to make me come out of retirement. Boy, you just don't know."

I felt his body move so I put the gun to his head again. "I'm not playing! Don't fucking move!" I screamed.

"You want out of this relationship that bad that you'd kill me? You hate me that much, Carin?" he asked, his eyes welling up with fake tears, his voice shaking.

"I'm so tired of seeing your fucking ass cry, Monty. *So tired of it*. What the hell are you crying for now, huh? Let me guess, because you love me so much? You don't love me, look what you did to me. Look at how you treat me!"

I didn't want to cry mainly because I didn't want the tears to blur my vision and have Monty make a move. I was going to kill his ass in here yet.

Monty

The cold look in Carin's eyes was just like the look that I had seen Harriet give me before she killed my father. It was so eerily similar. She looked just as bruised as Harriet, too, even worse. Carin could kill me right now and walk away a free woman. I couldn't let that happen. She was holding that gun like a pro. And what did she mean about she did a bid before? I didn't know whether to take her seriously or not. Right now I just wanted her to get that gun out of my face and boy when she did I was going to give that ass a good thrashing. For now I had to keep her calm. She was looking real deranged.

"Carin, just put that gun down. If you want to go you can go but put that gun down. You don't know what you're doing."

"How you figure? You think I never used one of these things before?"

"You'd shoot me, Carin?"

"'Til it's empty."

"Carin, put this gun down now!"

Carin

"I'm not going to take anything that is in this house. I am walking out of here the way I came and I was better off then. I don't want nor do I need shit that you ever bought me. You didn't make me so you *damn sure can't break me*." I reached for my car keys behind me with the gun still aiming. "I am leaving you, Monty. This is it. I let you beat on me long enough. I think you've had enough fun at my expense."

His eyes held a confused glare as if he didn't know who I was, as if I just robbed him of something. I said nothing as I closed the bedroom door slowly and whisked down the steps. I knew that our bedroom window was facing the front of the building so I kept my guard up as I exited the building. I looked up and true to form Monty was there, halfway out the window. He just glared at me. I walked backward, gun stashed in my shirt. I jogged across the street, hopped in my car, and sped off quickly.

16

Carin

I whizzed through traffic quickly getting horns honked at me and middle fingers thrown up at me but I didn't care. Monty was a slickster and he probably jumped right in his car behind me and was following me with his piece so I had to make sure I had the advantage. I checked in at the Sheraton in Queens right off of the Conduit and took a shower. I ordered room service, sat back, and relaxed my mind. I ate ice cream and turned on the television. I began to involuntarily laugh wickedly. I would call Missy and Jetta as soon as my bruises healed so that I could meet up with them. I needed love from my friends right about now, not sympathy or judgment. I figured that I could go stay at Missy's until I figured out my next move. Her house was the only place that he couldn't find.

***

Sharon orchestrated a plot for me to get all of my clothes out of the house. She met me at work and got my key and one day while Monty was gone for an entire day she and Pamela went in and packed up all of my clothes, jewelry, and underclothes. I didn't tell them where I was staying but I did meet them to get all of my things. Later on that week I made an appointment to get my hair done. In about ten days I was looking brand new. It was amazing what a few nights' sleep without worry could do for your skin. While my dad and Tyra were at work, I brought most of my clothes home and put them in my walk-in closet. I had so much stuff it was unreal. Once I felt I was ready to be seen, I called a meeting with my girls because I hadn't seen them in a while. We all decided to meet up at the South Street Seaport. As I waited for them, a handsome gentleman walked up to me. I wasn't in the mood to entertain anybody but he was not giving up.

"Can I buy you another iced tea?"

"Sure," I heard myself say. As he turned his head to talk to the waiter I checked him out. Clean nails, dapper how I like my men, handsome, I could tell from his Bvlgari watch he had expensive taste. I relaxed a little bit when I realized he wasn't some slouch and began smiling a little. It didn't hurt to flirt. We talked for about twenty minutes and I found out that he was from

Brooklyn but lived in Queens, he was thirty-four years old and lived alone. He asked if I needed company as I waited for my girlfriends and I said yes. We spoke some more, then I realized that it was getting late.

"So, Carin, can I call you sometime?" he asked as we stood out in the open smiling at one another.

"I don't really know if I'm ready to start dating. I just got out of something pretty serious."

"No pressure, sweetheart, so did I. But we all need a friend, right?"

"Yeah, you're right about that." I laughed nervously. It felt weird talking to another man after so many years.

"If it was Monty you'd wait!" I heard Jetta joke from behind me. Missy stood behind her waiting in line for a hug.

Haman smiled and waved to the girls.

"Ladies, this is Haman. Haman, these are my two best friends, Jetta and Missy."

"Nice to meet you both. Okay, so I guess you won't need that walk to your car then?"

"But thank you." I smiled.

"I'll call you. Nice meeting you ladies." He walked off.

I watched him walk away and I immediately gave Jetta his number. "Hold it for me, just in case." I smiled.

"Oh, you know I will."

"If you have to hide it then why do it?" Missy threw in.

I hugged both of my girls tight and escorted them back to my table.

"You both look good! So tell me what's been going on?"

"You too, so what is up, Miss Thing? I see you got a new bag, new shoes, and all that!" Jetta said excitedly.

"So what brings us here?" Missy asked.

I took a deep breath. "As you both know, Monty beats me. Well, he used to. We got into our last fight ten days ago and I have been living out of a hotel until I figured out my next move. I didn't call you guys immediately because I wasn't doing too well and I didn't want either of you to see me in the state that I was in. I had a lot of time to rest and think about what's important and I miss my girls is all. It seems as if we don't hang anymore. I miss my friends and I just wanted to see you guys before Monty found my ass again." I laughed. They didn't. "I know it's a crazy situation that I'm in but it'll work out. In the meantime, Missy, since he doesn't know where you live, I wanted to know if I could stay with you for a while. Half of my things are at my father's house but I still have things back at the hotel. I really don't want to go back to living with them again. I like being out on my own. Besides, Monty is searching high and low looking for me and he doesn't know where you live but he will stalk me outside of my father's building. I don't need a lot of time at your house. Just two months to save up my rent and security then I'm gone."

"You are a trooper! I'm so sorry that you're going through all of this, mama," Jetta admired.

"You make things so much harder than they have to be. Well, you can stay with me but only for a week," Missy snapped.

I eyed Missy as she looked me up and down.

"Never mind, Missy, it's okay. Besides, I know you have a man and I don't want to interfere."

"But if you need a place to stay and she's your girl, how could she let some man interfere with that?" Jetta said. She was right but it didn't matter. Missy had her mind made up.

"I said that she can stay for a week. But right now Drew is out of town on business and when he gets back I'm sure he's not going to want to see some other woman in the house since he spends so much time at my house, that's all."

"She said she needed two months, how you gon' offer her a week? You're a bitch, Missy."

"I'm good, Missy, don't even worry about it." I smiled but I was hurt at how she had been acting toward me, as if I had done something to her.

"You can stay with me if you'd like," Jetta offered.

"Jetta, you live across the hall from my father." I chuckled.

"Still, I'm your friend so I am offering my home. Besides, Kenny has an extra bedroom at his apartment in Harlem. You are more than welcome to get low up there if you want to. I'm sure he won't have a problem with that. You shouldn't have to be in some hotel when you have two friends who live alone."

"I don't play that shit," Missy said.

"Play what?" Jetta asked.

"Having some other woman in my house when my man is there. Friend or no friend, that shit is trouble."

Jetta shook her head in disgust. "Insecurity is such an ugly trait. You probably know that your man would be into Carin so you don't want her to stay. Don't let me tell it. Besides, Drew doesn't even seem like the kind of man to get down like that. It's you that's acting all phony and shit."

"I'm not even studying that shit, please." Missy fanned her hand.

"You are so fucking ugly inside, Missy, and I knew that from the day I met you. You walk around acting like you're so green and pure, you ain't shit, you fucking hypocrite."

"I'm not understanding why you're being so malicious toward me, Jetta," Missy said as condescendingly as she could. She was batting her eyes and smirking. I wanted to smack her in the face.

"You're wack, Missy. Straight up and down wack."

Missy stood there holding her bag, waiting for someone to say something, but there was nothing else to say. Missy thought she was better than me because of my situation. It was clear as day.

"I don't know why you're over there acting like Carin is a damn disease or some shit like Drew don't be abusing your ass!" Jetta shot out.

"You need to shut the hell up because you have no idea what you're talking about."

"Please, he calls you black, fat, sloppy, and everything under the sun and you walk around here like you're all high and mighty because you have bruises no one can see. At least Carin is real about her shit. And what about that ol' pedophile father of yours? So much for religion, you're a fucking hypocrite, Missy, and I can't give a fuck about you. Carin won't say it but I will. Shit, as much shit as you talk about Carin I'd feel bad letting her stay with me if I were you too."

"Talking about me to who?" I asked.

"Anybody who would listen, especially her man, so of course she doesn't want you to come to her house. Her man is there and she's probably insecure that he would want you. I mean, you're fly, pretty, and everything she wants to be, everything her man wants in a woman. Missy is jealous of you, period, yeah, I said it!"

An awkward silence followed.

"Missy is always going off about how you're letting Monty kick your ass because he keeps you up with the Jones's and how stupid you are and how ghetto you are and she even told her man that you were a ghetto-ass bitch and how back in the day you used to rob and steal just to be fly, that you would sell your soul to be fly. Shit, and if what she say about your past is true you know I'm not lying because you never told me that shit," Jetta said.

"You said that, Missy?"

Missy was too busy staring at Jetta as if she was trying to put root on her and Jetta was looking at me, satisfied. The two of them always did this shit to eliminate the other from the picture, but they always wound up hurting me.

"You said that, Missy?" I asked again.

"I just think you can do better and I did not use those exact words," she said.

I immediately became defensive.

"I always knew you were jealous of me, Missy. You're jealous of my tenacity and strength. You struggle so much with your appearance and your childhood drama and your family that you try your best to shit on me so that I can feel beneath you. You can never be me, Missy, and you can never break me, ever. I'm cool though. Gloat in my distress, mama."

"You believe that crock of shit, Carin? Jealous of what? You getting your ass kicked or your deadbeat mother? Girl, please, that's that liquor talking, which, by the way, you need to lay off of. Furthermore, Jetta is only dickriding you because she wants your shoes and clothes and she wants to be like you. Jetta don't give a fuck about you like that! I've known you since we were thirteen years old."

"Bitch, if you could fit her shit maybe she'd give you some too!" Jetta spat out.

"That's all you got, Missy? You couldn't wait to find something on me to throw at me, huh? Is that all you got? I consider you a friend so I won't go there with you, Missy, because as hurt as I am, one day I hope we can resolve this but if I open my mouth and get in your ass the way that Carin Douglas can get in someone's ass, we will never ever be friends again. You're living in hell enough as is. I'm out of here." I snatched up my purse.

"I wanted better for you, Carin, because you are my friend. We go back to the ninth grade. I could never be jealous of you. Why would you even fix your mouth to say something like that? Our sisterhood was never based on any kind of competition because you and I come from different lifestyles and you know this," Missy said, walking behind me. I turned around quickly.

"Different lifestyles? How so? You grew up in East New York, bitch! You don't come from no privileged background! What, because you live in Long Island now you forgot where you came from? Bitch, you live in the hood in Long Island! You're so fucking busy running from reality and shit you totally forgot who you are! Your parents are fake-ass holy rollers, your father is a pedophile, your mother is an alcoholic, and your man is not even attracted to you! What lifestyle Missy? The one in your mind that you wish you had? Maybe it's a misunderstanding because I don't understand it. The last time I checked we all came from the fucking ghetto and the only reason why your ass worked so much was because you didn't want to be home with your crazy-ass parents."

"Let's not talk about parents, Carin. At least mine wanted me."

"Yeah? Well your father probably wants to fuck you and your mother just wants you so you can give her money to support her habit, you dumb bitch."

"In here? Ya fucked up, girl, *gone!*" she said, tapping her temple.

"Missy, get your fat ass from in front my face, I can't stand the sight of you. Jetta, call me, girl, I'm out!" I was hurt that Missy was talking about me but fuck her hating ass. I was tired of her giving me dirty looks all the time anyway. She wasn't a friend, she was just someone who stood close to me to make sure I failed. But if she knew me she'd know better than that.

Jetta ran behind me. Missy was with her.

"I see what this is, yawl sit back and talk shit about me? What did you guys come out here for? To see if I looked fucked up? Well surprise! It's me, Carin, still fly, still pretty as shit and that ain't never gon' change so stop wishing, and, Missy, you know me better than anybody. I'm a survivor, baby. This shit ain't gon' last forever, B!" I said, yanking my arm hard from Jetta's grasp. I hit the alarm on my car and hopped in, letting them eat my dust.

I cried as I drove on the FDR back to the hotel.

I was hurt as hell by Missy but right now I had other things on my mind. For one, I had a psycho looking for me, and two, I couldn't tell my

father that I was staying in a hotel. I just wanted
to work this out on my own. The more I told, the
more questions would be asked. I just wanted to
bow out gracefully and move on with my life.

When he asked me why half of my things were
there, I simply told him that I had too much
stuff and needed a place to put them. Monty
hadn't caught up to me yet because he didn't
know where I was staying. My boss gave me
emergency time off so for the past month I was
just laying low at the hotel. The only person who
knew where I was was Jetta. She would come by
and spend nights with me. We would sit up in my
hotel room and bug out for hours. One night in
particular right before Christmas she showed up
bearing gifts.

"For all of the fly shit you handed down to me
that was unworn and even only worn once, I say
thank you, girl." She handed me a pretty name
plate necklace set in white gold. "I couldn't afford no platinum but, shit, it ain't silver," she
laughed.

"Aw, Jetta, you are the shit, girl. Thank you so
much, mama." I smiled.

"I'm not done. I also got you this here
certificate. Go have you a day at the spa, girl, get
your hair done, facials, mani, pedi, get your body
rubbed down because I know you surely can use
it, sis."

"Thank you, Jetta, you didn't have to do that for me. I don't even have anything for you."

"You've given me enough and nothing is better than your friendship. You're a real bitch, Carin, and I'm so sorry that all of this shit is happening to you. I don't know how you deal with it, but I know that there is a lesson and a reason that you're going through this. Maybe one day you'll be a spokesperson for domestic violence or something, I don't know. All I do know is that I have your back, me and the man above. I'm here for you and I spoke with Kenny. That back room is yours if you ever need it, mama. Don't be too proud." She smiled warmly.

All I could do was shake my head. I felt so vulnerable and scared.

"Listen, I know you and Missy have been friends for a long time and I'm the new girl on the scene. But I love you like a sister just as much if not even more than Missy, and yeah, I'm sorry you two fell out but you needed to know how much she dogs you, man. Be it out of jealousy or not she is always talking shit about you then smiling in your face and I don't think it's cool."

"It's all right, Jetta. I mean, when you go through things you see who your true friends are. I got love for Missy, I always will. Will we ever speak again? I don't know. Right now as you can imagine, I have much bigger issues in my life than Missy's friendship. Now, with all of these gifts, you didn't bring no liquor?"

"Oh, of course I did!" she said, digging into her oversized leather bag.

"Pick, you want Henny, Moet, or Bacardi Limon?"

I tapped my chin and contemplated. "Hmmm, let's pop some champagne with my saddity ass." I laughed.

"So do you plan on going to your father's for Christmas? I'm sure they would love to see you there."

"Yeah, I'm going. I just hope Monty doesn't show his ass, good Lord what's wrong with him?"

"I don't know, girl. That nigga is straight bonkers. I mean, he my boy and all but we can't be cool with him treating you like this. It's crazy. I mean, do you even love him anymore, Carin?"

"I don't know how I feel. I just know I feel trapped. Like now I'm free but am I? He's going to find me soon you know."

"So why not just go home to your father and tell him everything and let him protect you? You know he will! Quit your job, lay low, relax, go to church, get the word, get a new life, and go lay up under that fine ass Haman. How is he doing?"

"He's fine. We talk often." I smiled. Jetta was smiling devilishly.

"What?"

"He hit that yet?" She giggled as she sipped Moet out of a plastic cup.

"No, I'm not ready for that. I need to close one door before I open another."

"I feel you. You're strong, Carin. It's going to be okay. Let me know if I can do anything to make things easier for you."

"Okay, thanks. Now enough of this Hallmark moment, let's get fucked up and watch some movies."

"The Wiz is on!" Jetta squealed.

"Look at my boy Mike Jackson. I don't give a fuck what he did to his face he is still the damn King, I love him! You can't win chile, go 'head Mike."

"Look at Diana bald-headed ass," Jetta cracked.

"Diana look crazy as shit, don't she?"

"Indeed."

"But my boy Mike? They better leave Mike alone."

"Yeah, go fuck with Tito or something." Jetta laughed.

I joined in. Tonight was the best night I had in a long time.

The holidays were upon us and everyone was just happy to have me around. Nobody knew that I was on the lam, living out of a hotel and had snuck over so that I could spend Christmas with my family. I just kept praying that Monty didn't show up and ruin everything.

Weeks had gone by and I was feeling great! I gained ten pounds, I was smiling again, and I was sleeping well at night. Mr. Hathaway was crooning my all-time favorite Christmas song, "This Christmas." I stuffed my face as I sang with my dad next to me throwing back eggnog and Remy like it was water.

Tyra and her best friend, Dale, began clearing up the dishes, and me, Kim, and Jetta held court in the kitchen, spiking the eggnog. It was Christmas and the mood was right. This was the first Christmas I had had with my family alone in years.

"So Carin, I notice that you are still wearing your ring. You plan on getting back with Monty?" Tyra asked.

"No! I just think it's a pretty ring, you know. I like wearing it. It keeps the lames away," I said, loading the dishwasher.

"Well good riddance to that crazy son of a so-and-so. He was nuts," Dale said. I hit her playfully but toasted to that.

"Monty was all right, he just needed to fix that problem of his," Jetta said, siding with Monty.

"What problem? Look, wasn't nothing all right about Monty. The man been crazy and Carin just had to find that shit out the hard way. It's nothing; there are plenty of other fish in the sea," Tyra said.

"You never know what a person is really going through; don't be so quick to judge the man. He might be going through something," Jetta kept on.

"Physical abuse is not right no matter how you try to slice it," Dale threw in.

"Thank you," Tyra said, satisfied.

"I might need a session, Doctor." I said to Dale, who was a psychiatrist.

"Anytime you ready, honey," she offered.

"It's free, right?"

"For you, *yes*." She chuckled.

"I'd just die if Farrod put his hands on me," Kim said.

"Well, my son was raised to respect women so if he laid hands on you he must have reason," Tyra said.

"I know that's right. So, Carin, are you seeing anybody right now?" Dale smiled at me.

"I met someone a while back but right now I'm just taking it easy. Being with Monty took a lot out of me, you know?"

"I'm sure," Tyra agreed.

"What do you think went wrong to make him just start abusing you like that?"

I shook my head slowly. "I have no idea. It just started happening. I can't even tell you about any signs that I've seen or anything like that. I just woke up one day and he was a monster."

"The first time he hit you, you didn't know then?" Dale asked.

"I mean, I was upset and I know that it was wrong but I just didn't think it would go this far or that he would ever hit me again. We were arguing and I was in his face carrying on and he kind of smacked me but that was it."

"That was more than enough. I'm just glad that you got out of that situation. I can't even imagine the things that he has done or said to you that you haven't told. But you'll be fine, baby," Tyra assured me.

"Carin, there is somebody at the door for you!" I heard Farrod yell out.

"What if it's Monty?" Jetta squealed. "What if he's back with a bunch of I love yous and I'm sorrys and shit like that?"

"Jetta, shut the hell up, nobody wants his psycho ass back here!" Tyra laughed.

"I'm calling po-po if he's at the door," Dale said, sipping her eggnog. The three of them heckled behind me as we walked out of the kitchen and to the front door. I heard Tyra ask Farrod who it was and he shrugged. "Some nigga."

I opened the door nervous as hell only to find Haman standing there with a gift box and a bottle of wine. "Merry Christmas." He smiled. He was looking handsome in a cream sherling coat with a skull cap on.

"Hey, how are you? I wasn't expecting you."

"I hope this is not a bad time."

"No come on in, please make yourself comfortable. Everybody, this is my friend, Haman."

Everybody said their hellos and my father just sat there shuffling cards, looking him up and down.

"Daddy, this here is my friend, Haman." I smiled. My father stood up and shook his hand.

"Nice to meet you," Haman said, and handed me the wine and box.

I shook it then opened it.

"You love jewelry so." He smiled.

It was the most beautiful jewelry box I had ever seen and it was big!

"Thank you, Haman," I smiled and offered him a seat and some eggnog. In a matter of minutes he was at the table with Farrod, my father, Dale's husband, and Jetta's boyfriend playing cards while the women sat off to the side drinking and stuffing our faces with the leftovers.

My father and Haman hit it off immediately. I'm sure anyone was better than Monty to him. They talked about everything men could talk about. It helped that Haman was older, more mature, and a hard worker. He fit in perfectly. As the men talked, us women stood off to the side gossiping about the new man in the house.

"He is fine! You hear me? That right there is a fine-ass young man, yes, Lord!" Dale said.

"Who you telling, damn, what does he do, how old is he?"

"He's thirty-four, he's an architect, and he lives alone, no kids, no drama, a little too good to be true if you ask me."

"Shit, you better quit playing. That is what you call prime real estate, little girl. He is nice and mature for you, older, seasoned, yes, yes, yes we have us a winner, yes!" Tyra laughed.

"Shhh, he might hear you." I laughed.

Jetta stood to the side, biting her bottom lip. "Kenny is going to put foot to your ass, girl, calm down!" I laughed.

"As long as he doesn't shut my eye so that I can't see that fine-ass man sitting next to him. Carin, what are you waiting for to bag that up and make him your husband?"

Dale gave her a high five.

"I know you have to be horny as all hell!" Kim, Farrod's woman finally spoke up.

"I'm not thinking about sex."

"Well, whatever the case may be, I like him. My spirit takes to him. Monty gave me bad vibes from the door. I don't know if it was that eye or what."

"Yes, wasn't that spooky?" Jetta said.

"Listen, I know he was not the best boyfriend. But there were so many good things about him. I don't hate him, you know. I don't take the things he put me through personally." I shrugged.

"That's your vagina talking. He must have had some good dick," Tyra said. "Let me tell you something, when you get older that dick won't mean a thing to you. What matters most is how that man makes you feel with one touch, one look, and one kiss. It's how you feel when you hear his name, it's how you feel when you go to sleep next to him at night. Dick comes a dime a dozen. Find you a man who will take care of this and this." She pointed to her head and heart.

"I feel you but dammit he has to bring dick, too!" Dale said. We all laughed at that one.

17

Carin

After the New Year, I deemed it safe to go back to work. It was cold on this day as I opted to take the train. I put on my long, copper-colored fur coat with the head wrap to match. I was bundled up nice and warm as I walked to the train station thinking about what Jetta said about quitting my job. I knew my father would hold me down especially if I was leaving Monty so it wasn't an issue of money. It was never an issue of how to get money with me. I gave myself one more month to stay at the hotel then I was going to find my own apartment. I stopped and got the paper as usual and some plain M&Ms and sat on the platform until the train came. For whatever reason the train was extremely crowded so I had to stand up for the duration of my ride, and that was not a good feeling with my riding boots on. Holding on to the bar with one hand and reading the paper with the other was no easy task as the train jerked and the lights flickered on and off. Everyone had on their heavy coats so it made the ride that much more frustrating.

"When I get your fucking ass home, I'ma wile you out!" he snarled in my ear. I stopped breathing. My body froze up. It was a scene straight out of a Lifetime movie as I wondered how the hell he found me on this crowded F train. "Where are you going, huh? Who lives on the F line, it better not be some nigga, Carin, that's my word," he whispered in my ear. I couldn't say anything because my heart was in throat. My eyes welled up with tears and I wished I had told my father what was going on.

"We are going back to wherever the fuck you coming from."

We got off and went to the other side so that we could wait for the train.

"I can't wait to see where you were going." He smiled at me wickedly. He didn't say a word to me. He just followed me, giving me a few feet. I hailed a cab outside of the train station and took it to the Sheraton off of the conduit.

"You going to a fucking hotel?" His eyes widened.

"I know what you're thinking but it's not that." I kept walking. The concierge smiled at me as I came in. I smiled back and wanted to scream for him to call 911 but instead I just kept walking and took the elevator up to the third floor.

"It's been months since I've heard from you or seen you. Everybody asking for you and I don't have shit to tell them. I'm fucking embarrassed, Carin. What the fuck do you take me for," Monty said, and slammed my head against the door before I could enter the room. I dropped my key card and dropped to my knees. He picked up the card, opened the door, and dragged me in by my hair. He looked around the room for a while then told me to get up as he unzipped his black fur jacket. He tossed his skull cap on the bed and choked me up against the wall and began slapping me ferociously.

"Just let me go!" I screamed and clawed at his face.

"If somebody hears you and calls the cops that's your fucking ass!" he snarled, and slapped me again.

I held my face so that I wouldn't catch any bruises for anyone to see. "How the fuck did you get your clothes, where the fuck you been all of this time it's been months?" he asked as I cried.

"Your mother and Sharon gave them to me one day while you were out of town or something. Just leave me alone! I don't want to be with you anymore, I hate your fucking ass!"

"Oh yeah?" he said, and kicked me in my back. I felt my skin split. My shirt was sticking to my back, that meant blood.

"You out here impressing some next nigga with the shit I bought you, bitch? Get your fucking dumbass up and let's go home. I can't believe you had me looking for your fucking bum ass all this time. You weren't at work?"

"No."

"So you were up in the hotel all this time doing nothing? You think I'm stupid? Who is this nigga you fucking, Carin?"

I got up off of the floor happy that I gave Jetta Haman's number to hold because I knew Monty would go searching through my things. My head was pounding and I could feel my eye getting swollen. "Pack up your shit and let's go now. Fucking dummy, hurry up! Talking about you don't want to be with me. Who else is gonna want your ass?" he demanded from a corner chair while smoking a cigarette.

When we got home, Jomar and Ski were on the stoop waiting as if they knew that I was the hunted. So for them to see me, I was embarrassed.

I didn't even speak I just dragged my bags up the stairs angrily. I heard Monty tell them that he'd be back down in a few. He came up behind me as I was taking my clothes off. He touched my back. "Damn, I didn't mean to kick you that hard. Let me see your back." I stood there and let him examine the damage. I wanted him dead as I looked in the mirror and counted the whelps on my face. He left the room and came back with alcohol, peroxide, and gauze. I stood in front of him in my panties as he cleaned my large wound and covered it.

"You might need some stitches on that, baby. If you want to go to the hospital call me, I'm going downstairs for a few. Put those clothes up tomorrow and get some rest. You got to go to work tomorrow." He headed out.

When morning came I felt pure exhaustion. I reached from under the covers and took two Ibuprofens. I didn't want to go to work today but I'd be damned if I was going to stay home with Monty all day. My little dream was over. My freedom snatched from me just like that. My power gone, my hopes up in smoke. I was almost free from the devil and just like that it was over. I was in this bubble just wishing someone would save me. It seemed as if no matter how loud I screamed, no one could hear me. The answer was simple, I needed to save myself. I needed to open up my mouth and say something. My boss would be disappointed when he saw my bruises, as he was rooting for me. Everyone would be disappointed, which was why I didn't tell anyone that I attempted to leave him, in case I wound up back with him. It was very cold outside so I stopped at the corner store as usual for a cappuccino, a pack of Trident, and a newspaper. I even decided to drive my car to work. I wanted to put on some music and just ride. I wanted to be alone and not have to deal with public transportation. I was on my way to the register when a conversation that I overheard deterred me.

"Monty got a whole lot of money and his wife wears some heavy jewelry, too, he bought her a big-ass diamond engagement ring and she wears it *every day*," one voice said.

"He keeps it in his closet under his clothes, that's what Jack said."

"How you know Jack telling the truth?"

"'Cause he said he went with Monty to withdraw the money from the bank about a week ago. Monty wanted Jack to hold him down. He said that Monty took out a hundred grand."

"So why Jack ain't stick em?"

"You know Jack is buns."

They laughed. I couldn't move. Jack ate in my house, I cooked dinner for him and he cut Monty's hair, he rode with Monty most mornings to take me to work if we saw him on the block after taking his daughter to school. That was his boy. I peeked through the Enfamil and Beech Nut rice but I could not see who they were. The voices sounded familiar but I couldn't figure out who it was. I saw a green jersey on one of the guys and a black T-shirt on the other. I couldn't see the third one. I didn't want them to see me but they were not budging from in front of the store and I was not leaving until they did.

"His wife normally comes out the house around this time going to work. We can hit that nigga up when she leaves for work," Green Jersey said.

"That's a good idea but how we gon' get up in the crib?" said Black T-shirt.

"I don't know, snatch up his wife and make her take us in the house, you know, put the burner to her, shake her up." Green Jersey laughed. They all began laughing after that.

"You ever seen his girl?" the third one asked.

"Yeah, she nice, *real* nice."

"How he get all that paper, hustling?" Invisible Man asked.

"Nah, heard it was some lawsuit shit."

"How much he got from the suit?"

"Close to a mill if not a mill."

"*Woo hoo,* he holding!" Green Jersey said, excited. He was no doubt the ringleader.

"All that dough and he still live in the hood?" said Black T-shirt.

"He got a condo in Queens."

"Well, we need to get to the crib in Queens then. That's probably where the stash really is!" one of them said.

"Ain't no way we can pull that off, nobody knows where he lives, but right here in the hood. We know for a fact he keeps dough in his mom's crib."

"Which is why he needs to get got!" Green Jersey said and they all laughed. *Told Monty we needed to stay up off this block but nooooo he wanna sit around flossing all day.*

"What time does his wife get home, we need some of her shit, too."

"Leave wifey out of it. No women, no kids."

"Yo, you got the hots for her or some shit?"

"She nice, man, that's all, I see her going to work and just doing her thing and I got sisters and a wife, man, I wouldn't want niggas involving mine into no jux."

"True, true."

"Man, fuck all that sensitive thug shit!" Green Jersey said. "She comes home from work at around nine or ten, school or some shit. I don't like shorty no way. I came to the crib and she be acting like she was disgusted with me being there, fuck that. He goes to pick her up most of the time. We need *her* to get to him. He love that bitch to death."

"Fuck it, I'm down for whatever. You?"

"Whatever, man."

Monty deserved whatever came his way. But since I lived there too I needed to let him know what was going to go down so he could protect us both. In my mind I tried to plan my own escape so that if and when shit hit the fan I would have no parts of it. When they left the store, I ran in the opposite direction to let Monty know what was about to go down.

"Get up, get up!" I said frantically as I burst through our bedroom door. He got up and rubbed his eyes.

"Shouldn't you be on your way to work?" he said, rolling over and putting his back to me.

"Listen, I was in the store and I heard some guys talking about running up in here!" I said, pushing him on his back.

"What dudes, what are you talking about, Carin?"

"The corner store, they didn't see me, one had on a Greenbay Packers jersey, the other had on a black T-shirt and a do-rag, and I didn't see the other one. They said they were on their way to Jack's house to find out where you keep your stash. I heard them from the back of the store."

"Hold up," he said, sitting up. "You heard somebody talking about running up in *this house?*"

"Yes, and they were scheming on my jewelry, too!"

"Come on, I'm taking you to work." He got out of the bed and put on his sweats. He lit a cigarette and puffed it harder than I had ever seen him do and got on the phone and headed into the den so I would not hear him.

Ten minutes later we went outside to the car and a little dark-skinned guy was in front of Monty's truck. He gave Monty a pound and said hello to me. I smiled back.

We drove around the corner and got out in front of Jack's building. Monty ran upstairs to see if anybody was in Jack's house. About five minutes later he came back, pulling hard on his cigarette. He jumped in the car and slammed the door and looked into my eyes.

"You know Tuan from down Rockaway who used to come to the house?" he asked me.

"Yeah."

"Him and his cousin and some other dude are the ones. All of them are upstairs in Jack's house."

"How you wanna handle this?" the quiet guy asked.

"Not in front of my wife," Monty said and pulled off.

We drove to the city quietly as I contemplated how I was going to get out of this situation before anything happened.

Monty picked me up from work in the same clothes from this morning. I didn't say anything to him. I just got in the car and sat quietly and so did he. We let the radio play to keep us from having to say anything to one another. I just wanted to go home and go to sleep. But Monty had other plans. He went in as soon as we pulled up on the block.

"I've been meaning to ask you. What did you go to jail for? You never told me that you did a bid."

"My past has nothing to do with you and me." I wasn't about to tell Monty shit. I got out of the car and stomped up the front steps. He came behind me.

"I knew you weren't going to tell me so I took it upon myself to investigate. Conspiracy to murder and armed robbery, huh?" The tone in his voice suggested that I tell him something. If I knew Monty, he was not letting this go. I stood in the doorway of our home, wishing I could just shut my eyes tight and disappear but every time I closed my eyes all I could see was Ashanti's eyes staring up at me. It had been a long time since I saw her face in my mind. I shook my head real quick.

"You all right?" he asked. He wasn't really concerned. He was ready to hear about the old Carin. Still I stayed quiet. I wasn't going to volunteer anything.

"Talk to me, Carin, I'm not about to ask you again."

I took a deep breath.

"A long time ago I use to run with these guys from Brownsville. One of them was a stick-up kid. My mother, you know she wasn't really on her job like that and I had to get money the best way I knew how so the guy put me on to run with him."

"Mmm-hmm, I'm listening."

"So we use to go on sticks together, that's all. Five-O caught up to us and he took the heat for everything."

"Brownsville, huh? I know a lot of people from Brownsville. What's his name?"

"Monty, come on now. I don't feel comfortable giving out names and all of that."

"What the fuck is his name?" he asked me again.

"Panama," I gave up quickly.

"Panama. Tall, light skin, green eyes?"

"Yeah."

"I know Panama." Monty sipped his beer. I sat there wondering what else he knew.

"You use to fuck with Panama? Tell the truth."

"Yes."

Monty had a way of making me think he knew something when he probably didn't. Either way I wasn't taking a chance by lying.

"What kind of dudes did you all rob?"

"Drug dealers, weed spots, whoever was getting money."

"You fucked him?" he said, looking at me now. His eyes wild and angry.

"No, I swear I didn't."

"Never? He kissed you, fingered you, any of that shit?"

What the fuck does that matter?

"We kissed, all the time. He was my boyfriend."

"So why you ain't fuck him?"

"I was a virgin, you know that you were my first."

"I don't know if shit you told me was true," he mumbled. "So you were doing sticks and all that. So you knew about that Cat shit?"

Oh, God, say it ain't so. How does he know these damn people?

"Cat? I'm not sure. We got a lot of people."

"Cat was my man from East New York. We grew up together. They said Panama and some bitch bodied him. That was you?" Monty said, looking at me. He was smiling at me nervously as if he wasn't sure what to feel about me at this moment. I wasn't sure if I should say anything. My head began to hurt and my mouth got dry.

"Carin, that was my man, you hear me? We grew up from babies, he called my mother Mommy, and he lived in my house at one time. Him and his girl used to stay with us back in the day before he started getting real money. You was down with that shit, Carin?" he said, getting up off the stoop. He stood right in front of me.

I looked up at him, still hugging my knees nervously. It was cold outside and I wanted to go in the house.

"Can we take this upstairs?"

Monty ignored my request.

"That was you, Carin?" he said and slammed the bottle down to the concrete, breaking it.

"No," I said.

"You are fucking lying and you know I can find out, right?"

"Monty, what the hell do you want from me!" I said, standing up.

"I want to know what kind of bitch I'm dealing with.

What are you into, Carin? You wanna set me up, rob me too, huh? Is this why you're with me? What the fuck! Tell me everything right fucking now!" he was screaming. I looked around.

"Monty, cool it, all right?" I whispered. "I was young. I did what I had to do."

"You did what you had to do. So when you met me you just forgot to tell me that you went to prison for a year, you forgot to tell me that you had a body and attempted murder on your hands, huh? That you was running around robbing people, fucking with niggas to set them up to get robbed and shit. So you had everything to do with that little shorty getting popped, too, huh?"

"No, I didn't have anything to do with that. I didn't even know Ashanti like that. Panama and his man brought her to me so that we could go set up Cat, I just met her that day."

"What happened that day, Carin. Nobody knows what happened that day. *Nobody*. Cat is dead and his man disappeared, Simone won't talk to nobody! What the fuck happened that day?"

"We went on one of our usual jobs. Ashanti went in the house first. Cat girl let her in I guess because they were cool with her brother. I went in after her and pretended like she was messing with my man and that I was there to find out.

When I got to the door I pulled out and barged inside the crib." I could see Monty's face all distorted and confused. He was looking at me like he wanted to choke me. He stood in front of me with one foot up on the stoop with his arms folded listening intently. I leaned back. I wasn't sure what he was going to do. He had tears in his eyes.

"I'm listening." He sniffled.

"Cat came out, it's all so blurry to me now but I think Cat came out and tried to press me once he found out why I was there and Ashanti put the heat to him. We got out of the house with the money and guns and after that shit just got funky, Monty. I didn't even know Ashanti was dead until we were about to pull off and I realized how quiet she was. I still have nightmares about her to this day. Her eyes were staring up at me. She had a big gunshot wound to the head." I began sobbing.

"I cannot believe this shit. They found her body in the woods somewhere like months later. You knew that they did that to her?"

"I'm not a fucking animal. Stop talking to me like I did this shit. Cat was aiming his gun at me so I shot him, what else was I supposed to do. Nobody had seen it coming but me. I had to protect all of us!" I said, standing up.

"How in the fuck did you not remember to tell me this shit, huh? How the fuck did this just slip your mind. Oh, and by the way I did time, huh?"

"That is a part of my life that I rather not divulge. You think I just run around telling people I did a bid? You think I'm proud of that shit, Monty?"

Monty rubbed his head while holding his fitted cap in his hand. "Cat was my brother, Carin. My wife-to-be is a fucking gangsta. I knew I couldn't trust your grimey slut ass, you fucking wicked bitch."

"I was just trying to eat. I wasn't trying to be some gangsta bitch or anything like that," I said softly.

He stared at me for a while. "You deserve everything you get, Carin. You are a fucking con artist acting like you're so innocent and helpless when in all actuality you use people to get to where you have to go. You used me so that you could maintain an image. I'm buying you all of this fly shit so that your bum ass could look good not knowing that you probably set me up. Shit, you're probably setting me up now!"

"Used you for an image? I never asked you to buy me shit, you chose to do all of this!" I defended myself. I was tired of Monty acting like he made me. "You forced your life on me! I never needed you. When you met me I had shopping bags with thousands of dollars worth of shit in it, what the fuck are you talking about? I was always working, always independent, and everything you bought me I fucking deserve! Furthermore, nothing can compensate for the way you treat me!"

Monty just looked at me and sucked his teeth. He fanned his hand off at me and dismissed me.

It was no use even arguing with Monty, he already had it all figured out so I stood quiet.

"Take your ass upstairs, when I figure out what to do with you I'll be up there."

18

Carin

Monty hadn't talked to me in days since I revealed my story to him. He would let me see his face when I came home from work and he would sit out on the stoop all night drinking but would never spend any alone time with me. I decided that I would go out. He said he didn't care but made sure he handed me the keys to his truck. I knew he only let me drive it as it had some sort of tracking device.

My mind quickly went to Haman who was home waiting for me. I was tired and every day at work I spoke to Haman and found a friend in him. He offered his ear and his couch if I needed it. He was a gentlemen, he took me to lunch some days when I wasn't too nervous to go, he sent flowers that made me feel guilty. He told me that he was just trying to make me feel beautiful. I needed a break from the rumors of stick-ups, the haunted dreams, and the guilt for taking a life, so yesterday when he requested to see me I happily obliged. I had already called my dad who said he and Tyra would be inside not answering phones anyway. So the plan was to park the truck then cab it to Haman's. I called a cab as soon as I parked on my dad's block and waited in the truck until a cab arrived. I requested a Lincoln Town Car with dark tints to take me from Jersey to Queens.

This was my first time going to Haman's house. I was very nervous yet I felt at home. His apartment was warm and cozy. I sought comfort immediately and took my shoes off. He smiled and handed me a glass of wine. For hours we sat and spoke of everything from movies to clothes to avoid the topic of my relationship. It felt so good to be in his arms as he rubbed my back like a baby. He knew my pain.

"You know, Carin, you don't ever have to go back there. Now, I don't know everything but I know enough to know that you're probably not safe. You can stay with me, no strings attached."

"I made it this far so I'll be okay," I said with my eyes closed. I wanted him to keep on convincing me to leave. But he respected my privacy and said nothing more. He continued rubbing me.

"I want to make love to you so bad. I just don't want to complicate things." He kissed my ear lobe. Instantly my back arched and I moaned. But I said nothing. "Let me love you, Carin."

"Soon," I moaned.

Haman turned me to face him then laid me on his couch. He planted my body with the softest kisses on earth from head to toe. All I could do was cry. He felt so good.

"I'm a good man, Carin. I won't treat you the way he treats you. I promise you that," he said between kisses.

"I know. Nobody would."

I laid in his arms for about an hour then real-ized that I needed to get home. Reluctantly, I called a cab.

The house was pitch black when I got there. I turned all of the lights on in the front of the apartment, scared that Monty was going to jump out at me. He was like the boogey man. After a few moments I realized that he wasn't home so I put on my pajamas and curled up in the bed doz-ing off, thinking about Haman's kisses.

I woke up several times throughout the night because Monty hadn't reached home yet. As I walked to the bathroom, around 7:00 A.M., Monty was coming through the door. I started to run back to my bed but decided against it. When he opened the door I was in his face. I grabbed him by his shirt and hemmed him up against the wall.

"Where the fuck were you, Monty?"

"Yo, get off me," he said, attempting to pry my tiny hands off of him but to no avail.

"You're spending nights out now? Huh? Are you stupid or something?"

"First of all I was out with Rick, we got drunk and I fell asleep in his crib. You didn't know if I was okay or nothing, you just automatically assume that I was out with some chick, right? I didn't see my fucking cell ringing all night so where the fuck where you that you couldn't call?"

"Don't try to flip this shit around. Why else would you be coming home at this hour, Monty?" I said, letting him go. He walked off into our bedroom talking shit.

"I wasn't with a chick and unless you can prove me to be lying, take what I say and drop it," he said, grabbing me.

"Get off me." I turned my back. I waited for him to beg me for sex as usual, but a few minutes later he was asleep. I lay next to him staring at the ceiling, trying to fight the urge to run in the kitchen, boil some water and scorch his ass.

***

The next night, while I was ironing my work clothes, Monty was hustling around the apartment, getting dressed. It was Valentines Day eve. I started not to say anything but he was not about to act like he was single on my watch so I intervened. If he was going to make my life miserable then I would do the same to him.

"Where do you think you're going on the eve of a holiday?" I put the iron down and put my hand on my hips. Monty was not leaving the house tonight and I meant that shit. I was ready to throw down and have a knock-down drag-out fight with him.

He ignored me as he continued getting dressed. I stood there watching him stuff a wad of money wrapped in a rubberband in his pocket. He popped a Trident in his mouth and headed out the door.

"Don't wait up," he said and tried to walk out that easily. He was dressed to kill in beige silk pants, a cream button-up shirt, chocolate brown Salvatore Ferragamo shoes, his gold Rolex and his three-quarter copper-colored mink coat. I snatched the plug from the iron out of the socket and ran down after him with the iron in my hand; he was already at the bottom of the steps walking out the door. I launched the hot iron at him and he ducked.

"Carin, I swear to my mother if that iron would have hit me . . . Go the fuck to sleep, yo, I'll see you in the morning." He kept walking out the door. Though it was February, I ran down behind him not caring that I had on a long lavender silk nightgown.

"Monty!" I yelled from the top stoop as he walked up the block toward his Lexus. I could see people looking at me but I didn't give a shit. Barefoot and not paying attention to the onlookers I was blind with rage. The scent of his Gucci cologne hit me with each step I tried to take to get closer to him. When I reached him, Monty turned around and barked.

"Look at you outside like this, making a fool of me. You see this shit, look around you!" he yelled at me. I stood frozen, I played myself. He pointed sharply. "Take your ass in the house; I will be back *when I get back.*"

"Don't get in that car," I said.

"Or what?" he asked me as he opened the door.

"Do not get in that fucking car." I socked him in his defected eye. "Don't disrespect me like this, Monty. I deal with enough of your shit in the house. Do not disrespect me like this."

"Carin," he started through clenched teeth, "I am going to . . . You are embarrassing us, Carin, outside in lingerie, on the corner, and do you know how many fuckin' people are looking at you right now? Look around, stupid!"

"Everybody knows that the eve of a major holiday is when a man goes out with his mistress. You got the nerve to be fucking dressed to the fucking nines about to step out on me? You must be fucking smoking! Get your fucking ass upstairs, Monty, I'm not going for this shit, uh-uh!"

"As a matter of fact, fine, I won't go out. You will be sorry you asked me to stay home. Let's go, dummy!" He pushed me up the block by my neck as everybody watched. I was humiliated. I could see Peaches and her girls laughing at me.

Monty took off his clothes, he was pissed. He took of his beige silk shirt angrily and laid it on top of his honey brown Kenneth Cole slacks. *Where is he going?*

He unfastened his diamond bracelet but left on his gold watch. He stood in front of me with a beige wife beater on and beige Hilfiger boxers. *Damn, down to the drawers he was dressing for this bitch,* I thought.

"What the fuck is so important that you made such a fool out of us?" he said, inching closer to me.

He had the nerve to be disgusted with me. Who was I to feel inadequate around him? I decided that he could go out after all, remembering the sweet thing who always gave me a shoulder to cry on. I was going to kick it up a notch and start fucking with Haman's hard body. Fuck it, I was getting my ass beat on the regular for nothing, why not give him a reason to put his hands on me? If he wanted to keep me here then he would have to pay such as he made me pay, constantly for a debt I didn't owe.

"You know what, Monty? I'm better than this. I don't have to beg you for shit, you need me. You're the one who dragged me back here because you can't fucking function without me. You would fall the fuck to pieces without me. This money don't mean shit, I was fine before I fucking met your ass. So go run around with the raggedy black bitch, I will not be here when you get back, you fucking woman beater. You're a maggot, a pussy, a fucking bitch!" I said, and spat at him.

Monty reached out and grabbed me by my throat and punched me so hard that I needed ten stitches over my left eye. When the officers in the hospital asked me what had happened, I foolishly told them that I fell because I knew that if Monty went to jail, he'd come home and whoop my ass even worse.

"You wanted me home for the holiday, you got me home. Happy Valentines Day," he said, step-

ping over me as I screamed loud enough to wake
the dead.

Monty

The next morning on Valentine's Day I woke up
and watched Carin as she slept, her left eye swollen shut, colored in blues, purples and greens, a
bandage covering her brow where she had to get
ten stitches over her left eye to close the wound
that I caused. As we drove home, she quietly
stared out the window with tears rolling down her
face crying quietly. How could I even say sorry
after breaking the skin on her beautiful face? I
didn't recognize the man I had become so I knew
that Carin had't either. I left her asleep this morning and headed out in the cold to get her some
Valentines Day gifts. When I got home, Carin was
still in the bed but watching television, the covers
half way over her face. It was going on four in the
evening. She didn't flinch when I walked in with
all my bags, Ski bringing up the rear with more. I
went to the grocery store and got things to cook
and went to Bloomingdales and spent at least
$3,000 on clothes. I brought her flowers, candy,
and jewelry. I was going to treat Carin the way I
use to. I was going to make her a home cooked
dinner and light the house up with candles, play
soft music, and make love to my wife to be. After

I put away the groceries, I brought the bags in the room and sat on the edge of the bed. The longer I watched her the more she began to cry. I pulled the sheets from off of her and sat her up on my lap like a baby. She wrapped her arms around my neck and sobbed into my shoulder. I began to cry too. I rubbed her back as we both silently wondered what happened to us.

"I'm so sorry baby doll. Ain't no way in hell I should be treating you like this Carin I'm so sorry." I cried into her bosom. She squeezed me tighter.

"You still love me, I know you do baby and I keep breaking your heart. I'm a fuck up Carin. I love you more than anything. I'm supposed to be protecting you and I keep hurting you."

We held one another for a while longer then I reached over for the bags.

"Look, daddy bought you a whole bunch of gifts to make you feel pretty again baby." I said and pulled out a few outfits complete with designer shoes and bags to match.

"Try them on." I tried to make her smile. She tried them on quietly as I complimented her and clapped for her like she was on the runway. When she got down to her last outfit I pulled out a jewelry box and handed her a diamond charm bracelet with our initials, hearts and stars hanging from it. I placed it on her pretty little wrist.

"I'm going to lavish you with everything from now on. Not just when I fuck up but all the time like I use to."

Carin didn't talk. She had nothing to say to me at this point. The look in her eyes told me that she was devastated. I was going to do everything I could to restore her faith in me.

As the evening went on, Carin still didn't talk. She just sat on the sofa as I instructed and watched television while I cooked. I had slow jams playing and tried to make small talk with her but she just sat on the sofa and sipped champagne laughing at whatever was on the television. I prepared chicken parm with salad for our dinner and I baked a chocolate on chocolate cake, her favorite. I pulled out the dinner table and placed a red table cloth on it and dimmed the lights while we ate. I held Carin's hand and led the grace. She said amen and ate still not talking. I held back tears as I looked at what I did to her face. She was still beautiful underneath the huge blemish, her skin clear, her frame petite and curvaceous under a pretty grayish blue long silk gown that I purchased for her to wear tonight. We ate silently as the slow jams played and she sipped champagne chewing her food still crying. It was tearing me apart. I cleared the table once we were done and turned the television off. Carin was lying on the sofa with her eyes closed wincing at the pain over her eye.

I lifted my lady up and carried her into the bedroom where I planned on making love to her all night long.

I turned the music up and lit more candles then crawled beside my woman, slowly peeling off the strap on her gown to reveal her small ample breast. Her breasts were so pretty, soft, small, and full. I sucked on her nipples thirstily but slow as R. Kelly crooned in the background about not being able to sleep without his woman in his life. I felt the same.

"Stop." Carin finally spoke.

"Why?" I breathed. She had no words. "Shhh" I said softly. "Just let me make love to you it's been so long since we've made love."

She didn't fight me. She closed her eyes and began to cry some more. She was breaking my heart. I kissed her tears away and stripped her down to the bare necessities and I laid with my woman and cupped her face, kissing her bruised eye, stroking her pretty short hair.

"You're so perfect." I looked into her eyes. She kept her head hung low trying not to look at me but I forced her to.

"Why you keep crying Carin? Talk to me baby doll."

"I'm scared of you that's why!" She blurted out. I squeezed her so tight.

"I just want to squeeze this pain right out of you Carin. Don't be scared of me baby, nah this shit ain't cool. You know I would protect you from anything."

"Yeah, but whose going to protect me from you?" She sobbed into my chest. She stuck me with her comment. I didn't know what else to do.

"Let's make some babies Carin. It's time. Let's go get married, make some babies, and be in love. I want to be the man you fell in love with."

I lay my woman down and dove head first into that innocent love that I know she gave only to me despite the hell I put her through. She rubbed my head as I ate her then pulled me up to her face where we kissed passionately. With each stroke I promised her better days, better nights, a better life, better times, and a better me. She began rubbing my back the minute I entered her. I loved when she rubbed my back, I missed my woman. While the music played in the background and the candles burned out, I made love to the love of my life until sunrise praying that she didn't leave me.

19

Carin

Over the past four months, Monty had not laid a hand on me since the Valentine Day massacre. Things were pretty quiet around the house and we spent all of our time in Queens. Being in an abusive relationship was like a drug. You knew it wasn't good for you but when it got good you feigned to get that feeling back. So you put yourself through hell to get that fix. Monty made sure that he whisked me out of there quickly before anyone could see what he had done to me on February thirteenth. I eventually wound up quitting my job. I couldn't stand the humiliation anymore and I needed the rest. I spent most of my days home, sleeping, doing things around the house, shopping, visiting my father when my appearance allowed me to, and hanging out with Jetta. I had a few more classes to finish before I graduated with my associate's degree but I needed a break. I was tired. Monty stayed in

Brooklyn out of my way most of the time. I was trapped in this relationship and needed to find a way out. Something had to give. Most times when he'd leave to go to Brooklyn, in my mind I'd plan my escape but then I'd be reminded of the last time he found me. I was thinking that maybe we could break up like normal couples do. You know, have the sit down and the "This is not working out" speech. I laughed at my naïveté.

But I was afraid that if I tried to leave, the next time he caught me he'd kill me. He often told me that there was no way out. He wasn't starting over, he wasn't willing to see me with anyone else, and if I wanted to go I could but it would be in a body bag. I needed to be untraceable when I left. Quitting my job was the best thing I could have done. My next move would be to get low somewhere, anywhere. My thoughts were interrupted upon hearing Monty's keys. I began doing the dishes, anything to not look at him. I couldn't stand the sight of him, even four months after the fact.

"Put some clothes on, dirty, we going to Brooklyn to chill out," he said happily. He was in a "good mood."

"I don't want to go." I said calmly. He hugged me from behind and kissed my neck softly then started rubbing my breasts through my silk gown. I closed my eyes and thought about Haman, wondering what he felt like. My thoughts took me away as Monty picked me up and put me on the kitchen counter and laid me down. "You're so beautiful to me still. I'm still in love with you, baby."

I wanted to blurt out *I don't feel the same about you, you fucking psycho*. But instead I said nothing. I closed my eyes and began picturing Haman, reminiscing on his sweet tender kisses and his invitation to love. I was going to make time soon to give this man my body and my heart as soon as it was healed up and ready for serving.

He stripped quickly then crawled on top of me. Then reality hit, he was not Haman. "Knock-knock, open up for Daddy," he whispered. I remembered how that used to turn me on so much. I kept my eyes closed and continued picturing another man as Monty slow grinded me to orgasm. I moaned in delight.

After he sexed me I took a shower, threw on my Sergio Valente's since they were back in style and rode shotgun to Brooklyn to face the peanut gallery.

Monty and I sat on his stoop with some of his friends and his aunt Sharon, laughing and joking. The day was going well, everyone was laughing and even the neighborhood hood rats stayed in their place. Monty got up to go to the corner store and asked all of us if we needed something.

"Water for me," I said. He said okay and walked off. Sharon, Jomar, Ski, and I got into a heated debate about who was the better rapper, Biggie or Jay-Z. "I'm riding with Big," I said.

"Why, because he's dead? That nigga Jay is nicer than Big cousin, sorry," Ski said.

"Well, shit, who got more money? That's who I'm rolling with!" Sharon joked.

"Obviously, Jay does now, shit, besides, Big ain't have no real money. Puff was raping his ass." I put my two cents in. Jomar agreed as he kept his eye on the black Camry creeping up the block. I got up to stretch and also looked at the car. Soon, the four of us were looking, wondering why this car was creeping. Ski automatically went and stood on the side of the stoop so that he could be closer to his piece that he kept behind a rock. Jomar brazenly kept his hammer on his hip like most Jamaicans did. Like nothing, they both kept talking, but concentrated on the black car. The car stopped directly across the street and I saw Tionne get out. Her friends stood outside the car as she boldly walked up to my stoop. She waved to Peaches and some other girls then walked up to me. She said hello to Sharon who ignored her.

"Hello, everybody, is Monty around?" she asked.

Then her eyes met mine. She just couldn't let the day go by without incident. Nobody had seen me in a while so I'm sure they had put the call in that I was still on the scene once they saw me. I'm sure everyone thought that I was gone.

"Where's my man Monty at?" she had the gall to ask Ski. Ski didn't say anything; he just looked at me and shook his head. "Oh, so you gon' act like me and you ain't cool, Ski? Like you don't come over and eat at my house when that nigga Monty is there?" She laughed. She was coming to start some shit and I was not up for it. She sized me up and couldn't stop staring at me. I took two steps down off of the stoop. Jomar stood up and turned to face me.

"Carin," was all he said and shook his head no.

"So you actually brought your trifling ass to my house?" I said.

"Bitch, I been coming to your house, please. Like you ain't catch me in your fucking bed and you stayed with that nigga. You'sa dumb-ass bitch." She flung her hair.

She backed up and looked up the block. Monty was frozen on the corner. When he saw me looking he came walking. He swaggered down the block toward us probably wondering what to do.

I went upstairs to get my car keys. I wasn't about to put up with this. They could have this. I hit the alarm and walked toward my car when Sharon ran up to me. "You are not going to let this bitch come on your block and disrespect you, are you?"

"She's right. I let this nigga get away with murder. You think I'm going to be out here fighting over him? Nah, that ain't my style, Sharon. I'm out here in Chanel sneakers, stacks on my neck, hundreds covering my eyes, and about to pull off in my Lexus. You think I'm going to humiliate myself by fighting that fucking hood rat? It's obvious that your nephew made it to where this bitch thinks she can come over here and disrespect me. If Monty respected me then everybody else would. I'm out of here." I opened my door.

"I hear you, Carin, but don't leave. You're looking like a real sucker right now."

"I don't give a fuck, Sharon. Look, I know I'm not a sucker by a long shot. I have nothing to prove. I'm out, hon. I'll get with you later." I hopped in my car and slammed the door. Monty jogged up to the car and stopped me as I was about to pull off.

"Yo, roll the window down, yo. Where you going?"

"Back to Queens."

"Get out the car you not going anywhere. Fuck this bitch coming over here starting trouble."

"I'm good Monty. I don't want to be out here." I felt my temper rising and I needed to get out of here before something bad happened to someone.

"Carin, get out of the car. You're not going anywhere."

"Monty. Please let me go home. Really, I'm a little tired, baby."

"No." He opened my door. He grabbed my hand and began hugging me. "I'm not going to let nobody disrespect you, Carin. I know I put you through hell but that's me and you, baby. I'm not letting some bitch come between us. I told you I got you for life and that I've changed, baby. When I hit you on Valentines Day and busted your eye open I swore to God that I'd never ever put my hands on you again and I meant it. Come on, how long has it been? I meant it, Carin. Now come on, sit on this stoop with your pretty fly-ass self and come get these bitches mad. That's all it is they just mad."

I hesitantly walked back to the stoop and put my back to Tionne and her friends who were on the stoop clucking like the birds they were. They were talking loud and reckless, trying to get a rise out of me.

"She is off the chain, Monty, you need to check that bitch for real," Sharon said.

Monty fanned her off and kept talking to his friends, trying his best to ignore her. But we couldn't. She needed to be slapped and stopped. The more she talked the more aggravated I got. I stood up and looked over at the stoop to see where she was standing. She was right at the bottom like the ring leader putting on a show. I rushed past Jomar and tackled Tionne to the ground. I heard Monty yelling for me to get off of her, I felt people pulling me off of her, but this woman's behavior was unacceptable. Someone had to pay for the hell Monty put me through at home. I know he didn't beat on any of his little girlfriends like he beat on me, so I would do the job for him. She deserved this ass whooping I was giving her and then some. Someone succeeded in pulling me off of her. I had a handful of her hair in my hand and my knuckles were bleeding. No, it was the blood from her mouth. Monty finally picked me up and carried me to the steps.

"Carin, no!" he said, pointing in my face like I was a child. I ignored him. His ass was next, but right now, I had to send this bitch a very important message.

Her friends who had come along for the ride were all standing around cursing and carrying on. That meant nothing to me, I wanted to throw down. Sharon was still sitting on the steps cool, waiting for a third party to get involved.

"Dirty jealous bitches, I'm calling you out, all of you!"

Monty grabbed me around the waist.

"Carin, you done lost your fucking mind?" he whispered.

"Why the *fuck* did she think she had the right to come here and disrespect me?"

"I ain't going nowhere, bitch!" Tionne said.

"You're making a fool out of me." I slapped Monty hard across his face.

A crowd had formed by now and everyone watched me as I poked my finger in Monty's face. He stood firm and tall looking me in the eye.

"As if I don't deal with enough of your shit in the house, you're out here sleeping around with *this?*" I said, looking at Tionne who was still holding her mouth.

At this moment it was much deeper than Tionne or any other broad. This was personal between my man and me.

"Carin, let's go upstairs."

"No, I'm not going no fucking where, Monty! I want to make sure I put an end to this shit to-night since you obviously can't. I been quiet long enough!"

"Carin, let's go!" he threatened.

"The bully tactic is not working today. You are going to tell me right now what the fuck is going on or I'm going to start swinging, again!"

"He has been messing with me for the past eight years on and off, he helps me with my kids and everything, ain't that right, Money Man?" she clucked.

He stepped back and looked at me. "Carin, I don't spend money on nobody but you. You know I'd never break the code, baby."

He then turned his attention to Tionne. "Why did you come here? This is my wife, you understand? Nobody and I mean *nobody* comes before her, you understand? So what did you come here for? Huh? What did you call yourself doing Tionne, huh?" I was waiting for him to tear her a new asshole like he had done to me so many times. But he wasn't budging.

"It's like that, Monty?" she said, smiling smugly.

"Yeah, it's like that so get the fuck outta here," he said. She gave me an evil glare that I matched.

"Fuck you, Monty! He ain't worth it!" her friend yelled. He fanned his hand off and grabbed me by my wrist.

"Upstairs now!" he said through clenched teeth. Monty dragged me upstairs by my wrist and slammed the door once we were inside.

"You mutherfucka you . . . Eight years you been dealing with this bitch, eight years!"

Monty started rubbing his head and digging his hands in his pockets nervously.

"And now the bitch thinks she has the right to come to my house and step to me and my man on my block in front of everybody. I mean, damn, Monty, what are you going to do to me next? Have a baby on me? Leave me for the bitch? What? It doesn't get no more disrespectful than this!"

"Carin, I'll handle this." He walked out.

"You're not going to stop dealing with her after eight years!" I yelled to his back.

"Carin, I said I'll handle it, all right?" he said, slamming the door so hard the walls shook.

No, I'ma handle this shit.

Monty was talking to Tionne when I came down behind him and stood in the hallway to see what he was going to do. She walked up to him trying to grab his hand. Monty violently jerked his hand away.

"Tionne, you need to raise up outta here," he said, looking up at our window, not knowing I was downstairs in the hallway peeking.

"Can I talk to you privately?" she asked.

"No! Get the fuck outta here, man. You wrong for coming over here, you wrong."

"Monty, baby, come on." She reached for him again. I lost my mind. Like a raging bull I ran out of the house.

I pulled a .380 out from behind me. Everyone started screaming. I cocked it back and backed her down against a hooptie and put the gun to her forehead.

"How bad you want Monty? Tell me?" I said to her through clenched teeth.

She shook her head.

"If I hear your name again, you are going to feel a hot one in your ass. You and this nigga right here!" I said and looked at Monty who looked shocked, turned on, mad, and scared all at once. Now that he knew of my past, he knew that this could go either way.

"Let her go, Carin," he said calmly.

I smacked her in the side of her head with the butt of the gun, not hard enough to break skin but hard enough to leave a knot and a headache. Ski took the gun from me and disappeared. Tionne took the opportunity to swing at me, she got one good hit then I grabbed her and banged her head against the car repeatedly. The ass whooping ended with her under a car. Monty then grabbed her by her neck and slammed her down to the ground. Her eyes went wide.

"If I ever see your face again I'm going to kill you, you got it?" he said.

"I'm telling my brother." She squirmed out of Monty's grasp.

"I'll kill that nigga too," he said. She got up and walked to the car while her friends yelled obscenities to Monty and me. Peaches stood at the top of her stoop looking scared. I pointed at her.

"You bitch, you're next," I promised. This time she didn't smirk or say anything slick. She kindly backed up into her hallway.

Tionne got in the driver's side and sped off. I stood there for a while trying to gain my composure. I grabbed a bottle of water out of the brown paper bag Monty had brought from the store earlier. Everyone whispered around me.

Monty blamed me now for the beef between him and his friend Barry, so he was walking around hemming and hawing all day after I beat Tionne's ass. I couldn't believe that he found it in his fucking heart to blame me for defending myself and finally snapping.

He finally left the house at around four in the afternoon and I was glad he hadn't come home yet. I didn't want to see his lying-ass face anywhere near me. Overall the building was quiet and I was here practicing frying chicken because I had nothing else better to do. I sipped the bottle of Cristal that had been in the pantry forever and I put my music on. It had been a while since I listened to some nice tunes and just relaxed. I was feeling mighty fine tonight despite the events that surrounded me. I gave myself a facial, a mani, and pedi, then I felt Monty coming. He stomped up the steps two at a time like Godzilla. I chose to ignore him. Had he not been fucking around none of this would have happened. He didn't see it that way, though. He never saw things in the right light when he was involved. He came in the house and stood before me with both hands in his pockets. While we stood there in a thick silence, I tried to smell what he had been drinking. He had no idea that I mapped him out that way and played him according to what he sipped on. White liquor made him horny, dark liquor made him violent, and champagne made him spend money.

"Are you cooking or burning up some shit?" he asked, half serious, half joking.

I ignored him but held the handle ready to wop him with it if I had to, hot oil and all. But for now I was just trying to scrape the chicken out of the pan.

"I need to get some better pots," I mumbled.

He sucked his teeth and took his cap off, pointing it at me as he talked.

"You would think by now your ass knew how to boil water, and then you wonder why I eat at everyone else's house."

"What you drinking on tonight?" I asked casually as I toyed with the chicken with a long-handled fork.

"Henny, why?"

I cringed.

"Damn," he said, picking up the pot and slamming it back down. "I was hungry, too."

"You been out all day and you didn't eat? You didn't even call me to ask me to cook."

"Do I have to tell you to cook? Damn, Carin, it's not rocket science. You live with a man, you make sure he eats and that he busts a nut at least once a day if not twice, that's all you gotta do. Shit, I got bitches ready to cook for me all day every day and you in here burning chicken?"

"Go wherever you need to go, Monty, if you're *that* hungry."

"You being a smart ass?" he said and walked up to me. "You're standing in the kitchen, in Chanel slippers that cost more than most of these bitches' spring jackets. Donna Karan silk pajamas not the hood shit that everybody else has, wearing a diamond Cartier jewelry set worth a good five Gs, *easy*, with an eighty dollar haircut, sipping on a three hundred dollar bottle of Cristal, listening to a two thousand dollar stereo system, sleeping on a

one thousand dollar mattress, wearing an engagement ring that can easily be a down payment on
a house, and probably got a one hundred dollar
Gucci thong up your ass *right now*." He walked
up to me and sniffed me. "And let's not forget the
damn bath and body set you washed your ass with
that costs over four hundred because out of nowhere you want to wash your ass with *caviar*, like
you Halle Berry or some shit, so that makes you
worth a good . . . He had the nerve to go and get a
calculator and total me up. "$14,130! And I didn't
include the taxes! And I can't get a decent fucking
meal when I come home?" he yelled.

"I figured you ate while you were out is all—"
I said.

"Fifteen Gs, my girl is not even going out! You
in your crib and you are wearing and using fifteen
Gs worth of shit. You got bitches who can't even
get fifteen dollars from a nigga and they cook
Thanksgiving feasts every single night for they
man and you're here, chillin', don't even have to
work, down to your socks and the toothbrush you
use is high maintenance, and I can't get a meal.
Well, I'll be damned, you should feel like shit,
Carin."

I turned the stove off, this was going to be
a long night. I walked into the bedroom and
quickly slid my jewelry off. I didn't want him to

pop or break anything. He took off his hat and shirt and kept on his sweats and wife beater. He slid his feet into his Gucci flip-flops and walked into the kitchen. I waited. He was leaning against the counter, smoking a cigarette, and sipping the Cristal I had in the cup on the counter. I began putting the pots away wondering what Hennessy mixed with Crystal could do to a person.

"I'm hungry, Carin."

I looked at the clock. It was eleven at night.

"We have cold cuts."

"I'm not going on a class fucking trip!" He sat on the sofa.

"Monty, there is nothing to eat." I made him a sandwich: turkey, tomato, mayo, cheese, mustard on whole wheat, how he liked it. I handed it to him then walked back to the kitchen and took out the chicken for tomorrow's dinner.

"What the fuck I'ma do with a sandwich, Carin?" He threw it at me, hitting me square in the face. I backed up and picked the sandwich off of the ground.

"Cook something, Carin, *now!*" he said, and slapped me across the face. I jumped back to avoid getting smacked hard but it stung just the same. "Cook something now or *I'll cook you*, I'll make it hot in here, I'm telling you, you got an hour to whip some shit up that tastes good or it's on. One hour!" he yelled, and slammed the bedroom door. I jumped in my car and headed to the 24-hour Pathmark to get something to cook, talking to Haman the entire time. I told him to get that spare room ready for me because I'd be coming soon.

20

Carin

Peaceful was what I felt this morning and that's how I knew that a big change was coming. It was going to be a change that I couldn't prepare myself for, I just had to be ready when it came. The morning was silent and still. I was actually able to think clearly today for some reason. I opened my eyes and just lay there in my king-sized bed. I never felt so lonely and down. I was a fool. I had come to that conclusion many times before but this morning the revelation had come to me full throttle. I was a fool, I was a dumb bitch, I was all of those things I had been called and it was becoming harder to deal with my reality. I contemplated suicide over and over again. It seemed like that was the only way I could get out of the hell I was living in. I quickly erased those silly thoughts and replaced them with more positive ones. I began thinking about my future and how beautiful I knew that my life could be. I had everything going for me. *He's just a man, he is just a man,* I said to myself. *Don't let him hinder you, live your life.* Non-stop since childhood I couldn't seem to find inner peace. After busting Tionne's ass, the fight continued upstairs between me and Monty. Though it was only verbal at first, it was enough for me, to have blame put on me. I was wrong for pulling out a gun on her and according to him, I took it too far. I couldn't believe that he was taking her side so I hauled off and smacked him with an empty Cristal bottle, and of course, not one to back down from a fight with a girl, Monty commenced to ass kicking. So much for him never hitting me again.

I sat up and stretched long and hard as the wheels in my mind turned. *You're better than this Carin, you know better so do better, you been through worse than this, just go, run and don't look back!* I kept telling myself knowing that there was power in the word.

When Monty left this morning he told me that he would be gone all day and to not call him as he didn't want to be bothered with me. I was more than cool with that hoping he'd drink while driving and kill himself on the Jackie Robinson. I wouldn't even cry, and I'd skip the funeral too. I thought about escaping but knowing Monty he had someone watching me or he wasn't too far. I called my dad to see what he was doing. I needed to hear his voice. He was still asleep when I called. "Is this a bad time?"

"No, baby, you okay?"

"Yeah, just missing you that's all. I was going to come see you later on."

"Oh, of course, baby. But how's everything?"

"I'm fine, I'm cool," I said, trying to sound upbeat. The words were stuck in my throat for me to beg my daddy to come save me. What was wrong with me? Why was I so afraid of this man? I just wanted it to be over. I wanted us to be how we were. I wanted to go back in time when we laughed and talked and loved and were friends. I hated that things turned out to be this way.

"Where's Monty?"

"He left this morning. I'm here alone."

"So come on over."

"Okay, Daddy, let me get it together. I'll be there later on. I love you."

"Love you too, princess," he said in his sleepy voice.

But who was I kidding. I was battered and bruised and could not go to my father's house. I couldn't go anywhere looking like this. I was twenty-six years old with no job, no friends, no life, no nothing anymore. My desire to live life to the fullest had faded. I needed a do-over. I needed a breakthrough. I didn't know where to start or what to do. My phone rang interrupting my thoughts. It was probably Monty checking in on me. "Hello."

"Hi, may I talk to Carin, please."

"Speaking, who this."

"Hey, it's Missy."

I hadn't talk to her in a year and quite frankly I didn't miss her. I saw Missy for who she really was over these past few years and I didn't like it. You know what they say, the first time someone shows you who they are, believe them. I sat quietly waiting for her to speak, I had no apologies to give out.

"You there?" she asked upon my silence.

"Yeah, I'm here, what's good?"

"How have you been, it's been a while since we've talked. You crossed my mind so I just wanted to know if you were okay?"

"Same ol' same ol'. What's good with you?"

"Not much. I'm here. You know Drew and I broke up a few months back."

"Sorry to hear that."

"Yeah, it was for the best. How are things with you and Monty?"

"Could be better."

"Look, I don't know if you need a friend right now or if things finally went back to normal for you, but I'm here if you need me. I'm sorry for the way I treated you, Carin. I mean that. I've worried and wondered about you for a long time and prayed for your well being, sis. I hope you can forgive me. I recognize my part in this. I'm sorry."

"It's cool, Missy."

"Listen, why don't you come over . . . if you can, and I'll make us a dinner and we can just kick it."

"That sounds like a great idea. I'll see you shortly."

"Cool." She hung up.

I needed to get out of the house and see something different, which was the only reason I headed over to Missy's. I knew that if she looked at me wrong or said anything condenscending she was going to get dealt with. But I had this surreal will to forgive people and so with that I headed over to Missy's just as I was, not trying to hide my unhappiness because that wasn't the kind of person I was. I was real and with that I expected real results.

"Hey." I walked past her nonchalantly as if I had groceries and good news, but all I had was a face and neck full of bruises. She was silent. She ran to the stereo and turned it off then turned off her pots. She sat next to me and held my hand.

I just sat there wondering where the good times had gone.

"I'm so sorry for criticizing you instead of being there for you as a friend. I should have never turned my back to you or put my nose up at you. I just didn't know how to be there for you and accept what you were going through. I'm so sorry. It was so foolish of me to hate on you over material items and not understand the hell you had in your heart and at home. I'm so sorry." She hugged me, it hurt, I winced, and she hugged me harder, I cried. *Hard.*

"Not that he needs a reason to hit you but what happened, mama?"

I gave her the run down of everything she missed up to the current events.

"I'm so tired, Missy." I sobbed heavily.

"So leave, come stay with me. Drew is out of the picture. You were right, he had no respect for me. Monty doesn't know where I live."

"He'll find out."

"No, he won't, Carin. You've come too far to let some man beat on you. I mean, look at you!" She pulled away from me to examine me. "I can only imagine the bruises I can't see."

I stripped for her so she wouldn't have to imagine. She began to cry. She grabbed my hand and extended my arm, touching each bruise.

"He punches through my soul, Missy. God he hurts me so bad when he hits me, I mean it hurts, and it feels like death. I get numb and he just punches and punches and punches me over and over. Sometimes I think he doesn't even know that he is punching me. He can't possibly know that he is hurting me. I never know when or how or why he just does." I began to bawl. "The pain is enough to make me pass out! And all I can think is, Monty, I love you stop hitting me, I love you, don't hurt me, I love you! And he just keeps on. God, it kills me every day. I'm dying, Missy, I'm dying." I whispered.

My friend was at a loss for words. I sobbed, my chest and shoulders heaving.

"Missy, help me, I gotta get away." I let out a bloodcurdling scream.

Missy wrapped her entire body around me and began to squeeze me tight. "Missy, hold me, please!"

"You're not going home tonight."

"I have to Missy, Monty is not trying to hear me staying out."

"Fuck him right now." She got up, and came back with comfortable house clothes.

"I know they are too big but dammit they comfortable, and you don't need anything close-fitting on your bruises. I'll get some ice, you want a drink?"

"Yeah."

"I have wine."

"Bring the bottle."

"You got it."

By the time she fixed my drink, I was drifting off to sleep, because it's the only freedom I knew and I needed to be free . . . *now*.

I woke up with a headache. Missy was at her computer with her hair pinned up, biting on a pencil, typing away. She had soft music playing and was sipping on a glass of water with lemon. I lay there for a while watching her, wondering where my mental freedom had gone, then sat up and stretched. It hurt. She turned upon hearing me.

"Hey you, I thought you were dead, you know what time it is?"

"No, enlighten me."

"It's twelve in the afternoon and your father called. He is worried about you because your man called looking for you."

"What did you tell my father?"

"Well, I told him that you were here, that we went out and you fell asleep. I told him that Monty had just called me and knows where you are."

"I have to call Monty."

"Be my guest." She turned back to her studies. I knew Monty was going to raise the roof when I called and if he did I'd just stay out another night. I wasn't up for his bullshit. He didn't have a care in the world when I told him I was at Missy's house. He told me to just bring my ass home.

When I got home he wasn't even there. He himself didn't come home last night. I didn't care to wonder where he was. I was going to call Haman to see how he was doing. I put on a gray sweat suit and my red and gray Airs with one of Monty's red Yankee caps. The day was gloomy like it was going to rain and I didn't feel like doing my hair anyway. I just felt defeated and tired and wanted someone, anyone to take me away from my misery. Besides, Haman didn't care about all that dress-up stuff. I pulled the tomboy look off very well each time so it was nothing. I put on lip gloss and my small hoop earrings. I was comfortable. I stood on the top of the stoop and stretched again, looking around to see if he was anywhere to be found. His truck was gone. I ran back upstairs and got the keys to his Lexus because mine was easily spotted because of the color. Nobody had a cranberry-colored one. Black-on-black was everywhere. I decided not to beep him or call him but to just go so he could wonder where I was for a change. Fuck how mad he would be when I got back. It was time to step out.

I backed out of the driveway and turned on the radio to Hot 97. "Be Happy" by Mary J. was playing. I turned it up and headed down the block. I made a slow careful turn and was on my way to the BQE heading to Queens to see Haman. Monty had tints, thank God, so I was reclined back in a cool-like stance, riding with one hand on the wheel the other on my temple, getting my gangster lean on to the side, in deep thought like I seen him do so many times. All this time I thought he was frontin' but this was really comfortable. I opened the glove compartment for some tissue to clean my shades that I had in my purse and saw a joint. I put on my Dior shades and lit the joint and smoked it on my way to Queens. The radio was playing good jams back to back and I started to feel kind of good. I was in a zone while Luther was crooning in the back, "Don't you remember you told me you loved me baby . . ."

"Stop breaking my fucking heart, Monty, stop!" I yelled and banged the steering wheel with my fist. Tears formed in the corners of my eyes. I thought back to Tionne and how long he had been seeing her, the girls on the block taunting me, my father, Ashanti's eyes. So many things were going through my mind. The music was getting me too emotional so I hit CD and let the songs get picked randomly. I turned my radio up loud when

I heard the beat to Zapp's "Computer Love" come on, and Biggie's throaty voice. "Uh, when I met ya I admit my first thought was a trick!" I yelled, and started bopping, trying to lift my mood. This was me and Monty's shit! "Lie together cry together I swear to God I hope we fuckin' die together!" I yelled and started laughing and my high took a turn for the better. I put the song on repeat and decided to ride out to that until I reached Queens. I just wished things could go back to the way they were. But too much damage had been done. I'd never look at him through the same eyes that I did years ago. I looked at my huge diamond engagement ring and wondered what it meant if he was going to cheat on me. Soon the tears made my vision blurry and I was high. Traffic getting on the BQE was bananas. I dabbed my eyes and eased up in my seat to see what the hold up was. Traffic seemed to be flowing. It was the car in front of me that wasn't moving, the car beside me wasn't moving, *and* the car in back of me wasn't moving. I looked around erratically and belligerently ready to curse out the drivers and ask them where the hell they got their licenses from. The passenger of the car in front of me got out, his hat pulled down eerily low. The driver in the car on my left lowered his window. I looked through my rearview mirror and both the driver and the passenger got out and ran to my car. I figured I was too high to understand what happened with these men, it must have been some serious road rage for all of them to be getting out of their cars. I started to roll my window down to ask the guy in the front to please move his car but before I can press the button for the window, gunshots rang out. I screamed loudly. Since I was small I was able to slide over my seat and hide under the backseat. The gunshots kept erupting and glass was shattered everywhere. "Oh my God, somebody help me!" I screamed. I held my hands over my head and screamed.

I heard someone open the car door. The would-be murderer grabbed me by the neck of my shirt so violently my fitted cap fell off, and he put the gun to my head. It was then I realized that this was no road rage. My brown eyes looked up at him and his face told me that he had no idea I was a woman until now. I was stuck when my eyes met Barry's. He pushed the gun up against my forehead tighter, then looked at me. I was lying on the backseat of the car. My lips trembled and my bladder got weak. Tears fell down my cheeks. I didn't want to die this way, not now, not so young, not like this. Flashbacks of Ashanti and Cat came to my mind. This was my karma. I looked him in his eyes. He was contemplating what he should do. He wanted to shoot me, I knew it. I felt it in his tremble. I know, I been there, but I also knew this kind of hesitance could backfire. I just closed my eyes and asked the Lord to forgive me for my sins because here I come. My bladder gave out as he cocked his tool back and then . . . Bom! Bom! Bom!

Cars began screeching, people were screaming, my windshield and driver's side window were shot out. He dropped my chain as he fled. He almost got away with a $2,000 chain. Then there was complete silence except my cries and Biggie's thunderous voice.

"And when I find them they life is to an end, they killed my best friend . . ." he yelled over Zapp's "Computer Love" beat through the car radio.

"Are you okay in there, is anyone in there?" a voice asked. I trembled with fear under the backseat. When the person opened the car door, glass fell everywhere. I heard crowds of people surrounding the car. I was scared to death; my urine-soaked sweats would not lie.

"You a'ight?" a young street boy said, extending his hand to me. I didn't respond. He slid in the backseat and picked me up. "You hit? You good?" he asked, tapping me hard.

"Damn, somebody wanted that nigga dead, that's some ol' godfather shit!" a bystander said, peeking into the car.

"Get out the car, let me check you," the boy said.

"Someone is alive in there?" I heard someone else ask.

"Thank you, Jesus," someone else added.

I got out of the car and it seemed as if a sea of millions was standing around. I heard cop cars and ambulances in the distance. I was right by Fort Greene projects and it seemed as if the entire project was outside today.

"Oh, shit, it's a woman! Miss, you okay?" the boy said to me as I took my cap off.

I backed up from the BQE exit and turned down Park Avenue leaving the cops behind. I was a nervous wreck and didn't want to drive another block. So I parked on a side street on Woodbine and Broadway getting my second wind. Bullet holes were on the driver's side of the car. All of the windows except the back window were broken. I wasn't too far from home so I started the car up again and headed home.

It was dark out when I got home and everyone had migrated to our stoop. Monty was sitting outside in deep conversation with Ski and Jomar, probably trying to figure out where I was. A few other guys were off to the side talking shit and laughing. Some girls were leaning on a car in front of the house. The Puerto Rican family from across the street were forty deep as usual playing dominoes. When I pulled up slowly, Monty, always on point, looked to see who was creeping down his block. When he recognized that it was me, he stood up and ran to the car. He threw his hands in the air.

"Carin! What the fuck happened?"

He walked around his car slowly and his mouth hit the floor. "What . . . the fuck . . . ? Yo!" he said signaling for his boys to come over and look. I got out slowly, leaving the engine running and I ran to his arms. He hugged me tight with his eyes still on his car.

"What the fuck happened? Where did you go? Yo, Ski, turn off the car, park it! What the fuck happened to you?" he said, escorting me to the stoop.

His friends crowded around me as I sat on the stoop and sobbed heavily. I didn't care about my urine-stained pants. They waited patiently for me to speak. I told him every detail from me getting dressed to go to Queens to "see Missy" to getting stopped as I was about to get on the BQE. The stoop was quiet. Monty picked me up and brought me upstairs, leaving his friends behind. When one of them tried to come up he barked orders. "Don't *nobody* come around me and my wife right now, *no fucking body*, get off of my stoop, get the fuck outta here!" he yelled as Ski came in the house behind us.

Monty carried me to the bathroom as I was cradled in his arms, he sat on the edge of the tub, set the bath and began stripping me like an infant. I couldn't stop crying and shaking. Monty was pissed. The veins in his neck and forehead pulsating never lied. He didn't speak a word and he was barely breathing. He concentrated on getting the water just right and held me in his arms until the tub was full. He placed me in the tub gently as my body heaved up and down. He washed the cuts I received from the broken glass and cleaned glass particles out of my hair and ears. He didn't say a word, he didn't ask me anything, he just breathed heavier the harder I cried.

21

Monty

Barry was a dead man whenever I caught his ass. I was so mad I couldn't even think straight. Day and night for the past three days, me, Rick, and two of his cousins rode around trying to find Barry or anybody close to him. It seemed as if everyone had disappeared and rightfully so. They knew that once I started I didn't stop. It didn't matter what time of the day it was, we were riding around, sending messages to passersby letting them know that Barry had a price on his head. I even went to his barbershop and told the barber to let Barry know when I see him he was a dead man so he better kill me first if he caught me. Rick and his cousins were with me in the living room trying to figure out how we were going to catch up with these niggas while Carin lay in the bedroom still shaken up. She hadn't opened her mouth to talk in four days. She barely ate anything and I had to force her to go wash her ass. She wasn't taking any calls and she wasn't having any visits. I tried to get Sharon to talk to her but she wouldn't even converse with her. She was numb. I saw death in her eyes. I had to do something. I knew Carin wanted to leave me and at this point I wanted her to leave me too. Things had gotten way out of control and it would never be the same again. I hurt her too many times, I put her in harm's way, I disrespected her, I caused her pain. But no one would understand how much I really and truly loved Carin. She meant the world to me. She meant so much to me that I tried to scare her into being with me. My insecurities made me treat her that way. When I knew things had gone too far I began to make her too afraid to leave. It was my only option. I couldn't live without her. I needed her more than she could ever know. It was no fault of hers the way I treated her but it was too late to try to explain that to her. She'd never believe me. She'd never understand how much I loved her and how much I wished I could erase all the damage I had done to her. The last thing I would do is make things right between us then set her free. For what it was worth, I wanted her to leave this relationship feeling loved, if that was possible. I didn't want her to run away from us but walk with her head up high. I wanted her to leave me the same way she came, pure. I would tell anybody who would listen that I loved Carin with all of my heart and soul. But no one believed me anymore.

"You know where he lives, right?" Rick asked.

"Yeah, man, but ain't no telling who he got with him. He stay with a bunch of li'l niggas in his crib. Right now Barry ain't around. He low with his right now. He fucked up."

"What about his sister?" Rick's cousin asked.

"I'ma ring that bitch neck when I catch her. I can't believe this shit happened."

"How's my girl doing?" Rick asked of Carin.

"She ain't talk to nobody in days, B. She won't eat, she just sits up in that bed all day just staring at the walls, her face expressionless," I said somberly.

"Let me try and talk to her." Rick stood up.

"Son, I'm telling you she won't even talk to Sharon and that's her girl! She's not budging."

Rick asked my permission to enter my bedroom. I told him to go 'head but it was of no use. I went in the kitchen to pour myself some water while he attempted to get Carin to talk.

Carin

I was numb. I couldn't believe I had come that close to death. So many times when Monty would beat me I thought that was death. But, no, I was wrong. The minute that I was able to get my mind right I was getting the hell out of here. Right now I couldn't move. I could only cry and pray for God to open up my soul and pour His love down inside of me. I prayed for Him to put me in that position one more time to be free, and I promised Him that I would not look back and if I ever did that I would not ask Him for his guidance ever again.

"Hey, Carin," Rick said softly, appearing in the doorway with a smile. He had a glass of water in his hand. "May I come in?"

Unable to talk I said nothing, I just stared at him. My eyes softened and he made his way into my bedroom. He pulled up a chair and sat in front of me. "Here." He offered me the water. I took it and guzzled it thirstily. My throat was burning because I had barely drunk anything in days.

"It's been a while."

"You want some more?" he asked me.

"No."

"I'm just coming in here to check on you. You know I got love for you, Carin, and you been through hell, baby.

You not talking, eating, what's up, you trying to kill yourself slowly?" he whispered.

"No, your boy is," I said somberly.

"I wish I could take the pain away, C. I know the shit he does to you ain't right, and I feel dumb saying this, but that man loves you."

I cringed at him. "Well, I'd hate to know how he treats me if he stopped loving me."

"We are going to do everything we can to find Barry and settle this shit. Carin, just know that they weren't looking for you. Nobody is out to kill you so don't fear for your life in that way."

"I have feared for my life every day for the past five years, every time that man beats me I fear that one blow is going to kill me, Rick." I began to cry.

"Shhh." He pulled my head to his chest. "It's going to be okay. I'm going to make sure nobody harms you anymore, Carin. Come on, ma, get up out this bed. I miss seeing you smile. Come on." He pulled the covers off of me. I was dressed in Monty's boxers and a wife beater, my hair unkempt, circles around my eyes, my body a dull canvas of black-and-blues that never healed correctly, scars and stitches. My bones ached and my head hurt.

"You need a nice vacation or something. Why don't you and one of your friends go away real quick so you can clear your mind?" he suggested.

"If I go on vacation I'm never coming back."

"Good, don't. Get away from this shit. Get away from Monty and all of this bullshit. Come on, get out of the bed."

Rick helped me out of the bed and on to my feet. My legs hurt from being in the bed for three days only getting up to pee. Slowly we walked into the living room where Monty was conversing with two strange guys who stood up and took their hats off upon my entrance. I said nothing as I headed straight to the shower where I stayed for about a half-hour, lathering my body in fine moisturizers. I tweezed my eyebrows and washed my hair. Monty came into the bathroom with a pair of leggings and a T-shirt for me.

"Glad to see you up, baby. How you feeling?"

"I'm a'ight," I said with salt.

"So what Rick say to you to get you out of bed?"

"Nothing that no one else said. Maybe it was his timing," I lied. Rick and I had always been close but Monty would beat me from here to El Segundo if he knew that. He had my back and checked on me all the time. He knew Monty wasn't shit and he wasn't phony about it, either. Though he never snitched on his boy he treated me in a fashion that let me know he was on my side. I respected him for that.

"You hungry? You want some Spanish food?"

"No."

Monty reached out and pulled me to him and hugged me tight. "I'm so sorry, baby. For every and anything, I'm sorry." He held me tight for a while until I pushed him off.

"I can't breathe." I began putting my clothes on. I walked out of the bathroom feeling refreshed a little bit.

"Better, much better, ma!" Rick said as soon as I came out of the bathroom. I plopped on the couch next to him and looked around. "So, what's next, what are we going to do about this situation?"

"We on the job, ma. Why don't we all go out and get some food and drinks, how about that?"

"She still won't eat, I tried to treat her to Spanish food just now," Monty said.

"Let's go to City Island!" I said to Rick.

"Who's driving all the way out there?" Monty chuckled.

"I can go for some City Island," Rick's cousins cosigned.

"Whatever the lady wants. City Island it is," Rick said. Monty gave him a snarl.

"Okay, let me go get pretty." I disappeared into my bedroom and began humming a song as I looked in my closet. Monty came in behind me and closed the door. He sat on the bed and watched me as I pulled out a pair of black skinny pants that hugged every curve, a Bebe tank top and peep-toe shoes. I laid out a jewelry set and began undressing.

"So Rick runs shit now?" he asked. I ignored him and kept getting dressed.

"You wanna fuck Rick now?" he ignorantly asked. I continued getting dressed. Once I was fully dressed I stepped into my heels and instantly felt sexy. I tried to walk out and Monty grabbed my arm.

"What now, what?" I asked annoyed. "You can't stand for anybody to show me love, can you? I gotta be fucking somebody because they are nice to me? Get the fuck off of my arm, Monty, I'm sick of your ass already, shit." And with that I stepped into the living room and told the fellas, "Let's go." One by one they filed out, complimenting my outfit as they passed me to go downstairs.

Panama

It felt good to step out of Green Correctional Facility after so long. As soon as I hit Port Authority, I called my man Tuan to tell him to make sure he had a bag of some thing to puff and some pussy in the car. For the last six months of my bid he kept telling me about some dude from around the way that he wanted to get. I had been hearing about this nigga named Money Monty through half of my bid and here it was, my man wanted us to stick him up. Everybody kept telling me I'd know him if I saw him but I doubted it. Rumor had it he had a price on my head for Cat's murder. *We'll see.*

I still had on my prison pants and Tuan was already talking about committing another crime. "Damn, nigga, can I get home, get some ass, take a shower, eat a meal first? You ready to send me back up the creek and shit."

"You want pussy? Nigga, you better focus on getting this paper! You can't get pussy without paper. Bitches ain't tryin'a hear that shit," Tuan said.

"You ain't change a bit," I said as he hopped into the hooptie and began driving.

I took a deep breath thinking that I just came home and already I was on some bullshit. I was wishing that my man G.O. was home but he got violated at the board and had to serve another year.

"What it do, son, you tryin'a take this nigga money or what?"

"Yeah, I'm in it, I'm in it, when?" I said, thinking of Carin.

She would be perfect for this kind of job. I had plans to find her and see how she was doing and if she was doing bad I had a job for her. I had written her several times once I knew she had come home but she never responded. I couldn't blame her. Carin had a lot going for her and it was only right she cut all ties and move on with her life.

Carin

We had a ball at City Island last night. Everybody had gotten piss drunk and we laughed all night. I didn't say but two words to Monty but kept my conversation general. I spoke to everyone. The only quiet time we had was in the car when he held my hand and played slow jams, obviously trying to set some kind of mood. I in turn popped in a mix tape and decided I wanted to hear rap music. I wasn't in no lovey-dovey mood.

Monty woke me up to tell me to lock the door, that he was going to Ralphies to buy some sneakers. He asked me if I wanted a pair. I shrugged. He sucked his teeth and said he'd be back. Right after Monty left I began separating the laundry so that I could get all of my clothes washed and put up. I was leaving his black ass once and for all and was not coming back. I loaded bags of clothes in his Range Rover and decided for safety reasons I needed to put a burner in the truck. You never knew what kind of jam you'd find yourself in these days. I was done dropping off bags and as soon as I got upstairs, the door bell rang hungrily. Frustrated, I looked out the window and didn't see anybody. I didn't even see any strange cars on the block so I figured it was somebody who lived in the building. I ran downstairs and was greeted by Tuan and another guy. They smiled at me and stared for a second or two. I froze. I knew that something was about to happen but I didn't know what. My mind was telling me to run up the stairs as fast as I could but I couldn't move.

"Can I help you?" I asked with attitude. It was about to go down and I was alone. I was scared but couldn't show any fear. I just wanted to make it out of this situation alive. I didn't even have time to react as Tuan put me in a choke hold and dragged me upstairs. They closed the door and waited for me to show them the money. I took a deep breath and thought about what I was going to do next. I had never been on this end of the stick. I started thinking about things that I could do to get popped. I thought about all the victims I had the drop on and the dumb suspicious things they would do to get me tight and get them gun butted or slapped with iron. I try to avoid doing anything dumb at all costs.

Tuan kept looking at me lustfully. I hope they didn't plan on raping me, too. I could see the envy in their eyes as they looked around the apartment. "He got a beeper or a phone? Call him and tell him you need him to come home," Tuan said angrily. He tossed the expensive phone at me and I paged Monty using code 100 which meant "heat." He only kept a beeper after all of this time just for this kind of situation. I paged him so he knew what it was but Tuan and his friend thought that I was calling him.

"He's not picking up," I said.

"Keep calling him!" Tuan demanded. I dialed his pager for the fifth time and left our code, praying that he'd call back.

"I thought you guys were friends," I said squarely.

"Friends?" they both said in unison and laughed.

"Well, I know I've seen *you* in my house before," I said to Tuan.

"Shut the fuck up," he demanded. I shook in an exaggerated motion as if he scared me. He looked apologetic.

"Just as long as he ups the dough and doesn't act like a cowboy, nobody gets hurt," The other guy whose name I learned to be Jeekie said. Tuan kept his eyes on me.

"You a fine bitch, you know that?"

I stared at him.

"I see why Monty keeps you in the house." He licked his lips. "When this is all over maybe I can toss a few dollars at you and you'll come flockin' my way."

Monty called back before I could say something smart.

Monty

My hip was buzzing mad. I knew it was Carin rushing me, but I saw my man on the way to the sneaker store and kicked it with him for about forty-five minutes. But she kept beeping me so I looked. I saw code 100 and got nervous. I stopped dead in my tracks and dropped the sneakers on the floor and just stared at my pager. I only kept a pager so that she could beep me in case of an emergency and no one would know. She was the only person who had the number, it was for her. I felt that I owed Carin my life as much hell as I put her through and I would never put my hands on her again. I know she didn't believe me but I meant it this time. I was going to get help. My mother was looking for a good therapist for me.

I didn't want to be like this anymore. She kept beeping me, 100-911, 100-911. Carin wouldn't play like that. She knew the seriousness of using 911 or even 100. I dialed hard and quick. Carin picked up, sounding normal.

"C, whaddup." I didn't know the situation, if someone was listening or not.

My heart was beating fast as she spoke slow and deliberately. I had to pay attention.

"What is taking you so long?" she said sweetly.

"I'll be there in a minute. You good?"

"*No*"

"What's up, talk to me, Carin, what are you talking about? You lost me now," I snapped. I had to think and ask her the right questions. I got quiet.

"What's up, baby?" I asked her again.

"I don't know, just don't get that *green jersey* that I saw in the store the other day. Throwbacks are played out."

"Green jersey? What green jersey?"

She was silent.

"Okay, listen, Carin, how many people are in the house with you?" I asked. "Two should be fine. I can save some for later, baby, hurry up."

"In my room?"

"Yes."

"They got guns, Carin, how many?"

"Yeah, get me two biscuits and a medium Coke, oh, and a large so I can freeze it."

"So that's two guns, one big one and one medium one. Carin, nobody is around and I don't have no heat on me," I yelled angrily. I was sick to my stomach. I started banging the phone against the wall. "Fuck fuck fuck!"

"Yes, you do," she said.

"Just give them the money. You know my combination, give it to them I don't want them to hurt you baby, shit!" I punched the phone some more. Shit shit shit!

"Yes, you do, it's in the car. I started packing because I was bored when you left and I put them all in there. But let me go now, baby, I'll see you in a few."

"What's in the trunk? What, Carin?"

She was quiet.

"Is something in the trunk?"

"Yeah."

"Which car, the Range?"

"Yeah, and bring my CDs upstairs, too." Then the phone went dead. I didn't know what to do. All I knew was that my girl and my money were in that house and I needed them both, one more than the other.

Carin

Tuan grabbed the phone from me and slammed it down.

"Is he coming?"

"Yes, he's on his way," I said, sitting on the bed, hoping Monty understood what I was saying to him. I saw that the two goons were getting restless and I hoped that they didn't start doing anything stupid like Panama used to do. The longer he had to wait to get what he came for, the more ignorant he'd act, pistol whipping folk, smacking them around, torturing them. That was the part I hated the most. I just wanted the money and then to be gone. I was waiting to hear Monty run up the steps. He was taking too long and I was really getting scared. These cats were looking thirsty.

"What did he say, how long?" Jeekie asked.

"He said ten minutes, he is on his way."

"Yo, bag up some jewelry, some guns, or *something*. Take that ring off, ma." Tuan waved his gun recklessly. I stalled because I didn't want to be near the door when Monty came in. Jeekie was unarmed. I had a trick for him. Finally, I could hear Monty running up the steps.

Panama

After Tuan and Jeekie went inside the building, I waited five minutes then came inside. I ran up the steps and waited in the dark on the stairs with my ski mask on. Monty wasn't home so they wanted me to be in the dark in his hallway waiting for him. I was thinking about how after we got the hundred stacks, I was going to put the drop on Tuan and Jeekie and take it all. I was hungry. My thoughts got interrupted at the sounds of keys. I backed up into the shadows of the stairwell as Monty came running up the steps, singing. Long icy chain swinging, diamond earrings, this nigga had to get got. Soon as he put the key in his apartment door I rolled up behind him. I took the gun out of his hand and put the burner to the back of his neck. "You know what this is."

Monty

This was not part of the plan. I thought everybody was inside. I wondered what they did to Carin. The first thing I could see when I entered the house was that Carin was nowhere to be found. I had my hands up in a surrendering fashion and yelled her name.

"Carin, where you at, baby?"

"In here, Monty!" she yelled out. I didn't detect any fear in her voice. I know she was scared, because, shit, I was.

"You know what this is, the safe, the guns, the dough or your wife is broccoli," Tuan said with the gun to Carin's head.

The site of that shit made me sick to my stomach.

"Just let her go. You ain't gotta do this. You my man," I said.

"Nah, I ain't ya man. The *safe*, the *dough*! Get the dough!" Tuan said, cocking his weapon back.

Carin

Monty was not acting now. I could see the fear in his eyes. He was looking at me, I was looking past him to let him know the other guy was in the other room. But it didn't matter because this guy with the ski mask on came from out of nowhere. Tuan choked me hard and pushed me on to the bed then pointed the gun at Monty. "Go get the cash!"

"Monty, do what they say," I said, knowing what a hard-head Monty could be.

"You stupid motherfucka you think you gon' live after this?" Monty raised up.

Baby, no! Now is not the time for you to be super thug. Please just give them the money.

Tuan walked up to Monty and hit him in the nose with the gun. Monty hit the floor.

"I'm not fucking playing. Go get the cash now!" he yelled. I was scared now. Monty got up holding his nose. He looked at me.

"Yo, hold the bitch down and let me take care of this," Tuan yelled out to his two goons then followed Monty to the back of the house. We eyed one another. He turned his head away.

"Why are you guys doing this?" I asked. Jeekie said nothing. He put his head down. The dude with the ski mask stepped up to me and looked at me.

"You're a fucking coward, take the fucking mask off!" I snarled. He just stood there looking at me.

"Have a seat, shorty," he said calmly.

"I ain't having shit, fuck you, take your mask off!" I said again. I remembered how brazen Panama was. He'd just run up on people, no mask no nothing. He didn't care and in some strange way I admired him for that. But this coward right here? He had on all black with his mask hiding everything.

"I don't want you to get hurt, sit down."

Jeekie walked up to me and slapped me. "Sit the fuck down, bitch."

Ski mask turned around and pushed him. "Don't fuckin hit no girls, you crazy?"

"Fuck you, this bitch is outta pocket!"

While they bickered, I took that quick second to reach back and retrieve my weapon from the side of the bed.

"Why are you guys doing this?" I asked again, this time gun pointing. Ski mask backed up and Jeekie stood frozen.

"Yeah, now this is what you're going to do. You're going to walk slowly to the back of the house with your boy and if you try anything *you're* going to be broccoli, got it?"

"Yeah," they both said and walked to the back where Monty was emptying out the $150,000 he had just withdrawn from his account. Tuan was holding a plastic bag open with one hand and pointing his gun with the other as Monty emptied jewelry and all into the bag. He was hurt and mad, I could tell. His pride was shot, he was getting robbed in front of me. He stood up and looked at Tuan.

"This is good, let's go." Tuan said and turned to leave.

He met the barrel of my gun instead.

"Oh you got you a real live bitch, huh? Go 'head, shoot me, bitch." He laughed.

I cocked it back. Tuan smirked at me.

"Drop the bag." I popped him in his gun hand. He dropped his gun and yelled out to Jeekie who was standing there, frozen. I turned around and put the drop on Ski mask and Monty snatched up Tuan's piece and aimed it at Jeekie.

"Now, this is some shit. This is a real bad predicament. What are we going to do now?" Monty asked sarcastically. Jeekie swiftly pulled a gun from the small of his back, aimed at me to shoot. Before he could squeeze, Ski mask popped him. I ducked and screamed.

Monty ducked and scooped me up, pushing me behind him. Jeekie hit the floor and Tuan tried to rush past Monty and me like a football player. We tackled him to the ground and Monty put the gun in his mouth. I put mine to Ski mask's nuts wondering why he shot his man for me as if that was going to save him. Jeekie lay on the floor, squirming.

"You, take your fucking mask off," I said, both guns pointing at him now. It got quiet.

"Panama, pop this bitch!" Tuan yelled like an animal.

Panama

I couldn't believe it. I couldn't let Carin know that it was me under this mask. But it was too late. I knew that Carin would pop me if she had to, so I had no choice but to peel my mask off. Her eyes held shock, disbelief, pain but she kept her feet in the ground, kept her hand tight on that trigger I noticed. She didn't budge as she stared at me with her mouth wide open.

Carin

I couldn't even bring myself to say anything. I was scared to death. I shook off the nostalgia. This was an unfortunate situation, but it was me, him, or Monty.

Monty

I kept my eye on Tuan who was on the floor trembling, his man was curled up in a ball holding his stomach, bleeding. I didn't care if he died or not, fuck 'em. What was more confusing was that Panama was in my house. I began to wonder if Carin had set me up for how I treated her all of this time. I wanted to aim my gun at her but I couldn't.

"You killed Cat right?" I aimed my gun at Panama.

Someone knocked at the door. It was Ski.

"You heard them shots?" Ski said, coming in. I backed up with my gun.

Tuan made a sudden move. Panama looked at me then Carin. Carin had the drop on Panama still. All I could pray for now is that she not get soft and begin to feel all nostalgic. There was no nostalgia to this shit. Then again, was this a setup? It was me against everybody in this room right now. I didn't trust anybody. One soft move and she was going to get us killed. Carin looked at me, I looked at her. I knew that she knew what I was thinking. I was trying to read her eyes. They held no malice, no pain, no "fuck you." She was focused. She was trying to tell me to stay on point with her eyes. She held her pistol tight. But Carin was a pro at this kind of thing. I didn't know what to think.

"Carin, you with me, baby." I pointed my gun at her. Her eyes widened. "What are you doing?"

"You set me up, bitch?"

She shook her head as slowly as possible.

"You know this nigga Panama, don't you, don't you?"

"Monty, you know what this is. Don't do this. I haven't seen Panama since the nineties. I didn't even know that he was home," she said through clenched teeth.

"I can't trust you, Carin. I don't know why you're here." I cocked back my weapon.

"Son, what are you doing?" Ski asked.

"This bitch killed Cat."

"What?"

"Yeah, her and this nigga here."

Ski looked confused.

"I'll explain later. Carin, drop your fucking piece now. Drop that shit or I'ma pop you. I don't want to but I will."

She hesitated. "Monty, I don't know what is going on. But don't make me drop this piece. I can't."

Everybody in the house seemed to have a tool on them pointing it at somebody at this point.

"I'ma count to three and I'ma pop you if you don't drop it. One . . . two . . ."

POP!

Carin

Panama shot Monty in the shoulder and Monty in turn let off six shots that dropped Panama to the ground. Tuan lay on the floor aiming the gun. Ski kicked the gun out of Tuan's hand. Jeekie was left unattended because he was "hurt" and with that he ran up on me and pumped one in my stomach close range then tried to run.

I felt the burning in my side. I closed my eyes and played dead. I had no idea what was going on but I wasn't dying, not today. I could hear Monty screaming, I could hear shots around me, I didn't know what I'd find when I opened my eyes. But I felt Monty covering me, crying, praying in my ears and it was keeping me alive.

He was praying for me not to die, he was saying sorry for everything, he was promising me the world, the stars, the sun if I just lived another day. Then I felt his arms release me and he laid me down. I heard him say a few words, I heard shots, I heard Ski on the phone calling 911. Monty thought I was dead. But I was just tired from it all, tired from running, thinking, hurting, crying, and needing. I just wanted to lie down peacefully. My head dropped to the side and my eyes lowered in pain. But before they did they focused on Panama who was on the floor, no doubt dead. I shut my eyes tight to stop the tears from flowing. I began to sob. I was hurting for him, hurting for me.

Monty

"It's okay. Help is on the way."

"I'm dying, Monty, I'm dying," she whispered.

"No, you're not, baby. Just hold on."

"Panama is dead?"

"Don't worry about him, baby, you just hold on." She was bleeding profusely. I pressed a pile of T-shirts down on her wound as I bled from the shoulder. "Help is coming, baby."

"I hate you. Why couldn't you be dead. Why Panama? Why me? Why don't you die," she whispered, then fell into unconsciousness.

Carin

I remembered being on the gurney and Monty towering over me with tears in his eyes trying to look so brave. Tuan and Jeekie were also on gurneys but handcuffed to the rails. As clear as day I could see them place a sheet over Panama's handsome face. Through the tiny slits in my eyes, tears fell long and hard for my friend. It seemed as if the entire world was outside of our house as the paramedics rolled me outside. Cops were everywhere and Pamela was demanding answers. The kids were screaming and Ski was being led out in cuffs.

I slept most of the night in the hospital but when I woke up, Monty was there prepping me so that I could talk to the detectives. It was already laid out. Ski had no priors so he would take the rap. Monty had the money so he'd pay for the lawyers and keep money on his books. All I knew was that three armed men came into our home and we did what we had to do to spare our lives. My father showed up to the hospital with flowers and a tear-stained face with Tyra, Missy, Jetta, and Farrod bringing up the rear.

"Princess, how you doing, baby, you okay, baby?" he cooed at me. I shook my head slowly. I was in pain from being shot in the stomach. The bullet in my stomach passed through not damaging me, but it hurt like hell.

"What are the doctors saying, honey?" he asked. When Monty tried to answer my father went off. He slammed Monty's body up against the wall and delivered two body blows. Farrod and a nurse pulled my father off of him.

"I should have killed you when I had the fucking chance." My father's voice boomed through the small hospital room. Monty said nothing. He just wiped his face with a rag he had in his hand. My father fluffed my pillows and sat me up.

"I brought you some food," Jetta said, pulling a small table up to my bed and laying out the food on a paper plate.

"Thank you." I smiled faintly.

"I got it from here, son, you can excuse yourself," My father said to Monty.

"I just want to make sure she's all right."

"What part of get the fuck out don't you understand? It's over between you and Carin, there ain't shit else for you to do here. Get the fuck out of here!" My father yelled in Monty's face. "You know something, I should pump two in your fucking ass and see how you like it, bitch."

"I didn't want this to happen," was all Monty could say.

"You're a fucking disgrace of a man. Get out of my fucking sight and don't ever let me catch you

around my daughter again ever in this lifetime.
You two are through! I don't want to hear shit
about love and what had happened or none of
that shit!"

I wished I could intervene and say something,
but what more was there to say? My father was
right and I was happy that it was finally over.
As much pain as I was in, I was happy as I ate
my pasta slowly, not even looking Monty's way.
Monty and I had been together six long years,
through blood, sweat, and tears, literally. I had
no more to give. I was tired. It was over.

22

Carin

Three Months Later . . .

It occurred to me today that I was an angel sent from God. He used me as an example of perseverance, strength, and wisdom and for that I could not be mad at anything that I had gone through. All I knew was that I was free and today was one of those days I slept a little longer, lounged around, and collected myself. I didn't have to do anything that I didn't want to. My mind crossed Haman and I thought about how he and I had really been getting along, and for the first time in a long time, I was really getting on with my life for real. Haman came to New Jersey at least four days a week to check on me and bring me things. He was an angel. He read me scriptures out of the Bible and brought stacks of DVDs to my house. Jetta and Missy were there all the time, too, especially Jetta since she lived across the hall. I was recovering nicely and just happy to be alive. Ski caught a 3-9 for manslaughter, and last I heard, Monty was living in Red Lion, PA, in his town home, and had a girlfriend already. I could only pray for her. He was going to beat that girl silly for not being me.

I still couldn't grasp the lingo of the good book, but God knew my heart, I prayed to Him through good and bad, I believed in Him and for that reason alone He protected me. How else could I have made it through the things that I have endured and still have my sanity intact? My mind ran across Panama. *Damn.* I couldn't even go to the funeral but I did watch the procession from afar as I sat in my car with dark shades on. I still hurt every day behind that whole Panama situation. May he rest in peace.

PART THREE

Seasoned

Carin

My black wrap dress fit me nicely as it hugged my ever-spreading hips and thick thighs. I sat with my legs crossed feeling sexy with my hair in a sexy, jet black cut. My eyebrows were arched to perfection and I had an arch in my back. My face was done up in Chanel and my man sat across from me, handsome, calm, and secure in his skin. I picked up the menu and finally decided on the roasted duck, potatoes, and wild rice. Haman ordered lamb. We dined at the Red Eye on Sixtieth and Lexington this evening as Stevie Wonder made a guest appearance, playing the piano. The waitress took our orders and placed a bottle of Dom Perignon on the table.

I had never told Haman I loved him, this entire year and a half that we officially dated. It seemed as if we didn't have to exchange those words. He had to know I loved him for all that he'd done for me. And I had to know that he loved me for sticking around through the hell I had gone through. He was my angel and I was never letting him go.

"What are you thinking about, Carin?" he asked me knowingly. My eyes turned to dew as I stared at him.

"I love you, baby, that's all."

He squeezed my hand gently from across the table and sighed as if he had been waiting to hear that.

"We make beautiful music together."

"Yes, we do." I smiled.

He was so gentle with me, the way he held my hand, the way he kissed me, looked at me, wanted me, needed me.

"I don't see how a man could ever put his hands on you in any other way other than to caress your body and love you. I mean, the things you have endured over the years and the fact that you are still so beautiful and you just grew from your experiences and didn't let it fuck up what you stand for, I had to love you. You are a strong woman, just the kind of woman that *any* man needs."

"Thank you for being there for me even when you didn't have to be, Haman. You put up with a lot of my nonsense. You must have thought I was such a fool for going through all of that hell with Monty."

"No . . . well, yeah, but that's all water under the bridge now. I won't judge you. I just want to love you and make it all go away."

"You have, baby, trust me. I don't know what I'd do without you."

"You will never know, because I'm never leaving you, baby. We made it through the worst part. Now let's just enjoy life. Here's to us," he said, pouring both of us drinks. I raised my glass.

"To life, love, respect, and God." I smiled.

"Amen to that." He smiled. We sipped and kissed. This was love.

My days with Haman were filled with bliss and love. He helped me find my own place once my father finally trusted me enough to let me go and saw that Haman had my back. He cooked for me at night, he took me to work and picked me up. He sent me flowers just because, he held me while watching movies, stroked my hair while sitting on park benches. We went to museums and art shows, we watched the Discovery Channel and comedies together and on Saturday mornings, providing the weather was nice, we'd ride out to Prospect Park and go jogging, then lie out on the grass and take a nap. Haman had freed my mind, body, and soul and I could never let him know that though I loved him, I feared him. I didn't trust that he would remain this way forever. I was waiting for the real him to show up.

All I needed to hear were harps playing this morning as the sun shone on my face while Haman delicately and succulently devoured every inch of my body under the morning sun. We were in my canopy bed as he flipped me around and kissed me all over, stretching my limbs as he made love to my every crevice. I could only smile at the joy he brought me whenever he was around. *I can live with this forever,* I thought as he slid his tongue into my mouth and sucked all around my face like a lap dog. He wouldn't let me join in, he just took over. "Let me love you." He moaned as he entered me from the side. I held on to the pillows and bit my bottom lip tenderly as he stroked me to his own rhythm, like he had a song playing in his mind.

"I wanna get on top." I moaned.

Haman wasted no time pulling me on top of him as I lay flat, grinding my body on him slowly, surely.

"I love you," he said, kissing my face.

"I know," was all I could say. Haman switched positions with me once more, this time him on top, placing my legs on his shoulders. He started stroking me gently, placing his fingers in my mouth as I sucked hungrily. I caught a glimpse of us in the mirror. My body looking beautiful, unbruised, golden brown, and creamy as it should. The sun was shining, I was nearing orgasm, and I was in love.

We lay there in our nakedness for a while when my phone began to ring. I saw that it was my father so I answered breathlessly.

"Yes, Daddy."

"Don't 'yes, Daddy' me. You got plans for today?"

"No, why?"

"Why don't you and Haman come over. Tyra is cooking and we can play some cards or something."

I put the phone down. "You want to go to my father's later for dinner and cards?"

"Yeah, sure, baby, it's whatever."

"Okay, Daddy, see you around six."

"Good, later princess." He hung up. I rolled over and helped myself to another serving of loving.

"Haman, you are such a cheater!" I yelled out and pushed the cards off the table. My father was cracking up and high fiving Haman. Tyra shook her head and put her cards on the table.

"You see this shit? Do you see this? Damn women always have to accuse somebody of cheating just because they're losing. Spades is a man's game, little girl," My father said.

"Daddy, please, I am the Spades Queen! I got kicked out of school for playing spades so much!"

"Oh, please, tell me about her childhood!" Haman laughed. I looked at my father and we both burst out laughing.

"Trust me, you don't want to know," I said.

"Besides, I wasn't around for her childhood. Carin and I got acquainted and she came to live with me when she was eighteen," my father said somberly.

I touched my father's leg. "But, Daddy, you were there when I needed you most, and you been here ever since." I winked. He smiled.

"But from what I was told from her mother! *Sheeeeeeeet* this girl was a hot mess just running around into all kinds of shit."

I shook off the thoughts of my past. Ashanti tried to creep back into my head. I closed my eyes tight and began shaking without realizing it. "You okay, baby?" Haman asked.

I popped my eyes open to see my father, Tyra, and Haman staring at me.

"Yeah, my chest just burns a little bit. Let me get some water. Yawl want anything out the kitchen?" I said, getting up.

"I'm good," Daddy said.

"Bring me some ice, baby!" Tyra shouted out. I opened the freezer door as my hip vibrated. I didn't recognize the 717 area code. "Hello."

"Hey, Carin?"

"Yeah this is she," I said, balancing my phone and the ice tray. I was on my way into the living room when I heard his name.

"It's Monty, how have you been?"

I backed up into the kitchen.

"Hey, what's up?" *What do you want, Monty, Lord, boy just let me live!*

"Everything is cool, how you?"

"I'm fine."

"You sound a little busy right now, is this a bad time?"

"Yeah. I'm at my father's house and I have company."

"Is your man there or something?"

"Yes."

"Okay, well, this is my number. It's been a while since I've talked to you, you know I had something I wanted to say to you but it has to be in person. I'll be in town for about four days. I'll be staying at the Marriot in the city. If you can find the time to get away for us to just do lunch so I can talk to you, that'll be cool, you know?"

"I don't know, Monty. I mean it's been a long time and I think we need to just let sleeping dogs lie."

"Carin, I'm not trying to push up on you or get you back, I swear. I just want to tell you something that I never got the chance to tell you. No pressure from me, baby, you got my word on that."

I held the phone to my ear as Haman and Tyra walked in talking and laughing. I perked up and began to end my call.

"Okay, so I'll give you a call later to let you know what's up!"

"All right then, later." He hung up easily.

Monty

I wanted Carin back bad. I bit my bottom lip and shook as I thought about another man entering Carin and pleasing her the way only I had for so many years. This man was getting the better part of Carin. She was grown now, seasoned, and free of any drama. I wanted that Carin. I had the young Carin, the ride or die faithful Carin. Now I wanted the woman Carin, and I was willing to do whatever it took to get her back. I couldn't force it or she'd run, so I figured I'd take my time, gain her trust, and make her feel comfortable. Then I'd push up.

Carin

I didn't know why I was here. I guess, curios-
ity got the best of me. Besides, he couldn't stop
telling me how urgent it was for him to see me.
It had been two years since I'd seen him or even
heard his voice. I spoke to Sharon and Pamela
once in a while but other that I had no dealings
with anybody attached to Monty. I should have
hated him for the hell he put me through but I
didn't. I guess I spent so much time in pain and
hating him when we were together that I felt no
need to still hold malice in my heart now that it
was over. I was happy in my life and could only
pray he found the same because he obviously
had demons. I prayed on it, I slept on it, and
I let it go a long time ago. Ironically enough, I
knew that the way Monty treated me was not
a reflection of the kind of woman that I was. I
was young, influential, and caught up but those
days were over. I wanted to see what he wanted.
I was secure in my relationship and I knew that
I didn't have any intimate feelings for Monty
anymore. I rode out to the city blasting my Tupac
CD. I put "So Many Tears" on repeat as I maneu-
vered in traffic on Broadway, finally pulling up to
the valet at the Marriott. I checked my appearance in the mirrored elevators as I rode up to the

twenty-third floor. The hallways were quiet as I tried to find his room. 2309 was safely nestled in a corner, in the cut.

Monty came to the door visibly intoxicated, his eyes red, his smile wide and his cologne slapping me all over the damn hallway. He extended his large, diamond bracelet–clad wrist toward me and gently pulled me inside. He was so big. He had ballooned to 221 pounds! He had always maintained the weight of 185. He closed the door and hugged me tight. At first I resisted. I didn't want the hug to feel this good. But it did and I soon found myself hugging him tight, rocking from side to side. There was no doubt that Monty felt like home. After a long moment, he kissed the top of my head and let me go.

"Sup, C?" he joked and tapped my arm.

"Sup, son!" I said and tapped his jaw playfully with my fist. I wanted to keep this visit as platonic as possible.

"Henny?" he offered. Not one to ever turn down a drink, I obliged, "Yeah, I'll do Henny. I'm hungry as hell, Monty, can we order some food?"

"I knew you would be hungry so I went out to Victors up the block and got some creamy fettuccine shrimp with wine sauce, your favorite."

"Garlic bread?" I smiled.

"No doubt." He relieved me of my jacket.

"That's what's up. So what is up with you staying up in the hotel in this big-ass room? You think you jigga or somebody?"

"Baby, you know how I do. I'm the muh-fuckin' president."

"So I met this next chick though. She seems a'ight, her name is Lindsey, and she's a phle-botomist. The only thing about honey is that she knows *way too many niggas*. I can't keep my eye on all of them, you know? I don't know who knows me and all that shit. Any given moment some nigga ringing her bell or some shit. So I kind of fell back from honey. I'm thinking of coming back to New York."

I shook my head vigorously because I had food in my mouth.

"No, *hell no*. Stay your ass right back in P.A. All because nobody is talking doesn't mean that they are sleeping, Monty. You should know better than that."

"C, if niggas wanna get me they gon' get me. But I can't hide forever. P.A. is not for me. Besides, that shit is turning into New York. It's niggas from up top all up and through P.A. You can't hide out there because everybody is trying to hide. You liable to run into a nigga you got beef with right up in the mountains and shit because he hiding from somebody *he got beef with*. I can go on the low, Long Island or something. I don't have to come back to BK or Queens."

"You are going to do what you want, Monty, but I'm telling you that I don't think you should go back to New York. If you were to get got in P.A. it would have happened already. Stay your ass out of the spotlight."

"You don't want anything to happen to your baby?" he flirted.

"Of course I don't want anything to happen to you," I said seriously as I finished up my food and washed it down with a glass of water.

"You'sa fucking pig, Carin."

I wiped my mouth with my hands and belched. We both fell out laughing.

"Look, I need to get some things off of my chest. I mean, I know that this won't erase everything that I put you through but just allow me to say this to you, Carin. I am still in love with you and I know there is no hope for me and you. I'm surprise you even showed up. I never deserved you. I don't deserve to be with anybody because I don't know how to act. I can admit that. But you were so special in your own little way. You were like a little me. I felt that the minute I laid eyes on you in the mall that day. I saw something in your eyes. I saw your need for love, a need for something real, and I wasted no time trying to be the one to make you happy. I was lonely too because I didn't know who was in my life because of love or money. I knew you didn't know anything about that. You were pure and innocent so I put my money on you. I hurt you in ways that I know I'm going to pay for dearly, if not me then my kids. Either way that karma is gonna come back on me, baby. I just want to say that for every time I ever hit you, made you cry, broke you heart, said any bullshit, did anything to cause you pain, from the bottom of my heart, Carin, I am so, so sorry, man. If there is anything you need in this world, whether you have a man or not, you call me. As long as I'm alive you will never ever want for anything, you hear me?" he said, holding my hand and staring me in my eyes.

"I forgive you, Monty. I been forgave you," I said, tapping his hand.

"This is not about you forgiving me. This is about me acknowledging that what I did to you was wrong. You will never ever forget what I did to you. I had no business putting those kinds of memories in your head. You are precious, Carin. You're a precious, precious woman. You are everything a woman should be and I'm sorry, baby. I am so sorry I just want you to know this, please." He touched his heart.

"I feel you, Monty. We are good." I extended myself for a hug.

We stood up and hugged for a long time. He stepped back and looked at me. "Damn, man, you got all thick and shit." He grinned.

"That's that good loving I'm getting. I'm happy, Monty. Really." I smiled.

"I'm happy for you and I mean that. You look well. You deserve it, baby. So who's this man you're seeing?"

"He's a nice guy. He treats me well, I have no complaints. He's an architect, he has no children, he's handsome, classy, mild mannered. I can't complain at all."

"How long have you been seeing him?"

"About a year-and-a-half seriously now."

"That's good. He's a lucky man. I see you found someone right after me, huh?"

I smiled. I thought about Haman and it brought a smile to my face. He was a gem. I was in love and I was safe. There was no better feeling in the world.

After talking to Monty for a while I realized that it was time for me to go. There was nothing else for Monty and me to talk about. I finished my glass of Hennessey then made the announcement that I was ready to go. Monty looked at his watch.

"It's still early. Come on, have some drinks with me for old time's sake. You don't have to run from me, Carin, I'm safe, I respect your relationship. I just know that this was it for me, you know? You might not see me for a long time, if ever again."

"I guess I can stay for a little while. Haman thinks I'm out with Jetta so he's not expecting me home anytime soon."

"Good, good." Monty poured me another drink. We spent the entire evening watching pay-per-view movies and reminiscing on the good times and people around the way. Before I knew it I was fucked up, asking Monty to wake me up at a certain time so I could go home, but first I needed to sleep this alcohol off.

Monty

It was about midnight and Carin was knocked out. I knew she would be, that's why I didn't stop her from throwing back the drinks. I didn't want her to get in trouble with her man but at the same time, fuck him. Her phone kept buzzing. I saw that it was Jetta.

"Hello," I whispered, walking into the bathroom.

"Monty?"

"Yeah, Jetta, whaddup girl!"

"Nothing how you been?" She sounded really happy to hear my voice.

"I'm good, baby, I'm good. What's up with you?"

"I'm hanging in there. I'm supposed to be covering for her but she won't answer her phone. Her man keeps calling me but I'm not going to answer the phone until I talk to her. Where is she?"

"She's sleeping. I'll wake her up in a few."

"Monty, you are so full of shit." Jetta laughed.

"No, you got my word, I'll let her know." I chuckled.

"Cool, I'll call you back in five minutes to see what happened."

I hung up with Jetta and scrolled through her phone book. I found Haman's name and number and decided to send him a text.

Baby if you're up, meet me at my house in about 2 hours. I got a surprise for you. Just hit me back and let me know if you'll be up and ready to come over.

When Haman replied no doubt! with a smiley face, I erased all messages and records of Haman calling and went to wake Carin up.

24

Carin

I was so drunk I let Monty drive my car home. I figured if Monty wanted to make a move, he would have had his way in the hotel so I felt safe. He whipped through traffic like a madman, switching lanes and doing eighty on the expressway to get me home. I wanted to throw up. "So when are you coming back to N.Y.?" I slurred. I could see Monty smiling with ridicule, then he said, "In two weeks."

I had no thoughts of seeing Haman tonight. I would just call him in the morning to let him know that I got too drunk to see him. I just wanted to lay down.

Monty

Carin was trying to act like she was sober but she wasn't. She couldn't even talk without slurring or nodding off like a fiend. She leaned against her front door and almost fell. I held her up and tapped her pockets for her keys. I then dug in her Gucci waist band and found them. I let her in her home and turned the lights on.

"I'ma turn the shower on for you, sit." I made my way around her apartment, trying to locate the bathroom and shower. I turned on her room lights and found her panty drawer. I pulled out a pretty, black lace teddy and held it up.

I went back to the living room and looked around, admiring her place. Carin had her head back and her mouth open when I came back into the living room. I straddled her.

"Baby, get up and take a shower and drink this." I dropped two Motrins in her mouth. She accepted and sipped the water. I pulled her sneakers off and pulled her shirt over her head, careful not to mess up her nice short "do," then I led her naked body to the bathroom and put her in the shower. I bathed her nicely, wrapped her in a towel, and carried her to the bedroom. At this point Carin was coherent but not enough to care about what I was doing. I looked around her heavily filled dresser for a nice fragrance and decided to go with Clinique's Happy. *I can't believe she still wears this shit.*

I took my time lotioning her body. I rubbed each thigh for a duration of time; her legs were always my favorite part of her body. "Knock Knock," I whispered seductively. Carin shifted her position in the bed, slightly opening her legs. Immediately, I got erect at the sight of her pussy. I watched her for a while, contemplating if I should violate. Carin opened her legs wider and grabbed my head as soon as she felt me breathing near that area. I got so excited I stripped down and climbed on top of her but didn't want to violate Carin. *This is the type of shit bitches get killed over, I wouldn't want nobody doing this shit to my girl.* I knew Carin was caught up, I knew she didn't want to do this. Not wanting her to wake up though, I put the head of my raw penis to her opening. "Knock Knock." Carin grabbed my neck and held on so I let myself in.

Being with Carin was so good, always so good. I knew she was up as she lay in my arms content, breathing heavily. Tonight she beat the high score and made me feel a way I had never felt. She wouldn't stop kissing my lips and telling me she loved me, She held on to my neck and rested her lips on my Adam's apple as she breathed on me, with one leg thrown over my hip. I rubbed her ass with my free hand. I could hear the knocking on the door. A part of me, a big part of me felt bad for what I did to Carin, but I'm a selfish nigga so. . . .

"Haman, baby, who's at the door," she slurred. I could smell the liquor coming out her pores.

"It's Monty, baby."

Carin backed up away from me and opened her eyes slowly. They were bloodshot. "Monty?"

I got up and threw my velour suit back on but didn't get a chance to put my sneakers on. I lit a cigarette and waltzed my way to the door. I knew this was going to be a long night. When I was halfway to the door I heard Carin call out, "Monty!" But she was pissed.

"Somebody is at the door," I said nonchalantly.

"I will get it!" she said, quickening her steps but by then it was too late, my hand was on the knob.

Haman

I was smiling from ear to ear when I heard the locks open. My smile faded when I saw this dude standing in the doorway puffing on a cigarette. I looked him up and down and walked in the apartment.

"Who the fuck are you?"

The dude took a pull of his cigarette first then smirked at me. He took another pull, then another, and then he put the cigarette out comfortably in the ashtray next to the love seat. He kept his eye on me the entire time. Carin came out of the room in the sexy teddy that I bought for her last year. "What the fuck you got on Carin?" I heard myself seethe.

Carin

"Haman!" I said, and tried to cover myself. I looked at Monty who was walking past me to go in my bedroom. I grabbed his arm. "Where are you going? You better tell my man what the fuck is going on!" I yelled. I didn't even know half of what happened. How did Monty wind up in my bed? My head was spinning and I felt sick. I had too much to drink. I stood there alone looking at Haman, my love. He was mad.

"I should smack the shit out of you, but you done had enough of that with this nigga, huh?" He snarled and walked up to me.

"What the fuck is going on here?"

I was at a loss for words and I was half drunk still. Monty came out of the room with his sneakers on.

"You were out with him all day?" Haman questioned.

"I was with Jetta and then I—"

"Carin, don't lie to me, how did you wind up with him?" he said, stepping up to me.

"I called her and she met me in the city," Monty offered.

"My man, I'm not even interested in nothing you have to say." Haman stepped right up in Monty's face. I stood there holding my scantily clad body. Monty stood erect, staring eye to eye with Haman.

"Ain't nuttin, Haman, right?" Monty said. Haman bit his lip.

"You did something with him tonight, Carin?" he asked.

"No." I shook my head. Monty put his head down and began digging in his pockets for nothing. Haman walked past us and went into the bedroom. I looked at Monty with scared eyes. He looked back at me unapologetic. "Fuck him," he mouthed.

I didn't want to argue with him right now.

"Carin!" Haman yelled. I walked into the bedroom. He was standing there pointing at my bed. "You're telling me that you didn't do anything with this man tonight?" he yelled.

"My man, chill out," Monty said, walking up to Haman.

"Who the fuck is talking to you?"

"Haman, it's not what you think. I had too much to drink and I'm still drunk now. I don't even know what happened." I felt like a dummy. Why did I even agree to meet up with Monty?

"Every time I'm near you it's nothing but fucking trouble, Monty, trouble! I want you out of my fucking house!" I yelled.

Monty just looked through me then looked at Haman. "Nothing happened, Haman. She wouldn't have sex with me. She was too drunk and too in love with you."

"I look stupid to you?" he said, stepping to Monty again with his fists balled.

"Chill out, pretty boy," Monty taunted.

"Please, please, yawl. Haman, baby, I swear I didn't. Yes, I saw him, yes, he came home with me only because I was drunk. I swear he just drove me home. I don't know what happened in that room, but I do know that I did not have sex with him."

"You want the truth?" Monty asked. I looked at Monty. Haman folded his arms.

"I tried to get some from her, tried to turn her on, but ain't nothing pop off." Monty shrugged his shoulders. "She loves you, man, she used to love me like that too." Monty put his fitted on and zipped up his jacket. "I'm gone, Carin, back out of town, probably won't be back for a minute."

I couldn't say shit to Monty. I was so damn furious with him. Monty nodded his head at Haman and winked at me when he wasn't looking.

"What were you thinking being with him, Carin?" Haman asked as soon as the door slammed.

I shook my head. "I swear to you, I did not have sex with Monty. I love you baby."

"You didn't sleep with him?"

"No."

"How did he wind up here then?"

"I was with Jetta today, but Monty called and said he was in town. We were right by one another so I told Jetta to come with me. It was innocent. I got so drunk and he brought me home."

"So how did you wind up wearing this shit and why couldn't Jetta drive you home?"

I shook my head slowly. "I don't even know. I just remember us all laughing and drinking and having a good time. Next thing you know he was driving me home."

"You were laughing and having a good time with this man who used to beat on you and put his feet on you? How did he even know where you lived to drive you home if you were too drunk to tell him?"

"I don't know! Maybe he looked at my license and saw my address, baby, I don't know."

"You got so drunk that you don't remember how you got undressed, how you got home, or if somebody put their dick in you or not."

"No." I grabbed his hand and walked him to my couch. "Baby, please, let's not blow this out of proportion.

Haman stood there, unbuttoning his jeans. "Well, come give me what you called me over here for then."

"I didn't call you over here."

"You were that drunk you don't remember that, either?" he said, showing me the text in his cell phone. "That's you right?"

I tried to think but I didn't remember sending Haman the text message. "Come over here," he said with his dick in his hands. He sat down and held himself.

"You want to have sex with me because you think I had sex with Monty?" I wanted to cry.

"No, I want to have sex with my beautiful lady after she has been out drinking. You gotta be horny by now." He smiled devilishly. I walked up to him and held my breath. I began doing Kegel exercises with my vagina. I squeezed it tight as possible and lowered myself on him. He stared into my eyes as I lowered my body down on to him. I couldn't let him know how much pain I was in.

"Now come on, ride me good, Carin, unless of course this pussy of yours is not in the mood."

I ignored him and did what I had to do to keep my man.

When he came, he came in me and wrapped his arms around my waist. He whispered in my ear.

"I know you fucked him, Carin. I know," he said through clenched teeth.

25

Carin

It had been almost a month since the Monty incident and though Haman hadn't said a thing about it to me since that night he was acting strange. He never touched me again after that night and seemed kind of standoffish. This was a man who made love to me on sight and now thirty days had gone by and he hadn't touched me once. I was in Haman's house, watching him as he tidied up as if he didn't have a care in the world, smiling at me occasionally and asking me what was wrong. I could tell that he had something on his mind though.

"Haman, can you please talk to me about that night if it's still bothering you? I can't help but to think that things have changed between us since then. "

"Did something happen? You said you didn't fuck him, right?" he snapped, right on point.

"I didn't! Haman we have *never* had any drama and I don't want it to start now," I pleaded. I was so mad at Monty for doing this. He wasn't returning my calls because he knew how pissed I was at him but every chance I got I cursed his ass out on voice mail.

"It takes this quick to ruin trust." Haman snapped his fingers. "But you know what, Carin? I can't stop you from doing what you want to do, your heart is still with ol' boy. I can't run you down and I love you, woman, I do," he said, turning toward me. "But I will not beg you to stay; I will *not* follow you around. I'm a good man and I don't have to do that shit to keep a woman. The right one will find me."

"Oh, so I'm not the one for you now, Haman?"

"I don't know anymore. Deep down in my heart I know something did happen. I'm trying to trust you but it's hard. So please stop bringing the shit up, it'll take time for me to even shake the memory out of my mind. I mean, he did eat ya pussy, you think I'm cool with that?"

"I never told you that he ate my pussy, I don't even remember what happened that night!"

"You smelled like sex, Carin."

I put my head down.

"Just chill out, woman. If nothing happened then stop acting all nervous. Let the shit blow over. Trust me it will."

I got up, unsure, and went to make myself a cup of tea. I was heartbroken and realized how much I didn't want to lose Haman and had no idea what to do. I stood in the kitchen watching the water boil over in a daze, wondering if I was going to lose the man I loved over one mistake that I seemed to make over and over again.

26

Carin

The first couple of days that I had not called Haman, I was shocked that he in turn had not called me either to check on me. *Damn near a week!* I couldn't take it anymore so I called him. He picked up sounding as if he was asleep. "Is this a bad time?" I asked with attitude.

"No, not at all, how you been?" he asked curtly.

"I've been fine. I mean, I could have been dead and buried Haman."

"So could I."

"Did I do something to you?" I cried out knowing damn well what I did and felt like shit.

"Carin . . ." Haman started, taking a deep breath. "I know you fucked Monty. I know you did and as much as I'm trying to shake that shit off I can't."

"Haman, don't do this. I'm on my way to see you."

"For what? I'm leaving," he said unconvincingly.

I hung up and headed for my car.

When I reached his house, I found him in this huge closet organizing it. He began talking as soon as he heard my footsteps.

"All week, I thought about it, I cried over it, I rationalized, I forgave you, hated you, loved you all over again. Then I woke up about two days ago realizing I hadn't heard from you . . . but the shit was, I didn't care if I ever heard from you again. I called my mother and asked her what I should do. She told me to take my time and to not let pride make my decision. Then you called and my heart palpitated and I said damn she's just a woman in love with another man, this is life, right? Forgive her. But then I heard your lying ass voice and it just sent me over the edge again. So many times I could have cheated but said nah, Carin would never do that to me and I brushed these women off, pay them no mind 'cause to me? I have everything I need at home. But my home has been burglarized. This nigga took something from me, something I thought was just for me, and you let someone else literally come between us." Haman spoke quietly as he lightly dropped my pretty clothes in a pile. I watched him in a wrinkled white tee, grey sweats, and flip-flops. His face handsome and scruffy, his wavy dark ceasar thick and in need of cutting.

My head began to hurt. "I didn't have sex with him, Haman. I swear to God I didn't."

He began lightly tossing my lotions and perfumes in a bag.

"Haman, why don't you believe me?"

"Because I can't forget the pain in your eyes when you had sex with me Carin. You were in so much pain and your pussy was wide open! A man can't tell when a woman cheats, but if it was just moments before? Hell, yeah, Carin, I couldn't even feel shit. My dick was swimming in you like I was fucking a pool of water and I ain't no li'l nigga. My dick ain't *never* swim in you *ever*. It was loose *and* you were in pain. Carin, your pussy gets swollen after sex," he said, stepping to me. I braced myself. "I would never hit you, ever, you don't have to back up from me. You was too drunk to even know how swollen your shit was. I was hurt but I fucked you anyway, trying to hurt you, but I just wound up hurting myself. Anyway, the point is I know you fucked Monty. You felt the need to be with him behind my back then go on with him, Carin."

"I don't want Monty, I want you!" I said, quietly starting to cry. Haman had resumed tossing my things into a pile on his bed. He left the room and went into the kitchen to get more bags. I followed him like a puppy. Haman poured himself some water and turned to come back to the bedroom but I was right on his heels, we were now eye to eye. "I'm hurt, Carin. I'm *real real* hurt, you understand me? So you need to just get your things and raise up out my crib."

"I'm not leaving here. I love you, and I made a mistake, baby. I swear all I want is you."

"So *you did* fuck him."

"Why are you doing this to me?"

Haman just chuckled at me and quickly threw my things in bags then headed to the front door. I ran in front of him and stopped at the door, holding on to the knob. "We need to talk about this."

"I'm a grown-ass man. I don't have time for some little girl who can't grow the fuck up and leave her past alone. You don't want a man to love you. You want drama. Drama is love to you and I can't give you that."

"I don't want drama, Haman, I want you. I swear to you. Please, can we talk about this?"

"Ain't nuttin' to talk about, kitten. You fucked up, now move out of my way."

"Haman, please, can we just talk for a minute. Please sit," I said, sitting down and tapping a spot next to me. He looked at me for a minute. I know he could see how sorry I was for the pain I had caused but it wasn't his problem. Haman walked to the sofa, leaned over, and dug his hand in my pocket, snatching his keys then stiffly grabbing my wrist and dragging me to the door.

"I want you out my house and out of my life. Go be with that nigga, let him whoop your ass and don't call me when he does." He opened the door, tossing me and my bags out onto the stoop. He slammed the door so hard my body jerked.

I stood in shock. I didn't even breathe as I looked around to see if anyone had witnessed the disrespect. I could feel Haman on the other side of the door; all I could do was cry and beg him to please open up. Then I heard him walking way. I eventually picked up my bags and threw them in the backseat. I sat in the car for a while with my head on the steering wheel, bawling outrageously. "God, please don't let me lose him. Please."

Carin

The pain in my chest was so severe that I thought I was having a minor heart attack. I had to take deep shallow breaths because my chest was cramped up. My head was hurting so bad that it hurt to blink. I sat in my apartment with all of my lights off listening to Chrisette Michelle, dialing Haman's number over and over again until it finally started going straight to voice mail. I left music on his voice mail, poetry, and I even typed a letter and emailed it to him. I did everything but admit that I slept with Monty. I wasn't going to give in.

I felt like a fool and it pained me to tell Missy, Tyra, and Jetta what I had done. But I couldn't hold it in. I had to talk about it. They decided that I needed some cheering up so they all came over to my house.

I had to swear Tyra to secrecy because I didn't want my father to know. They showed utter shock when I told them what I had done.

"What in the hell made you sleep with Monty again?" Tyra said.

"I swear to you I was so drunk I don't even remember anything."

"So Haman isn't talking to you at all? When was the last time you two spoke?" Jetta asked.

"It's been about two weeks officially now but it's been shady ever since last month when this happened. I feel so lost right now."

No one said anything. There was nothing they could say.

"I think Haman just needs some time to himself to kind of shake things off. You know how a man is with his pride and everything. Give him some time. That man loves you, he'll come around," Missy said. I wish it were true but Haman wasn't coming back.

"It gets even more complicated guys. I'm pregnant."

"What?" Tyra said.

"By who?" Jetta gawked.

I shrugged. "I don't know." I sobbed.

"Say what now? You don't know? How you don't know?" Tyra said.

"I was with them both that night. I'm seven weeks. I don't know whose baby it is."

"Okay, this is some real live bullshit. Are you going to keep it?" Jetta asked.

"I've never had an abortion."

"There is a first time for everything, girl, you don't want to risk having the spawn of Satan's baby!" Missy said. Tyra laughed at that.

"Girl, you are a fool! But seriously, Carin, she is right. You can't tell Haman this is his baby and not be sure. What are you going to do?"

"I'm keeping my baby. Secretly, I have always wanted a child and the entire time I was with Monty it never happened. My gut tells me it's Haman's."

"So are you going to tell him?" Jetta said.

"He won't talk to me."

"Give me his number," Tyra said, pulling out her cell phone.

When Haman picked up, Tyra excused herself and went into the kitchen to talk to him. After about five minutes she resurfaced.

"He agreed to see you only because you have some more things at his house. He told me you can come as long as I come with you and wait in the car because if you overstay your welcome he will not hesitate to put you out."

"Damn." Missy shook her head.

"So when are we going?" I said, just wanting to take a glimpse at him. I was sick without him.

"Let's go now before he changes his mind. We all might as well ride. Carin, put on something nice and get out of these nasty-ass clothes you been in all week and pray this man has a heart."

27

Carin

Haman let me in and he seemed annoyed. I couldn't understand why he was going so hard. I stood for a while as he lay on the sofa with one hand behind his head, sipping a Corona.

"You waiting for me to tell you to sit?" he asked.

Not wanting to rock the boat, I sat at his feet and stared at him.

"What I'm about to tell you isn't easy for me, Haman. But I'm asking that before you react, before you respond, please think before you speak and please do not let your emotions and or pride answer for you."

I could tell that I got Haman's attention now. He stared at me for a while then sat up. With his hands dangling between his legs, he looked at me and said, "*What.*" Then sipped his beer, looking at me again.

"I'm pregnant."

I smiled as I said it. It felt good coming out of my mouth and at this moment there wasn't anything Haman could say to take away this feeling that I had right now. The idea of being a mother tickled me and I wasn't afraid. I had support, I just didn't want to be a single mother after coming so far.

"How do you know?" he asked. I dug in my purse and handed him the test. Haman looked at it and tapped his hand with it.

"A baby." He lay back down. I held my breath and closed my eyes. I opened them when I felt his hand on mine.

"What do you want to do?"

"I'm keeping the baby, Haman, I am not having an abortion," I said with an attitude.

"I didn't ask you to have no motherfuckin' abortion, I asked you what do you want to do?"

"Well, what about us? We're not even on speaking terms."

"Carin, I'm not even sure if this baby is mine." He got up and stretched casually then sat back down. "Is this baby mine?" he said, looking down at me on the sofa.

"What kind of question is that, Haman, of course the baby is yours!"

"Carin, you had sex with your ex."

I went to say something but he put his hand up and silenced me.

"Don't even start that lying shit again. You had sex with your ex, did you use condoms, yes or no."

"Haman, this baby is yours."

"You didn't use condoms, did you?"

"I'm telling you I did not even sleep with him, why won't you believe me?" I said, standing up.

"I told you what I felt. But you're taking it to the grave that you didn't sleep with Monty."

"I did not sleep with him, Haman, that is what I been trying to tell you."

He stood up and rubbed his face out of frustration as I watched his every move. "So you're having my baby?" he asked, a little more light-hearted.

"This changes nothing for now, Carin. I'll go with you to every appointment, I'm here for you. But I still need to sort out my feelings. But if nothing else I know you'll be a great mother and I'm happy you're having a baby." he hugged me. I began crying tears of relief.

"I was raised by a good woman, I got morals, I'm here for you, Carin, I'm here for my child no matter what *our* outcome is," he said, holding me.

"Haman I love you, and I promise you can trust me. I'll give you your space but you can trust me, know this. I want us to raise this child

together in the same house. It's the right thing
to do. "

At that moment the decision was made, I
knew there was nothing on earth more important than family.

As time went on, my stomach grew so perfect
and round. I knew that my baby would be perfect. My hair had grown out, my face was full and
unblemished and my smile was bright. Haman
and I spent every night together once I began
to show and there was no greater feeling in the
world than having my man's hands wrapped
around my belly at night or waking up to his
kisses on my stomach. It was a first for us both.

But when I became eight months pregnant
Tyra brought the reality to me that there was
a huge chance that this baby might not be Haman's and that he needed to take a paternity test.

"I can't ask Haman to take a test, are you kidding me?" I said with my feet kicked up on an
ottoman in my house.

"No, but you can ask Monty to take it."

"I don't ever want to see his rat ass again. Hell
no."

"Carin, you need to do this. You cannot live
your life wondering if Haman is the father."

"It doesn't even matter, Tyra. Haman is the father no matter who the father is so let's just pray that this child looks like me so we can all move the hell on."

"What are you going to do if Haman decides to take a test? You know that in the back of his mind he is feeling a way about this baby. If he asks you for a test what are you going to say?"

"I am going to tell him no, now can we just move on?"

"You think he's going for that? Suit yourself, Carin, but you know what the right thing to do is. Haman doesn't deserve that kind of disrespect and that karma is going to come back strong on you, baby girl, so make it easy on yourself."

Monty

I didn't know what Carin wanted to see me for but since I was in New York for the weekend visiting Rick, I told her that I'd meet her by Green Acres Mall, at Foot Locker.

The only people I saw in the store were a white couple and a fat lady with long hair paying for her purchase, so I called Carin to rush her. I had shit to do. She told me she was paying for her sneakers and she was coming. I looked in the store again and almost dropped my phone when

the fat lady turned around and I saw that it was
Carin.

"Close your mouth. We got a problem on our
hands," she said as soon as she came up to me.

My face was stuck. "What's up? You pregnant?"

"No, I drank too much. What the fuck does it
look like?"

"Wait, hold up, why are you coming at me with
all this fucking attitude. What's the problem?"

"The problem is I don't know if it's your baby
or if it's my man's, so I need you to take a paternity test."

"Why can't you ask ol' boy to take the test?"

"Because if I ask him then he is going to know
that I had sex with you, genius."

"So he didn't figure that shit out that night?"

"Look, Monty, I came here so you can see me
live and in color with a stomach. When I have
this baby I need for you to come by the hospital
and do me this favor, can you do that for me,
please?"

"Yeah, I can do that for you." I prayed that the
baby was mine. "Can you open your coat so I can
see your stomach?"

She lightened up and opened her down coat
revealing the biggest stomach I had ever seen.
"Oh my God, look at this shit. Yo, I have to swing
you by Rick's so he can see this."

"No, I really need to get going, Monty."

"Carin, please, he lives ten minutes away. Can you wait for him to come so he can see you? He's been asking about you."

"Tell him to hurry up. I have things to do and I'm hungry."

"Let's go to Ponderosa's so I can feed you. He can meet us there."

28

Carin

I began to cry for no reason at all. It was a
mixture of life being so beautiful mixed with
the anxiety of knowing that something would
go wrong. I was lying on my back, the only position comfortable for me to sleep in. It was a dark
night and it was storming outside. Haman, my
handsome good man, slept so peacefully as I felt
so guilty for being so tainted. He slept with one
hand on my large stomach. I put my hand on top
of his and watched him. He was an angel to me.
My heart went out to him. I was torn, damaged
goods and still doing dumb fucking shit to cause
myself harm. Here he was in love with me and I
was carrying a baby that might not be his. I cried
and prayed every day. God knows I made a mistake, I didn't mean it, I asked him to please spare
me. I didn't know as of yet if he heard my cries.

"You okay, baby?" Haman woke up and asked
me.

I didn't even know I was crying. I was sniffling hard. I had so much to say to Haman. He sat up and turned the lights on.

"Baby, what is it?"

The moment he asked I cried harder. I was overflowing with emotion. I had some things I had to get off my chest. Haman got up and got me some water and a warm rag. He wiped my face and fed me water. I wanted him to stop. He was too damn good.

"Talk to me, baby. What is it sweetheart?" he asked. His eyes held so much sincerity and kindess, a kindness that only a child could exhibit. I kept crying and he began to hold me tight. He put my head on his chest and let me cry. He always knew what to do.

"Baby, what's wrong?"

"If you reach to give me something I flinch!" I belted out.

"I don't understand." He stared into my eyes.

"If you raise your hand to hug me, or to get the remote I jump, I flinch, I think you're going to hit me! I can't do this. I can't do this shit, Haman! I don't even know how to make love to you the way you deserve. I'm programmed . . . I'm programmed to fuck you how I fucked him. He's in my mind, I can't get him out of my head, like he has me brainwashed, and it's not fair to you.

I don't deserve you!" I cried. Haman hugged me tighter.

"I would never ever put my hands on you unless it's to love you and caress you. You don't ever have to flinch at me. That part of your life is over, Carin, trust me. We will get through this if you want to, but you have to want it. You have to let it go. It's going to take time and I'm here for you. It's not easy and you been through a lot, come on now give yourself some credit."

I shook my head.

"Haman, you don't understand. I have fucking nightmares of this man beating me and beating me and beating me to death. Baby, I need help."

"If you need help then we can make that happen, we can go to counseling or church, whatever you feel you need, but please calm yourself down. My baby is in your belly and we have to make sure she's okay, or he, right?"

I began to cry harder. I didn't even know whose baby it was.

"Just put your arms around me and hold me, tell me that this is going to be over soon."

Haman lay on his back and put me on top of him like a baby. I turned to an angle so that I didn't have to lie on my stomach. But he held on to me tight.

"I hate to see you suffer like this, Carin. But it's up to you. I can give you my all but it's up to you to let it go. It's over. Life is good. I'm here, you're having a baby, your past is gone, baby. Live, okay? Live for me, for the baby, but finally, live for you."

His words were so soothing it put me at ease. I continued to cry myself to sleep.

The next afternoon, born by Cesarean section, Nina-Simone Douglas came into the world weighing seven pounds six ounces. When I awakened I was in my room surrounded by family and friends, flowers and cards, and a smiling Haman holding his baby girl.

Sharon came up to me first. "Hey, how are you?" She smiled.

"In pain," I whispered.

"I called to check on you and didn't get an answer so I called your father's house and he said you were in labor."

"She is so beautiful but Haman won't let anybody hold her!" Missy joked.

"In a minute, in a minute." He smiled, getting up.

"She doesn't look like anybody yet," Jetta cooed over Haman's shoulder.

My father stood by me rubbing my hair and forehead.

"Haman, can I hold my baby, please?" I winced as I tried to sit up. Sharon and Tyra helped me up and adjusted my bed. Haman brought the pretty brown baby over to me, wrapped up in yellow blankets. I stared at her for a long time trying to see if I saw any of Monty's traits. I tried not to ruin this moment with her fear of paternity so I smiled. But the tears soon began to fall and Sharon squeezed my hand. Haman stepped in and rubbed my back.

"It's okay, kitten, you'll be okay. You want me to hold Nina?"

"No, no I got her, I got her." I tried to gain my composure. I kissed the tiny baby repeatedly, saying I love you.

"I'm a mother." I smiled.

"Shit, you think that's something, I'm a grandmother as fine as I am!" Tyra said.

"You don't look nowhere *near* as good as me," Daddy snapped back.

"In your dreams, go take them tight-ass jeans off like you ride a motorcycle."

"My jeans are not tight and nobody said anything about that bullshit Clair Huxtable sweater you got on."

Tyra was cracking up with her hands on her hips. "Clair Huxtable? Okay, Eric Estrada. Look at his jacket yawl, looking like an extra from CHiPs," she said, picking up his leather jacket.

"My coat cost more than your weave!" he said.

Tyra feigned seriousness as she stroked her extra-long natural tresses. "You are out of line, this is *not* a weave!"

"Might not be, but them leggings you got on? Time to clean the furniture with 'em, woman."

The entire room including the woman that was in the bed next to me was laughing.

Nina-Simone began getting fussy so I pulled out a breast. "You're breast feeding?" Jetta asked.

"I am so jealous right now. It's six weeks right?" Haman joked.

Sharon smiled. "Let me get out of here. Pamela said she is going to swing by tomorrow. Call me if you need me, okay? Darren and Tyra, nice seeing you guys again. Haman, it's been a pleasure."

"It's been so long, don't be a stranger," my father said sincerely. He used to have a thing for Sharon on the low. Tyra smiled and waved.

Haman walked up to me and kissed my forhead. "You and my daughter are so beautiful. I am the luckiest man alive." He smiled like a proud father. "My family is flying in tomorrow." He gushed like a little boy. I smiled too, but behind my smile I feared the worse.

***

I never did call Monty once the baby was born but he left threatening messages on my voice mail telling me that I better not be keeping his child from him. But months had gone by and Nina-Simone looked a lot like me and for right now I was glad and feeling and knowing in my heart that this was Haman's baby. Pamela had called on several occasions asking me to bring the baby over but I didn't feel too right about that. I didn't want Haman to even hear me being associated with Monty or his family right now. But one day Monty and his mother just showed up at my door unannounced. I looked through the peephole and paused for second in shock. Then I opened the door, smiling.

"Hey what are you guys doing here?" I smiled, happy that Haman was at work.

"Where she at, didn't I tell you I'd cause a fucking scene if you tried to play me? This baby is six months and you been ducking and dodging making excuses. Where she at?" Monty fumed as he barged in.

"Lower your damn voice, she is in my room sleeping. Hey, Pamela," I said, hugging her.

"Hey, baby, you looking good, so how's the li'l mama?"

"She's fine, greedy, big, *long*." I smiled as Monty brought the baby out of the room. She was awake and cooing at him.

"Asleep my ass," Monty grumbled and started kissing Nina on her neck. Pamela reached her arms out. "Let me see her, let me see this baby."

"This baby looks just like Monty when he was a child. Look," she said, pulling out a baby picture. I shook my head as I looked at it. I saw some resemblance, but no. Life was good right now. I was a stay-at-home mom and my baby's daddy made $100,000 a year. He paid all the bills, he didn't hit me, he didn't curse at me, he loved me, he needed me, and he kept me safe.

"Carin, baby girl, just let me take a paternity test. Look, I'll take it and homeboy don't even have to know and if it's his, then fine; if it's not, then you got some explaining to do. The most you'll have to deal with is a broken heart and time will heal that. It's a win-win situation for you, Carin."

Monty passed the baby over to his mother as Pamela held Nina close to her and began kissing her.

"She even has my son's fingers. This is my grandbaby, I don't care what nobody says. Monty, look, that is your mouth."

"Damn, she does look like me."

"Well, do your boyfriend and Monty look alike?" Pamela asked.

"Please, Ma, who looks like me, I'm a fine-ass dude. But this li'l mama right here? She looks like me, yes, she does," he said in his baby voice.

***

Monty, Pamela, and I sat in the doctor's office waiting to be called. One at a time, they called in Monty first, then me and the baby.

"I have to warn you that the results take three to five days to come back," the stubby Spanish doctor informed us.

"Why we gotta wait so long? On *Maury* that shit takes a day!" Monty said.

"If you paid attention you'd see that they have on different clothes when they come back. It takes days," I said nervously. My hands were sweating and shaking so bad I couldn't even hold Nina.

"You can either come in for the results or you can call in or we can mail them to you."

"I think we should come in together," I suggested.

"Nah, have them mail it to you, Carin, call me and I'll come to your crib and we can open it together."

We took our tests and I quickly got the hell out of dodge. I was struggling with Nina in her car seat so Monty took her from me. "Let me help you to your car."

I handed her over and smiled at my pretty little baby who was dressed in a lavender and yellow Rocawear short set, with yellow socks and white Reeboks that Monty had bought for her, with her hair in little rubber bands parted in squares. "She is so fat!" Monty said, putting her in the car. He strapped her in and squatted outside the car. Pamela got in the backseat and I stood behind Monty.

"I really, *really* hope you are my daughter." Monty kissed Nina on her cheeks over and over. He got up from his squat and faced me. "I know that it's fucked up for you and ol' boy, and I'm sorry for all of this confusion and shit, but dammit, you belong with me, you know that shit, Carin. Me and you? Come on, man. All these years and look where we are, taking paternity tests. It was meant to be, baby. But whatever the outcome is, I'm happy for you and I'm here for you. You and li'l mama over here." He smiled. I decided not to respond to him but instead got in the car.

Monty

After Carin dropped me and my mother off at home, I stayed there for a while to talk to her about everything that had been going on inside of me. I was getting older and I didn't want to live my life as a cowboy watching my back any more. I wanted deeply to just have a family, chill, take family trips, be a man, provide for my wife and kids and just live life happily ever after. Me,

Ski, my mother, Sharon, and my sister Yvonne sat in the living room thinking of how happy we would be if the baby was ours. The family was ready for a new addition.

"How are you going to see the baby if your living in P.A.?" my mother asked me.

"I'll take Carin out there with me ma. My child is going to live with me. I'm not with that baby mother shit. Carin and I been through too much so if that baby is mine we are going to Vegas to get married point black period and I'm done."

My mother and Sharon glanced at one another.

"Yeah but Monty, you need to get that hand situation in order nephew. You can't be beating on Carin around the baby and all that." Sharon said.

"Son it pains my heart to know that you beat on that child the way you use to. I can't even imagine how she felt going through something like that and it's a shame because she loves you so much."

"I love her too and I promise you that I will never in my life lay a hand on another woman again. I look at Lindsey and can't imagine hitting her for any reason. With Carin I was young and dumb and I apologized to her so many times. I'd spend the rest of my life trying to make that shit up to her for real."

"Well I can only pray for the both of you. Personally I think she'd be crazy as hell to take you back, baby or not but it's on her. You just need to focus on being a father if this child is yours. If it's meant for you and Carin to be together you will." My mother said.

"I miss her. We use to have fun together." Sharon said.

"Yeah, cooking out on your fire escape, drinking, playing cards." I smiled reminiscing on the good days when we were young, fly, flashy and happy.

We all sat around silent for a while probably thinking about back in the days when all was good in the world, when Carin and I were in love and inseparable. Then I changed. It's my fault and everyone knows it.

"Carin is good people, she still family no matter what though." Ski said trying to lighten the mood. I decided not to dwell on "back when" any longer. It was aching my heart.

"Well I gotta boogie yawl. I have to get back to P.A. to my lady. She's begging the kid to come back home. I'll be back through for the fourth. Yawl cooking out?"

"You already know!" Sharon said getting up too.

"Ski you riding back to PA with me?"

"Yeah."

I hugged my mother tight and told her I loved her.

"I love you too son be safe, see you in a few days."

I peeled off some money and told her and my sister to split it then me and Ski burnt up the highway and headed to P.A. Once I reached Pennsylvania, I dropped Ski off to the house and got my piece, something I always did when visiting Lindsey because of the dudes that kept company around her house. I called Lindsey and told her I was home and that I'd be to her in 20 minutes. She told me to take my time that her cousins from Brooklyn was there with their kids.

"Your cousins from Brooklyn? What part of Brooklyn?"

"You know I don't know Brooklyn I can't even tell you. I just know there's a bunch of projects where they live. I use to go there as a kid. Anyway my cousin is here with her kids and her brother."

"Well do your family thing; I'm not coming if you got company."

"No come, I want you to meet them okay baby? Be nice to me and I'll be nice to you." She flirted.

"You know exactly what to say to a nigga huh?" I laughed.

"I knew you'd see things my way"

"Yeah, fo' sho. I'll be to you in a minute." I smiled when I hung up with Lindsey. She was so pleasant to be around.

Instead of running back out I decided to shower, change clothes and spray my body with Jean Paul Gautier cologne. Lindsey loved that on me. I tucked my Ruger in the small of my back and grabbed my car keys. I called Rick on my way out.

Rick answered the phone all sarcastic. "Say word? Is this my boy calling me?" Rick joked.

"Rick whaddup my dude I know it's been a minute!"

"Whaddup, where you been at man? My mother was even asking about you too, you good?"

"Tell mama love I'm good and I'll see her soon!"

"Nah for real you good, it's been a while." Rick asked.

"Yeah man I'm good been in and out of New York taking care of this li'l situation."

"What, beef?"

"Nah Carin."

"Carin." Rick sang. "Carin you still getting up with ole C-Murda?" I laughed at the nick name the boys had for Carin behind her back.

"Yeah and she might have a li'l girl for me man."

"Word? Oh that's love man I hope that works out for you, when will you know?"

"I should be hearing from her either tonight or no later than tomorrow. I really hope this baby is mine. We went and took a test and all that."

"So what are you doing out in P.A. then if Carin is going to call you?"

"My redbone up here wanted to see me and all that so I came home to check her but I'm gone 'til November tomorrow."

"I hear you, I hear you well good luck on that Carin shit, that's a good look."

"Yeah if its mine, son I'm going right to City Hall and doing it, fuck it."

"Yeah this has been going on since what, when you met C?"

"A long time man. If the baby is mine, that's it, we out. She so pretty too. You have to see shorty."

"She looks like you? Do you feel that she's yours?"

"I don't know. I'm up in the air with it."

"Wow, that's deep son. Make sure you call me tomorrow and let me know about the baby situation and all that. Come check me when you come back up top."

"I'll hit you up and come through. Tell your mother I love her and to make me some smothered turkey wings."

"Fuh sho."

"Ahiet man, one."

I pushed on the gas driving a little faster. The more I thought about Lindsey the more eager I became. I pulled up to Lindsey's crib and it was like double the amount of guys outside. I hit the alarm on my car and got out. I felt the heat was on my back as I walked into Lindsey's building. I could hear them heckling as I walked inside. My temper couldn't take that kind of fuckery.

"You know them niggas outside?" I asked her as I peered through the window.

While she was looking out the window I was already calling my cousin Ski who had just come home and was in my house asleep. I kept calling the house until he answered.

"Whaddup." He said his voice still groggy.

"Come to Lindsey crib, come heavy."

"What's up? What happened?" I could hear his voice becoming more alert.

"It is not that serious!" Lindsey said. I ignored her.

"It's on, I don't know what but get to Lindsey crib now and come heavy. Make sure you and cali come." I spoke of my calico.

"I'll be there in fifteen minutes." Ski said hopping out of the bed. He brushed his teeth real quick and threw on his fitted and some sweats.

"Call Whop and Nate since they live right up the way." I said and hung up.

"Where's your cousins at? They out there?"

"No, my boy cousin went to the store right before you came and his sister is outside smoking a cigarette now come on baby, relax. Why do you have to bring that Brooklyn shit to my house? Nobody is thinking about you!" Lindsey said as I flipped my phone shut.

"Yeah? Shit you don't know me woman. A lot of niggas is thinking about me. You just don't know. So who's all them niggas outside?"

Lindsey sucked her teeth and folded her arms. I was hot and got even hotter when I heard a bunch of arguing outside. I ran to the window and saw my li'l man Whop, Nate and two other dudes arguing with the dudes outside.

"Yo, I'll be back."

"Don't go out there!" Lindsey yelled behind me.

"I'll be back."

I ran outside and broke up the monotony of what these cats do all day, argue and bullshit. I told Whop and Nate to head up the hill and get low till Ski got here. A real big dude that I never saw around Lindsey's way before stepped to me.

"Yo, my man you from up top right?"

I didn't respond I just sized him up.

"Then you should know the code son, mind ya fuckin business."

I didn't know what was going on. All I knew was Ski needed to hurry up because Whop and Nate looked shook. I reached for my weapon and put it to big man's head because I felt that he was about to put the drop on me first. He put his piece to my chest. We stood like that for a minute. All I could hear was Lindsey whining in the background saying it's not that serious for us to put our guns away.

Where the fuck was Ski?

Lindsey stood off in the distance. I could hear her crying.

"Can you please just put the guns away please? It's not that serious" her soft voice spoke in the background.

I felt big man's patience running out. Big man pushed me away and fired his gun. On the way down I let off three shots then my head crashed on the floor.

The last thing I heard was Lindsey screaming. My eyes were closed. I heard the scuffle of feet, more gun shots and cars screeching. I kept my eyes closed and prayed quickly as I knew my time was running out. I felt my self going under. I asked God for forgiveness for all the wrong I've done and for him to protect my family from any harm. I opened my eyes one last time and could see Tionne standing there and next to her was Barry.

"Hold on baby, help is coming" Lindsey sniffled. But I couldn't hold on. Lindsey's face was so pretty and sad at the same time.

"Monty baby, please hold on, help is coming."

I tried to smile. I tried to hold on at least until Carin called me with the good news. I knew that me leaving this earth meant that Nina was mine. I hope that was enough for my family to carry on, because I was gone. My eyes lowered as Barry and Tionne watched me go under for reassurance.

29

Carin

My fourth of July was great. Me, Haman, and Nina-Simone went to the promenade out in Brooklyn and got first row on the balcony of one of Haman's coworkers who fixed appetizers for us and drinks.

Nina clapped and cooed at the bright fireworks. She was so beautiful. My life was beautiful. My man was beautiful, everything was just perfect.

I was so tired and half drunk when we got home that I wound up crashing the minute we got in the house. Haman gave Nina a much-needed bath. Her body was filled with ice cream and lollipops. I was too tired to even bathe so I just stripped down to my panties and curled up in bed when Tyra began blowing up my cell phone.

"Carin, baby, get up," she said softly into the phone.

"Hmm?" I asked, half asleep.

"Have you spoken to Pamela?"

"Yeah, like two days ago," I slurred. She was quiet.

"So you didn't speak to her tonight at all?"

"No, Tyra, why? Can't this wait 'til tomorrow?"

"No, call her, she needs to talk to you."

"Did she say what it was about?"

I knew Pamela was just stressing me for the paternity test. I'd deal with that tomorrow.

"Carin, baby, I am so sorry."

"About what?"

"Pamela called me and told me to tell you . . . that, um . . . they, well *someone* killed her baby."

"What baby?"

"Her baby son," she said in a barely audible whisper.

"Who, Monty?"

"Yes, Carin."

"What, who told her that?" I said, sitting up.

"I don't know, but call her and find out what's going on."

I stopped breathing. I stood there with my heart in my throat. "Tyra, are you sure?" My eyes began to water. I sat up and turned the lights on as Haman entered the bedroom with Nina over his shoulder, sleeping. He looked in my face and immediately got concerned. I began to cry.

"What happened, baby?" he asked me as I dropped the phone. He picked it up and Tyra told him what happened. He promised her he'd take care of me and hung up.

"Carin, kitten, are you okay?" he asked me softly. I stared at him, trying to find a hint of happiness in his eyes that Monty was dead. I saw nothing but concern. "You need to call his mother or something?"

"Yes," I whispered. He handed me my phone and I dialed, slowly.

"Pamela, is it true? Tell me it's a rumor," I spoke quickly.

"No, baby, it's true . . . Monty is dead," she said matter-of-factly.

The words rang in my head over and over.

"Pamela, how do you know this?"

"Brandon called me crying, he saw the whole thing. He was arguing with some guy and next thing you know guns were drawn and now my son is dead, one shot to the chest," she said, speaking of his cousin Ski.

I sat on the edge of my bed, too shocked to cry, too hurt to talk. I wasn't sure of how to feel. Should I feel sad because a life was lost or relieved because a monster was dead? It wasn't real. I refused to believe what Pamela was telling me. I could hear her calling my name but I could not answer.

"Carin, baby, you there?"

"Yeah, I'm here, I just don't understand Pamela, what do you mean he's dead?"

"It's real. Listen, we have to get the obituary together as soon as possible so could you please bring some pictures? I know you have plenty. Oh, and bring my baby over too, I need her right now. I need you both. You hear me? Did you find out if the baby is his?"

"Yeah, I'll, um, see you tomorrow."

"Come over here with us. I couldn't find you yesterday. You're the last to know and we are all here waiting for you so come on over, baby, and don't forget the pictures. Try to get some rest then come over when you wake up, okay, pootie?"

"Okay," I said, choking on what seemed to be nothing. There was a deafening silence on the phone. It was five in the morning and Pamela was telling me some shit that I just would not accept. This could not be happening. It wasn't real. I had to see it to believe it. I had to get on the phone and tell *somebody something*.

The first person I called was Rick. He began yelling and screaming and then the phone went dead. I called Missy next. Her phone kept ringing and ringing and I kept hitting redial. *Come on, girl, answer please.*

"Hello," she asked groggily.

"Missy, he is dead, he is dead!" I exploded.

"What, who is this?

"Somebody killed, Monty!"

"Who?"

"Monty!"

"*What!* No, Carin, are you sure?" she sympathized, dragging her words for emphasis.

"Yeah, I just spoke to his mother."

"Where is Haman?"

"He's here. Look, I'm just spreading the news while I have it in me. I'll call you later."

"Yes, if you need me, please call me, I'm here."

I knew Haman didn't want to sit with me while I looked through my things so he took Nina in the spare room and they closed the door while I looked through the boxes of pictures slowly and deliberately. Each photo held a memory that I would cherish. I had photos of us on vacation, in the clubs, on the stoop, on his motorcycle, photos of him sleeping, photos of us laughing, crying, in love, talking, eating dinner. With each photo I came across it became harder to believe that he was dead. I couldn't cry. I was torn between emotions.

I didn't want to go to Pamela's house in shambles so I took a long hot shower and put on something nice. I did my makeup and combed my hair. Missy dropped me off and Haman had to go to work so I took Nina-Simone with me. Jomar, Ski, Rick, and Monty's uncle, Theo, were all standing outside when I pulled up. Jomar helped me out the car with my bags and Rick took Nina from me and immediately began checking her out and kissing her.

Pamela was sitting there in a pretty silk nightgown as usual with her long hair combed back. She was beautiful but tired. Sharon was in the corner wearing shades, looking at photos of Monty and some loose women. I turned my head as Sharon scooped up the pictures out of respect and put them away. I handed Pamela the bag of pictures that I had of Monty. "There has to be *something* in there that you'll want to use on his obituary."

"Right now I just want to hug my baby. Hi baby!" she said and kissed Nina all over. Everyone seemed so calm. I guess they were all cried out from the night before. I just sat there quietly as they all cooed over Nina. Sharon kept shooting glances my way and I kept avoiding her eyes. I know she wanted to come and hug me but I just wasn't ready. I got up and walked to the kitchen to get a glass of water because my chest started to tighten. I passed through our old bedroom and looked on the wall where he carved "Monty and Carin for life" on one of our drunken home video nights. I found myself sitting on our old bed in a daze. Sharon came out and sat next to me.

"Let it out, Carin, please, we all did, it's okay." She eased down in a seat next to me.

"I haven't accepted it yet, Sharon, so I can't let it out." I got up to get my water. She was trying to get my emotions out but I couldn't. When I came back in the bedroom it was filled with a few of his friends. Rick's eyes were bloodshot.

"You gotta be strong," I said.

He held my hand and stared at me then shook his head in disbelief. "This is not real, man, my boy is gone. I just spoke to him the other night. He was supposed to come out here and check me after getting up with you," he whispered. I let go of his hand and turned to find Nina. He was about to break down and I couldn't stand to see it. There waiting was a line of his boys wanting to hug me and ask me if I was okay. I avoided them all. Monty hadn't been my man in a long time but no matter how far the distance or how many years had passed, everyone would always link Monty and me together no matter what.

Pamela was waiting for me to stop running from her. I hated to see her so hurt, she was so good to everyone.

Everyone was buzzing around talking about what happened and I just sat there, totally lost and confused. Pamela kept rocking Nina in her arms. Everyone kind of did their own thing so I got up and pulled Ski to my bosom. I rubbed his back. He needed it.

"I was on my way, Carin." He began to bawl.

"He knew something was about to happen and he called me. He told me to come and I got there as soon as I could. When I got there nobody was around except for Lindsey and some corner boys. I was on my way, Carin, man, I was on my way to hold him down," he said, wrapping his arms around me.

"It's not your fault, Ski."

I continued holding Ski until he was ready to let go. He wiped his eyes with his T-shirt and backed out of the room.

"My heart is breaking, that shit seems so foul."

"Just know that my nephew loved you more than anything in this world, Carin, you do know that, right? You and my nephew shared so much and you knew him better than anyone. Everyone knows that. He loved you girl, those other women, his new girl, she meant nothing, not compared to you. You can cry, Carin, just let it out." Sharon said.

"I can't, for some reason, I can't."

"So just know that and hold that close to your heart, he will always be with you. We are all hurting and Monty was a complex man." She laughed then continued. "But you figured him out, you got in his heart and nobody has accomplished that, *nobody*."

As much as he beat me, as much as I hated him and prayed that he died, it pained me that he was actually dead, but I just couldn't cry. I was all cried out over Monty.

The day of his wake it took me all morning to get dressed. I walked around the house and did every and anything to avoid this day but to no avail. I got dressed in a black pencil skirt and black top, my hair was pulled back in a bun and I donned a pair of vintage Dior shades that Monty purchased for me about eight years prior. Nina was with my father and I was home alone. I put on the radio as I glossed my lips and heard Luther singing about a woman that he was with. He loved her, had good times with her, but she just wasn't the woman that had his heart. I recognized it as the song Monty dedicated to me along with about four or five others. I began to sing, "I'd rather be beside you in a storm, than safe and warm by myself."

It was raining hard outside and it was cold in July, as if the entire world was crying with me as I held on to my windowsill for support. I was weak. I hadn't eaten the entire week since I found out about his death. I hadn't shed a tear yet. I just felt fucked up inside. Maybe because I wasn't grieving the way people thought I should. A part of me knew that this was how Monty's life was going to end. His karma came back hard and strong. He had demons and he no longer had to fight them. He was resting, hopefully in peace, and not giving any trouble wherever he was lying. I was a nervous wreck and had no idea what to do so I picked up a pen and paper and began to write. I shot straight from the hip and didn't even re-read what I wrote, and with that I rolled up a picture of Monty and me in the small paper and tucked it in my purse.

The place was packed as expected. There were women and children everywhere. I opted to stand outside with Monty's cousin Joy and kick it with her for a while. The line was long so I cut through and went to sit next to Pamela and Sharon in the front row.

From where I was sitting I could see his large diamond earrings. He looked handsome in a navy blue suit and colorful tie. He was dapper as always. The service was mellow and not ghetto fabulous. A few women that I'm sure had flings with him were at his coffin crying for the Lord. They had no idea what loving Monty and being loved by Monty consisted of. They were just something he did to get over me. But Pamela informed me that the light-skinned thick woman who just entered was his current girlfriend.

She entered the place gracefully dressed in a navy blue linen shirt dress and her hair in soft barrel curls. She stood there watching his lifeless body then wiped her face. She scanned the room then walked up to Pamela and Sharon who greeted her warmly. She then came up to me.

"Hi, I'm Lindsey, you're Carin?"

"Yes."

"I heard so much about you. Saw so many pictures of you. I just wanted to extend my condolences to you. I know that the two of you were very close. I'm so sorry." She began to tear up. I hugged her warmly. She was a good girl.

"I'm going to leave now. I just wanted to stop by and pay my respects," she said.

"Thank you for coming."

She nodded and made her way to the door but stopped as I made my way to the coffin. The closer I got to his body the weaker I felt. Out of nowhere I felt Missy's arm around mine and Joy on the other, Lindsey had her hand lightly on my back. I guess seeing him up close and personal had an effect on me that I wasn't prepared for.

"Get off of me," I whispered to Missy and Joy who were holding me back. They backed up respectfully but stood close. It's as if the entire funeral home got quiet and waited to see the show. I leaned in closer to him and slid my note and picture under his body but then I got stuck in that position and began holding him. I lay my head on his chest as I did many nights hoping to hear a heartbeat.

"Monty, get up, baby, get out of this damn coffin." I still couldn't cry. I just wanted this nightmare to end. There was too much pain and heartache going on around me. I wanted it to stop. I ran my fingers down to his large hands. My other hand caressed the top of his head.

"Monty, all of the times I wished you dead I didn't mean it, I swear!" That's when I began to cry.

I felt an arm pulling me away so I wrapped my arms around Monty's body even tighter. I kissed his face as I did many nights when I just wanted to show affection. I was hoping he'd blush and smile like he always did when I did that. I kissed his hard cold lips, his cheeks, his head, his face, and every part of him as my arms stayed wrapped around his body. I was hoping my kisses would bring him back to life. Traces of my "Beaux" M·A·C gloss were all over his face. I wouldn't move.

"Carin, please, come on, it's all right," his cousin whispered.

I slowly released my arms from under his body and held on to the edge of his coffin. My tears were hard, fast, and steady. I wiped them away so that I could see his face. He was so damn handsome and peaceful. "You 'sleep, Monty? Get up, baby," I cried. I prayed that maybe my tears would hit his skin and wake him up. Or maybe he'd realized how devastated I was and change his mind about going to heaven or he'd wake up, snatch me in the coffin, and close it, taking me with him. I shook my head in disbelief as my chest heaved up and down, hard and quickly. I ran my fingers down the middle of his face lightly as he always did to me.

"You know he'd take you with him if it was up to him, you know that, right, Carin?" Rick assured me as he wiped his own tears. Pamela came behind me and picked me up delicately. I felt another pair of arms wrap themselves around me and it was his grandmother. She rocked me in her arms and told me it was going to be okay but I knew it wasn't. Arms were carrying me out to get air and to the car. They could only be God's because I had no strength. Pamela slapped my face gently and grabbed me by my chin.

"Carin, get a hold of yourself. You go home and get some rest, you hear me?"

I began to cry harder as arms reached out to hug me and comfort me. Lindsey sat next to me and held my hand.

"Carin, you gotta pull it together. You gotta go home and take care of that baby. Can you drive home?" she asked sweetly, dabbing at her eyes with a napkin. I stood up and wiped my face. I straightened out my clothes and slicked back my hair. "I'm good."

She gave me one last embrace and disappeared to go on with her life, like I needed to.

The funeral had to be worse than anything. The friends were all there waiting for the family to come in. I paired up with Sharon and walked down with her. I knew that they would close that coffin soon and I'd never see him again. I stood over him and got a warning look from Pamela to not do what I did yesterday. I looked at him one last time.

"Well, Monty, this is it. I hope you prayed to God before you took your last breath. I hope you made it to heaven boy," I said, and leaned down to kiss his lips one last time. I had so much more to say but there just wasn't enough time to say it all. I stood there frozen for a second, staring at his lifeless body wondering how someone could take a life, then I thought about the life that I took many years ago. I shook it off and blew my Monty a kiss before I walked away from him. I blindly walked to my seat and sat down. Soon after, the thud of the casket closing and a woman singing, "His Eye is on the Sparrow" sent chills through my body. The ride in the hearse with his family was torture. A procession of cars followed us to New Jersey to where he would be buried. As the pastor spoke, I looked at his coffin. I began to feel nauseated. I stood next to Sharon this time as Missy and Joy again held me. As they lowered his body I leaned in closer and closer to see how far he'd go. Then just like that, that part of my life was over.

30

Haman

I felt real bad for Carin and even for Monty. I mean, I had nothing personal against the man, I just didn't like the fact that he thrived off of Carin's nostalgia for them. I knew she loved and wanted nothing more than to be with me, but sometimes she would get caught up in her past that I obviously don't know as much about as I thought I did. But nevertheless, I loved Carin and I recognized her as a real good woman, and now we had this baby together. Today she was at the burial and hadn't been home in days. Nina stayed with me and I'd taken some days off to just hold the baby down while Carin got her mind right. I planned on being there for her through this for as long as she needed me. I knew what it was like to lose a soulmate.

I got her spare key and decided to clean her house, pay off her bills, and kind of redecorate her crib. I checked her mailbox and began sorting out her bills, paying off her credit cards, her phone bill, her light and gas, and realized that we'd save so much more money if we just lived together. I wanted my daughter next to me every night anyway. It's how things should be. I needed to swallow my pride and take that next step. So the minute she got her head right I'd propose the idea of living together. I know I had a challenge ahead because Carin loved her apartment and loved her space and independence. Things that were not bills, I put to the side as I didn't want to invade her privacy, but one envelope in particular that read Nina-Simone Douglas-Adams c/o Carin Douglas from Brooklyn Paternity Lab got my attention. I put it down and stared at it for a while and my head began spinning all over again. Too scared to open it, I left it there for Carin. I'd wait for her to come home and let her open it for me.

Carin

"Carin, I know this is not the time, but you need to go home and find out if my son is the father of your child," Pamela said in the limo ride home from Rosehill Cemetery.

I ignored her and kept my eyes closed. I didn't want to see anymore grief stricken faces. I wished Pamela would just shut the hell up.

"You have to be strong for this little one. Come here, baby." Pamela pulled my head into her bosom. I was sobbing uncontrollably. Yvonne rubbed my knee and wiped her own tears.

Once we reached Brooklyn, I called to check on Nina and Haman. Haman said Nina was with his mother and that he was out picking up some things for the house and he'd see me later. After eating a large plate of food (the first time I had really eaten anything since I learned of Monty's death a week ago), I gave hugs to the immediate and extended family and decided to head home. Once I got in the car, I had a few more breakdowns, having to pull over every once in a while. I finally made it home safely and sat in the car for a few moments to collect myself.

Pulling up in front of my apartment, I remembered immediately to check the mailbox. It was empty, which was strange. I knew I had to have received mail. Yet I went inside with my head throbbing to see Haman sitting comfortably on the sofa. I smelled food in the distance.

"I cooked for you and everything. The house is clean, I paid off all your bills for two months. I didn't want you to worry about anything right now. How you feelin', kitten?" He extended his arms to me. On cue I began to bawl. The pain was just too much to bear.

"Haman, I am so sorry, but please I need you to just hold me and be there for me, I know you didn't like Monty and I know . . ."

Haman shushed me. "Don't say another word. You lost someone you love, Carin, I'm not an ignorant man. I know you're in pain. You've known this man your entire adult life." He rocked my thunderous cries down to a heaving sob. Haman reached behind him for the box of tissues and began wiping my tears. He shushed me some more as I settled down. Easing up from under me, he laid me down on a pillow and began to undress me, taking off my tights and black dress. Once I was down to my panties and bra, I curled up with my face smothered in the pillow. Haman couldn't hear me cry but my body jerked violently as I tried to hold back. "Let it out, baby." He knelt next to me. "Go on, let it out, mama." My body jerked violently for about twenty seconds, then I let out a loud deep sigh. I was done for now. "You wanna eat?" he asked.

"No, but some water and some Motrin, baby, please."

"You got it."

"Thank you for paying off all of my bills and such. I appreciate that," I said.

"It's nothing, baby." Haman smiled. "Oh, Carin, I forgot, one more thing." He handed an envelope to me. The yellow business envelope frightened me. My whirlwind of emotions started all over again. I looked at Haman. He grabbed my wrist. "I want to know why you lied to me, kitten."

I shook my head. "I can't do this, Haman. If you want to leave me then go! Go! I won't let you sit here and torture me, dammit, I'm not going to do this! Just go, leave me now!" I stood up. Haman grabbed my arm hard and pulled me back down to the sofa.

"Not until you open that envelope to let me know if Nina is mine," he said coldly.

I tore at the envelope to open it. I didn't give a fuck at this point. I wasn't about to sit there and let Haman torture me when I was already going through it. If he was going to leave now would be the time because I was numb.

31

Carin

The weeks and months following Monty's funeral got harder and harder to deal with. The reality of him being dead didn't hit me until later on. I was ashamed of the pain I felt behind his death knowing I should hate him. But I just didn't feel that way, so I cried in the dark away from prying eyes and accusing souls. I cried when nobody was around to judge me. I didn't speak to Pamela much because it hurt too much to have any dealings with her. I called her when I knew she wasn't home and left messages on the machine, then never answered the phone when she returned my call. I just wanted her to know that I loved her and that I was okay. My heart was broken beyond repair and a lot of people couldn't understand why. They would ask me, "How could you love a man that treated you so fucked up? You're stupid for feeling the way that you do."

I thought about the ridicule that I received over the years in my face and behind my back. I thought about the girls who laughed at me, the men who thought I was stupid, and the ones who turned their backs on me, and friends who talked about me instead of helping me. But I felt no malice because I went through everything so that I could become the woman I was today. Besides, it was my life and the only person responsible for me was me. God chooses a path for all of us to follow and He knew that I had to learn the hard way or I would have never learned. Some say I was stupid, dumb, had low self-esteem, and didn't love myself, but I disagree. I loved myself more than you could imagine and I just wanted everybody to love me just as much.

When love is true and it's real, you will always love that person though you may not like what they have done to you. And when you find it in your heart to forgive, it's almost as if the wrong they have done has never happened. That is the power and the point of forgiveness. It helps one heal and move on. I was so caught up in the "now" that I hated Monty while he was doing those things to me. But once it was over, I felt no need to give him the power or the control by hating him and allowing him to saturate my mind or heart any longer. The God in me allowed me to forgive him and move on. Being his friend was not in the plans, it just happened. I guess I knew that no matter what, Monty provided that stability in my life, which was the only thing I ever wanted. So though it was tainted, it was stable. And now my crutch was gone. That poison was gone, that make-believe idea of love was gone. I had lost myself in pain the fight to survive and totally lost sight of what was important: me. But Monty was in my head, my heart, and my dreams, and in every word I spoke, and it was time to settle these feelings. I just didn't know where to start. The only thing that kept me strong was my faith in God and my daughter. Every time I thought about how far I'd come it made me feel better. I thought about the life I took long ago and the lives I lost in turn. Karma had come.

I thought about countless women around me who were beaten by men who claimed to love them, and in turn lost their lives or lost their souls. Some of them had to go to shelters and witness protection programs. Some of them got burned in the face with lye so no other man would find them attractive. Some got crippled or stuck in marriages and with babies. Some never found a way out of that hell. Some got so comfortable in their pain that they thought there was nothing better outside of those relationships. Some women even wound up in jail for life for killing the men who struck them. But I was blessed to have escaped all of that and even made amends with my abuser, forgave him, and was blessed enough to even find love again in myself and with another man.

As I rocked my daughter in my arms I thought about my mother and how we hadn't talked since I was eighteen. I wondered if she would have ever been there for me the way that I needed had she been in my life and known that a man was abusing me. I was happy that I would never know the answer to that. I wanted to reconcile with my mother one day. I wanted her to know Nina-Simone and be a part of her life. I figured if I could forgive Monty after the hell he put me through, then I could, no doubt, forgive my mother. I kissed my daughter and vowed to be a better mother to her than my mother was to me. I forgave my mother for all that she didn't do for me. She was just a woman with a broken bitter heart. She reacted to her circumstances the way she deemed right. I couldn't take it personal. Monty was a reflection of how he was raised and the things he saw. I couldn't take it personal.

I thought about Chauncey and Sinny, Tron and Panama. All of the men I loved loved me for their own reasons. Chauncey was looking for a

mother and a nurturer. Panama was looking for
his mother's love, Monty was looking for revenge
for his father's demise. He was angry.

He tried to buy me and put me on a pedestal
and when he realized that I was not perfect he
knocked me down with his fists and couldn't
stop, and Haman just wanted to save me from it
all. But the answer was in me to save myself.

I thought about the days I stared out of my
project window, feeling uninspired, looking for
my father, wanting love, needing love, and having no idea how to fill that void so I did whatever I had to do to feel loved. I ran the streets,
I smoked drugs, I drank heavily, I numbed myself. The days Monty beat me, I stayed because
I wanted him to know and see that I was no
quitter, that I loved him, that I was down, that
I understood the changes men go through such
as I understood why my father left, but I almost
risked my life for that love. So I couldn't be mad
at him because I chose to stay.

I rode with Panama through the streets because I was a soldier. I wanted to be what my
mother was not or what I thought she wasn't until I got older and took the time to hear her story.
At that moment I realized that I was my mother
and she indeed was a soldier.

I took a deep breath and I let the past go finally.
Monty was dead, Panama was dead, my father

was here, my past was dead, and my daughter was born. I was able to see a part of me that was pure, innocent, and untainted, and I planned on keeping her that way. I was a grown woman, with a child, with a life that I needed to live, no longer on the run, no longer searching, needing, or living in fear, no longer putting a man at the wheel of my car but letting God be my driver to my ultimate destiny. I was nobody's victim.

I learned that love is driven by fear when you're in a violent relationship. You love the idea of things being good again, you're in love with what once was, you're giving love so that you can receive love in return, but that man that is beating you will never stop beating you no matter how much you love him, because he doesn't love himself. He hates himself so much that he tries to destroy everything around him because he feels that he is not worthy of those things. He hates himself and in turn he will hate you and he will show it in each blow, each slap, each kick or punch. There is nothing you can say or do to make him stop, he will never stop. So there is no use in sacrificing your time or heart in trying to make him change. Perhaps I was crying out for something. As much as I felt like I had it all together, something was missing to allow this man to beat on me the way he did. Perhaps I wanted to love a man the way I wish I was loved, with loyalty and stability. I sacrificed myself, my body, my loyalty for the sake of another. But people won't love you the way that you love them. You can't expect that. You have to love without a limit for your own reasons, never to get something in return. I never loved to get in return. I loved to give joy, to give hope, to give promise, to give stability, stability, stability. As I looked at my baby girl I shivered at the thought of a man hitting her and me not giving my life to make sure that relationship ended. Because of the pain that I endured I knew that my daughter would not have to and so with that I smiled and was at ease. I didn't go through that pain in vain. I survived so that I could teach. My advice to anyone who goes through this is to first and foremost not be ashamed to seek help and to let someone know what is going on. Even if you don't leave right away, it is important to let your loved ones know what is going on so that they can be of some assistance. I felt bad for the women who were next in line hungry to be me. They were the ones that were lost, they were the ones willing to sell their soul and risk their lives for superficial things. I know my worth and with that I decided to not let anything or person infiltrate my happiness or sanity ever again no matter what. I, Carin Douglas, had finally come into my own without needing a "Clyde" on my side to validate me. I found my Clyde in the most High and in my daughter's eyes. I had unique size shoes that no one could walk in. I had been through it all before the age of thirty and had a long promising life to live. No more pain, no more putting myself in harm's way, no more settling, no more fighting, no more Bonnie, no more riding, or dying. It was time to love and be loved. Yeah, I was down for that.

Epilogue

Missy was getting Nina-Simone dressed as we waited for Jetta so that we could all go to the mall. "Nina looks so much like her father, she is just adorable."

"Isn't she though?" I beamed smacking Nina playfully on the butt. I couldn't believe that she was already going on two years old. I was elated that Nina-Simone turned out to be Haman's child. But deep down in my heart I knew that she was. My baby girl was conceived in love. My body wouldn't produce a child from Monty. God wasn't about to latch me on to that man for life. He had other plans for me and bigger than that he had other plans for my child. He knew that she deserved to grow up in a loving, two-parent home and being afforded the opportunities that I wasn't.

"Stop!" she whined, running into the kitchen.

"She is such a drama queen." I fanned her off and started straightening up.

"What happened?" Haman said, picking her up as he came out of the kitchen.

"Mommy hit me!" she pointed to me.

Missy chuckled getting up from off the floor.

"She did? I'ma get her," Haman whined with Nina playfully then winked at me.

I winked back as Haman turned his back to take Nina in the kitchen for a snack so that she would feel better. As they walked away, I silently thanked God for sparing my life and sanity over the years, my loving and trusting husband for being a good man and a great father, the power of forgiveness, and the strength to deal with it all. I was happy, I was focused, and I was determined to not let the past get in the way of my happiness ever again. I was strong and I knew what needed to be done. I had positive people around me and I no longer suffered from nostalgia. Motherhood was the greatest joy and I knew exactly how to play my role, and if I had to do it all again I wouldn't change a thing, because my past built my future. I was at peace with me and had finally come full circle.